D1388882

INTRODUCTION

I think I can probably claim some of the credit for introducing H. P. Lovecraft to the British reading public. After his death from cancer in 1937, Lovecraft was in danger of being totally forgotten. Fortunately, his friends – and disciples – August Derleth and Donald Wandrei decided to launch a small publishing firm, simply to keep his work in print. During his lifetime, it had appeared in pulp magazines – mostly *Weird Tales* – and his efforts to issue a hardcover volume of his works were a failure, with the exception of a short novel called *The Shadow Over Innsmouth*, which appeared in the year before his death, and which sold only 150 copies before the publisher went bankrupt. Arkham House, founded by Derleth and Wandrei, issued the first collection of Lovecraft, *The Outsider And Others*, in 1939, and two more volumes over the following ten years. Outside America, Lovecraft remained unknown.

In 1959, I stayed overnight at a farm in Corfe Castle, Dorset, with my friend Mark Helfer, an American who had married the farmer's daughter. It was on his bookshelf that I found the volume *The Outsider And Others*, the cheap paper already yellow and smelling of mould. Since my own first book had been called *The Outsider*, I was intrigued, and before I fell asleep, read its opening story, "In The Vault", a gruesome little tale about a mortuary keeper who hacks off a corpse's feet to make it fit his coffin, and whose own feet are gnawed by a vengeful corpse as he tries to escape from a burial vault.

It brought back powerfully the atmosphere of old copies of *Weird Tales* that I had read while staying with an aunt in Doncaster at the age of ten or so. *Weird Tales*, published in Chicago, was not devoted to the usual stories of mystery and imagination in the manner of Poe and Le Fanu; although the title was inspired by Poe, its editor preferred crude physical horror – the first issue (1923) had a cover illustration of a man and woman writhing in the grip of a giant octopus. I recall a story called "Cats Are Uncanny", about someone who does something horrible to a cat, and who ends floating in the lily pond with his throat torn out and claw marks all over his chest. And I can remember feeling equally nauseated at a story called "The Mound", about an underground realm peopled by descendants of the Aztecs, and guarded by disfigured surface-dwellers who have made the mistake of seeking treasure in the mound that forms the entrance to the underworld – horrible creatures with stumps of arms and legs. This, I learned later, was written by a friend of Lovecraft called Zealia Bishop, and revised by him.

Now I have to admit that, as I renewed acquaintance with Lovecraft's work – Mark Helfer was kind enough to lend me the book – I found myself experiencing some of the rather queasy misgivings that I had felt eighteen years earlier. At the age of ten I had felt instinctively that this was a kind of pornography of violence that was designed to appeal to a kind of sickness in the reader. Now I felt much the same – that Lovecraft was a "case history" rather than a literary figure. Yet it was obvious that the peculiar violence and morbidity of his work was a typical "outsider"'s reaction against a world he found crude and unbearable. In the 19th Century, the romantic poets had dreamed of fairyland, and wilted away (or even committed suicide) because they were unable to find it. You might say that Lovecraft had given up feeling sad about the failure of his dreams and turned nasty.

As we left Mark Helfer's, I began talking to my wife Joy about Lovecraft and the psychology of horror stories, comparing him with Thomas Lovell Beddoes (who wrote imitation Elizabethan tragedies full of gruesome horrors, and committed suicide), Sheridan Le Fanu and M. R. James. Suddenly, I saw that I had the material for a new book. The result was *The Strength To Dream*, written in 1961 and published the following year. It was, as far as I know, the first time anyone had published anything about Lovecraft in England. Lovecraft paperbacks began to appear in the mid-sixties, and soon he was a cult among the young.

The Strength To Dream begins with Lovecraft, but the opinion I express of him is not high. *"He began as one of the worst and most florid writers of the 20th Century, but finally developed a certain discipline and economy."* Yet in spite of my irritation with his overblown style, there was something about him that continued to fascinate me. When I was in Providence, Rhode Island, in the autumn of 1961, I spent some hours in the library at Brown University (which Lovecraft calls Miskatonic) reading Lovecraft's journals and letters, then went back to look at the house where he had lived. I also found the address of Arkham House in a book catalogue, and wrote to ask them what books by Lovecraft were still in print. I received back a friendly letter from August Derleth, who had read my *Outsider*, and entered into a correspondence with him. As a result, I toned down some of the harsher comments about Lovecraft in the American edition of *The Strength To*

Dream. And when Derleth suggested I should write a "Lovecraft novel" for Arkham House, I produced *The Mind Parasites*, which has been in print ever since.

Howard Philips Lovecraft was born on 20 August, 1890 in Providence, Rhode Island – a small provincial town of the type guaranteed to suffocate any person of talent. He was a nervous and delicate only child, whose father died of syphilis when Howard was seven.

Lovecraft spent most of his childhood in bed, reading. His mother withdrew him from school at the age of eight, and he devoted the next two years to devouring every book he could lay his hands on – with particular attention to writers of horror like "Monk" Lewis. He also began writing stories with titles like "The Mystery Of The Graveyard".

Finally back at school, he developed a passionate interest in science, and began reading books on astronomy. Paradoxically, he did not believe in the 'occult' or supernatural, regarding it throughout his life as superstitious nonsense. His later work was a kind of self-created mythology aimed at expressing his dislike of modern civilisation. (When in New York in the 1920s he talked indignantly about the "loathsome Asiatic hordes who drag their dirty carcasses over streets where white men once moved"; but his disgust applied to the whole human race, and he talked about the "miserable vermin called human beings".)

After two and a half years of high school he had another "nervous collapse", and spent the next five years at home suffering from headaches, indigestion and boredom – which induced a permanent state of lethargy. The writings of Nietzsche – another sick recluse – aroused his admiration. But, like Nietzsche, he lacked the "joyful wisdom" of the "Overman"; all the photographs show the same pale, unhappy face – there is not one with a smile. And he was twenty-seven years old before he wrote his first typically "Lovecraftian" story, "Dagon", in which a shipwrecked mariner finds himself on an island that has been created in some recent seismic convulsion, thrown up from the seabed; there he sees an enormous monolith with strange carvings, and is horrified when a scaly humanoid creature emerges from the sea and flings its arms around the monument. Lovecraft had finally created his own distinctive realm, where strange ancient civilisations lie buried under layers of mud and slime, and their sinister former inhabitants stir uneasily in their sleep...

Two years later, influenced by Lord Dunsany (a now forgotten fantasist), he began writing tales about strange cities that sound not unlike Rider

Haggard, and have more than a touch of science fiction. But the most typical story of this early period is "The Outsider", about a man who grows up alone in an underground den, and only discovers – when he finally encounters a mirror – that he is a horrible, misshapen monster. (Lovecraft's mother had often told him he was ugly.)

In 1924, when he was thirty-four, he married and moved to New York. He had met Sonia Greene, seven years his senior, at a writers' convention; she was a Russian Jewess, and took the initiative in the courtship. But the shrinking recluse found married life too much for him, and after two years, fled back to Providence. By now he had become a regular contributor to *Weird Tales*, and in fact, was at one point responsible for the magazine's survival. In 1924 sales were so poor that it was about to cease publication. Then a sinister little story called "The Loved Dead" – written by C. M. Eddy and revised by Lovecraft – caused such an outcry that the magazine was withdrawn from the bookstalls, and sales of the next issue rocketed. It was a tale about a necrophile who ends as a sex killer, and the erotic overtones are as powerful as in Bram Stoker's *Dracula*. It makes it suddenly clear that the basic force behind all Lovecraft's work is disguised sexual frustration, which emerges in a form of violent or sadistic fantasy, in which horrible, sinister creatures wreak havoc in the daylight world of boredom and ordinariness.

"The Call Of Cthulhu", still his most famous story, was written in 1926. It was in this tale that Lovecraft found his true voice and his true subject; like William Blake, he had finally created his own mythology. He was to work within this mythology for the remainder of his short life. Together with "The Dunwich Horror" and "The Colour Out Of Space", it is among his finest work.

In the early 1930s he became so discouraged at his lack of success that he decided to give up writing; Derleth cheered him up by getting one of his stories accepted, and he pressed on. But there was another and deeper problem. In his forties, Lovecraft was recovering from the adolescent fever that had produced the Cthulhu mythos; he was growing up, and the thought of slimy horrors that chewed off people's head no longer made his flesh creep. "The Shadow Over Innsmouth" reveals this increasing conflict; it is an attempt to extend the concept of the early story "Dagon" to the Cthulhu mythos, but Lovecraft was no longer able to immerse himself in that twilight realm of sinister corruption and degeneration; he was ceasing to believe in his own "nasties". A long fantasy called "Through The Gates Of The Silver Key", in which his hero Randolph Carter visits a planet of "squamous" creatures, actually sounds like tongue-in-cheek self-parody. And in "The Shadow Out Of Time", written in 1934, it finally becomes clear that Lovecraft has outgrown his morbidity, and turned into a science fiction writer who can be compared with Wells and Verne. It could be said that Lovecraft had finally achieved what he had aimed at all his life. Because he found the real world so boring, he had attempted to create his own private hothouse in which his soul could blossom like an exotic flower. He succeeded so well that he ceased to be a world-weary "outsider", and became a widely admired writer with dozens of friends and correspondents; he even began to enjoy travel. Ironically, this new success undermined his creative impulse, which had been based on sickness and rebellion. "The Shadow Out Of Time" was to my mind his last major work. It is arguable that the cancer that killed him three years later sprang out of a sense of confusion and bewilderment, a failure to grasp what had happened.

The psychologist Abraham Maslow coined the term "deficiency needs" to explain the problem of characters like Lovecraft. A child who lacks certain vitamins will grow up stunted and undernourished, perhaps with some bone disease like rickets. A human being who lacks certain mental vitamins will grow up suffering from spiritual undernourishment. The novels of the Brontë sisters sprang out of their loneliness and frustration in a moorland parsonage, with no close male companionship except their alcoholic brother. If Emily had been seduced by the local blacksmith's assistant at the age of sixteen, she would have felt no need to create Heathcliff in *Wuthering Heights*.

On the other hand, the creative impulse that led Dostoevsky to create *Crime And Punishment* was not based on "deficiency needs", but on a deep sensitivity to human misery, and a craving to *understand*, the most powerful of human drives. Tolstoy once called him "the hospital muse", but there can be no doubt that his sickness is founded on a kind of strength.

There is no point in denying that most of Lovecraft's work sprang out of deficiency needs, and that for that reason, has a narrow and suffocating quality. Yet it is impossible not to admire the sheer toughness that enabled him to survive years of invalidism and loneliness, and to leave behind such a powerful body of work. He is the last of the great romantic "outsiders", and his work marks the end of an era. There can be no doubt that, in spite of his obvious faults, we have to classify Lovecraft as a man of genius.

–COLIN WILSON

CRAWLING CHAOS

SELECTED WEIRD FICTION
Volume One: 1917-1927

H P LOVECRAFT

DAGON

I am writing this under an appreciable mental strain, since by tonight I shall be no more. Penniless, and at the end of my supply of the drug which alone makes life endurable, I can bear the torture no longer; and shall cast myself from this garret window into the squalid street below. Do not think from my slavery to morphine that I am a weakling or a degenerate. When you have read these hastily scrawled pages you may guess, though never fully realise, why it is that I insist I have forgetfulness or death.

It was in one of the most open and least frequented parts of the broad Pacific that the packet of which I was supercargo fell a victim to the German sea-raider. The great war was then at its very beginning, and the ocean forces of the Hun had not completely sunk to their later degradation; so that our vessel was made a legitimate prize, whilst we of her crew were treated with all the fairness and consideration due us as naval prisoners. So liberal, indeed, was the discipline of our captors, that five days after we were taken I managed to escape alone in a small boat with water and provisions for a good length of time.

When I finally found myself adrift and free, I had but little idea of my surroundings. Never a competent navigator, I could only guess vaguely by the sun and stars that I was somewhat south of the equator. Of the longitude I knew nothing, and no island or coastline was in sight. The weather kept fair, and for uncounted days I drifted aimlessly beneath the scorching sun; waiting either for some passing ship, or to be cast on the shores of some habitable land. But neither ship nor land appeared, and I began to despair in my solitude upon the heaving vastnesses of unbroken blue.

The change happened whilst I slept. Its details I shall never know; for my slumber, though troubled and dream-infested, was continuous. When at last I awaked, it was to discover myself half sucked into a slimy expanse of hellish black mire which extended about me in monotonous undulations as far as I could see, and in which my boat lay grounded some distance away.

Though one might well imagine that my first sensation would be wonder at so prodigious and unexpected a trans-formation of scenery, I was in reality more horrified than astonished; for there was in the air and in the rotting soil a sinister quality which chilled me to the very core. The region was putrid with the carcasses of decaying fish, and of other less describable things which I saw protruding from the nasty mud of the unending plain. Perhaps I should not hope to convey in mere words the unutterable hideousness that can dwell in absolute silence and barren immensity. There was nothing within hearing, and nothing in sight save a vast reach of black slime; yet the very completeness of the stillness and the homogeneity of the landscape oppressed me with a nauseating fear.

The sun was blazing down from a sky which seemed to me almost black in its cloudless cruelty; as though reflecting the inky marsh beneath my feet. As I crawled into the stranded boat I realised that only one theory could explain my position. Through some unprecedented volcanic upheaval, a portion of the ocean floor must have been thrown to the surface, exposing regions which for innumerable millions of years had lain hidden under unfathomable watery depths. So great was the extent of the new land which had risen beneath me, that I could not detect the faintest noise of the surging ocean, strain my ears as I might. Nor were there any seafowl to prey upon the dead things.

For several hours I sat thinking or brooding in the boat, which lay upon its side and afforded a slight shade as the sun moved across the heavens. As the day progressed, the ground lost some of its stickiness, and seemed likely to dry sufficiently for travelling purposes in a short time. That night I slept but little, and the next day I made for myself a pack containing food and water, preparatory to an overland journey in search of the vanished sea and possible rescue.

On the third morning I found the soil dry enough to walk upon with ease. The odour of the fish was maddening; but I was too much concerned with graver things to mind so slight an evil, and set out boldly for an unknown goal. All day I forged steadily westward, guided by a far-away hummock which rose higher than any other elevation on the rolling desert. That night I encamped, and on the following day still travelled toward the hummock, though that object seemed scarcely nearer than when I had first espied it. By the fourth evening I attained the base of the mound, which turned out to be much higher than it had appeared from a distance; an intervening valley setting it out in sharper relief from the general surface. Too weary to ascend, I slept in the shadow of the hill.

I know not why my dreams were so wild that night; but ere the waning and fantastically gibbous moon had risen far above the eastern plain, I was awake in a cold perspiration, determined to sleep no more. Such visions as I had experienced were too much for me to endure again. And in the glow of the moon I saw how unwise I had been to travel by day. Without the glare of the parching sun, my journey would have cost me less energy; indeed, I now felt quite able to perform the ascent which had deterred me at sunset. Picking up my pack, I started for the crest of the eminence.

I have said that the unbroken monotony of the rolling plain was a source of vague horror to me; but I think my horror was greater when I gained the summit of the mound and looked down the other side into an immeasurable pit or canyon, whose black recesses the moon had not yet soared high enough to illumine. I felt myself on the edge of the world; peering over the rim into a fathomless chaos of eternal night. Through my terror ran curious reminiscences of *Paradise Lost*, and of Satan's hideous climb through the unfashioned realms of darkness.

As the moon climbed higher in the sky, I began to see that the slopes of the valley were not quite so perpendicular as I had imagined. Ledges and outcroppings of rock afforded fairly easy foot-holds for a descent, whilst after a drop of a few hundred feet, the declivity became very gradual. Urged on by an impulse which I cannot definitely analyse, I scrambled with difficulty down the rocks and stood on the gentler slope beneath, gazing into the Stygian deeps where no light had yet penetrated.

All at once my attention was captured by a vast and singular object on the opposite slope, which rose steeply about a hundred yards ahead of me; an object that gleamed whitely in the newly bestowed rays of the ascending moon. That it was merely a gigantic piece of stone, I soon assured myself; but I was conscious of a distinct impression that its contour and position were not altogether the work of Nature. A closer scrutiny filled me with sensations I cannot express; for despite its enormous magnitude, and its position in an abyss which had yawned at the bottom of the sea since the world was young, I perceived beyond a doubt that the strange object was a well-shaped monolith whose massive bulk had known the workmanship and perhaps the worship of living and thinking creatures.

Dazed and frightened, yet not without a certain thrill of the scientist's or archaeologist's delight, I examined my surroundings more closely. The moon, now near the zenith, shone weirdly and vividly above the towering steeps that hemmed in the chasm, and revealed the fact that a far-flung body of water flowed at the bottom, winding out of sight in both directions, and almost lapping my feet as I stood on the slope. Across the chasm, the wavelets washed the base of the Cyclopean monolith; on whose surface I could now trace both inscriptions and crude sculptures. The writing was in a system of hieroglyphics unknown to me, and unlike anything I had ever seen in books; consisting for the most part of conventionalised aquatic symbols such as fishes, eels, octopi, crustaceans, molluscs, whales, and the like. Several characters obviously represented marine things which are unknown to the modern world, but whose decomposing forms I had observed on the ocean-risen plain.

It was the pictorial carving, however, that did most to hold me spellbound. Plainly visible across the intervening water on account of their enormous size, were an array of bas-reliefs whose subjects would have excited the envy of a Doré. I think that these things were supposed to depict men – at least, a certain sort of men; though the creatures were shewn disporting like fishes in the waters of some marine grotto, or paying homage at some monolithic shrine which appeared to be under the waves as well. Of their faces and forms I dare not speak in detail; for the mere remembrance makes me grow faint. Grotesque beyond the imagination of a Poe or a Bulwer, they were damnably human in general outline despite webbed hands and feet, shockingly wide and flabby lips, glassy, bulging eyes, and other features less pleasant to recall. Curiously enough, they seemed to have been chiselled badly out of proportion with their scenic background; for one of the creatures was shewn in the act of killing a whale represented as but little larger than himself. I remarked, as I say, their grotesqueness and strange size; but in a moment decided that they were merely the imaginary gods of some primitive fishing or seafaring tribe; some tribe whose last descendant had perished eras before the first ancestor of the Piltdown or Neanderthal Man was born. Awestruck at this unexpected glimpse into a past beyond the conception of the most daring anthropologist, I stood musing whilst the moon cast queer reflections on the silent channel before me.

Then suddenly I saw it. With only a slight churning to mark its rise to the surface, the thing slid into view above the dark waters. Vast, Polyphemus-like, and loathsome, it darted like a stupendous monster of nightmares to the monolith, about which it flung its gigantic scaly arms, the while it bowed its hideous head and gave vent to certain measured sounds. I think I went mad then.

Of my frantic ascent of the slope and cliff, and of my delirious journey back to the stranded boat, I remember little. I believe I sang a great deal, and laughed oddly when I was unable to sing. I have indistinct recollections of a great storm some time after I reached the boat; at any rate, I know that I heard peals of thunder and other tones which Nature utters only in her wildest moods.

When I came out of the shadows I was in a San Francisco hospital; brought thither by the captain of the American ship which had picked up my boat in mid-ocean. In my delirium I had said much, but found that my words had been given scant attention. Of any land upheaval in the Pacific, my rescuers knew nothing; nor did I deem it necessary to insist upon a thing which I knew they could not believe. Once I sought out a celebrated ethnologist, and amused him with peculiar questions regarding the ancient Philistine legend of Dagon, the Fish-God; but soon perceiving that he was hopelessly conventional, I did not press my inquiries.

It is at night, especially when the moon is gibbous and waning, that I see the thing. I tried morphine; but the drug has given only transient surcease, and has drawn me into its clutches as a hopeless slave. So now I am to end it all, having written a full account for the information or the contemptuous amusement of my fellow men. Often I ask myself if it could not all have been a pure phantasm – a mere freak of fever as I lay sun-stricken and raving in the open boat after my escape from the German man-of-war. This I ask myself, but ever does there come before me a hideously vivid vision in reply. I cannot think of the deep sea without shuddering at the nameless things that may at this very moment be crawling and floundering on its slimy bed, worshipping their ancient stone idols and carving their own detestable likenesses on submarine obelisks of water-soaked granite. I dream of a day when they may rise above the billows to drag down in their reeking talons the remnants of puny, war-exhausted mankind – of a day when the land shall sink, and the dark ocean floor shall ascend amidst universal pandemonium.

The end is near. I hear a noise at the door, as of some immense slippery body lumbering against it. It shall not find me. God, *that hand!* The window! The window!

THE CRAWLING CHAOS

(with Elizabeth Berkeley)

Of the pleasures and pains of opium much has been written. The ecstasies and horrors of De Quincey and the *paradis artificiels* of Baudelaire are preserved and interpreted with an art which makes them immortal, and the world knows well the beauty, the terror and the mystery of those obscure realms into which the inspired dreamer is transported. But much as has been told, no man has yet dared intimate the *nature* of the phantasms thus unfolded to the mind, or hint at the *direction* of the unheard-of roads along whose ornate and exotic course the partaker of the drug is so irresistibly borne. De Quincey was drawn back into Asia, that teeming land of nebulous shadows whose hideous antiquity is so impressive that "the vast age of the race and name overpowers the sense of youth in the individual", but farther than that he dared not go. Those who *have* gone farther seldom returned; and even when they have, they have been either silent or mad. I took opium but once – in the year of the plague, when doctors sought to deaden the agonies they could not cure. There was an overdose – my physician was worn out with horror and exertion – and I travelled very far indeed. In the end I returned and lived, but my nights are filled with strange memories, nor have I ever permitted a doctor to give me opium again.

The pain and pounding in my head had been quite unendurable when the drug was administered. Of the future I had no heed; to escape, whether by cure, unconsciousness, or death, was all that concerned me. I was partly delirious, so that it is hard to place the exact moment of transition, but I think the effect must have begun shortly before the pounding ceased to be painful. As I have said, there was an overdose; so my reactions were probably far from normal. The sensation of falling, curiously dissociated from the idea of gravity or direction, was paramount; though there was a subsidiary impression of unseen throngs in incalculable profusion, throngs of infinitely diverse nature, but all more or less related to me. Sometimes it seemed less as though I were falling, than as though the universe or the ages were falling past me. Suddenly my pain ceased, and I began to associate the pounding with an external rather than internal force. The falling had ceased also, giving place to a sensation of uneasy, temporary rest; and when I listened closely, I fancied the pounding was that of the vast, inscrutable sea as its sinister, colossal breakers lacerated some desolate shore after a storm of titanic magnitude. Then I opened my eyes.

For a moment my surroundings seemed confused, like a projected image hopelessly out of focus, but gradually I realized my solitary presence in a strange and beautiful room lighted by many windows. Of the exact nature of the apartment I could form no idea, for my thoughts were still far from settled, but I noticed vari-coloured rugs and draperies, elaborately fashioned tables, chairs, ottomans, and divans, and delicate vases and ornaments which conveyed a suggestion of the exotic without being actually alien. These things I noticed, yet they were not long uppermost in my mind. Slowly but inexorably crawling upon my consciousness and rising above every other impression, came a dizzying fear of the unknown; a fear all the greater because I could not analyse it, and seeming to concern a stealthily approaching menace; not death, but some nameless, unheard-of thing inexpressibly more ghastly and abhorrent.

Presently I realized that the direct symbol and excitant of my fear was the hideous pounding whose incessant reverberations throbbed maddeningly against my exhausted brain. It seemed to come from a point outside and below the edifice in which I stood, and to associate itself with the most terrifying mental images. I felt that some horrible scene or object lurked beyond the silk-hung walls, and shrank from glancing through the arched, latticed windows that opened so bewilderingly on every hand. Perceiving shutters attached to these windows, I closed them all, averting my eyes from the exterior as I did so. Then, employing a flint and steel which I found on one of the small tables, I lit the many candles reposing about the walls in arabesque sconces. The added sense of security brought by closed shutters and artificial light calmed my nerves to some degree, but I could not shut out the monotonous pounding. Now that I was calmer, the sound became as fascinating as it was fearful, and I felt a contradictory desire to seek out its source despite my still powerful shrinking. Opening a portiere at the side of the room nearest the pounding, I beheld a small and richly draped corridor ending in a carven door and large oriel window. To this window I was irresistibly drawn, though my ill-defined apprehensions seemed almost equally bent on holding me back. As I approached it I could see a chaotic whirl of waters in the distance. Then, as I attained it and glanced out on all sides, the stupendous picture of my surroundings burst upon me with full and devastating force.

I beheld such a sight as I have never beheld before, and which no living person can have seen save in the delirium of fever or the inferno of opium. The building stood on a narrow point of land – or what was *now* a narrow point of land – fully three hundred feet above what must lately have been a seething vortex of mad waters. On either side of the house there fell a newly washed-out precipice of red earth, whilst ahead of me the hideous waves were still rolling in frightfully, eating away the land with ghastly monotony and deliberation. Out a mile or more there rose and fell menacing breakers at least fifty feet in height, and on the far horizon ghoulish black clouds of grotesque contour were resting and brooding like unwholesome vultures. The waves were dark and purplish, almost black, and clutched at the yielding red mud of the bank as if with uncouth, greedy hands. I could not but feel that some noxious marine mind had declared a war of extermination upon all the solid ground, perhaps abetted by the angry sky.

Recovering at length from the stupor into which this unnatural spectacle had thrown me, I realized that my actual physical danger was acute. Even whilst I gazed, the bank had lost many feet, and it could not be long before the house would fall undermined into the awful pit of lashing waves. Accordingly I hastened to the opposite side of the edifice, and finding a door, emerged at once, locking it after me with a curious key which had hung inside. I now beheld more of the strange region about me, and marked a singular division which seemed to exist in the hostile ocean and firmament. On each side of the jutting promontory different conditions held sway. At my left as I faced inland was a gently heaving sea with great green waves rolling peacefully in under a brightly shining sun. Something about that sun's nature and position made me shudder, but I could not then tell, and cannot tell now, what it was. At my right also was the sea, but it was blue, calm, and only gently undulating, while the sky above it was darker and the washed-out bank more nearly white than reddish.

I now turned my attention to the land, and found occasion for fresh surprise; for the vegetation resembled nothing I had ever seen or read about. It was apparently tropical or at least sub-tropical – a conclusion borne out by the intense heat of the air. Sometimes I thought I could trace strange analogies with the flora of my native land, fancying that the well-known plants and shrubs might assume such forms under a radical change of climate; but the gigantic and omnipresent palm trees were plainly foreign. The house I had just left was very small – hardly more than a cottage – but its material was evidently marble, and its architecture was weird and composite, involving a quaint fusion of Western and Eastern forms. At the corners were Corinthian columns, but the red tile roof was like that of a Chinese pagoda. From the door inland there stretched a path of singularly white sand, about four feet wide, and lined on either side with stately palms and unidentifiable flowering shrubs and plants. It lay toward the side of the promontory where the sea was blue and the bank rather whitish. Down this path I felt impelled to flee, as if pursued by some malignant spirit from the pounding ocean. At first it was slightly uphill, then I reached a gentle crest. Behind me I saw the scene I had left; the entire point with the cottage and the black water, with the green sea on one side and the blue sea on the other, and a curse unnamed and un-nameable lowering over all. I never saw it again, and often wonder... After this last look I strode ahead and surveyed the inland panorama before me.

The path, as I have intimated, ran along the right-hand shore as one went inland. Ahead and to the left I now viewed a magnificent valley comprising thousands of acres, and covered with a swaying growth of tropical grass higher than my head. Almost at the limit of vision was a colossal palm tree which seemed to fascinate and beckon me. By this time wonder and escape from the imperilled peninsula had largely dissipated my fear, but as I paused and sank fatigued to the path, idly digging with my hands into the warm, whitish-golden sand, a new and acute sense of danger seized me. Some terror in the swishing tall grass seemed added to that of the diabolically pounding sea, and I started up crying aloud and disjointedly, "Tiger? Tiger? Is it Tiger? Beast? Beast? Is it a Beast that I am afraid of?" My mind wandered back to an ancient and classical story of tigers which I had read; I strove to recall the author, but had difficulty. Then in the midst of my fear I remembered that the tale was by Rudyard Kipling; nor did the grotesqueness of deeming him an ancient author occur to me. I wished for the volume containing this story, and had almost started back toward the doomed cottage to procure it when my better sense and the lure of the palm prevented me.

Whether or not I could have resisted the backward beckoning without the counter-fascination of the vast palm-tree, I do not know. This attraction was now dominant, and I left the path and crawled on hands and knees down the valley's slope despite my fear of the grass and the serpents it might contain. I resolved to fight for life and reason as long as possible against all menaces of sea or land, though I sometimes feared defeat as the maddening swish of the uncanny grass joined the still audible and irritating pounding of the distant breakers. I would frequently pause and put my hands to my ears for relief, but could never quite shut out the detestable sound. It was, as it seemed to me, only after ages that I finally dragged myself to the beckoning palm tree and lay quiet beneath its protecting shade.

There now ensued a series of incidents which transported me to the opposite extremes of ecstasy and horror; incidents which I tremble to recall and dare not seek to interpret. No sooner had I crawled beneath the overhanging foliage of the palm, than there dropped from its branches a young child of such beauty as I never beheld before. Though ragged and dusty, this being bore the features of a faun or demigod, and seemed almost to diffuse a radiance in the dense shadow of the tree. It smiled and extended its hand, but before I could arise and speak I heard in the upper air the exquisite melody of singing; notes high and low blent with a sublime and ethereal harmoniousness. The sun had by this time sunk below the horizon, and in the twilight I saw an aureole of lambent light encircled the child's head. Then in a tone of silver it addressed me: "It is the end. They have come down through the gloaming from the stars. Now all is over, and beyond the Arinurian streams we shall dwell blissfully in Teloë." As the child spoke, I beheld a soft radiance through the leaves of the palm tree, and rising greeted a pair whom I knew to be the chief singers among those I had heard. A god and goddess they must have been, for such beauty is not mortal; and they took my hands, saying, "Come, child, you have heard the voices, and all is well. In Teloë beyond the Milky Way and the Arinurian streams are cities all of amber and chalcedony. And upon their domes of many facets glisten the images of strange and beautiful stars. Under the ivory bridges of Teloë flow rivers of liquid gold bearing pleasure-barges bound for blossomy Cytharion of the Seven Suns. And in Teloë and Cytharion abide only youth, beauty and pleasure, nor are any sounds heard, save of laughter, song, and the lute. Only the gods dwell in Teloë of the golden rivers, but among them shalt thou dwell."

As I listened, enchanted, I suddenly became aware of a change in my surrounding. The palm tree, so lately overshadowing my exhausted form, was now some distance to my left and considerably below me. I was obviously floating in the atmosphere; companioned not only by the strange child and the radiant pair, but by a constantly increasing throng of half-luminous, vine-crowned youths and maidens with wind-blown hair and joyful countenance. We slowly ascended together, as if borne on a fragrant breeze which blew not from the earth but from the golden nebulae, and the child whispered in my ear that I must look always upward to the pathways of light, and never backward to the sphere I had just left. The youths and maidens now chanted mellifluous choriambics to the accompaniment of lutes, and I felt enveloped in a peace and

22

happiness more profound than any I had in life imagined, when the intrusion of a single sound altered my destiny and shattered my soul. Through the ravishing strains of the singers and the lutanists, as if in mocking, daemoniac concord, throbbed from gulfs below the damnable, the detestable pounding of that hideous ocean. And as those black breakers beat their message into my ears I forgot the words of the child and looked back, down upon the doomed scene from which I thought I had escaped.

Down through the aether I saw the accursed earth turning, ever turning, with angry and tempestuous seas gnawing at wild desolate shores and dashing foam against the tottering towers of deserted cities. And under a ghastly moon there gleamed sights I can never forget; deserts of corpselike clay and jungles of ruin and decadence where once stretched the populous plains and villages of my native land, and maelstroms of frothing ocean where once rose the mighty temples of my forefathers. Around the northern pole steamed a morass of noisome growths and miasmal vapours, hissing before the onslaught of the ever-mounting waves that curled and fretted from the shuddering deep. Then a rending report clave the night, and athwart the desert of deserts appeared a smoking rift. Still the black ocean foamed and gnawed, eating away the desert on either side as the rift in the centre widened and widened.

There was now no land left but the desert, and still the fuming ocean ate and ate. All at once I thought even the pounding sea seemed afraid of something, afraid of dark gods of the inner earth that are greater than the evil god of waters, but even if it was it could not turn back; and the desert had suffered too much from those nightmare waves to help them now. So the ocean ate the last of the land and poured into the smoking gulf, thereby giving up all it had ever conquered. From the new-flooded lands it flowed again, uncovering death and decay; and from its ancient and immemorial bed it trickled loathsomely, uncovering nighted secrets of the years when Time was young and the gods unborn. Above the waves rose weedy remembered spires. The moon laid pale lilies of light on dead London, and Paris stood up from its damp grave to be sanctified with star-dust. Then rose spires and monoliths that were weedy but not remembered; terrible spires and monoliths of lands that men never knew were lands.

There was not any pounding now, but only the unearthly roaring and hissing of waters tumbling into the rift. The smoke of that rift had changed into steam, and almost hid the world as it grew denser and denser. It seared my face and hands, and when I looked to see how it affected my companions I found they had all dis-appeared. Then very suddenly it ended, and I knew no more till I awaked upon a bed of convalescence. As the cloud of steam from the Plutonic gulf finally concealed the entire surface from my sight, all the firmament shrieked at a sudden agony of mad reverberations which shook the trembling aether. In one delirious flash and burst it happened; one blinding, deafening holocaust of fire, smoke, and thunder that dissolved the wan moon as it sped outward to the void.

And when the smoke cleared away, and I sought to look upon the earth, I beheld against the background of cold, humorous stars only the dying sun and the pale mournful planets searching for their sister.

NYARLATHOTEP

Nyarlathotep... the crawling chaos... I am the last... I will tell the audient void... I do not recall distinctly when it began, but it was months ago. The general tension was horrible. To a season of political and social upheaval was added a strange and brooding apprehension of hideous physical danger; a danger widespread and all-embracing, such a danger as may be imagined only in the most terrible phantasms of the night. I recall that the people went about with pale and worried faces, and whispered warnings and prophecies which no-one dared consciously repeat or acknowledge to himself that he had heard. A sense of monstrous guilt was upon the land, and out of the abysses between the stars swept chill currents that made men shiver in dark and lonely places. There was a demoniac alteration in the sequence of the seasons – the autumn heat lingered fearsomely, and everyone felt that the world and perhaps the universe had passed from the control of known gods or forces to that of gods or forces which were unknown.

And it was then that Nyarlathotep came out of Egypt. Who he was, none could tell, but he was of the old native blood and looked like a Pharaoh. The *fellahin* knelt when they saw him, yet none could say why. He said he had risen up out of the blackness of twenty-seven centuries, and that he had heard messages from places not on this planet. Into the lands of civilisation came Nyarlathotep, swarthy, slender, and sinister, always buying strange instruments of glass and metal and combining them into instruments yet stranger. He spoke much of the sciences – of electricity and psychology – and gave exhibitions of power which sent his spectators away speechless, yet which swelled his fame to exceeding magnitude. Men advised one another to see Nyarlathotep, and shuddered. And where Nyarlathotep went, rest vanished, for the small hours were rent with the screams of nightmare. Never before had the screams of nightmare been such a public problem; now the wise men almost wished they could forbid sleep in the small hours, that the shrieks of cities might less horribly disturb the pale, pitying moon as it glimmered on green waters gliding under bridges, and old steeples crumbling against a sickly sky.

I remember when Nyarlathotep came to my city – the great, the old, the terrible city of unnumbered crimes. My friend had told me of him, and of the impelling fascination and allurement of his revelations, and I burned with eagerness to explore his uttermost mysteries. My friend said they were horrible and impressive beyond my most fevered imaginings; that what was thrown on a screen in the darkened room prophesied things none but Nyarlathotep dared prophesy, and in the sputter of his sparks there was taken from men that which had never been taken before yet which shewed only in the eyes. And I heard it hinted abroad that those who knew Nyarlathotep looked on sights which others saw not.

It was in the hot autumn that I went through the night with the restless crowds to see Nyarlathotep; through the stifling night and up the endless stairs into the choking room. And shadowed on a screen, I saw hooded forms amidst ruins, and yellow evil faces peering from behind fallen monuments. And I saw the world battling against blackness; against the waves of destruction from ultimate space; whirling, churning, struggling around the dimming, cooling sun. Then the sparks played amazingly around the heads of the spectators, and hair stood up on end whilst shadows more grotesque than I can tell came out and squatted on the heads. And when I, who was colder and more scientific than the rest, mumbled a trembling protest about "imposture" and "static electricity", Nyarlathotep drove us all out, down the dizzy stairs into the damp, hot, deserted midnight streets. I screamed aloud that I was *not* afraid; that I never could be afraid; and others screamed with me for solace. We swore to one another that the city *was* exactly the same, and still alive; and when the electric lights began to fade we cursed the company over and over again, and laughed at the queer faces we made.

I believe we felt something coming down from the greenish moon, for when we began to depend on its light we drifted into curious involuntary marching formations and seemed to know our destinations though we dared not think of them. Once we looked at the pavement and found the blocks loose and displaced by grass, with scarce a line of rusted metal to shew where the tramways had run. And again we saw a tram-car, lone, windowless, dilapidated, and almost on its side. When we gazed around the horizon, we could not find the third tower by the river, and noticed that the silhouette of the second tower was ragged at the top. Then we split up into narrow columns, each of which seemed drawn in a different direction. One disappeared in a narrow alley to the left, leaving only the echo of a shocking moan. Another filed down a weed-choked subway entrance, howling with a laughter that was mad. My own column was sucked toward the open country, and presently I felt a chill which was not of the hot autumn; for as we stalked out on the dark moor, we beheld around us the hellish moon-glitter of evil snows. Trackless, inexplicable snows, swept asunder in one direction only, where lay a gulf all the blacker for its glittering walls. The column seemed very thin indeed as it plodded dreamily into the gulf. I lingered behind, for the black rift in the green-litten snow was frightful, and I thought I had heard the reverberations of a disquieting wail as my companions vanished; but my power to linger was slight. As if beckoned by those who had gone before, I half-floated between the titanic snow-drifts, quivering and afraid, into the sightless vortex of the un-imaginable.

Screamingly sentient, dumbly delirious, only the gods that were can tell. A sickened, sensitive shadow writhing in hands that are not hands, and whirled blindly past ghastly midnights of rotting creation, corpses of dead worlds with sores that were cities, charnel winds that brush the pallid stars and make them flicker low. Beyond the worlds vague ghosts of monstrous things; half-seen columns of unsanctified temples that rest on nameless rocks beneath space and reach up to dizzy vacua above the spheres of light and darkness. And through this revolting graveyard of the universe the muffled, maddening beating of drums, and thin, monotonous whine of blasphemous flutes from inconceivable, unlighted chambers beyond Time; the detestable pounding and piping whereunto dance slowly, awkwardly, and absurdly the gigantic, tenebrous ultimate gods – the blind, voiceless, mindless gargoyles whose soul is Nyarlathotep.

FROM BEYOND

Horrible beyond conception was the change which had taken place in my best friend, Crawford Tillinghast. I had not seen him since that day, two months and a half before, when he told me toward what goal his physical and metaphysical researches were leading; when he had answered my awed and almost frightened remonstrances by driving me from his laboratory and his house in a burst of fanatical rage, I had known that he now remained mostly shut in the attic laboratory with that accursed electrical machine, eating little and excluding even the servants, but I had not thought that a brief period of ten weeks could so alter and disfigure any human creature. It is not pleasant to see a stout man suddenly grown thin, and it is even worse when the baggy skin becomes yellowed or greyed, the eyes sunken, circled, and uncannily glowing, the forehead veined and corrugated, and the hands tremulous and twitching. And if added to this there be a repellent un-kemptness, a wild disorder of dress, a bushiness of dark hair white at the roots, and an unchecked growth of white beard on a face once clean-shaven, the cumulative effect is quite shocking. But such was the aspect of Crawford Tillinghast on the night his half coherent message brought me to his door after my weeks of exile; such was the spectre that trembled as it admitted me, candle in hand, and glanced furtively over its shoulder as if fearful of unseen things in the ancient, lonely house set back from Benevolent Street. That Crawford Tillinghast should ever have studied science and philosophy was a mistake. These things should be left to the frigid and impersonal investigator for they offer two equally tragic alternatives to the man of feeling and action; despair, if he fail in his quest, and terrors unutterable and unimaginable if he succeed. Tillinghast had once been the prey of failure, solitary and melancholy; but now I knew, with nauseating fears of my own, that he was the prey of success. I had indeed warned him ten weeks before, when he burst forth with his tale of what he felt himself about to discover. He had been flushed and excited then, talking in a high and unnatural, though always pedantic, voice.

"What do we know," he had said, "of the world and the universe about us? Our means of receiving impressions are absurdly few, and our notions of surrounding objects infinitely narrow. We see things only as we are constructed to see them, and can gain no idea of their absolute nature. With five feeble senses we pretend to comprehend the boundlessly complex cosmos, yet other beings with a wider, stronger, or different range of senses might not only see very differently the things we see, but might see and study whole worlds of matter, energy, and life which lie close at hand yet can never be detected with the senses we have. I have always believed that such strange, inaccessible worlds exist at our very elbows, *and now I believe I have found a way to break down the barriers.* I am not joking. Within twenty-four hours that machine near the table will generate waves acting on unrecognized sense-organs that exist in us as atrophied or rudimentary vestiges. Those waves will open up to us many vistas unknown to man, and several unknown to anything we consider organic life. We shall see that at which dogs howl in the dark, and that at which cats prick up their ears after midnight. We shall see these things, and other things which no breathing creature has yet seen. We shall overleap time, space, and dimensions, and without bodily motion peer to the bottom of creation."

When Tillinghast said these things I remonstrated, for I knew him well enough to be frightened rather than amused; but he was a fanatic, and drove me from the house. Now he was no less a fanatic, but his desire to speak had conquered his resentment, and he had written me imperatively in a hand I could scarcely recognize. As I entered the abode of the friend so suddenly metamorphosed to a shivering gargoyle, I became infected with the terror which seemed stalking in all the shadows. The words and beliefs expressed ten weeks before seemed bodied forth in the darkness beyond the small circle of candle light, and I sickened at the hollow, altered voice of my host. I wished the servants were about, and did not like it when he said they had all left three days previously. It seemed strange that old Gregory, at least, should desert his master without telling as tried a friend as I. It was he who had given me all the information I had of Tillinghast after I was repulsed in rage. Yet I soon subordinated all my fears to my growing curiosity and fascination. Just what Crawford Tillinghast now wished of me I could only guess, but that he had some stupendous secret or discovery to impart, I could not doubt. Before I had protested at his unnatural pryings into the unthinkable; now that he had evidently succeeded to some degree I almost shared his spirit, terrible though the cost of victory appeared. Up through the dark emptiness of the house I followed the bobbing candle in the hand of this shaking parody on man. The electricity seemed to be turned off, and when I asked my guide he said it was for a definite reason.

"It would be too much... I would not dare," he continued to mutter. I especially noted his new habit of muttering, for it was not like him to talk to himself. We entered the laboratory in the attic, and I observed that detestable electrical machine, glowing with a sickly, sinister violet luminosity. It was connected with a powerful chemical battery, but seemed to be receiving no current; for I recalled that in its experimental stage it had sputtered and purred when in action. In reply to my question Tillinghast mumbled that this permanent glow was not electrical in any sense that I could understand.

He now seated me near the machine, so that it was on my right, and turned a switch somewhere below the crowning cluster of glass bulbs. The usual sputtering began, turned to a whine, and terminated in a drone so soft as to suggest a return to silence. Meanwhile the luminosity increased, waned again, and assumed a pale, *outré* colour or blend of colours which I could neither place nor describe. Tillinghast had been watching me, and noted my puzzled expression.

"Do you know what that is?" he whispered, "*that is ultra-violet.*" He chuckled oddly at my surprise. "You thought ultra-violet was invisible, and so it is – but you can see that and many other visible things *now*.

"Listen to me! The waves from that thing are waking a thousand sleeping senses in us; senses which we inherit from aeons of evolution from the state of detached electrons to the state of organic humanity. I have seen the truth, and I intend to show it to you. Do you wonder how it will seem? I will tell you." Here Tillinghast seated himself directly opposite me, blowing out his candle and staring hideously into my eyes. "Your existing sense-organs – ears first, I think – will pick up many of the impressions, for they are closely connected with the dormant organs. Then there will be others. You have heard of the pineal gland? I laugh at the shallow endocrinologist, fellow-dupe and fellow-parvenu of the Freudian. That gland is the great sense organ of organs – *I have found out*. It is like sight in the end, and transmits visual pictures to the brain. If you are normal, that is the way you ought to get most of it... I mean you get most of the evidence *from beyond*."

I looked about the immense attic room with the sloping south wall, dimly lit by rays which the every-day eye cannot see. The far corners were all shadows, and the whole place took on a hazy unreality which obscured its nature and invited the imagination to symbolism and phantasm. During the interval that Tillinghast was silent I fancied myself in some vast incredible temple of long-dead gods; some vague edifice of innumerable black stone columns reaching up from a floor of damp slabs to a cloudy height beyond the range of my vision. The picture was very vivid for a while, but gradually gave way to a more horrible conception; that of utter, absolute solitude in infinite, sightless, soundless space. There seemed to be a void, and nothing more, and I felt a childish fear which prompted me to draw from my hip pocket the revolver I always carried after dark since the night I was held up in East Providence. Then, from the farthermost regions of remoteness, the sound softly glided into existence. It was infinitely faint, subtly vibrant, and unmistakably musical, but held a quality of surpassing wildness which made its impact feel like a delicate torture of my whole body. I felt sensations like those one feels when accidentally scratching ground glass. Simultaneously there developed something like a cold draught, which apparently swept past me from the direction of the distant sound. As I waited breathlessly I perceived that both sound and wind were increasing; the effect being to give me an odd notion of myself as tied to a pair of rails in the path of a gigantic approaching locomotive. I began to speak to Tillinghast, and as I did so all the unusual impressions abruptly vanished. I saw only the man, the glowing machines, and the dim apartment. Tillinghast was grinning repulsively at the revolver which I had almost unconsciously drawn, but from his expression I was sure he had seen and heard as much as I, if not a great deal more. I whispered what I had experienced and he bade me to remain as quiet and receptive as possible.

"Don't move," he cautioned, "for in these rays we are able to be seen as well as to see. I told you the servants left, but I didn't tell you how. It was that thick-witted house-keeper – she turned on the lights downstairs after I had warned her not to, and the wires picked up sympathetic vibrations. It must have been frightful – I could hear the screams up here in spite of all I was seeing and hearing from another direction, and later it was rather awful to find those empty heaps of clothes around the house. Mrs Updike's clothes were close to the front hall switch – that's how I know she did it. It got them all. But so long as we don't move we're fairly safe. Remember we're dealing with a hideous world in which we are practically helpless... *Keep still!*"

The combined shock of the revelation and of the abrupt command gave me a kind of paralysis, and in my terror my mind again opened to the impressions coming from what Tillinghast called *"beyond"*. I was now in a vortex of sound and motion, with confused pictures before my eyes. I saw the blurred outlines of the room, but from some point in space there seemed to be pouring a seething column of unrecognizable shapes of clouds, pene-trating the solid roof at a point ahead and to the right of me. Then I glimpsed the temple-like effect again, but this time the pillars reached up into an aerial ocean of light, which sent down one blinding beam along the path of the cloudy column I had seen before. After that the scene was almost wholly kaleidoscopic, and in the jumble of sights, sounds, and unidentified sense-impressions I felt that I was about to dissolve or in some way lose the solid form. One definite flash I shall always remember. I seemed for an instant to behold a patch of strange night sky filled with shining, revolving spheres, and as it receded I saw that the glowing suns formed a constellation or galaxy of settled shape; this shape being the distorted face of Crawford Tillinghast. At another time I felt the huge animate things brushing past me and occasionally *walking or drifting through my supposedly solid body*, and thought I saw Tillinghast look at them as though his better trained senses could catch them visually. I recalled what he had said of the pineal gland, and wondered what he saw with this preternatural eye.

Suddenly I myself became possessed of a kind of augmented sight. Over and above the luminous and shadowy chaos arose a picture which, though vague, held the elements of consistency and permanence. It was indeed somewhat familiar, for the unusual part was superimposed upon the usual terrestrial scene much as a cinema view may be thrown upon the painted curtain of a theater. I saw the attic laboratory, the electrical machine, and the unsightly form of Tillinghast opposite me; but of all the space unoccupied by familiar objects not one particle was vacant. Indescribable shapes both alive and otherwise were mixed in disgusting disarray, and close to every known thing were whole worlds of alien, unknown entities. It likewise seemed that all the known things entered into the composition of other unknown things, and vice versa. Foremost among the living objects were inky, jellyish monstrosities which flabbily quivered in harmony with the vibrations from the machine. They were present in loathsome profusion, and I saw to my horror that they *over-lapped*; that they were semi-fluid and capable of passing through one another and through what we know as solids. These things were never still, but seemed ever floating about with some malignant purpose. Sometimes they appeared to devour one another, the attacker launching itself at its victim and instantaneously obliterating the latter from sight. Shudderingly I felt that I knew what had obliterated the unfortunate servants, and could not exclude the things from my mind as I strove to observe other properties of the newly visible world that lies unseen around us. But Tillinghast had been watching me, and was speaking.

"You see them? You see them? You see the things that float and flop about you and through you every moment of your life? You see the creatures that form what men call the pure air and the blue sky? Have I not succeeded in breaking down the barrier; have I not shown you worlds that no other living men have seen?" I heard his scream through the horrible chaos, and looked at the wild face thrust so offensively close to mine. His eyes were pits of flame, and they glared at me with what I now saw was overwhelming hatred. The machine droned detestably.

"You think those floundering things wiped out the servants? Fool, they are harmless! But the servants are gone, aren't they? You tried to stop me; you discouraged me when I needed every drop of encouragement I could get; you were afraid of the cosmic truth, you damned coward, but now I've got you! What swept up the servants? What made them scream so loud?... Don't know, eh! You'll know soon enough. Look at me – listen to what I say – do you suppose there are really any such things as time and magnitude? Do you fancy there are such things as form or matter? I tell you, I have struck depths that your little brain can't picture. I have seen beyond the bounds of infinity and drawn down daemons from the stars... I have harnessed the shadows that stride from world to world to sow death and madness... Space belongs to me, do you hear? Things are hunting me now – the things that devour and dissolve – but I know how to elude them. It is you they will get, as they got the servants... Stirring, dear sir? I told you it was dangerous to move, I have saved you so far by telling you to keep still – saved you to see more sights and to listen to me. If you had moved, they would have been at you long ago. Don't worry, they won't *hurt* you. They didn't hurt the servants – it was the *seeing* that made the poor devils scream so. My pets are not pretty, for they come out of places where aesthetic standards are – *very different*. Disintegration is quite painless, I assure you – *but I want you to see them*. I almost saw them, but I knew how to stop. You are curious? I always knew you were no scientist. Trembling, eh. Trembling with anxiety to see the ultimate things I have discovered. Why don't you move, then? Tired? Well, don't worry, my friend, *for they are coming...* Look, look, curse you, look... it's just over your left shoulder..."

What remains to be told is very brief, and may be familiar to you from the newspaper accounts. The police heard a shot in the old Tillinghast house and found us there – Tillinghast dead and me unconscious. They arrested me because the revolver was in my hand, but released me in three hours, after they found it was apoplexy which had finished Tillinghast and saw that my shot had been directed at the noxious machine which now lay hopelessly shattered on the laboratory floor. I did not tell very much of what I had seen, for I feared the coroner would be sceptical; but from the evasive outline I did give the doctor told me that I had undoubtedly been hypnotized by the vindictive and homicidal madman.

I wish I could believe that doctor. It would help my shaky nerves if I could dismiss what I now have to think of the air and the sky about and above me. I never feel alone or comfortable, and a hideous sense of pursuit sometimes comes chillingly on me when I am weary. What prevents me from believing the doctor is this one simple fact – that the police never found the bodies of those servants whom they say Crawford Tillinghast murdered.

THE PICTURE IN THE HOUSE

Searchers after horror haunt strange, far places. For them are the catacombs of Ptolemais, and the carven mausolea of the nightmare countries. They climb to the moonlit towers of ruined Rhine castles, and falter down black cobwebbed steps beneath the scattered stones of forgotten cities in Asia. The haunted wood and the desolate mountain are their shrines, and they linger around the sinister monoliths on un-inhabited islands. But the true epicure in the terrible, to whom a new thrill of unutterable ghastliness is the chief end and justification of existence, esteems most of all the ancient, lonely farmhouses of backwoods New England; for there the dark elements of strength, solitude, grotesqueness and ignorance combine to form the perfection of the hideous.

Most horrible of all sights are the little unpainted wooden houses remote from travelled ways, usually squatted upon some damp, grassy slope or leaning against some gigantic outcropping of rock. Two hundred years and more they have leaned or squatted there, while the vines have crawled and the trees have swelled and spread. They are almost hidden now in lawless luxuriances of green and guardian shrouds of shadow; but the small-paned windows still stare shockingly, as if blinking through a lethal stupor which wards off madness by dulling the memory of unutterable things.

In such houses have dwelt generations of strange people, whose like the world has never seen. Seized with a gloomy and fanatical belief which exiled them from their kind, their ancestors sought the wilderness for freedom. There the scions of a conquering race indeed flourished free from the restrictions of their fellows, but cowered in an appalling slavery to the dismal phantasms of their own minds. Divorced from the enlightenment of civilization, the strength of these Puritans turned into singular channels; and in their isolation, morbid self-repression, and struggle for life with relentless Nature, there came to them dark furtive traits from the prehistoric depths of their cold Northern heritage. By necessity practical and by philosophy stern, these folks were not beautiful in their sins. Erring as all mortals must, they were forced by their rigid code to seek concealment above all else; so that they came to use less and less taste in what they concealed. Only the silent, sleepy, staring houses in the back-woods can tell all that has lain hidden since the early days, and they are not communicative, being loath to shake off the drowsiness which helps them forget. Sometimes one feels that it would be merciful to tear down these houses, for they must often dream.

It was to a time-battered edifice of this description that I was driven one afternoon in November 1896, by a rain of such chilling copiousness that any shelter was preferable to exposure. I had been travelling for some time amongst the people of the Miskatonic Valley in quest of certain genealogical data; and from the remote, devious, and problematical nature of my course, had deemed it convenient to employ a bicycle despite the lateness of the season. Now I found myself upon an apparently abandoned road which I had chosen as the shortest cut to Arkham, overtaken by the storm at a point far from any town, and confronted with no refuge save the antique and repellent wooden building which blinked with bleared windows from between two huge leafless elms near the foot of a rocky hill. Distant though it is from the remnant of a road, this house none the less impressed me unfavourably the very moment I espied it. Honest, wholesome structures do not stare at travellers so slyly and hauntingly, and in my genealogical researches I had encountered legends of a century before which biased me against places of this kind. Yet the force of the elements was such as to overcome my scruples, and I did not hesitate to wheel my machine up the weedy rise to the closed door which seemed at once so suggestive and secretive.

I had somehow taken it for granted that the house was abandoned, yet as I approached it I was not so sure, for though the walks were indeed over-grown with weeds, they seemed to retain their nature a little too well to argue complete desertion. Therefore instead of trying the door I knocked, feeling as I did so a trepidation I could scarcely explain. As I waited on the rough, mossy rock which served as a door-step, I glanced at the neighbouring windows and the panes of the transom above me, and noticed that although old, rattling, and almost opaque with dirt, they were not broken. The building, then, must still be inhabited, despite its isolation and general neglect. However, my rapping evoked no response, so after repeating the summons I tried the rusty latch and found the door unfastened. Inside was a little vestibule with walls from which the plaster was falling, and through the doorway came a faint but peculiarly hateful odour. I entered, carrying my bicycle, and closed the door behind me. Ahead rose a narrow staircase, flanked by a small door probably leading to the cellar, while to the left and right were closed doors leading to rooms on the ground floor.

Leaning my cycle against the wall I opened the door at the left, and crossed into a small low-ceiled chamber but dimly lighted by its two dusty windows and furnished in the barest and most primitive possible way. It appeared to be a kind of sitting-room, for it had a table and several chairs, and an immense fireplace above which ticked an antique clock on a mantel. Books and papers were very few, and in the prevailing gloom I could not readily discern the titles. What interested me was the uniform air of archaism as displayed in every visible detail. Most of the houses in this region I had found rich in relics of the past, but here the antiquity was curiously complete; for in all the room I could not discover a single article of definitely post-revolutionary date. Had the furnishings been less humble, the place would have been a collector's paradise.

As I surveyed this quaint apartment, I felt an increase in that aversion first excited by the bleak exterior of the house. Just what it was that I feared or loathed, I could by no means define; but something in the whole atmosphere seemed redolent of unhallowed age, of unpleasant crudeness, and of secrets which should be forgotten. I felt disinclined to sit down, and wandered about examining the various articles which I had noticed. The first object of my curiosity was a book of medium size lying upon the table and presenting such an antediluvian aspect that I marvelled at beholding it outside a museum or library. It was bound in leather with metal fittings, and was in an excellent state of preservation; being altogether an unusual sort of volume to encounter in an abode so lowly. When I opened it to the title page my wonder grew even greater, for it proved to be nothing less rare than Pigafetta's account of the Congo region, written in Latin from the notes of the sailor Lopez and printed at Frankfurt in 1598. I had often heard of this work, with its curious illustrations by the brothers De Bry, hence for a moment forgot my uneasiness in my desire to turn the pages before me. The engravings were indeed interesting, drawn wholly from imagination and careless descriptions, and represented negroes with white skins and Caucasian features; nor would I soon have closed the book had not an exceedingly trivial circumstance upset my tired nerves and revived my sensation of disquiet. What annoyed me was merely the persistent way in which the volume tended to fall open of itself at Plate XII, which represented in gruesome detail a butcher's shop of the cannibal Anziques. I experienced some shame at my susceptibility to so slight a thing, but the drawing nevertheless disturbed me, especially in connection with some adjacent passages descriptive of Anzique gastronomy.

I had turned to a neighbouring shelf and was examining its meagre literary contents – an eighteenth century Bible, a *Pilgrim's Progress* of like period, illustrated with grotesque woodcuts and printed by the almanack-maker Isaiah

Thomas, the rotting bulk of Cotton Mather's *Magnalia Christi Americana*, and a few other books of evidently equal age – when my attention was aroused by the unmistakable sound of walking in the room overhead. At first astonished and startled, considering the lack of response to my recent knocking at the door, I immediately afterward concluded that the walker had just awaked from a sound sleep, and listened with less surprise as the footsteps sounded on the creaking stairs. The tread was heavy, yet seemed to contain a curious quality of cautiousness; a quality which I disliked the more because the tread was heavy. When I had entered the room I had shut the door behind me. Now, after a moment of silence during which the walker may have been inspecting my bicycle in the hall, I heard a fumbling at the latch and saw the panelled portal swing open again.

In the doorway stood a person of such singular appearance that I should have exclaimed aloud but for the restraints of good breeding. Old, white-bearded, and ragged, my host possessed a countenance and physique which inspired equal wonder and respect. His height could not have been less than six feet, and despite a general air of age and poverty he was stout and powerful in proportion. His face, almost hidden by a long beard which grew high on the cheeks, seemed abnormally ruddy and less wrinkled than one might expect; while over a high forehead fell a shock of white hair little thinned by the years. His blue eyes, though a trifle bloodshot, seemed inexplicably keen and burning. But for his horrible unkemptness the man would have been as distinguished-looking as he was impressive. This unkemptness, however, made him offensive despite his face and figure. Of what his clothing consisted I could hardly tell, for it seemed to me no more than a mass of tatters surmounting a pair of high, heavy boots; and his lack of cleanliness surpassed description.

The appearance of this man, and the instinctive fear he inspired, prepared me for something like enmity; so that I almost shuddered through surprise and a sense of uncanny incongruity when he motioned me to a chair and addressed me in a thin, weak voice full of fawning respect and ingratiating hospitality. His speech was very curious, an extreme form of Yankee dialect I had thought long extinct; and I studied it closely as he sat down opposite me for conversation.

"Ketched in by the rain, be ye?" he greeted. "Glad ye was nigh the haouse en' hed the sense ta come right in. I calc'late I was asleep, else I'd a heerd ye – I ain't as young as I uster be, an' I need a paowerful sight o' naps naowadays. Trav'lin fur? I hain't seed many folks 'long this rud sence they tuk off the Arkham stage."

I replied that I was going to Arkham, and apologized for my rude entry into his domicile, whereupon he continued.

"Glad ta see ye, young Sir – new faces is scurce arount here, an' I hain't got much ta cheer me up these days. Guess yew hail from Bosting, don't ye? I never ben thar, but I kin tell a taown man when I see 'im – we had one fer deestrick schoolmaster in 'eighty-four, but he quit suddent an' no-one never heerd on 'im sence –" here the old man lapsed into a kind of chuckle, and made no explanation when I questioned him. He seemed to be in an aboundingly good humour, yet to possess those eccentricities which one might guess from his grooming. For some time he rambled on with an almost feverish geniality, when it struck me to ask him how he came by so rare a book as Pigafetta's *Regnum Congo*. The effect of this volume had not left me, and I felt a certain hesitancy in speaking of it, but curiosity over-mastered all the vague fears which had steadily accumulated since my first glimpse of the house. To my relief, the question did not seem an awkward one, for the old man answered freely and volubly.

"Oh, that Afriky book? Cap't Ebenezer Holt traded me thet in 'sixty-eight – him as was kilt in the war." Something about the name of Ebenezer Holt caused me to look up sharply. I had encountered it in my genealogical work, but not in any record since the Revolution. I wondered if my host could help me in the task at which I was labouring, and resolved to ask him about it later on. He continued.

"Ebenezer was on a Salem merchant-man for years, an' picked up a sight o' queer stuff in every port. He got this in London, I guess – he uster like ter buy things at the shops. I was up ta his haouse onct, on the hill, tradin' hosses, when I see this book. I relished the picters, so he give it in on a swap. 'Tis a queer book – here, leave me git on my spectacles –" The old man fumbled among his rags, producing a pair of dirty and amazingly antique glasses with small octagonal lenses and steel bows. Donning these, he reached for the volume on the table and turned the pages lovingly.

"Ebenezer cud read a leetle o' this – 'tis Latin – but I can't. I had two er three schoolmasters read me a bit, and Passon Clark, him they say got draownded in the pond – kin yew make anything outen it?" I told him that I could, and translated for his benefit a paragraph near the beginning. If I erred, he was not scholar enough to correct me; for he seemed childishly pleased at my English version. His proximity was becoming rather obnoxious, yet I saw no way to escape without offending him. I was amused at the childish fondness of this ignorant old man for the pictures in a book he could not read, and wondered how much better he could read the few books in English which adorned the room. This revelation of simplicity removed much of the ill-defined apprehension I had felt, and I smiled as my host rambled on.

"Queer haow picters kin set a body thinkin'. Take this un here near the front. Hev yew ever seed trees like thet, with big leaves a-floppin' over an' daown? And them men – them can't be niggers – they dew beat all. Kinder like Injuns, I guess, even ef they be in Afriky. Some o'these here critters look like monkeys, or half monkeys an' half men, but I never heerd o' nothin' like this un." Here he pointed to a fabulous creature of the artist, which one might describe as a sort of dragon with the head of an alligator.

"But naow I'll show ye the best un – over here nigh the middle –" The old man's speech grew a trifle thicker and his eyes assumed a brighter glow; but his fumbling hands, though seemingly clumsier than before, were entirely adequate to their mission. The book fell open, almost of its own accord and as if from frequent consultation at this place, to the repellent twelfth plate showing a butcher's shop amongst the Anzique cannibals. My sense of restlessness returned, though I did not exhibit it. The especially bizarre thing was that the artist had made his Africans look like white men – the limbs and quarters hanging about the walls of the shop were ghastly, while the butcher with his axe was hideously incongruous. But my host seemed to relish the view as much as I disliked it.

"What d'ye think o' this – ain't never see the like hereabouts, eh? When I see this I told Eb Holt, *That's suthin' ta stir ye up an' make yer blood tickle.* When I read in Scripter about slayin' – like them Midianites was slew – I kinder think things, but I ain't got no picter of it. Hereabody kin see all they is to it – I s'pose 'tis sinful, but ain't we all born an' livin' in sin? – Thet feller bein' chopped up gives me a tickle every time I look at 'im – I hev ta keep lookin' at 'im – see whar the butcher cut off his feet? Thar's his head on thet bench, with one arm side of it, an' t'other arm's on the other side o'the meat block."

As the man mumbled on in his shocking ecstasy the expression on his hairy, spectacled face became indescribable, but his voice sank rather than mounted. My own sensations can scarcely be recorded. All the terror I had dimly felt before rushed upon me actively and vividly, and I knew that I loathed the ancient and abhorrent creature so near me with an infinite intensity. His madness, or at least his partial perversion, seemed beyond dispute. He was almost whispering now, with a huskiness more terrible than a scream, and I trembled as I listened.

"As I says, 'tis queer haow picters sets ye thinkin'. D'ye know, young Sir, I'm right sot on this un here. Arter I got the book off Eb I uster look at it a lot, especial when I'd heerd Passon Clark rant o'Sundays in his big wig. Onct I tried suthin' funny – here, young Sir, don't git skeert – all I done was ter look at the picter afore I kilt the sheep for market – killin' sheep was kinder more fun arter lookin' at it –" The tone of the old man now sank very low, sometimes becoming so faint that his words were hardly audible. I listened to the rain, and to the rattling of the bleared, small-paned windows, and marked a rumbling of approaching thunder quite unusual for the season. Once a terrific flash and peal shook the frail house to its foundations, but the whisperer seemed not to notice it.

"Killin' sheep was kinder more fun – but d'ye know, 'twan't quite *satisfyin'*. Queer haow a cravin' gits a holt on ye – As ye love the Almighty, young man, don't tell nobody, but I swar ter Gawd the picter begun ta make me *hungry fer victals I couldn't raise nor buy* – here, set still, what's ailin' ye? – I didn't do nothin', only I wondered haow 'twud be ef I *did* – They say meat makes blood an' flesh, an' gives ye new life, so I wondered ef 'twudn't make a man live longer an' longer ef 'twas *more the same* –" But the whisperer never continued. The interruption was not produced by my fright, nor by the rapidly increasing storm amidst whose fury I was presently to open my eyes on a smoky solitude of blackened ruins. It was produced by a very simple though somewhat unusual happening.

The open book lay flat between us, with the picture staring repulsively upward. As the old man whispered the words *"more the same"* a tiny splattering impact was heard, and something showed on the yellowed paper of the up-turned volume. I thought of the rain and of a leaky roof, but rain is not red. On the butcher's shop of the Anzique cannibals a small red spattering glistened picturesquely, lending vividness to the horror of the engraving. The old man saw it, and stopped whispering even before my expression of horror made it necessary; saw it and glanced quickly toward the floor of the room he had left an hour before. I followed his glance, and beheld just above us on the loose plaster of the ancient ceiling a large irregular spot of wet crimson which seemed to spread even as I viewed it. I did not shriek or move, but merely shut my eyes. A moment later came the titanic thunderbolt of thunderbolts; blasting that accursed house of unutterable secrets and bringing the oblivion which alone saved my mind.

THE OUTSIDER

That night the Baron dreamt of many a wo;
And all his warrior-guests, with shade and form
Of witch, and demon, and large coffin-worm
Were long be-nightmared.

—Keats

Unhappy is he to whom the memories of childhood bring only fear and sadness. Wretched is he who looks back upon lone hours in vast and dismal chambers with brown hangings and maddening rows of antique books, or upon awed watches in twilight groves of grotesque, gigantic, and vine-encumbered trees that silently wave twisted branches far aloft. Such a lot the gods gave to me – to me, the dazed, the disappointed; the barren, the broken. And yet I am strangely content and cling desperately to those sere memories, when my mind momentarily threatens to reach beyond to *the other*.

I know not where I was born, save that the castle was infinitely old and infinitely horrible, full of dark passages and having high ceilings where the eye could find only cobwebs and shadows. The stones in the crumbling corridors seemed always hideously damp, and there was an accursed smell everywhere, as of the piled-up corpses of dead generations. It was never light, so that I used sometimes to light candles and gaze steadily at them for relief, nor was there any sun outdoors, since the terrible trees grew high above the topmost accessible tower. There was one black tower which reached above the trees into the unknown outer sky, but that was partly ruined and could not be ascended save by a well-nigh impossible climb up the sheer wall, stone by stone.

I must have lived years in this place, but I cannot measure the time. Beings must have cared for my needs, yet I cannot recall any person except myself, or anything alive but the noiseless rats and bats and spiders. I think that whoever nursed me must have been shockingly aged, since my first conception of a living person was that of somebody mockingly like myself, yet distorted, shrivelled, and decaying like the castle. To me there was nothing grotesque in the bones and skeletons that strewed some of the stone crypts deep down among the foundations. I fantastically associated these things with everyday events, and thought them more natural than the coloured pictures of living beings which I found in many of the mouldy books. From such books I learned all that I know. No teacher urged or guided me, and I do not recall hearing any human voice in all those years – not even my own; for although I had read of speech, I had never thought to try to speak aloud. My aspect was a matter equally unthought of, for there were no mirrors in the castle, and I merely regarded myself by instinct as akin to the youthful figures I saw drawn and painted in the books. I felt conscious of youth because I remembered so little.

Outside, across the putrid moat and under the dark mute trees, I would often lie and dream for hours about what I read in the books; and would longingly picture myself amidst gay crowds in the sunny world beyond the endless forests. Once I tried to escape from the forest, but as I went farther from the castle the shade grew denser and the air more filled with brooding fear; so that I ran frantically back lest I lose my way in a labyrinth of nighted silence.

So through endless twilights I dreamed and waited, though I knew not what I waited for. Then in the shadowy solitude my longing for light grew so frantic that I could rest no more, and I lifted entreating hands to the single black ruined tower that reached above the forest into the unknown outer sky. And at last I resolved to scale that tower, fall though I might; since it were better to glimpse the sky and perish, than to live without ever beholding day.

In the dank twilight I climbed the worn and aged stone stairs till I reached the level where they ceased, and thereafter clung perilously to small footholds leading upward. Ghastly and terrible was that dead, stairless cylinder of rock; black, ruined, and deserted, and sinister with startled bats whose wings made no noise. But more ghastly and terrible still was the slowness of my progress; for climb as I might, the darkness overhead grew no thinner, and a new chill as of haunted and venerable mould assailed me. I shivered as I wondered why I did not reach the light, and would have looked down had I dared. I fancied that night had come suddenly upon me, and vainly groped with one free hand for a window embrasure, that I might peer out and above, and try to judge the height I had attained.

All at once, after an infinity of awesome, sightless, crawling up that concave and desperate precipice, I felt my head touch a solid thing, and I knew I must have gained the roof, or at least some kind of floor. In the darkness I raised my free hand and tested the barrier, finding it stone and immovable. Then came a deadly circuit of the tower, clinging to whatever holds the slimy wall could give;

till finally my testing hand found the barrier yielding, and I turned upward again, pushing the slab or door with my head as I used both hands in my fearful ascent. There was no light revealed above, and as my hands went higher I knew that my climb was for the nonce ended; since the slab was the trap-door of an aperture leading to a level stone surface of greater circumference than the lower tower, no doubt the floor of some lofty and capacious observation chamber. I crawled through carefully, and tried to prevent the heavy slab from falling back into place, but failed in the latter attempt. As I lay exhausted on the stone floor I heard the eerie echoes of its fall, hoped when necessary to pry it up again.

Believing I was now at prodigious height, far above the accursed branches of the wood, I dragged myself up from the floor and fumbled about for windows, that I might look for the first time upon the sky, and the moon and stars of which I had read. But on every hand I was dis-appointed; since all that I found were vast shelves of marble, bearing odious oblong boxes of disturbing size. More and more I reflected, and wondered what hoary secrets might abide in this high apartment so many aeons cut off from the castle below. Then unexpectedly my hands came upon a doorway, where hung a portal of stone, rough with strange chiselling. Trying it, I found it locked; but with a supreme burst of strength I overcame all obstacles and dragged it open inward. As I did so there came to me the purest ecstasy I have ever known; for shining tranquilly through an ornate grating of iron, and down a short stone passageway of steps that ascended from the newly found doorway, was the radiant full moon, which I had never before seen save in dreams and in vague visions I dared not call memories.

Fancying now that I had attained the very pinnacle of the castle, I commenced to rush up the few steps beyond the door; but the sudden veiling of the moon by a cloud caused me to stumble, and I felt my way more slowly in the dark. It was still very dark when I reached the grating – which I tried carefully and found unlocked, but which I did not open for fear of falling from the amazing height to which I had climbed. Then the moon came out.

Most demoniacal of all shocks is that of the abysmally unexpected and grotesquely unbelievable. Nothing I had before undergone could compare in terror with what I now saw; with the bizarre marvels that sight implied. The sight itself was as simple as it was stupefying, for it was merely this: instead of a dizzying prospect of treetops seen from a lofty eminence, there stretched around me on the level through the grating nothing less than the solid ground, decked and diversified by marble slabs and columns, and over-shadowed by an ancient stone church, whose ruined spire gleamed spectrally in the moonlight.

Half-unconscious, I opened the grating and staggered out upon the white gravel path that stretched away in two directions. My mind, stunned and chaotic as it was, still held the frantic craving for light; and not even the fantastic wonder which had happened could stay my course. I neither knew nor cared whether my experience was insanity, dreaming, or magic; but was determined to gaze on brilliance and gaiety at any cost. I knew not who I was or what I was, or what my surroundings might be; though as I continued to stumble along I became conscious of a kind of fearsome latent memory that made my progress not wholly fortuitous. I passed under an arch out of that region of slabs and columns, and wandered through the open country; sometimes following the visible road, but sometimes leaving it curiously to tread across meadows where only occasional ruins bespoke the ancient presence of a forgotten road. Once I swam across a swift river where crumbling, mossy masonry told of a bridge long vanished.

Over two hours must have passed before I reached what seemed to be my goal, a venerable ivied castle in a thickly wooded park, maddeningly familiar, yet full of perplexing strangeness to me. I saw that the moat was filled in, and that some of the well-known towers were demolished; whilst new wings existed to confuse the beholder. But what I observed with chief interest and delight were the open windows – gorgeously ablaze with light and sending forth sound of the gayest revelry. Advancing to one of these I looked in and saw an oddly dressed company indeed; making merry, and speaking brightly to one another. I had never, seemingly, heard human speech before and could guess only vaguely what was said. Some of the faces seemed to hold expressions that brought up incredibly remote recollections, others were utterly alien.

I now stepped through the low window into the brilliantly lighted room, stepping as I did so from my single bright moment of hope to my blackest convulsion of despair and realization. The nightmare was quick to come, for as I entered, there occurred immediately one of the most terrifying demonstrations I had ever conceived. Scarcely had I crossed the sill when there descended upon the whole company a sudden and unheralded fear of hideous intensity, distorting every face and evoking the most horrible screams from nearly every throat. Flight was universal, and in the clamour and panic several fell in a swoon and were dragged away by their madly fleeing companions. Many covered their eyes with their hands, and plunged blindly and awkwardly in their race to escape, overturning furniture and stumbling against the walls before they managed to reach one of the many doors.

The cries were shocking; and as I stood in the brilliant apartment alone and dazed, listening to their vanishing echoes, I trembled at the thought of what might be lurking near me unseen. At a casual inspection the room seemed deserted, but when I moved towards one of the alcoves I thought I detected a presence there – a hint of motion beyond the golden-arched doorway leading to another and somewhat similar room. As I approached the arch I began to perceive the presence more clearly; and then, with the first and last sound I ever uttered – a ghastly ululation that revolted me almost as poignantly as its noxious cause – I beheld in full, frightful vividness the inconceivable, indescribable, and unmentionable monstrosity which had by its simple appearance changed a merry company to a herd of delirious fugitives.

I cannot even hint what it was like, for it was a compound of all that is unclean, uncanny, unwelcome, abnormal, and detestable. It was the ghoulish shade of decay, antiquity, and dissolution; the putrid, dripping eidolon of unwholesome revelation, the awful baring of that which the merciful earth should always hide. God knows it was not of this world – or no longer of this world – yet to my horror I saw in its eaten-away and bone-revealing outlines a leering, abhorrent travesty on the human shape; and in its mouldy, dis-integrating apparel an unspeakable quality that chilled me even more.

I was almost paralysed, but not too much so to make a feeble effort towards flight; a backward stumble which failed to break the spell in which the nameless, voiceless monster held me. My eyes bewitched by the glassy orbs which stared loathsomely into them, refused to close; though they were mercifully blurred, and showed the terrible object but indistinctly after the first shock. I tried to raise my hand to shut out the sight, yet so stunned were my nerves that my arm could not fully obey my will. The attempt, however, was enough to disturb my balance; so that I had to stagger forward several steps to avoid falling. As I did so I became suddenly and agonizingly aware of the nearness of the carrion thing, whose hideous hollow breathing I half fancied I could hear. Nearly mad, I found myself yet able to throw out a hand to ward off the foetid apparition which pressed so close; when in one cataclysmic second of cosmic nightmarishness and hellish accident *my fingers touched the rotting outstretched paw of the monster beneath the golden arch.*

I did not shriek, but all the fiendish ghouls that ride the nightwind shrieked for me as in that same second there crashed down upon my mind a single fleeting avalanche of soul-annihilating memory. I knew in that second all that had been; I remembered beyond the frightful castle and the trees, and recognized the altered edifice in which I now stood; I recognized, most terrible of all, the unholy abomination that stood leering before me as I withdrew my sullied fingers from its own.

But in the cosmos there is balm as well as bitterness, and that balm is nepenthe. In the supreme horror of that second I forgot what had horrified me, and the burst of black memory vanished in a chaos of echoing images. In a dream I fled from that haunted and accursed pile, and ran swiftly and silently in the moonlight. When I returned to the churchyard place of marble and went down the steps I found the stone trap-door immovable; but I was not sorry, for I had hated the antique castle and the trees. Now I ride with the mocking and friendly ghouls on the night-wind, and play by day amongst the catacombs of Nephren-Ka in the sealed and unknown valley of Hadoth by the Nile. I know that light is not for me, save that of the moon over the rock tombs of Neb, nor any gaiety save the un-named feasts of Nitokris beneath the Great Pyramid; yet in my new wildness and freedom I almost welcome the bitterness of alienage.

For although nepenthe has calmed me, I know always that I am an outsider; a stranger in this century and among those who are still men. This I have known ever since I stretched out my fingers to the abomination within that great gilded frame; stretched out my fingers and touched *a cold and unyielding surface of polished glass*.

THE MUSIC OF ERICH ZANN

I have examined maps of the city with the greatest care, yet have never again found the Rue d'Auseil. These maps have not been modern maps alone, for I know that names change. I have, on the contrary, delved deeply into all the antiquities of the place, and have personally explored every region, of whatever name, which could possibly answer to the street I knew as the Rue d'Auseil. But despite all I have done, it remains a humiliating fact that I cannot find the house, the street, or even the locality, where, during the last months of my impoverished life as a student of metaphysics at the university, I heard the music of Erich Zann.

That my memory is broken, I do not wonder; for my health, physical and mental, was gravely disturbed throughout the period of my residence in the Rue d'Auseil, and I recall that I took none of my few acquaintances there. But that I cannot find the place again is both singular and perplexing; for it was within a half-hour's walk of the university and was distinguished by peculiarities which could hardly be forgotten by any one who had been there. I have never met a person who has seen the Rue d'Auseil.

The Rue d'Auseil lay across a dark river bordered by precipitous brick blear-windowed warehouses and spanned by a ponderous bridge of dark stone. It was always shadowy along that river, as if the smoke of neighbouring factories shut out the sun perpetually. The river was also odorous with evil stenches which I have never smelled elsewhere, and which may some day help to find it, since I should recognize them at once. Beyond the bridge were narrow cobbled streets with rails; and then came the ascent, at first gradual, but incredibly steep as the Rue d'Auseil was reached.

I have never seen another street as narrow and steep as the Rue d'Auseil. It was almost a cliff, closed to all vehicles, consisting in several places of flights of steps, and ending at the top in a lofty ivied wall. Its paving was irregular, sometimes stone slabs, sometimes cobblestones, and sometimes bare earth with struggling greenish-grey vegetation. The houses were tall, peaked-roofed, incredibly old, and crazily leaning backward, forward, and sidewise. Occasionally an opposite pair, both leaning forward, almost met across the street like an arch; and certainly they kept most of the light from the ground below. There were a few overhead bridges from house to house across the street.

The inhabitants of that street impressed me peculiarly. At first, I thought it was because they were all silent and reticent; but later decided it was because they were all very old. I do not know how I came to live on such a street, but I was not myself when I moved there. I had been living in many poor places, always evicted for want of money; until at last I came upon that tottering house in the Rue d'Auseil kept by the paralytic Blandot. It was the third house from the top of the street, and by far the tallest of them all.

My room was on the fifth storey; the only inhabited room there, since the house was almost empty. On the night I arrived I heard strange music from the peaked garret overhead, and the next day asked old Blandot about it. He told me it was an old German viol-player, a strange dumb man who signed his name as Erich Zann, and who played evenings in a cheap theatre orchestra; adding that Zann's desire to play in the night after his return from the theatre was the reason he had chosen this lofty and isolated garret room, whose single gable window was the only point on the street from which one could look over the terminating wall at the declivity and panorama beyond.

Thereafter, I heard Zann every night, and although he kept me awake, I was haunted by the weirdness of his music. Knowing little of the art myself, I was yet certain that none of his harmonies had any relation to music I had heard before; and concluded that he was a composer of highly original genius. The longer I listened, the more I was fascinated, until after a week I resolved to make the old man's acquaintance.

One night as he was returning from his work, I intercepted Zann in the hallway and told him that I would like to know him and be with him when he played. He was a small, lean, bent person, with shabby clothes, blue eyes, grotesque, satyr-like face, and nearly bald head; and at my first words seemed both angered and frightened. My obvious friendliness, however, finally melted him; and he grudgingly motioned to me to follow him up the dark, creaking and rickety attic stairs. His room, one of only two in the steeply pitched garret, was on the west side, toward the high wall that formed the upper end of the street. Its size was very great, and seemed the greater because of its extraordinary barrenness and neglect. Of furniture there was only a narrow iron bedstead, a dingy washstand, a small table, a large bookcase, an iron music-rack, and three old-fashioned chairs. Sheets of music were piled in disorder about the floor. The walls were of bare boards, and had probably never known plaster; whilst the abundance of dust and cobwebs made the place seem more deserted than inhabited. Evidently Erich Zann's world of beauty lay in some far cosmos of the imagination.

Motioning me to sit down, the dumb man closed the door, turned the large wooden bolt, and lighted a candle to augment the one he had brought with him. He now removed his viol from its moth-eaten covering, and taking it, seated himself in the least uncomfortable of the chairs. He did not employ the music-rack, but, offering no choice and playing from memory, enchanted me for over an hour with strains I had never heard before; strains which must have been of his own devising. To describe their exact nature is impossible for one unversed in music. They were a kind of fugue, with recurrent passages of the most captivating quality, but to me were notable for the absence of any of the weird notes I had overheard from my room below on other occasions.

Those haunting notes I had remembered, and had often hummed and whistled inaccurately to myself, so when the player at length laid down his bow I asked him if he would render some of them. As I began my request the wrinkled satyr-like face lost the bored placidity it had possessed during the playing, and seemed to show the same curious mixture of anger and fright which I had noticed when first I accosted the old man. For a moment I was inclined to use persuasion, regarding rather lightly the whims of senility; and even tried to awaken my host's weirder mood by whistling a few of the strains to which I had listened the night before. But I did not pursue this course for more than a moment; for when the dumb musician recognized the whistled air his face grew suddenly distorted with an expression wholly beyond analysis, and his long, old, bony right hand reached out to stop my mouth and silence the crude imitation. As he did this he further demonstrated his eccentricity by casting a startled glance toward the lone curtained window, as if fearful of some intruder – a glance doubly absurd, since the garret stood high and inaccessible above all the adjacent roofs, this window being the only point on the steep street, as the concierge had told me, from which one could see over the wall at the summit.

The old man's glance brought Blandot's remark to my mind, and with a certain capriciousness I felt a wish to look out over the wide and dizzying panorama of moonlit roofs and city lights beyond the hilltop, which of all the dwellers in the Rue d'Auseil only this crabbed musician could see. I moved toward the window and would have drawn aside the nondescript curtains, when with a frightened rage even greater than before, the dumb lodger was upon me again; this time motioning with his head toward the door as he nervously strove to drag me thither with both hands. Now thoroughly disgusted with my host, I ordered him to release me, and told him I would go at once. His clutch relaxed, and as he saw my disgust and offence, his own anger seemed to subside. He tightened his relaxing grip, but this time in a friendly manner, forcing me into a chair; then with an appearance of wistfulness crossing to the littered table, where he wrote many words with a pencil, in the laboured French of a foreigner.

The note which he finally handed me was an appeal for tolerance and forgiveness. Zann said that he was old, lonely, and afflicted with strange fears and nervous disorders connected with his music and with other things. He had enjoyed my listening to his music, and wished I would come again and not mind his eccentricities. But he could not play to another his weird harmonies, and could not bear hearing them from another; nor could he bear having anything in his room touched by another. He had not known until our hallway conversation that I could overhear his playing in my room, and now asked me if I would arrange with Blandot to take a lower room where I could not hear him in the night. He would, he wrote, defray the difference in rent.

As I sat deciphering the execrable French, I felt more lenient towards the old man. He was a victim of physical and nervous suffering, as was I; and my metaphysical studies had taught me kindness. In the silence there came a slight sound from the window – the shutter must have rattled in the night wind, and for some reason I started almost as violently as did Erich Zann. So when I had finished reading, I shook my host by the hand, and departed as a friend.

The next day Blandot gave me a more expensive room on the third floor, between the apartments of an aged money-lender and the room of a respectable upholsterer. There was no-one on the fourth floor.

It was not long before I found that Zann's eagerness for my company was not as great as it had seemed while he was persuading me to move down from the fifth storey. He did not ask me to call on him, and when I did call he appeared uneasy and played listlessly. This was always at night – in the day he slept and would admit no-one. My liking for him did not grow, though the attic room and the weird music seemed to hold an odd fascination for me. I had a curious desire to look out of that window, over the wall and down the unseen slope at the glittering roofs and spires which must lie outspread there. Once I went up to the garret during theatre hours, when Zann was away, but the door was locked.

What I did succeed in doing was to overhear the nocturnal playing of the dumb old man. At first I would tip-toe up to my old fifth floor, then I grew bold enough to climb the last creaking staircase to the peaked garret. There in the narrow hall, outside the bolted door with the covered keyhole, I often heard sounds which filled me with an indefinable dread – the dread of vague wonder and brooding mystery. It was not that the sounds were hideous, for they were not; but that they held vibrations suggesting nothing on this globe of earth, and that at certain intervals they assumed a symphonic quality which I could hardly conceive as produced by one player. Certainly, Erich Zann was a genius of wild power. As the weeks passed, the playing grew wilder, whilst the old musician acquired an increasing haggardness and furtiveness pitiful to behold. He now refused to admit me at any time, and shunned me whenever we met on the stairs.

Then one night as I listened at the door, I heard the shrieking viol swell into a chaotic babel of sound; a pandemonium which would have led me to doubt my own shaking sanity had there not come from behind that barred portal a piteous proof that the horror was real – the awful, inarticulate cry which only a mute can utter, and which rises only in moments of the most terrible fear or anguish. I knocked repeatedly at the door, but received no response. Afterward I waited in the black hallway, shivering with cold and fear, till I heard the poor musician's feeble effort to rise from the floor by the aid of a chair. Believing him just conscious after a fainting fit, I renewed my rapping, at the same time calling out my name reassuringly. I heard Zann stumble to the window and close both shutter and sash, then stumble to the door, which he falteringly unfastened to admit me. This time his delight at having me present was real; for his distorted face gleamed with relief while he clutched at my coat as a child clutches at its mother's skirts.

Shaking pathetically, the old man forced me into a chair while he sank into another, beside which his viol and bow lay carelessly on the floor. He sat for some time inactive, nodding oddly, but having a paradoxical suggestion of intense and frightened listening. Subsequently he seemed to be satisfied, and crossing to a chair by the table wrote a brief note, handed it to me, and returned to the table, where he began to write rapidly and incessantly. The note implored me in the name of mercy, and for the sake of my own curiosity, to wait where I was while he prepared a full account in German of all the marvels and terrors which beset him. I waited, and the dumb man's pencil flew.

It was perhaps an hour later, while I still waited and while the old musician's feverishly written sheets still continued to pile up, that I saw Zann start as from the hint of a horrible shock. Unmistakably he was looking at the curtained window and listening shudderingly. Then I half fancied I heard a sound myself; though it was not a horrible sound, but rather an exquisitely low and infinitely distant musical note, suggesting a player in one of the neighbouring houses, or in some abode beyond the lofty wall over which I had never been able to look. Upon Zann the effect was terrible, for, dropping his pencil, suddenly he rose, seized his viol, and commenced to rend the night with the wildest playing I had ever heard from his bow save when listening at the barred door.

It would be useless to describe the playing of Erich Zann on that dreadful night. It was more horrible than anything I had ever overheard, because I could now see the expression of his face, and could realize that this time the motive was stark fear. He was trying to make a noise; to ward something off or drown something out – what, I could not imagine, awesome though I felt it must be. The playing grew fantastic, delirious, and hysterical, yet kept to the last the qualities of supreme genius which I knew this strange old man possessed. I recognized the air – it was a wild Hungarian dance popular in the theatres, and I reflected for a moment that this was the first time I had ever heard Zann play the work of another composer.

Louder and louder, wilder and wilder, mounted the shrieking and whining of that desperate viol. The player was dripping with an uncanny perspiration and twisted like a monkey, always looking frantically at the curtained window. In his frenzied strains I could almost see shadowy satyrs and bacchanals dancing and whirling insanely through seething abysses of clouds and smoke and lightning. And then I thought I heard a shriller, steadier note that was not from the viol; a calm, deliberate, purposeful, mocking note from far away in the West.

At this juncture the shutter began to rattle in a howling night wind which had sprung up outside as if in answer to the mad playing within. Zann's screaming viol now outdid itself, emitting sounds I had never thought a viol could emit. The shutter rattled more loudly, unfastened, and commenced slamming against the window. Then the glass broke shiveringly under the persistent impacts, and the chill wind rushed in, making the candles sputter and rustling the sheets of paper on the table where Zann had begun to write out his horrible secret. I looked at Zann, and saw that he was past conscious observation. His blue eyes were bulging, glassy, and sightless, and the frantic playing had become a blind, mechanical unrecognizable orgy that no pen could even suggest.

A sudden gust, stronger than the others, caught up the manuscript and bore it towards the window. I followed the flying sheets in desperation, but they were gone before I reached the demolished panes. Then I remembered my old wish to gaze from this window, the only window in the Rue d'Auseil from which one might see the slope beyond the wall, and the city outspread beneath. It was very dark, but the city's lights always burned, and I expected to see them there amidst the rain and wind. Yet when I looked from that highest of all gable windows, looked while the candles sputtered and the insane viol howled with the night wind, I saw no city spread below, and no friendly lights gleamed from remembered streets, but only the blackness of space illimitable; unimagined space alive with motion and music, and having no semblance of anything on earth. And as I stood there looking in terror, the wind blew out both the candles in that ancient peaked garret, leaving me in a savage and impenetrable darkness with chaos and pandemonium before me, and the demon madness of that night-baying viol behind me.

I staggered back in the dark, without the means of striking a light, crashing against the table, overturning a chair, and finally groping my way to the place where the blackness screamed with shocking music. To save myself and Erich Zann I could at least try, whatever the powers opposed to me. Once I thought some chill thing brushed me, and I screamed, but my scream could not be heard above that hideous viol. Suddenly out of the blackness the madly sawing bow struck me, and I knew I was close to the player. I felt ahead, touched the back of Zann's chair, and then found and shook his shoulder in an effort to bring him to his senses.

He did not respond, and still the viol shrieked on without slackening. I moved my hand to his head, whose mechanical nodding I was able to stop and shouted in his ear that we must both flee from the unknown things of the night. But he neither answered me nor abated the frenzy of his unutterable music, while all through the garret strange currents of wind seemed to dance in the darkness and babel. When my hand touched his ear I shuddered, though I knew not why − knew not why till I felt of the still face; the ice-cold, stiffened, unbreathing face whose glassy eyes bulged uselessly into the void. And then, by some miracle, finding the door and the large wooden bolt, I plunged wildly away from that glass-eyed thing in the dark, and from the ghoulish howling of that accursed viol whose fury increased even as I plunged.

Leaping, floating, flying down those endless stairs through the dark house; racing mindlessly out into the narrow, steep, and ancient street of steps and tottering houses; clattering down steps and over cobbles to the lower streets and the putrid canyon-walled river; panting across the great dark bridge to the broader, healthier streets and boulevards we know; all these are terrible impressions that linger with me. And I recall that there was no wind, and that the moon was out, and that all the lights of the city twinkled.

Despite my most careful searches and investigations, I have never since been able to find the Rue d'Auseil. But I am not wholly sorry; either for this or for the loss in undreamable abysses of the closely-written sheets which alone could have explained the music of Erich Zann.

HERBERT WEST: REANIMATOR

I : FROM THE DARK

Of Herbert West, who was my friend in college and in other life, I can speak only with extreme terror. This terror is not due altogether to the sinister manner of his recent disappearance, but was engendered by the whole nature of his life-work, and first gained its acute form more than seventeen years ago, when we were in the third year of our course at the Miskatonic University medical school in Arkham. While he was with me, the wonder and diabolism of his experiments fascinated me utterly, and I was his closest companion. Now that he is gone and the spell is broken, the actual fear is greater. Memories and possibilities are ever more hideous than realities.

The first horrible incident of our acquaintance was the greatest shock I ever experienced, and it is only with reluctance that I repeat it. As I have said, it happened when we were in medical school, where West had already made himself notorious through his wild theories on the nature of death and the possibility of overcoming it artificially. His views, which were widely ridiculed by the faculty and by his fellow-students, hinged on the essentially mechanistic nature of life; and concerned means for operating the organic machinery of mankind by calculated chemical action after the failure of natural processes. In his experiments with various animating solutions he had killed and treated immense numbers of rabbits, guinea-pigs, cats, dogs, and monkeys, till he had become the prime nuisance of the college. Several times he had actually obtained signs of life in animals supposedly dead; in many cases violent signs; but he soon saw that the perfection of his process, if indeed possible, would necessarily involve a lifetime of research. It likewise became clear that, since the same solution never worked alike on different organic species, he would require human subjects for further and more specialized progress. It was here that he first came into conflict with the college authorities, and was debarred from future experiments by no less a dignitary than the dean of the medical school himself – the learned and benevolent Dr Allan Halsey, whose work in behalf of the stricken is recalled by every old resident of Arkham.

I had always been exceptionally tolerant of West's pursuits, and we frequently discussed his theories, whose ramifications and corollaries were almost infinite. Holding with Haeckel that all life is a chemical and physical process, and that the so-called "soul" is a myth, my friend believed that artificial reanimation of the dead can depend only on the condition of the tissues; and that unless actual decomposition has set in, a corpse fully equipped with organs may with suitable measures be set going again in the peculiar fashion known as life. That the psychic or intellectual life might be impaired by the slight deterioration of sensitive brain-cells which even a short period of death would be apt to cause, West fully realized. It had at first been his hope to find a reagent which would restore vitality before the actual advent of death, and only repeated failures on animals had shown him that the natural and artificial life-motions were incompatible. He then sought extreme freshness in his specimens, injecting his solutions into the blood immediately after the extinction of life. It was this circumstance which made the professors so carelessly sceptical, for they felt that true death had not occurred in any case. They did not stop to view the matter closely and reasoningly.

It was not long after the faculty had interdicted his work that West confided to me his resolution to get fresh bodies in some manner, and continue in secret the experiments he could no longer perform openly. To hear him discussing ways and means was rather ghastly, for at the college we had never procured anatomical specimens ourselves. Whenever the morgue proved inadequate, two local negroes attended to this matter, and they were seldom questioned. West was then a small, slender, spectacled youth with delicate features, yellow hair, pale blue eyes, and a soft voice, and it was uncanny to hear him dwelling on the relative merits of Christ Church Cemetery and the potter's field, because practically every body in Christ Church was embalmed; a thing of course ruinous to West's researches. I was by this time his active and enthralled assistant, and helped him make all his decisions, not only concerning the source of bodies but concerning a suitable place for our loathsome work. It was I who thought of the deserted Chapman farmhouse beyond Meadow Hill, where we fitted up on the ground floor an operating room and a laboratory, each with dark curtains to conceal our midnight doings. The place was far from any road, and in sight of no other houses, yet precautions were none the less necessary; since rumours of strange lights, started by chance nocturnal roamers, would soon bring disaster on our enterprise. It was agreed to call the whole thing a chemical laboratory if discovery should occur. Gradually we equipped our sinister haunt of science with materials either purchased in Boston or quietly borrowed from the college – materials carefully made unrecognizable save to expert eyes – and provided spades and picks for the many burials we should have to make in the cellar. At the college we used an incinerator, but the apparatus was too costly for our unauthorized laboratory. Bodies were always a nuisance – even the small guinea-pig bodies from the slight clandestine experiments in West's room at the boarding-house.

We followed the local death-notices like ghouls, for our specimens demanded particular qualities. What we wanted were corpses interred soon after death and without artificial preservation; preferably free from malforming disease, and certainly with all organs present. Accident victims were our best hope. Not for many weeks did we hear of anything suitable; though we talked with morgue and hospital authorities, ostensibly in the college's interest, as often as we could without exciting suspicion. We found that the college had first choice in every case, so that it might be necessary to remain in Arkham during the summer, when only the limited summer-school classes were held. In the end, though, luck favoured us; for one day we heard of an almost ideal case in the potter's field; a brawny young workman drowned only the morning before in Summer's Pond, and buried at the town's expense without delay or embalming. That afternoon we found the new grave, and determined to begin work soon after midnight.

It was a repulsive task that we undertook in the black small hours, even though we lacked at that time the special horror of graveyards which later experiences brought to us. We carried spades and oil-dark lanterns, for although electric torches were then manufactured, they were not as satisfactory as the tungsten contrivances of today. The process of unearthing was slow and sordid – it might have been gruesomely poetical if we had been artists instead of scientists – and we were glad when our spades struck wood. When the pine box was fully uncovered West scrambled down and removed the lid, dragging out and propping up the contents. I reached down and hauled the contents out of the grave, and then both toiled hard to restore the spot to its former appearance. The affair made us rather nervous, especially the stiff form and vacant face of our first trophy, but we managed to remove all traces of our visit. When we had patted down the last shovelful of earth we put the specimen in a canvas sack and set out for the old Chapman place beyond Meadow Hill.

On an improvised dissecting-table in the old farmhouse, by the light of a powerful acetylene lamp, the specimen was not very spectral looking. It had been a sturdy and apparently unimaginative youth of wholesome plebeian type

– large-framed, grey-eyed, and brown-haired – a sound animal without psychological subtleties, and probably having vital processes of the simplest and healthiest sort. Now, with the eyes closed, it looked more asleep than dead; though the expert test of my friend soon left no doubt on the score. We had at last what West had always longed for – a real dead man of the ideal kind, ready for the solution as prepared according to the most careful calculations and theories for human use. The tension on our part became very great. We knew that there was scarcely a chance for anything like complete success, and could not avoid hideous fears at possible grotesque results of partial animation. Especially were we apprehensive concerning the mind and impulses of the creature, since in the space following death some of the more delicate cerebral cells might well have suffered deterioration. I, myself, still held some curious notions about the traditional "soul" of man, and felt an awe at the secrets that might be told by one returning from the dead. I wondered what sights this placid youth might have seen in inaccessible spheres, and what he could relate if fully restored to life. But my wonder was not overwhelming, since for the most part I shared the materialism of my friend. He was calmer than I as he forced a large quantity of his fluid into a vein of the body's arm, immediately binding the incision securely.

The waiting was gruesome, but West never faltered. Every now and then he applied his stethoscope to the specimen, and bore the negative results philosophically. After about three-quarters of an hour without the least sign of life he disappointedly pronounced the solution inadequate, but determined to make the most of his opportunity and try one change in the formula before disposing of his ghastly prize. We had that afternoon dug a grave in the cellar, and would have to fill it by dawn – for although we had fixed a lock on the house we wished to shun even the remotest risk of a ghoulish discovery. Besides, the body would not be even approximately fresh the next night. So taking the solitary acetylene lamp into the adjacent laboratory, we left our silent guest on the slab in the dark, and bent every energy to the mixing of a new solution; the weighing and measuring supervised by West with an almost fanatical care.

The awful event was very sudden, and wholly unexpected. I was pouring something from one test-tube to another, and West was busy over the alcohol blast-lamp which had to answer for a Bunsen burner in this gasless edifice, when from the pitch-black room we had left there burst the most appalling and demoniac succession of cries that either of us had ever heard. Not more unutterable could have been the chaos of hellish sound if the pit itself had opened to release the agony of the damned, for in one inconceivable cacophony was centred all the supernal terror and unnatural despair of animate nature. Human it could not have been – it is not in man to make such sounds – and without a thought of our late employment or its possible discovery both West and I leaped to the nearest window like stricken animals; overturning tubes, lamp, and retorts, and vaulting madly into the starred abyss of the rural night. I think we screamed ourselves as we stumbled frantically toward the town, though as we reached the outskirts we put on a semblance of restraint – just enough to seem like belated revellers struggling home from a debauch.

We did not separate, but managed to get to West's room, where we whispered with the gas up until dawn. By then we had calmed ourselves a little with rational theories and plans for investigation, so that we could sleep through the day – classes being disregarded. But that evening two items in the paper, wholly unrelated, made it again impossible for us to sleep. The old deserted Chapman house had inexplicably burned to an amorphous heap of ashes; that we could understand because of the upset lamp. Also, an attempt had been made to disturb a new grave in the potter's field, as if by futile and spadeless clawing at the earth. That we could not understand, for we had patted down the mould very carefully.

And for seventeen years after that West would look frequently over his shoulder, and complain of fancied footsteps behind him. Now he has disappeared.

II : THE PLAGUE-DEMON

I shall never forget that hideous summer sixteen years ago, when like a noxious afrite from the halls of Eblis typhoid stalked leeringly through Arkham. It is by that satanic scourge that most recall the year, for truly terror brooded with bat-wings over the piles of coffins in the tombs of Christ Church Cemetery; yet for me there is a great horror in that time – a horror known to me alone now that Herbert West has disappeared.

West and I were doing post-graduate work in summer classes at the medical school of Miskatonic University, and my friend had attained a wide notoriety because of his experiments leading toward the revivification of the dead. After the scientific slaughter of uncounted small animals the freakish work had ostensibly stopped by order of our sceptical dean, Dr Allan Halsey; though

West had continued to perform certain secret tests in his dingy boarding-house room, and had on one terrible and unforgettable occasion taken a human body from its grave in the potter's field to a deserted farmhouse beyond Meadow Hill.

I was with him on that odious occasion, and saw him inject into the still veins the elixir which he thought would to some extent restore life's chemical and physical processes. It had ended horribly – in a delirium of fear which we gradually came to attribute to our own over-wrought nerves – and West had never afterward been able to shake off a maddening sensation of being haunted and hunted. The body had not been quite fresh enough; it is obvious that to restore normal mental attributes a body must be very fresh indeed; and the burning of the old house had prevented us from burying the thing. It would have been better if we could have known it was underground.

After that experience West had dropped his researches for some time; but as the zeal of the born scientist slowly returned, he again became importunate with the college faculty, pleading for the use of the dissecting-room and of fresh human specimens for the work he regarded as so overwhelmingly important. His pleas, however, were wholly in vain; for the decision of Dr Halsey was inflexible, and the other professors all endorsed the verdict of their leader. In the radical theory of reanimation they saw nothing but the immature vagaries of a youthful enthusiast whose slight form, yellow hair, spectacled blue eyes, and soft voice gave no hint of the super-normal – almost diabolical – power of the cold brain within. I can see him now as he was then – and I shiver. He grew sterner of face, but never elderly. And now Sefton has had the mishap and West has vanished.

West clashed disagreeably with Dr Halsey near the end of our last undergraduate term in a wordy dispute that did less credit to him than to the kindly dean in point of courtesy. He felt that he was needlessly and irrationally retarded in a supremely great work; a work which he could of course conduct to suit himself in later years, but which he wished to begin while still possessed of the exceptional facilities of the university. That the tradition-bound elders should ignore his singular results on animals, and persist in their denial of the possibility of reanimation, was inexpressibly disgusting and almost incomprehensible to a youth of West's logical temperament. Only greater maturity could help him understand the chronic mental limitations of the "professor-doctor" type – the product of generations of pathetic Puritanism, kindly, conscientious, and sometimes gentle and amiable, yet always narrow, intolerant, custom-ridden, and lacking in perspective. Age has more charity for these incomplete yet high-souled characters, whose worst real vice is timidity, and who are ultimately punished by general ridicule for their intellectual sins – sins like Ptolemaism, Calvinism, anti-Darwinism, anti-Nietzscheism, and every sort of Sabbatarianism and sumptuary legislation. West, young despite his marvellous scientific acquirements, had scant patience with good Dr Halsey and his erudite colleagues; and nursed an increasing resentment, coupled with a desire to prove his theories to these obtuse worthies in some striking and dramatic fashion. Like most youths, he indulged in elaborate day-dreams of revenge, triumph, and final magnanimous forgiveness.

And then had come the scourge, grinning and lethal, from the nightmare caverns of Tartarus. West and I had graduated about the time of its beginning, but had remained for additional work at the summer school, so that we were in Arkham when it broke with full demoniac fury upon the town. Though not as yet licensed physicians, we now had our degrees, and were pressed frantically into public service as the numbers of the stricken grew. The situation was almost past management, and deaths ensued too frequently for the local undertakers fully to handle. Burials without embalming were made in rapid succession, and even the Christ Church Cemetery receiving tomb was crammed with coffins of the unembalmed dead. This circumstance was not without effect on West, who thought often of the irony of the situation – so many fresh specimens, yet none for his persecuted researches! We were frightfully overworked, and the terrific mental and nervous strain made my friend brood morbidly.

But West's gentle enemies were no less harassed with prostrating duties. College had all but closed, and every doctor of the medical faculty was helping to fight the typhoid plague. Dr Halsey in particular had distinguished himself in sacrificing service, applying his extreme skill with whole-hearted energy to cases which many others shunned because of danger or apparent hopelessness. Before a month was over the fearless dean had become a popular hero, though he seemed unconscious of his fame as he struggled to keep from collapsing with physical fatigue and nervous exhaustion. West could not withhold admiration for the fortitude of his foe, but because of this was even more determined to prove to him the truth of his amazing doctrines. Taking advantage of the disorganization of both college work and municipal health regulations, he managed to get a recently deceased body smuggled into the university dissecting-room one night, and in my presence injected a new modification of his solution. The thing actually opened its eyes, but only stared at the ceiling with a look of soul-petrifying horror before collapsing into an inertness from which nothing could rouse it. West said it was not fresh enough – the hot summer air does not favour corpses. That time we were almost caught before we incinerated the thing, and West doubted the advisability of repeating his daring misuse of the college laboratory.

The peak of the epidemic was reached in August. West and I were almost dead, and Dr Halsey did die on the fourteenth. The students all attended the hasty funeral on the fifteenth, and bought an impressive wreath, though the latter was quite overshadowed by the tributes sent by wealthy Arkham citizens and by the municipality itself. It was almost a public affair, for the dean had surely been a public benefactor. After the entombment we were all somewhat depressed, and spent the afternoon at the bar of the Commercial House; where West, though shaken by the death of his chief opponent, chilled the rest of us with references to his notorious theories. Most of the students went home, or to various duties, as the evening advanced; but West persuaded me to aid him in "making a night of it". West's landlady saw us arrive at his room about two in the morning, with a third man between us; and told her husband that we had all evidently dined and wined rather well.

Apparently this acidulous matron was right; for about three A.M. the whole house was aroused by cries coming from West's room, where when they broke down the door they found the two of us unconscious on the blood-stained carpet, beaten, scratched and mauled, and with the broken remnants of West's bottles and instruments around us. Only an open window told what had become of our assailant, and many wondered how he himself had fared after the terrific leap from the second storey to the lawn which he must have made. There were some strange garments in the room, but West upon regaining consciousness said they did not belong to the stranger, but were specimens collected for bacteriological analysis in the course of investigations on the transmission of germ diseases. He ordered them burnt as soon as possible in the capacious fireplace. To the police we both declared ignorance of our late companion's identity. He was, West nervously said, a congenial stranger whom we had met at some downtown bar of uncertain location. We had all been rather jovial, and West and I did not wish to have our pugnacious companion hunted down.

That same night saw the beginning of the second Arkham horror – the horror that to me eclipsed the plague itself. Christ Church Cemetery was the scene of a terrible killing; a watchman having been clawed to death in a manner not only too hideous for description, but raising a doubt as to the human agency of the deed. The victim had been seen alive considerably after midnight – the dawn revealed the unutterable thing. The manager of a circus at the neighbouring town of Bolton was questioned, but he swore that no beast had at any time escaped from its cage. Those who found the body noted a trail of blood leading to the receiving tomb, where a small pool of red lay on the concrete just outside the gate. A fainter trail led away toward the woods, but it soon gave out.

The next night devils danced on the roofs of Arkham, and unnatural madness howled in the wind. Through the fevered town had crept a curse which some said was greater than the plague, and which some whispered was the embodied demon-soul of the plague itself. Eight houses were entered by a nameless thing which strewed red death in its wake – in all, seventeen maimed and shapeless remnants of bodies were left behind by the voiceless, sadistic monster that crept abroad. A few persons had half seen it in the dark, and said it was white and like a malformed ape or anthropomorphic fiend. It had not left behind quite all that it had attacked, for sometimes it had been hungry. The number it had killed was fourteen; three of the bodies had been in stricken homes and had not been alive.

On the third night frantic bands of searchers, led by the police, captured it in a house on Crane Street near the Miskatonic campus. They had organized the quest with care, keeping in touch by means of volunteer telephone stations, and when someone in the college district had reported hearing a scratching at a shuttered window, the net was quickly spread. On account of the general alarm and precautions, there were only two more victims, and the capture was effected without major casualties. The thing was finally stopped by a bullet, though not a fatal one, and was rushed to the local hospital amidst universal excitement and loathing.

For it had been a man. This much was clear despite the nauseous eyes, the voiceless simianism, and the demoniac savagery. They dressed the wound and carted it to the asylum at Sefton, where it beat its head against the walls of a padded cell for sixteen years – until the recent mishap, when it escaped under circumstances that few like to mention. What had most disgusted the searchers of Arkham was the thing they noticed when the monster's face was cleaned – the mocking, unbelievable resemblance to a learned and self-sacrificing martyr who had been entombed but three days before – the late Dr Allan Halsey, public benefactor and dean of the medical school of Miskatonic University.

To the vanished Herbert West and to me the disgust and horror were supreme. I shudder tonight as I think of it, shudder even more than I did that

morning when West muttered through his bandages,
"Damn it, it wasn't *quite* fresh enough!"

III : SIX SHOTS BY MOONLIGHT

It is uncommon to fire all six shots of a revolver with great suddenness when one would probably be sufficient, but many things in the life of Herbert West were uncommon. It is, for instance, not often that a young physician leaving college is obliged to conceal the principles which guide his selection of a home and office, yet that was the case with Herbert West. When he and I obtained our degrees at the medical school of Miskatonic University, and sought to relieve our poverty by setting up as general practitioners, we took great care not to say that we chose our house because it was fairly well isolated, and as near as possible to the potter's field.

Reticence such as this is seldom without a cause, nor indeed was ours; for our requirements were those resulting from a life-work distinctly unpopular. Outwardly we were doctors only, but beneath the surface were aims of far greater and more terrible moment – for the essence of Herbert West's existence was a quest amid black and forbidden realms of the unknown, in which he hoped to uncover the secret of life and restore to perpetual animation the graveyard's cold clay. Such a quest demands strange materials, among them fresh human bodies; and in order to keep supplied with these indispensable things one must live quietly and not far from a place of informal interment.

West and I had met in college, and I had been the only one to sympathize with his hideous experiments. Gradually I had come to be his inseparable assistant, and now that we were out of college we had to keep together. It was not easy to find a good opening for two doctors in company, but finally the influence of the university secured us a practice in Bolton – a factory town near Arkham, the seat of the college. The Bolton Worsted Mills are the largest in the Miskatonic Valley, and their polyglot employees are never popular as patients with the local physicians. We chose our house with the greatest care, seizing at last on a rather run-down cottage near the end of Pond Street; five numbers from the closest neighbour, and separated from the local potter's field by only a stretch of meadow land, bisected by a narrow neck of the rather dense forest which lies to the north. The distance was greater than we wished, but we could get no nearer house without going on the other side of the field, wholly out of the factory district. We were not much displeased, however, since there were no people between us and our sinister source of supplies. The walk was a trifle long, but we could haul our silent specimens undisturbed.

Our practice was surprisingly large from the very first – large enough to please most young doctors, and large enough to prove a bore and a burden to students whose real interest lay elsewhere. The mill-hands were of somewhat turbulent inclinations; and besides their many natural needs, their frequent clashes and stabbing affrays gave us plenty to do. But what actually absorbed our minds was the secret laboratory we had fitted up in the cellar – the laboratory with the long table under the electric lights, where in the small hours of the morning we often injected West's various solutions into the veins of the things we dragged from the potter's field. West was experimenting madly to find something which would start man's vital motions anew after they had been stopped by the thing we call death, but had encountered the most ghastly obstacles. The solution had to be differently compounded for different types – what would serve for guinea-pigs would not serve for human beings, and different specimens required large modifications.

The bodies had to be exceedingly fresh, or the slight decomposition of brain tissue would render perfect reanimation impossible. Indeed, the greatest problem was to get them fresh enough – West had had horrible experiences during his secret college researches with corpses of doubtful vintage. The results of partial or imperfect animation were much more hideous than were the total failures, and we both held fearsome recollections of such things. Ever since our first demoniac session in the deserted farm house on Meadow Hill in Arkham, we had felt a brooding menace; and West, though a calm, blond, blue-eyed scientific automaton in most respects, often confessed to a shuddering sensation of stealthy pursuit. He half felt that he was followed – psychological delusion of shaken nerves, enhanced by the undeniably disturbing fact that at least one of our reanimated specimens was still alive – a frightful carnivorous thing in a padded cell at Sefton. Then there was another – our first – whose exact fate we had never learned.

We had fair luck with specimens in Bolton – much better than in Arkham. We had not been settled a week before we got an accident victim on the very night of burial, and made it open its eyes with an amazingly rational expression before the solution failed. It had lost an arm – if it had been a perfect body we might have succeeded better. Between then and the next January we secured three more, one total failure, one case of marked muscular motion, and one rather shivery thing – it rose of itself and uttered a sound. Then came a period when luck was poor; interments fell off, and those that did occur were of specimens either too diseased or too maimed for us. We kept track of all the deaths and their circumstances with systematic care.

One March night, however, we unexpectedly obtained a specimen which did not come from the potter's field. In Bolton the prevailing spirit of Puritanism had outlawed the sport of boxing – with the usual result. Surreptitious and ill-conducted bouts among the mill-workers were common, and occasionally professional talent of low grade was imported. This late winter night there had been such a match; evidently with disastrous results, since two timorous Poles had come to us with incoherently whispered entreaties to attend to a very secret and desperate case. We followed them to an abandoned barn, where the remnants of a crowd of frightened foreigners were watching a silent black form on the floor.

The match had been between Kid O'Brien – a lubberly and now quaking youth with a most un-Hibernian hooked nose – and Buck Robinson, "The Harlem Smoke." The negro had been knocked out, and a moment's examination showed us that he would permanently remain so. He was a loathsome, gorilla-like thing, with abnormally long arms which I could not help calling fore-legs, and a face that conjured up thoughts of unspeakable Congo secrets and tom-tom poundings under an eery moon. The body must have looked even worse in life – but the world holds many ugly things. Fear was upon the whole pitiful crowd, for they did not know what the law would expect of them if the affair were not hushed up; and they were grateful when West, in spite of my involuntary shudders, offered to get rid of the thing quietly – for a purpose I knew too well.

There was bright moonlight over the snowless landscape, but we dressed the thing and carried it home between us through the deserted streets and meadows, as we had carried a similar thing one horrible night in Arkham. We approached the house from the field in the rear, took the specimen in the back door and down the cellar stairs, and prepared it for the usual experiment. Our fear of the police was absurdly great, though we had timed our trip to avoid the solitary patrolman of that section.

The result was wearily anti-climactic. Ghastly as our prize appeared, it was wholly unresponsive to every solution we injected in its black arm, solutions prepared from experience with white specimens only. So as the hour grew dangerously near to dawn, we did as we had done with the others – dragged the thing across the meadows to the neck of the woods near the potter's field, and buried it there in the best sort of grave the frozen ground would furnish. The grave was not very deep, but fully as good as that of the previous specimen – the thing which had risen of itself and uttered a sound. In the light of our dark lanterns we carefully covered it with leaves and dead vines, fairly certain that the police would never find it in a forest so dim and dense.

The next day I was increasingly apprehensive about the police, for a patient brought rumours of a suspected fight and death. West had still another source of worry, for he had been called in the afternoon to a case which ended very threateningly. An Italian woman had become hysterical over her missing child, a lad of five who had strayed off early in the morning and failed to appear for dinner – and had developed symptoms highly alarming in view of an always weak heart. It was a very foolish hysteria, for the boy had often run away before; but Italian peasants are exceedingly superstitious, and this woman seemed as much harassed by omens as by facts. About seven o'clock in the evening she had died, and her frantic husband had made a frightful scene in his efforts to kill West, whom he wildly blamed for not saving her life. Friends had held him when he drew a stiletto, but West departed amidst his inhuman shrieks, curses, and oaths of vengeance. In his latest affliction the fellow seemed to have forgotten his child, who was still missing as the night advanced. There was some talk of searching the woods, but most of the family's friends were busy with the dead woman and the screaming man. Altogether, the nervous strain upon West must have been tremendous. Thoughts of the police and of the mad Italian both weighed heavily.

We retired about eleven, but I did not sleep well. Bolton had a surprisingly good police force for so small a town, and I could not help fearing the mess which would ensue if the affair of the night before were ever tracked down. It might mean the end of all our local work – and perhaps prison for both West and me. I did not like those rumours of a fight which were floating about. After the clock had struck three the moon shone in my eyes, but I turned over without rising to pull down the shade. Then came the steady rattling at the back door.

I lay still and somewhat dazed, but before long heard West's rap on my door. He was clad in dressing-gown and slippers, and had in his hand a revolver and an electric flashlight. From the revolver I knew he was thinking more of the crazed Italian than of the police.

"We'd better both go," he whispered. "It wouldn't do not to answer it anyway, and it may be a patient – it would be like one of those fools to try the back door."

So we both went down the stairs on tiptoe, with a fear partly justified and partly that which comes only from the soul of the weird small hours. The rattling continued, growing somewhat louder. When we reached the door I cautiously unbolted it and threw it open, and as the moon streamed revealingly down on the form silhouetted there, West did a peculiar thing. Despite the obvious danger of attracting notice and bringing on our heads the dreaded police investigation – a thing which after all was mercifully averted by the relative isolation of our cottage – my friend suddenly, excitedly, and unnecessarily emptied all six chambers of his revolver into the nocturnal visitor.

For that visitor was neither Italian nor policeman. Looming hideously against the spectral moon was a gigantic misshapen thing not to be imagined save in nightmares – a glass-eyed, ink-black apparition nearly on all fours, covered with bits of mould, leaves, and vines, foul with caked blood, and having between its glistening teeth a snow-white, terrible, cylindrical object terminating in a tiny hand.

IV : THE SCREAM OF THE DEAD

The scream of a dead man gave to me that acute and added horror of Dr Herbert West which harassed the latter years of our companionship. It is natural that such a thing as a dead man's scream should give horror, for it is obviously not a pleasing or ordinary occurrence; but I was used to similar experiences, hence suffered on this occasion only because of a particular circumstance. And, as I have implied, it was not of the dead man himself that I became afraid.

Herbert West, whose associate and assistant I was, possessed scientific interests far beyond the usual routine of a village physician. That was why, when establishing his practice in Bolton, he had chosen an isolated house near the potter's field. Briefly and brutally stated, West's sole absorbing interest was a secret study of the phenomena of life and its cessation, leading toward the reanimation of the dead through injections of an excitant solution. For this ghastly experimenting it was necessary to have a constant supply of very fresh human bodies; very fresh because even the least decay hopelessly damaged the brain structure, and human because we found that the solution had to be compounded differently for different types of organisms. Scores of rabbits and guinea-pigs had been killed and treated, but their trail was a blind one. West had never fully succeeded because he had never been able to secure a corpse sufficiently fresh. What he wanted were bodies from which vitality had only just departed; bodies with every cell intact and capable of receiving again the impulse toward that mode of motion called life. There was hope that this second and artificial life might be made perpetual by repetitions of the injection, but we had learned that an ordinary natural life would not respond to the action. To establish the artificial motion, nocturnal life must be extinct – the specimens must be very fresh, but genuinely dead.

The awesome quest had begun when West and I were students at the Miskatonic University medical school in Arkham, vividly conscious for the first time of the thoroughly mechanical nature of life. That was seven years before, but West looked scarcely a day older now – he was small, blond, clean-shaven, soft-voiced, and spectacled, with only an occasional flash of a cold blue eye to tell of the hardening and growing fanaticism of his character under the pressure of his terrible investigations. Our experiences had often been hideous in the extreme; the results of defective reanimation, when lumps of graveyard clay had been galvanized into morbid, unnatural, and brainless motion by various modifications of the vital solution.

One thing had uttered a nerve-shattering scream; another had risen violently, beaten us both to unconsciousness, and run amuck in a shocking way before it could be placed behind asylum bars; still another, a loathsome African monstrosity, had clawed out of its shallow grave and done a deed – West had to shoot that object. We could not get bodies fresh enough to show any trace of reason when reanimated, so had perforce created nameless horrors. It was disturbing to think that one, perhaps two, of our monsters still lived – that thought haunted us shadowingly, till finally West disappeared under frightful circumstances. But at the time of the scream in the cellar laboratory of the isolated Bolton cottage, our fears were subordinate to our anxiety for extremely fresh specimens. West was more avid than I, so that it almost seemed to me that he looked half-covetously at any very healthy living physique.

It was in July, 1910, that the bad luck regarding specimens began to turn. I had been on a long visit to my parents in Illinois, and upon my return found West in a state of singular elation. He had, he told me excitedly, in all likelihood solved the problem of freshness through an approach from an entirely new angle – that of artificial preservation. I had known that he was working on a new and highly unusual embalming compound, and was not surprised that it

70

had turned out well; but until he explained the details I was rather puzzled as to how such a compound could help in our work, since the objectionable staleness of the specimens was largely due to delay occurring before we secured them. This, I now saw, West had clearly recognized; creating his embalming compound for future rather than immediate use, and trusting to fate to supply again some very recent and unburied corpse, as it had years before when we obtained the Negro killed in the Bolton prize-fight. At last fate had been kind, so that on this occasion there lay in the secret cellar laboratory a corpse whose decay could not by any possibility have begun. What would happen on reanimation, and whether we could hope for a revival of mind and reason West did not venture to predict. The experiment would be a landmark in our studies, and he had saved the new body for my return, so that both might share the spectacle in accustomed fashion.

West told me how he had obtained the specimen. It had been a vigorous man; a well-dressed stranger just off the train on his way to transact some business with the Bolton Worsted Mills. The walk through the town had been long, and by the time the traveller paused at our cottage to ask the way to the factories his heart had become greatly overtaxed. He had refused a stimulant, and had suddenly dropped dead only a moment later. The body, as might be expected, seemed to West a heaven-sent gift. In his brief conversation the stranger had made it clear that he was unknown in Bolton, and a search of his pockets subsequently revealed him to be one Robert Leavitt of St Louis, apparently without a family to make inquiries about his disappearance. If this man could not be restored to life, no one would know of our experiment. We buried our materials in a dense strip of woods between the house and the potter's field. If, on the other hand, he could be restored, our fame would be brilliantly and perpetually established. So without delay West had injected into the body's wrist the compound which would hold it fresh for use after my arrival. The matter of the presumably weak heart, which to my mind imperilled the success of our experiment, did not appear to trouble West extensively. He hoped at last to obtain what he had never obtained before – a rekindled spark of reason and perhaps a normal, living creature.

So on the night of July 18, 1910, Herbert West and I stood in the cellar laboratory and gazed at a white, silent figure beneath the dazzling arc-light. The embalming compound had worked uncannily well, for as I stared fascinatedly at the sturdy frame which had lain two weeks without stiffening I was moved to seek West's assurance that the thing was really dead. This assurance he gave readily enough; reminding me that the reanimating solution was never used without careful tests as to life; since it could have no effect if any of the original vitality were present. As West proceeded to take preliminary steps, I was impressed by the vast intricacy of the new experiment; an intricacy so vast that he could trust no hand less delicate than his own. Forbidding me to touch the body, he first injected a drug in the wrist just beside the place his needle had punctured when injecting the embalming compound. This, he said, was to neutralize the compound and release the system to a normal relaxation so that the reanimating solution might freely work when injected. Slightly later, when a change and a gentle tremor seemed to affect the dead limbs, West stuffed a pillow-like object violently over the twitching face, not withdrawing it until the corpse appeared quiet and ready for our attempt at reanimation. The pale enthusiast now applied some last perfunctory tests for absolute lifelessness, withdrew satisfied, and finally injected into the left arm an accurately measured amount of the vital elixir; prepared during the afternoon with a greater care than we had used since college days, when our feats were new and groping. I cannot express the wild, breathless suspense with which we waited for results on this first really fresh specimen – the first we could reasonably expect to open its lips in rational speech, perhaps to tell of what it had seen beyond the unfathomable abyss.

West was a materialist, believing in no soul and attributing all the working of consciousness to bodily phenomena; consequently he looked for no revelation of hideous secrets from gulfs and caverns beyond death's barrier. I did not wholly disagree with him theoretically, yet held vague instinctive remnants of the primitive faith of my forefathers; so that I could not help eyeing the corpse with a certain amount of awe and terrible expectation. Besides – I could not extract from my memory that hideous, inhuman shriek we heard on the night we tried our first experiment in the deserted farmhouse at Arkham.

Very little time had elapsed before I saw the attempt was not to be a total failure. A touch of colour came to cheeks hitherto chalk-white, and spread out under the curiously ample stubble of sandy beard. West, who had his hand on the pulse of the left wrist, suddenly nodded significantly; and almost simultaneously a mist appeared on the mirror inclined above the body's mouth. There followed a few spasmodic muscular motions, and then an audible breathing, and visible motion of the chest. I looked at the closed eyelids, and thought I detected a quivering. Then the lids opened, showing eyes which were grey, calm, and alive, but still unintelligent and not even curious.

In a moment of fantastic whim I whispered questions to the reddening ears; questions of other worlds of which the memory might still be present. Subsequent terror drove them from my mind, but I think the last one, which I repeated was: "Where have you been?" I do not yet know whether I was answered or not, for no sound came from the well-shaped mouth; but I do know that at that moment I firmly thought the thin lips moved silently, forming syllables which I would have vocalized as "only now" if that phrase had possessed any sense or relevancy. At that moment, as I say, I was elated with the conviction that the one great goal had been attained; and that for the first time a reanimated corpse had uttered distinct words impelled by actual reason. In the next moment there was no doubt about the triumph; no doubt that the solution had truly accomplished, at least temporarily, its full mission of restoring rational and articulate life to the dead. But in that triumph there came to me the greatest of all horrors – not horror of the thing that spoke, but of the deed that I had witnessed and of the man with whom my professional fortunes were joined.

For that very fresh body, at last writhing into full and terrifying consciousness with eyes dilated at the memory of its last scene on earth, threw out its frantic hands in a life and death struggle with the air; and suddenly collapsing into a second and final dissolution from which there could be no return, screamed out the cry that will ring eternally in my aching brain:

"Help! Keep off, you cursed little tow-head fiend – keep that damned needle away from me!"

V : THE HORROR FROM THE SHADOWS

Many men have related hideous things, not mentioned in print, which happened on the battlefields of the Great War. Some of these things have made me faint, others have convulsed me with devastating nausea, while still others have made me tremble and look behind me in the dark; yet despite the worst of them I believe I can relate the most hideous thing of all – the shocking, the unnatural, the unbelievable horror from the shadows.

In 1915 I was a physician with the rank of First Lieutenant in a Canadian regiment in Flanders, one of many Americans to precede the government itself into the gigantic struggle. I had not entered the army on my initiative, but rather as a natural result of the enlistment of the man whose indispensable assistant I was – the celebrated Boston surgical specialist, Dr Herbert West. Dr West had been avid for a chance to serve as surgeon in a great war, and when the chance had come he carried me with him almost against my will. There were reasons why I would have been glad to let the war separate us; reasons why I found the practice of medicine and the companionship of West more and more irritating; but when he had gone to Ottawa and through a colleague's influence secured a medical commission as Major, I could not resist the imperious persuasion of one determined that I should accompany him in my usual capacity.

When I say that Dr West was avid to serve in battle, I do not mean to imply that he was either naturally warlike or anxious for the safety of civilization. Always an ice-cold intellectual machine: slight, blond, blue-eyed, and spectacled: I think he secretly sneered at my occasional martial enthusiams and censures of supine neutrality. There was, however, something he wanted in embattled Flanders; and in order to secure it he had to assume a military exterior. What he wanted was not a thing which many persons want, but something connected with the peculiar branch of medical science which he had chosen quite clandestinely to follow, and in which he had achieved amazing and occasionally hideous results. It was, in fact, nothing more or less than an abundant supply of freshly killed men in every stage of dismemberment.

Herbert West needed fresh bodies because his life-work was the reanimation of the dead. This work was not known to the fashionable clientele who had so swiftly built up his fame after his arrival in Boston; but was only too well known to me, who had been his closest friend and sole assistant since the old days in Miskatonic University medical school at Arkham. It was in those college days that he had begun his terrible experiments, first on small animals and then on human bodies shockingly obtained. There was a solution which he injected into the veins of dead things, and if they were fresh enough they responded in strange ways. He had had much trouble in discovering the proper formula, for each type of organism was found to need a stimulus especially adapted to it. Terror stalked him when he reflected on his partial failures; nameless things resulting from imperfect solutions or from bodies insufficiently fresh. A certain number of these failures had remained alive – one was in an asylum while others had vanished – and as he thought of conceivable yet virtually impossible eventualities he often shivered beneath his usual stolidity.

West had soon learned that absolute freshness was the prime requisite for useful specimens, and had accordingly resorted to frightful and unnatural expedients in body-snatching. In college, and during our early practice together in the factory town of Bolton, my attitude toward him had been largely one of fascinated admiration; but as his boldness in methods grew, I began to develop a gnawing fear. I did not like the way he looked at healthy living bodies; and then there came a nightmarish session in the cellar laboratory when I learned that a certain specimen had been a living body when he secured it. That was the first time he had ever been able to revive the quality of rational thought in a corpse; and his success, obtained at such a loathsome cost, had completely hardened him.

Of his methods in the intervening five years I dare not speak. I was held to him by sheer force of fear, and witnessed sights that no human tongue could repeat. Gradually I came to find Herbert West himself more horrible than anything he did – that was when it dawned on me that his once normal scientific zeal for prolonging life had subtly degenerated into a mere morbid and ghoulish curiosity and secret sense of charnel picturesqueness. His interest became a hellish and perverse addiction to the repellently and fiendishly abnormal; he gloated calmly over artificial monstrosities which would make most healthy men drop dead from fright and disgust; he became, behind his pallid intellectuality, a fastidious Baudelaire of physical experiment – a languid Elagabalus of the tombs.

Dangers he met unflinchingly; crimes he committed unmoved. I think the climax came when he had proved his point that rational life can be restored, and had sought new worlds to conquer by experimenting on the reanimation of detached parts of bodies. He had wild and original ideas on the independent vital properties of organic cells and nerve tissues separated from natural physiological systems; and achieved some hideous preliminary results in the form of never-dying, artificially nourished tissue obtained from the nearly-hatched eggs of an indescribable tropical reptile. Two biological points he was exceedingly anxious to settle – first, whether any amount of consciousness and rational action might be possible without the brain, proceeding from the spinal cord and various nerve-centres; and second, whether any kind of ethereal, intangible relation distinct from the material cells may exist to link the surgically separated parts of what has previously been a single living organism. All this research work required a prodigious supply of freshly slaughtered human flesh – and that was why Herbert West had entered the Great War.

The phantasmal, unmentionable thing occurred one midnight late in March, 1915, in a field hospital behind the lines at St Eloi. I wonder even now if it could have been other than a demoniac dream of delirium. West had a private laboratory in an east room of the barn-like temporary edifice, assigned him on his plea that he was devising new and radical methods for the treatment of hitherto hopeless cases of maiming. There he worked like a butcher in the midst of his gory wares – I could never get used to the levity with which he handled and classified certain things. At times he actually did perform marvels of surgery for the soldiers; but his chief delights were of a less public and philanthropic kind, requiring many explanations of sounds which seemed peculiar even amidst that babel of the damned. Among these sounds were frequent revolver-shots – surely not uncommon on a battlefield, but distinctly uncommon in a hospital. Dr West's reanimated specimens were not meant for long existence or a large audience. Besides human tissue, West employed much of the reptile embryo tissue which he had cultivated with such singular results. It was better than human material for maintaining life in organless fragments, and that was now my friend's chief activity. In a dark corner of the laboratory, over a queer incubating burner, he kept a large covered vat full of this reptilian cell-matter; which multiplied and grew puffily and hideously.

On the night of which I speak we had a splendid new specimen – a man at once physically powerful and of such high mentality that a sensitive nervous system was assured. It was rather ironic, for he was the officer who had helped West to his commission, and who was now to have been our associate. Moreover, he had in the past secretly studied the theory of reanimation to some extent under West. Major Sir Eric Moreland Clapham-Lee, D.S.O., was the greatest surgeon in our division, and had been hastily assigned to the St Eloi sector when news of the heavy fighting reached headquarters. He had come in an aeroplane piloted by the intrepid Lieutenant Ronald Hill, only to be shot down when directly over his destination. The fall had been spectacular and awful; Hill was unrecognizable afterward, but the wreck yielded up the great surgeon in a nearly decapitated but otherwise intact condition. West had greedily seized the lifeless thing which had once been his friend and fellow-scholar; and I shuddered when he finished severing the head, placed it in his hellish vat of pulpy reptile-tissue to preserve it for future experiments, and proceeded to treat the decapitated body on the operating table. He injected new blood, joined certain veins, arteries, and nerves at the headless neck, and closed the ghastly aperture with engrafted skin from an unidentified specimen which had borne an officer's uniform. I knew what he wanted – to see if this highly organized body could exhibit, without its head, any of the signs of mental life which had distinguished Sir Eric Moreland Clapham-Lee. Once a student of reanimation, this silent trunk was now gruesomely called upon to exemplify it.

I can still see Herbert West under the sinister electric light as he injected his reanimating solution into the arm of the headless body. The scene I cannot describe – I should faint if I tried it, for there is madness in a room full of classified charnel things, with blood and lesser human debris almost ankle-deep on the slimy floor, and with hideous reptilian abnormalities sprouting, bubbling, and baking over a winking bluish-green spectre of dim flame in a far corner of black shadows.

The specimen, as West repeatedly observed, had a splendid nervous system. Much was expected of it; and as a few twitching motions began to appear, I could see the feverish interest on West's face. He was ready, I think, to see proof of his increasingly strong opinion that consciousness, reason, and personality can exist independently of the brain – that man has no central connective spirit, but is merely a machine of nervous matter, each section more or less complete in itself. In one triumphant demonstration West was about to relegate the mystery of life to the category of myth. The body now twitched more vigorously, and beneath our avid eyes commenced to heave in a frightful way. The arms stirred disquietingly, the legs drew up, and various muscles contracted in a repulsive kind of writhing. Then the headless thing threw out its arms in a gesture which was unmistakably one of desperation – an intelligent desperation apparently sufficient to prove every theory of Herbert West. Certainly, the nerves were recalling the man's last act in life; the struggle to get free of the falling aeroplane.

What followed, I shall never positively know. It may have been wholly an hallucination from the shock caused at that instant by the sudden and complete destruction of the building in a cataclysm of German shell-fire – who can gainsay it, since West and I were the only proved survivors? West liked to think that before his recent disappearance, but there were times when he could not; for it was queer that we both had the same hallucination. The hideous occurrence itself was very simple, notable only for what it implied.

The body on the table had risen with a blind and terrible groping, and we had heard a sound. I should not call that sound a voice, for it was too awful. And yet its timbre was not the most awful thing about it. Neither was its message – it had merely screamed, "Jump, Ronald, for God's sake, jump!" The awful thing was its source.

For it had come from the large covered vat in that ghoulish corner of crawling black shadows.

VI : THE TOMB-LEGIONS

When Dr Herbert West disappeared a year ago, the Boston police questioned me closely. They suspected that I was holding something back, and perhaps suspected even graver things; but I could not tell them the truth because they would not have believed it. They knew, indeed, that West had been connected with activities beyond the credence of ordinary men; for his hideous experiments in the reanimation of dead bodies had long been too extensive to admit of perfect secrecy; but the final soul-shattering catastrophe held elements of demoniac phantasy which make even me doubt the reality in what I saw.

I was West's closest friend and only confidential assistant. We had met years before, in medical school, and from the first I had shared his terrible researches. He had slowly tried to perfect a solution which, injected into the veins of the newly deceased, would restore life; a labour demanding an abundance of fresh corpses and therefore involving the most unnatural actions. Still more shocking were the products of some of the experiments – grisly masses of flesh that had been dead, but that West waked to a blind, brainless, nauseous animation. These were the usual results, for in order to reawaken the mind it was necessary to have specimens so absolutely fresh that no decay could possibly affect the delicate brain cells.

This need for very fresh corpses had been West's moral undoing. They were hard to get, and one awful day he had secured his specimen while it was still alive and vigorous. A struggle, a needle, and a powerful alkaloid had transformed it to a very fresh corpse, and the experiment had succeeded for a brief and memorable moment; but West had emerged with a soul calloused and seared, and a hardened eye which sometimes glanced with a kind of hideous and calculating appraisal at men of especially sensitive brain and especially vigorous physique. Toward the last I became acutely afraid of West, for he began to look at me that way. People did not seem to notice his glances, but they noticed my fear; and after his disappearance used that as a basis for some absurd suspicions.

West, in reality, was more afraid than I; for his abominable pursuits entailed a life of furtiveness and dread of every shadow. Partly it was the police he feared; but sometimes his nervousness was deeper and more nebulous, touching on certain indescribable things into which he had injected a morbid life, and from which he had not seen that life depart. He usually finished his experiments with a revolver, but a few times he had not been quick enough. There was that first specimen on whose rifled grave marks of clawing were later seen. There was also that Arkham professor's body which had done cannibal things before it had been captured and thrust unidentified into a madhouse cell at Sefton, where it beat the walls for sixteen years. Most of the other possibly surviving results were things less easy to speak of – for in later years West's scientific zeal had degenerated to an unhealthy and fantastic mania, and he had spent his chief skill in vitalizing not entire human bodies but isolated parts of bodies, or parts joined to organic matter other than human. It had become fiendishly disgusting by the time he disappeared; many of the experiments could not even be hinted at in print. The Great War, through which both of us served as surgeons, had intensified this side of West.

In saying that West's fear of his specimens was nebulous, I have in mind particularly its complex nature. Part of it came merely from knowing of the existence of such nameless monsters, while another part arose from apprehension of the bodily harm they might under certain circumstances do him. Their disappearance added horror to the situation – of them all West knew the whereabouts of only one, the pitiful asylum thing. Then there was a more subtle feat – a very fantastic sensation resulting from a curious experiment in the Canadian army in 1915. West, in the midst of a severe battle, had reanimated Major Sir Eric Moreland Clapham-Lee, D.S.O., a fellow-physician who knew about his experiments and could have duplicated them. The head had been removed, so that the possibilities of quasi-intelligent life in the trunk might be investigated. Just as the building was wiped out by a German shell, there had been a success. The trunk had moved intelligently; and, unbelievably to relate, we were both sickeningly sure that articulate sounds had come from the detached head as it lay in a shadowy corner of the laboratory. The shell had been merciful, in a way – but West could never feel as certain as he wished, that we two were the only survivors. He used to make shuddering conjectures about the possible actions of a headless physician with the power of reanimating the dead.

West's last quarters were in a venerable house of much elegance, overlooking one of the oldest burying grounds in Boston. He had chosen the place for purely symbolic and fantastically aesthetic reasons, since most of the interments were of the Colonial period and therefore of little use to a scientist seeking very fresh bodies. The laboratory was in a sub-cellar secretly constructed by imported workmen, and contained a huge incinerator for the quiet and complete disposal of such bodies, or fragments and synthetic mockeries of bodies, as might remain from the morbid experiments and unhallowed amusements of the owner. During the excavation of this cellar the workmen had struck some exceedingly ancient masonry; undoubtedly connected with the old burying ground, yet far too deep to correspond with any known sepulchre therein. After a number of calculations West decided that it represented some secret chamber beneath the tomb of the Averills, where the last interment had been made in 1768. I was with him when he studied the nitrous, dripping walls laid bare by the spades and mattocks of the men, and was prepared for the gruesome thrill which would attend the uncovering of centuried grave-secrets; but for the first time West's new timidity conquered his natural curiosity, and he betrayed his degenerating fibre by ordering the masonry left intact and plastered over. Thus it remained till that final hellish night, part of the walls of the secret laboratory. I speak of West's decadence, but must add that it was a purely mental and intangible thing. Outwardly he was the same to the last – calm, cold, slight, and yellow-haired, with spectacled blue eyes and a general aspect of youth which years and fears seemed never to change. He seemed calm even when he thought of that clawed grave and looked over his shoulder; even when he thought of the carnivorous thing that gnawed and pawed at Sefton bars.

The end of Herbert West began one evening in our joint study when he was dividing his curious glance between the newspaper and me. A strange headline item had struck at him from the crumpled pages, and a nameless titan claw had seemed to reach down through sixteen years. Something fearsome and incredible had happened at Sefton Asylum fifty miles away, stunning the neighbourhood and baffling the police. In the small hours of the morning a body of silent men had entered the grounds and their leader had aroused the attendants. He was a menacing military figure who talked without moving his lips and whose voice seemed almost ventriloquially connected with an immense black case he carried. His expressionless face was handsome to the point of radiant beauty, but had shocked the superintendent when the hall light fell on it – for it was a wax face with eyes of painted glass. Some nameless accident had befallen this man. A larger man guided his steps; a repellent hulk whose bluish face seemed half eaten away by some unknown malady. The speaker had asked for the custody of the cannibal monster committed from Arkham sixteen years before; and upon being refused, gave a signal which precipitated a shocking riot. The fiends had beaten, trampled, and bitten every attendant who did not flee; killing four and finally succeeding in the liberation of the monster. Those victims who could recall the event without hysteria swore that the creatures had acted less like men than like unthinkable automata guided by the wax-faced leader. By the time help could be summoned, every trace of the men and of their mad charge had vanished.

From the hour of reading this item until midnight, West sat almost paralyzed. At midnight the doorbell rang, startling him fearfully. All the servants were asleep in the attic, so I answered the bell. As I have told the police, there was no wagon in the street; but only a group of strange-looking figures bearing a large square box which they deposited in the hallway after one of them had grunted in a highly unnatural voice, "Express – prepaid." They filed out of the house with a jerky tread, and as I watched them go I had an odd idea that they were turning towards the ancient cemetery on which the back of the house abutted. When I slammed the door after them West came downstairs and looked at the box. It was about two feet square, and bore West's correct name and present address. It also bore the inscription, "From Eric Moreland Clapham-Lee, St Eloi, Flanders." Six years before, in Flanders, a shelled hospital had fallen upon the headless reanimated trunk of Dr Clapham-Lee, and upon the detached head which – perhaps – had uttered articulate sounds.

West was not even excited now. His condition was more ghastly. Quickly he said, "It's the finish – but let's incinerate – *this.*" We carried the thing down to the laboratory – listening. I do not remember many particulars – you can imagine my state of mind – but it is a vicious lie to say it was Herbert West's body which I put into the incinerator. We both inserted the whole unopened box, closed the door, and started the electricity. Nor did any sound come from the box, after all.

It was West who first noticed the falling plaster on that part of the wall where the ancient tomb masonry had been covered up. I was going to run, but he stopped me. Then I saw a small black aperture, felt a ghoulish wind of ice, and smelled the charnel bowels of a putrescent earth. There was no sound, but just then the electric lights went out and I saw outlined against some phosphorescence of the nether world a horde of silent toiling things which only insanity – or worse – could create. Their outlines were human, semi-human, fractionally human, and not human at all – the horde was grotesquely heterogeneous. They were removing the stones quietly, one by one, from the centuried wall. And then, as the breach became large enough, they came out into the laboratory in a single file; led by a stalking thing with a beautiful head made of wax. A sort of mad-eyed monstrosity behind the leader seized on Herbert West. West did not resist or utter a sound. Then they all sprang at him and tore him to pieces before my eyes, bearing the fragments away into that subterranean vault of fabulous abominations. West's head was carried off by the wax-headed leader, who wore a Canadian officer's uniform. As it disappeared I saw that the blue eyes behind the spectacles were hideously blazing with their first touch of frantic, visible emotion.

Servants found me unconscious in the morning. West was gone. The incinerator contained only unidentifiable ashes. Detectives have questioned me, but what can I say? The Sefton tragedy they will not connect with West; not that, nor the men with the box, whose existence they deny. I told them of the vault, and they pointed to the unbroken plaster wall and laughed. So I told them no more. They imply that I am either a madman or a murderer – probably I am mad. But I might not be mad if those accursed tomb-legions had not been so silent.

THE HOUND

In my tortured ears there sounds unceasingly a nightmare whirring and flapping, and a faint distant baying as of some gigantic hound. It is not dream – it is not, I fear, even madness – for too much has already happened to give me these merciful doubts.

St John is a mangled corpse; I alone know why, and such is my knowledge that I am about to blow out my brains for fear I shall be mangled in the same way. Down unlit and illimitable corridors of eldritch phantasy sweeps the black, shapeless Nemesis that drives me to self-annihilation.

May heaven forgive the folly and morbidity which led us both to so monstrous a fate! Wearied with the commonplaces of a prosaic world, where even the joys of romance and adventure soon grow stale, St John and I had followed enthusiastically every aesthetic and intellectual movement which promised respite from our devastating ennui. The enigmas of the Symbolists and the ecstasies of the pre-Raphaelites all were ours in their time, but each new mood was drained too soon, of its diverting novelty and appeal.

Only the sombre philosophy of the Decadents could help us, and this we found potent only by increasing gradually the depth and diabolism of our pene-trations. Baudelaire and Huysmans were soon exhausted of thrills, till finally there remained for us only the more direct stimuli of unnatural personal experiences and adventures. It was this frightful emotional need which led us eventually to that detestable course which even in my present fear I mention with shame and timidity – that hideous extremity of human outrage, the abhorred practice of grave-robbing.

I cannot reveal the details of our shocking expeditions, or catalogue even partly the worst of the trophies adorning the nameless museum we prepared in the great stone house where we jointly dwelt, alone and servantless. Our museum was a blasphemous, unthinkable place, where with the satanic taste of neurotic virtuosi we had assembled a universe of terror and decay to excite our jaded sensibilities. It was a secret room, far, far, underground; where huge winged daemons carven of basalt and onyx vomited from wide grinning mouths weird green and orange light, and hidden pneumatic pipes ruffled into kaleidoscopic dances of death the lines of red charnel things hand in hand woven in voluminous black hangings. Through these pipes came at will the odours our moods most craved; sometimes the scent of pale funeral lilies; sometimes the narcotic incense of imagined Eastern shrines of the kingly dead, and sometimes – how I shudder to recall it! – the frightful, soul-upheaving stenches of the uncovered grave.

Around the walls of this repellent chamber were cases of antique mummies alternating with comely, lifelike bodies perfectly stuffed and cured by the taxi-dermist's art, and with headstones snatched from the oldest churchyards of the world. Niches here and there contained skulls of all shapes, and heads preserved in various stages of dissolution. There one might find the rotting, bald pates of famous noblemen, and the fresh and radiantly golden heads of new-buried children.

Statues and paintings there were, all of fiendish subjects and some executed by St John and myself. A locked portfolio, bound in tanned human skin, held certain unknown and unnameable drawings which it was rumoured Goya had perpetrated but dared not acknowledge. There were nauseous musical instruments, stringed, brass, and wood-wind, on which St John and I sometimes produced dissonances of exquisite morbidity and cacodaemoniacal ghastliness; whilst in a multitude of inlaid ebony cabinets reposed the most incredible and unimaginable variety of tomb-loot ever assembled by human madness and perversity. It is of this loot in particular that I must not speak – thank God I had the courage to destroy it long before I thought of destroying myself!

The predatory excursions on which we collected our unmentionable treasures were always artistically memorable events. We were no vulgar ghouls, but worked only under certain conditions of mood, land-scape, environment, weather, season, and moonlight. These pastimes were to us the most exquisite form of aesthetic expression, and we gave their details a fastidious technical care. An inappropriate hour, a jarring lighting effect, or a clumsy manipulation of the damp sod, would almost totally destroy for us that ecstatic titillation which followed the exhumation of some ominous, grinning secret of the earth. Our quest for novel scenes and piquant conditions was feverish and insatiate – St John was always the leader, and he it was who led the way at last to that mocking, accursed spot which brought us our hideous and inevitable doom.

By what malign fatality were we lured to that terrible Holland churchyard? I think it was the dark rumour and legendry, the tales of one buried for five centuries, who had himself been a ghoul in his time and had stolen a potent thing from a mighty sepulchre. I can recall the scene in these final moments – the pale autumnal moon over the graves, casting long horrible shadows; the grotesque trees, drooping sullenly to meet the neglected grass and the crumbling slabs; the vast legions of strangely colossal bats that flew against the moon; the antique ivied church pointing a huge spectral finger at the livid sky; the phosphorescent insects that danced like death-fires under the yews in a distant corner; the odours of mould, vegetation, and less explicable things that mingled feebly with the night-wind from over far swamps and seas; and, worst of all, the faint deep-toned baying of some gigantic hound which we could neither see nor definitely place. As we heard this suggestion of baying we shuddered, remembering the tales of the peasantry; for he whom we sought had centuries before been found in this selfsame spot, torn and mangled by the claws and teeth of some unspeakable beast.

I remember how we delved in the ghoul's grave with our spades, and how we thrilled at the picture of ourselves, the grave, the pale watching moon, the horrible shadows, the grotesque trees, the titanic bats, the antique church, the dancing death-fires, the sickening odours, the gently moaning night-wind, and the strange, half-heard directionless baying of whose objective existence we could scarcely be sure.

Then we struck a substance harder than the damp mould, and beheld a rotting oblong box crusted with mineral deposits from the long undisturbed ground. It was incredibly tough and thick, but so old that we finally pried it open and feasted our eyes on what it held.

Much – amazingly much – was left of the object despite the lapse of five hundred years. The skeleton, though crushed in places by the jaws of the thing that had killed it, held together with surprising firmness, and we gloated over the clean white skull and its long, firm teeth and its eyeless sockets that once had glowed with a charnel fever like our own. In the coffin lay an amulet of curious and exotic design, which had apparently been worn around the sleeper's neck. It was the oddly conventionalized figure of a crouching winged hound, or sphinx with a semi-canine face, and was exquisitely carved in antique Oriental fashion from a small piece of green jade. The expression of its features was repellent in the extreme, savouring at once of death, bestiality and malevolence. Around the base was an inscription in characters which neither St John nor I could identify; and on the bottom, like a maker's seal, was graven a grotesque and formidable skull.

Immediately upon beholding this amulet we knew that we must possess it; that this treasure alone was our logical pelf from the centuried grave. Even had its outlines been unfamiliar we would have desired it, but as we looked more closely we saw that it was not wholly unfamiliar. Alien it indeed was to all art and literature which sane and balanced readers know, but we recognized it as the thing hinted of in the forbidden *Necronomicon* of the mad Arab Abdul Alhazred; the ghastly soul-symbol of the corpse-eating cult of inaccessible Leng, in Central Asia. All too well did we trace the sinister lineaments described by the old Arab daemonologist; lineaments, he wrote, drawn from some obscure supernatural manifestation of the souls of those who vexed and gnawed at the dead.

Seizing the green jade object, we gave a last glance at the bleached and cavern-eyed face of its owner and closed up the grave as we found it. As we hastened from the abhorrent spot, the stolen amulet in St John's pocket, we thought we saw the bats descend in a body to the earth we had so lately rifled, as if seeking for some cursed and unholy nourishment. But the autumn moon shone weak and pale, and we could not be sure.

So, too, as we sailed the next day away from Holland to our home, we thought we heard the faint distant baying of some gigantic hound in the background. But the autumn wind moaned sad and wan, and we could not be sure.

Less than a week after our return to England, strange things began to happen. We lived as recluses; devoid of friends, alone, and without servants in a few rooms of an ancient manor-house on a bleak and unfrequented moor; so that our doors were seldom disturbed by the knock of the visitor.

Now, however, we were troubled by what seemed to be a frequent fumbling in the night, not only around the doors but around the windows also, upper as well as lower. Once we fancied that a large, opaque body darkened the library window when the moon was shining against it, and another time we thought we heard a whirring or flapping sound not far off. On each occasion investigation revealed nothing, and we began to ascribe the occurrences to imagination which still prolonged in our ears the faint far baying we thought we had heard in the Holland churchyard. The jade amulet now reposed in a niche in our museum, and sometimes we burned a strangely scented candle before it. We read much in Alhazred's *Necronomicon* about its properties, and about the relation of ghosts' souls to the objects it symbolized; and were disturbed by what we read.

Then terror came.

On the night of September 24, 19–, I heard a knock at my chamber door. Fancying it St John's, I bade the knocker enter, but was answered only by a shrill laugh. There was no-one in the corridor. When I aroused St John from his sleep, he professed entire ignorance of the event, and became as worried as I. It was the night that the faint, distant baying over the moor became to us a certain and dreaded reality.

Four days later, whilst we were both in the hidden museum, there came a low, cautious scratching at the single door which led to the secret library staircase. Our alarm was now divided, for, besides our fear of the unknown, we had always entertained a dread that our grisly collection might be discovered. Extinguish-ing all lights, we proceeded to the door and threw it suddenly open; whereupon we felt an unaccountable rush of air, and heard, as if receding far away, a queer combination of rustling, tittering, and articulate chatter. Whether we were mad, dreaming, or in our senses, we did not try to determine. We only realized, with the blackest of apprehensions, that the apparently dis-embodied chatter was beyond a doubt *in the Dutch language*.

After that we lived in growing horror and fascination. Mostly we held to the theory that we were jointly going mad from our life of unnatural excitements, but sometimes it pleased us more to dramatize ourselves as the victims of some creeping and appalling doom. Bizarre manifestations were now too frequent to count. Our lonely house was seemingly alive with the presence of some malign being whose nature we could not guess, and every night that daemoniac baying rolled over the wind-swept moor, always louder and louder. On October 29 we found in the soft earth underneath the library window a series of footprints utterly impossible to describe. They were as baffling as the hordes of great bats which haunted the old manor-house in unprecedented and increasing numbers.

The horror reached a culmination on November 18, when St John, walking home after dark from the dismal railway station, was seized by some frightful carnivorous thing and torn to ribbons. His screams had reached the house, and I had hastened to the terrible scene in time to hear a whir of wings and see a vague black cloudy thing silhouetted against the rising moon.

My friend was dying when I spoke to him, and he could not answer coherently. All he could do was to whisper,

"The amulet – that damned thing–"

Then he collapsed, an inert mass of mangled flesh.

I buried him the next midnight in one of our neglected gardens, and mumbled over his body one of the devilish rituals he had loved in life. And as I pronounced the last daemoniac sentence I heard afar on the moor the faint baying of some gigantic hound. The moon was up, but I dared not look at it. And when I saw on the dim-lighted moor a wide-nebulous shadow sweeping from mound to mound, I shut my eyes and threw myself face down upon the ground. When I arose, trembling, I know not how much later, I staggered into the house and made shocking obeisance before the enshrined amulet of green jade.

Being now afraid to live alone in the ancient house on the moor, I departed on the following day for London, taking with me the amulet after destroying by fire and burial the rest of the impious collection in the museum. But after three nights I heard the baying again, and before a week was over felt strange eyes upon me whenever it was dark. One evening as I strolled on Victoria Embankment for some needed air, I saw a black shape obscure one of the reflections of the lamps in the water. A wind, stronger than the night-wind, rushed by, and I knew that what had befallen St John must soon befall me.

The next day I carefully wrapped the green jade amulet and sailed for Holland. What mercy I might gain by returning the thing to its silent, sleeping owner I knew not; but I felt that I must try any step conceivably logical. What the hound was, and why it had pursued me, were questions still vague; but I had first heard the baying in that ancient churchyard, and every subsequent event including St John's dying whisper had served to connect the curse with the stealing of the amulet. Accordingly I sank into the nethermost abysses of despair when, at an inn in Rotterdam, I discovered that thieves had despoiled me of this sole means of salvation.

The baying was loud that evening, and in the morning I read of a nameless deed in the vilest quarter of the city. The rabble were in terror, for upon an evil tenement had fallen a red death beyond the foulest previous crime of the neighbourhood. In a squalid thieves' den an entire family had been torn to shreds by an unknown thing which left no trace, and those around had heard all night a faint, deep, insistent note as of a gigantic hound.

So at last I stood again in the unwholesome churchyard where a pale winter moon cast hideous shadows and leafless trees drooped sullenly to meet the withered, frosty grass and cracking slabs, and the ivied church pointed a jeering finger at the unfriendly sky, and the night-wind howled maniacally from over frozen swamps and frigid seas. The baying was very faint now, and it ceased altogether as I approached the ancient grave I had once violated, and frightened away an abnormally large horde of bats which had been hovering curiously around it.

I know not why I went thither unless to pray, or gibber out insane pleas and apologies to the calm white thing that lay within; but, whatever my reason, I attacked the half-frozen sod with a desperation partly mine and partly that of a dominating will outside myself. Excavation was much easier than I expected, though at one point I encountered a queer interruption; when a lean vulture darted down out of the cold sky and peeked frantically at the grave-earth until I killed him with a blow of my spade. Finally I reached the rotting oblong box and removed the damp nitrous cover. This is the last rational act I ever performed.

For crouched within that centuried coffin, embraced by a closepacked nightmare retinue of huge, sinewy, sleeping bats, was the bony thing my friend and I had robbed; not clean and placid as we had seen it then, but covered with caked blood and shreds of alien flesh and hair, and leering sentiently at me with phos-phorescent sockets and sharp ensanguined fangs yawning twistedly in mockery of my inevitable doom. And when it gave from those grinning jaws a deep, sardonic bay as of some gigantic hound, and I saw that it held in its gory filthy claw the lost and fateful amulet of green jade, I merely screamed and ran away idiotically, my screams soon dissolving into peals of hysterical laughter.

Madness rides the star-wind… claws and teeth sharpened on centuries of corpses… dripping death astride a bacchanale of bats from night-black ruins of buried temples of Belial… Now, as the baying of that dead fleshless monstrosity grows louder and louder, and the stealthy whirring and flapping of those accursed web-wings closer and closer, I shall seek with my revolver the oblivion which is my only refuge from the unnamed and un-nameable.

THE FESTIVAL

Efficiut Daemones, ut quae non sunt, sic tamen quasi sint,
conspicienda hominibus exhibeant.

—Lacantius

I was far from home, and the spell of the eastern sea was upon me. In the twilight I heard it pounding on the rocks, and I knew it lay just over the hill where the twisting willows writhed against the clearing sky and the first stars of evening. And because my fathers had called me to the old town beyond, I pushed on through the shallow, new-fallen snow along the road that soared lonely up to where Aldebaran twinkled among the trees; on toward the very ancient town I had never seen but often dreamed of.

It was the Yuletide, that men call Christmas though they know in their hearts it is older than Bethlehem and Babylon, older than Memphis and mankind. It was the Yuletide, and I had come at last to the ancient sea town where my people had dwelt and kept festival in the elder time when festival was forbidden; where also they had commanded their sons to keep festival once every century, that the memory of primal secrets might not be forgotten. Mine were an old people, and were old even when this land was settled three hundred years before. And they were strange, because they had come as dark furtive folk from opiate southern gardens of orchids, and spoken another tongue before they learnt the tongue of the blue-eyed fishers. And now they were scattered, and shared only the rituals of mysteries that none living could understand. I was the only one who came back that night to the old fishing town as legend bade, for only the poor and the lonely remember.

Then beyond the hill's crest I saw Kingsport outspread frostily in the gloaming; snowy Kingsport with its ancient vanes and steeples, ridgepoles and chimney-pots, wharves and small bridges, willow-trees and graveyards; endless labyrinths of steep, narrow, crooked streets, and dizzy church-crowned central peak that time durst not touch; ceaseless mazes of colonial houses piled and scattered at all angles and levels like a child's disordered blocks; antiquity hovering on grey wings over winter-whitened gables and gambrel roofs; fanlights and small-paned windows one by one gleaming out in the cold dusk to join

Orion and the archaic stars. And against the rotting wharves the sea pounded; the secretive, immemorial sea out of which the people had come in the elder time.

Beside the road at its crest a still higher summit rose, bleak and windswept, and I saw that it was a burying-ground where black gravestones stuck ghoulishly through the snow like the decayed fingernails of a gigantic corpse. The printless road was very lonely, and sometimes I thought I heard a distant horrible creaking as of a gibbet in the wind. They had hanged four kinsmen of mine for witchcraft in 1692, but I did not know just where.

As the road wound down the seaward slope I listened for the merry sounds of a village at evening, but did not hear them. Then I thought of the season, and felt that these old Puritan folk might well have Christmas customs strange to me, and full of silent hearthside prayer. So after that I did not listen for merriment or look for wayfarers, kept on down past the hushed lighted farmhouses and shadowy stone walls to where the signs of ancient shops and sea taverns creaked in the salt breeze, and the grotesque knockers of pillared doorways glistened along deserted unpaved lanes in the light of little, curtained windows.

I had seen maps of the town, and knew where to find the home of my people. It was told that I should be known and welcomed, for village legend lives long; so I hastened through Back Street to Circle Court, and across the fresh snow on the one full flagstone pavement in the town, to where Green Lane leads off behind the Market House. The old maps still held good, and I had no trouble; though at Arkham they must have lied when they said the trolleys ran to this place, since I saw not a wire overhead. Snow would have hid the rails in any case. I was glad I had chosen to walk, for the white village had seemed very beautiful from the hill; and now I was eager to knock at the door of my people, the seventh house on the left in Green Lane, with an ancient peaked roof and jutting second storey, all built before 1650.

There were lights inside the house when I came upon it, and I saw from the diamond window-panes that it must have been kept very close to its antique state. The upper part overhung the narrow grass-grown street and nearly met the over-hanging part of the house opposite, so that I was almost in a tunnel, with the low stone doorstep wholly free from snow. There was no sidewalk, but many houses had high doors reached by double flights of steps with iron railings. It was an odd scene, and because I was strange to New England I had never known its like before. Though it pleased me, I would have relished it better if there had been footprints in the snow, and people in the streets, and a few windows without drawn curtains.

When I sounded the archaic iron knocker I was half afraid. Some fear had been gathering in me, perhaps because of the strangeness of my heritage, and the bleakness of the evening, and the queerness of the silence in that aged town of curious customs. And when my knock was answered I was fully afraid, because I had not heard any footsteps before the door creaked open. But I was not afraid long, for the gowned, slippered old man in the doorway had a bland face that reassured me; and though he made signs that he was dumb, he wrote a quaint and ancient welcome with the stylus and wax tablet he carried.

He beckoned me into a low, candle-lit room with massive exposed rafters and dark, stiff, sparse furniture of the seventeenth century. The past was vivid there, for not an attribute was missing. There was a cavernous fireplace and a spinning-wheel at which a bent old woman in loose wrapper and deep poke-bonnet sat back toward me, silently spinning despite the festive season. An indefinite dampness seemed upon the place, and I marvelled that no fire should be blazing. The high-backed settle faced the row of curtained windows at the left, and seemed to be occupied, though I was not sure. I did not like everything about what I saw, and felt again the fear I had had. This fear grew stronger from what had before lessened it, for the more I looked at the old man's bland face the more its very blandness terrified me. The eyes never moved, and the skin was too much like wax. Finally I was sure it was not a face at all, but a fiendishly cunning mask. But the flabby hands, curiously gloved, wrote genially on the tablet and told me I must wait a while before I could be led to the place of the festival.

Pointing to a chair, table, and pile of books, the old man now left the room; and when I sat down to read I saw that the books were hoary and mouldy, and that they included old Morryster's wild *Marvells Of Science*, the terrible *Saducismus Triumphatus* of Joseph Glanvil, published in 1681, the shocking *Daemonolatreia* of Remigius, printed in 1595 at Lyons, and worst of all, the unmentionable *Necronomicon* of the mad Arab Abdul Alhazred, in Olaus Wormius' forbidden Latin translation; a book which I had never seen, but of which I had heard monstrous things whispered. No-one spoke to me, but I could hear the creaking of signs in the wind outside, and the whir of the wheel as the bonneted old woman continued her silent spinning, spinning. I thought the room and the books and the people very morbid and disquieting, but because an old tradition of my fathers had summoned me to strange feastings, I resolved to expect queer things. So I tried to read, and soon became tremblingly absorbed by something I found in that accursed *Necronomicon*; a thought and a legend too hideous for sanity or consciousness, but I disliked it when I fancied I heard the closing of one of the windows that the settle faced, as if it had been stealthily opened. It had seemed to follow a whirring that was not of the old woman's spinning-wheel. This was not much, though, for the old woman was spinning very hard, and the aged clock had been striking. After that I lost the feeling that there were persons on the settle, and was reading intently and shudderingly when the old man came back booted and dressed in a loose antique costume, and sat down on that very bench, so that I could not see him. It was certainly nervous waiting, and the blasphemous book in my hands made it doubly so. When eleven struck, however, the old man stood up, glided to a massive carved chest in a corner, and got two hooded cloaks; one of which he donned, and the other of which he draped round the old woman, who was ceasing her monotonous spinning. Then they both started for the outer door; the woman lamely creeping, and the old man, after picking up the very book I had been reading, beckoning me as he drew his hood over that unmoving face or mask.

We went out into the moonless and tortuous network of that incredibly ancient town; went out as the lights in the curtained windows disappeared one by one, and the Dog Star leered at the throng of cowled, cloaked figures that poured silently from every doorway and formed monstrous processions up this street and that, past the creaking signs and antediluvian gables, the thatched roofs and diamond-paned windows; threading precipitous lanes where decaying houses overlapped and crumbled together; gliding across open courts and churchyards where the bobbing lanthorns made eldritch drunken constellations.

Amid these hushed throngs I followed my voiceless guides; jostled by elbows that seemed preternaturally soft, and pressed by chests and stomachs that seemed abnormally pulpy; but seeing never a face and hearing never a word. Up, up, up, the eery columns slithered, and I saw that all the travellers were converging as they flowed near a sort of focus of crazy alleys at the top of a high hill in the centre of the town, where perched a great white church. I had seen it from the road's crest when I looked at Kingsport in the new dusk, and it had made me shiver because Aldebaran had seemed to balance itself a moment on the ghostly spire.

There was an open space around the church; partly a churchyard with spectral shafts, and partly a half-paved square swept nearly bare of snow by the wind, and lined with unwholesomely archaic houses having peaked roofs and over-hanging gables. Death-fires danced over the tombs, revealing gruesome vistas, though queerly failing to cast any shadows. Past the churchyard, where there were no houses, I could see over the hill's summit and watch the glimmer of stars on the harbour, though the town was invisible in the dark. Only once in a while a lanthorn bobbed horribly through serpentine alleys on its way to overtake the throng that was now slipping speechlessly into the church. I waited till the crowd had oozed into the black doorway, and till all the stragglers had followed. The old man was pulling at my sleeve, but I was determined to be the last. Crossing the threshold into the swarming temple of unknown darkness, I turned once to look at the outside world as the churchyard phosphorescence cast a sickly glow on the hilltop pavement. And as I did so I shuddered. For though the wind had not left much snow, a few patches did remain on the path near the door; and in that fleeting backward look it seemed to my troubled eyes that they bore no mark of passing feet, not even mine.

The church was scarce lighted by all the lanthorns that had entered it, for most of the throng had already vanished. They had streamed up the aisle between the high pews to the trap-door of the vaults which yawned loathsomely open just before the pulpit, and were now squirming noiselessly in. I followed dumbly down the footworn steps and into the dark, suffocating crypt. The tail of that sinuous line of night-marchers seemed very horrible, and as I saw them wriggling into a venerable tomb they seemed more horrible still. Then I noticed that the tomb's floor had an aperture down which the throng was sliding, and in a moment we were all descending an ominous staircase of rough-hewn stone; a narrow spiral staircase damp and peculiarly odorous, that wound endlessly down into the bowels of the hill past monotonous walls of dripping stone blocks and crumbling mortar. It was a silent, shocking descent, and I observed after a horrible interval that the walls and steps were changing in nature, as if chiselled out of the solid rock. What mainly troubled me was that the myriad footfalls made no sound and set up no echoes. After more aeons of descent I saw some side passages or burrows leading from unknown recesses of blackness to this shaft of nighted mystery. Soon they became excessively numerous, like impious catacombs of nameless menace; and their pungent odour of decay grew quite un-bearable. I knew we must have passed down through the mountain and beneath the earth of Kingsport itself, and I shivered that a town should be so aged and maggoty with subterranean evil.

Then I saw the lurid shimmering of pale light, and heard the insidious lapping of sunless waters. Again I shivered, for I did not like the things that the night had brought, and wished bitterly that no forefather had summoned me to this primal rite. As the steps and the passage grew broader, I heard another sound, the thin, whining mockery of a feeble flute; and suddenly there spread out before me the boundless vista of an inner world — a vast fungous shore litten by a belching column of sick greenish flame and washed by a wide oily river that flowed from abysses frightful and unsuspected to join the blackest gulfs of immemorial ocean.

Fainting and gasping, I looked at that unhallowed Erebus of titan toadstools, leprous fire and slimy water, and saw the cloaked throngs forming a semi-circle around the blazing pillar. It was the Yule-rite, older than man and fated to survive him; the primal rite of the solstice and of spring's promise beyond the snows; the rite of fire and evergreen, light and music. And in the stygian grotto I saw them do the rite, and adore the sick pillar of flame, and throw into the water handfuls gouged out of the viscous vegetation which glittered green in the chlorotic glare. I saw this, and I saw something amorphously squatted far away from the light, piping noisomely on a flute; and as the thing piped I thought I heard noxious muffled flutterings in the foetid darkness where I could not see. But what frightened me most was that flaming column; spouting volcanically from depths profound and inconceivable, casting no shadows as healthy flame should, and coating the nitrous stone with a nasty, venomous verdigris. For in all that seething combustion no warmth lay, but only the clamminess of death and corruption.

The man who had brought me now squirmed to a point directly beside the hideous flame, and made stiff ceremonial motions to the semi-circle he faced. At certain stages of the ritual they did grovelling obeisance, especially when he held above his head that abhorrent *Necronomicon* he had taken with him; and I shared all the obeisances because I had been summoned to this festival by the writings of my forefathers. Then the old man made a signal to the half-seen flute-player in the darkness, which player thereupon changed its feeble drone to a scarce louder drone in another key; precipitating as it did so a horror unthinkable and unexpected. At this horror I sank nearly to the lichened earth, transfixed with a dread not of this or any world, but only of the mad spaces between the stars.

Out of the unimaginable blackness beyond the gangrenous glare of that cold flame, out of the tartarean leagues through which that oily river rolled uncanny, unheard, and unsuspected, there flopped rhythmically a horde of tame, trained, hybrid winged things that no sound eye could ever wholly grasp, or sound brain ever wholly remember. They were not altogether crows, nor moles, nor buzzards, nor ants, nor vampire bats, nor decomposed human beings; but something I cannot and must not recall. They flopped limply along, half with their webbed feet and half with their membranous wings; and as they reached the throng of celebrants the cowled figures seized and mounted them, and rode off one by one along the reaches of that unlighted river, into pits and galleries of panic where poison springs feed frightful and undiscoverable cataracts.

The old spinning woman had gone with the throng, and the old man remained only because I had refused when he motioned me to seize an animal and ride like the rest. I saw when I staggered to my feet that the amorphous flute-player had rolled out of sight, but that two of the beasts were patiently standing by. As I hung back, the old man produced his stylus and tablet and wrote that he was the true deputy of my fathers who had founded the Yule worship in this ancient place; that it had been decreed I should come back, and that the most secret mysteries were yet to be performed. He wrote this in a very ancient hand, and when I still hesitated he pulled from his loose robe a seal ring and a watch, both with my family arms, to prove that he was what he said. But it was a hideous proof, because I knew from old papers that that watch had been buried with my great-great-great-great-grandfather in 1698.

Presently the old man drew back his hood and pointed to the family resemblance in his face, but I only shuddered, because I was sure that the face was merely a devilish waxen mask. The flopping animals were now scratching restlessly at the lichens, and I saw that the old man was nearly as restless himself. When one of the things began to waddle and edge away, he turned quickly to stop it; so that the suddenness of his motion dislodged the waxen mask from what should have been his head. And then, because that nightmare's position barred me from the stone staircase down which we had come, I flung myself into the oily underground river that bubbled somewhere to the caves of the sea; flung myself into that putrescent juice of earth's inner horrors before the madness of my screams could bring down upon me all the charnel legions these pest-gulfs might conceal.

At the hospital they told me I had been found half-frozen in Kingsport Harbour at dawn, clinging to the drifting spar that accident sent to save me. They told me I had taken the wrong fork of the hill road the night before, and fallen over the cliffs at Orange Point; a thing they deduced from prints found in the snow. There was nothing I could say, because everything was wrong. Everything was wrong, with the broad windows showing a sea of roofs in which only about one in five was ancient, and the sound of trolleys and motors in the streets below. They insisted that this was Kingsport, and I could not deny it. When I went delirious at hearing that the hospital stood near the old churchyard on Central Hill, they sent me to St Mary's Hospital in Arkham, where I could have better care. I liked it there, for the doctors were broad-minded, and even lent me their influence in obtaining the carefully sheltered copy of Alhazred's objectionable *Necronomicon* from the library of Miskatonic University. They said something about a "psychosis", and agreed I had better get any harassing obsessions off my mind.

So I read that hideous chapter, and shuddered doubly because it was indeed not new to me. I had seen it before, let footprints tell what they might; and where it was I had seen it were best forgotten. There was no-one – in waking hours – who could remind me of it; but my dreams are filled with terror, because of phrases I dare not quote. I dare quote only one paragraph, put into such English as I can make from the awkward Low Latin.

"The nethermost caverns," wrote the mad Arab, *"are not for the fathoming of eyes that see; for their marvels are strange and terrific. Cursed the ground where dead thoughts live new and oddly bodied, and evil the mind that is held by no head. Wisely did Ibn Schacabao say, that happy is the tomb where no wizard hath lain, and happy the town at night whose wizards are all ashes. For it is of old rumour that the soul of the devil-bought hastes not from his charnel clay, but fats and instructs* the very worm that gnaws; *till out of corruption horrid life springs, and the dull scavengers of earth wax crafty to vex it and swell monstrous to plague it. Great holes secretly are digged where earth's pores ought to suffice, and things have learnt to walk that ought to crawl."*

WHAT THE MOON BRINGS

I hate the moon – I am afraid of it – for when it shines on certain scenes familiar and loved it sometimes makes them unfamiliar and hideous.

It was in the spectral summer when the moon shone down on the old garden where I wandered; the spectral summer of narcotic flowers and humid seas of foliage that bring wild and many-coloured dreams. And as I walked by the shallow crystal stream I saw unwonted ripples tipped with yellow light, as if those placid waters were drawn on in resistless currents to strange oceans that are not in the world. Silent and sparkling, bright and baleful, those moon-cursed waters hurried I knew not whither; whilst from the embowered banks white lotos-blossoms fluttered one by one in the opiate night-wind and dropped despair-ingly into the stream, swirling away horribly under the arched, carven bridge, and staring back with the sinister resignation of calm, dead faces.

And as I ran along the shore, crushing sleeping flowers with heedless feet and maddened ever by the fear of unknown things and the lure of the dead faces, I saw that the garden had no end under that moon; for where by day the walls were, there stretched now only new vistas of trees and paths, flowers and shrubs, stone idols and pagodas, and bendings of the yellow-litten stream past grassy banks and under grotesque bridges of marble. And the lips of the dead lotos-faces whispered sadly, and bade me follow, nor did I cease my steps till the stream became a river, and joined amidst marshes of swaying reeds and beaches of gleaming sand the shore of a vast and nameless sea.

Upon that sea the hateful moon shone, and over its unvocal waves weird perfumes breeded. And as I saw therein the lotos-faces vanish, I longed for nets that I might capture them and learn from them the secrets which the moon had brought upon the night. But when the moon went over to the west and the still tide ebbed from the sullen shore, I saw in that light old spires that the waves almost uncovered, and white columns gay with festoons of green seaweed. And knowing that to this sunken place all the dead had come, I trembled and did not wish again to speak with the lotos-faces.

Yet when I saw afar out in the sea a black condor descend from the sky to seek rest on a vast reef, I would fain have questioned him, and asked him of those whom I had known when they were alive. This I would have asked him had he not been so far away, but he was very far, and could not be seen at all when he drew nigh that gigantic reef.

So I watched the tide go out under that sinking moon, and saw gleaming the spires, the towers, and the roofs of that dead, dripping city. And as I watched, my nostrils tried to close against the perfume-conquering stench of the world's dead; for truly, in this unplaced and forgotten spot had all the flesh of the churchyards gathered for puffy sea-worms to gnaw and glut.

Over these horrors the evil moon now hung very low, but the puffy worms of the sea need no moon to feed by. And as I watched the ripples that told of the writhing of worms beneath, I felt a new chill from afar out whither the condor had flown, as if my flesh had caught a horror before my eyes had seen it.

Nor had my flesh trembled without cause, for when I raised my eyes I saw that the waters had ebbed very low, shewing much of the vast reef whose rim I had seen before. And when I saw that the reef was but the black basalt crown of a shocking eikon whose monstrous forehead was now shown in the dim moonlight and whose vile hooves must paw the hellish ooze miles below, I shrieked and shrieked lest the hidden face rise above the waters, and lest the hidden eyes look at me after the slinking away of that leering and treacherous yellow moon.

And to escape this relentless thing I plunged gladly and unhesitantly into the stinking shallows where amidst weedy walls and sunken streets fat sea-worms feast upon the world's dead.

THE RATS IN THE WALLS

On 16 July 1923, I moved into Exham Priory after the last workman had finished his labours. The restoration had been a stupendous task, for little had remained of the deserted pile but a shell-like ruin; yet because it had been the seat of my ancestors, I let no expense deter me. The place had not been inhabited since the reign of James the First, when a tragedy of intensely hideous, though largely un-explained, nature had struck down the master, five of his children, and several servants; and driven forth under a cloud of suspicion and terror the third son, my lineal progenitor and the only survivor of the abhorred line.

With this sole heir denounced as a murderer, the estate had reverted to the crown, nor had the accused man made any attempt to exculpate himself or regain his property. Shaken by some horror greater than that of conscience or the law, and expressing only a frantic wish to exclude the ancient edifice from his sight and memory, Walter de la Poer, eleventh Baron Exham, fled to Virginia and there founded the family which by the next century had become known as Delapore.

Exham Priory had remained untenanted, though later allotted to the estates of the Norrys family and much studied because of its peculiarly composite architecture; an architecture involving Gothic towers resting on a Saxon or Romanesque substructure, whose foundation in turn was of a still earlier order or blend of orders – Roman, and even Druidic or native Cymric, if legends speak truly. This foundation was a very singular thing, being merged on one side with the solid limestone of the precipice from whose brink the priory overlooked a desolate valley three miles west of the village of Anchester.

Architects and antiquarians loved to examine this strange relic of forgotten centuries, but the country folk hated it. They had hated it hundreds of years before, when my ancestors lived there, and they hated it now, with the moss and mould of abandonment on it. I had not been a day in Anchester before I knew I came of an accursed house. And this week workmen have blown up Exham Priory, and are busy obliterating the traces of its foundations. The bare statistics of my ancestry I had always known, together with the fact that my first American forebear had come to the colonies under a strange cloud. Of details, however, I had been kept wholly ignorant through the policy of reticence always maintained by the Delapores. Unlike our planter neighbours, we seldom boasted of crusading ancestors or other mediaeval and Renaissance heroes; nor was any kind of tradition handed down except what may have been recorded in the sealed envelope left before the Civil War by every squire to his eldest son for posthumous opening. The glories we cherished were those achieved since the migration; the glories of a proud and honourable, if somewhat reserved and unsocial Virginia line.

During the war our fortunes were extinguished and our whole existence changed by the burning of Carfax, our home on the banks of the James. My grand-father, advanced in years, had perished in that incendiary outrage, and with him the envelope that had bound us all to the past. I can recall that fire today as I saw it then at the age of seven, with the Federal soldiers shouting, the women screaming, and the negroes howling and praying. My father was in the army, defending Richmond, and after many formalities my mother and I were passed through the lines to join him.

When the war ended we all moved north, whence my mother had come; and I grew to manhood, middle age, and ultimate wealth as a stolid Yankee. Neither my father nor I ever knew what our hereditary envelope had contained, and as I merged into the greyness of Massachusetts business life I lost all interest in the mysteries which evidently lurked far back in my family tree. Had I suspected their nature, how gladly I would have left Exham Priory to its moss, bats and cobwebs!

My father died in 1904, but without any message to leave to me, or to my only child, Alfred, a motherless boy of ten. It was this boy who reversed the order of family information for although I could give him only jesting conjectures about the past, he wrote me of some very interesting ancestral legends when the late war took him to England in 1917 as an aviation officer. Apparently the Delapores had a colourful and perhaps sinister history, for a friend of my son's, Capt. Edward Norrys of the Royal Flying Corps, dwelt near the family seat at Anchester and related some peasant superstitions which few novelists could equal for wildness and incredibility. Norrys himself, of course, did not take them so seriously; but they amused my son and made good material for his letters to me. It was this legendry which definitely turned my attention to my transatlantic heritage, and made me resolve to purchase and restore the family seat which Norrys showed to Alfred in its picturesque desertion, and offered to get for him at a surprisingly reasonable figure, since his own uncle was the present owner.

I bought Exham Priory in 1918, but was almost immediately distracted from my plans of restoration by the return of my son as a maimed invalid. During the two years that he lived I thought of nothing but his care, having even placed my business under the direction of partners.

In 1921, as I found myself bereaved and aimless, a retired manufacturer no longer young, I resolved to divert my remaining years with my new possession. Visiting Anchester in December, I was entertained by Capt. Norrys, a plump, amiable young man who had thought much of my son, and secured his assistance in gathering plans and anecdotes to guide in the coming restoration. Exham Priory itself I saw without emotion, a jumble of tottering mediaeval ruins covered with lichens and honeycombed with rooks' nests, perched perilously upon a precipice, and denuded of floors or other interior features save the stone walls of the separate towers.

As I gradually recovered the image of the edifice as it had been when my ancestors left it over three centuries before, I began to hire workmen for the reconstruction. In every case I was forced to go outside the immediate locality, for the Anchester villagers had an almost un-believable fear and hatred of the place. The sentiment was so great that it was some-times communicated to the outside labourers, causing numerous desertions; whilst its scope appeared to include both the priory and its ancient family.

My son had told me that he was somewhat avoided during his visits because he was a de la Poer, and I now found myself subtly ostracized for a like reason until I convinced the peasants how little I knew of my heritage. Even then they sullenly disliked me, so that I had to collect most of the village traditions through the mediation of Norrys. What the people could not forgive, perhaps, was that I had come to restore a symbol so abhorrent to them; for, rationally or not, they viewed Exham Priory as nothing less than a haunt of fiends and werewolves.

Piecing together the tales which Norrys collected for me, and supplementing them with the accounts of several savants who had studied the ruins, I deduced that Exham Priory stood on the site of a pre-historic temple; a Druidical or ante-Druidical thing which must have been contemporary with Stonehenge. That indescribable rites had been celebrated there, few doubted, and there were un-pleasant tales of the transference of these rites into the Cybele worship which the Romans had introduced.

Inscriptions still visible in the sub-cellar bore such unmistakable letters as "DIV... OPS... MAGNA. MAT...", sign of the Magna Mater whose dark worship was once vainly forbidden to Roman citizens. Anchester had been the camp of the third Augustan legion, as many remains attest, and it was said that the temple of Cybele was splendid and thronged with worshippers who performed nameless ceremonies at the bidding of a Phrygian priest. Tales added that the fall of the old religion did not end the orgies at the temple, but that the priests lived on in the new faith without real change. Likewise was it said that the rites did not vanish with the Roman power, and that certain among the Saxons added to what remained of the temple, and gave it the essential outline it subsequently preserved, making it the centre of a cult feared through half the heptarchy. About 1000 A.D. the place is mentioned in a chronicle as being a substantial stone priory housing a strange and powerful monastic order and surrounded by extensive gardens which needed no walls to exclude a frightened populace. It was never destroyed by the Danes, though after the Norman Conquest it must have declined tremendously, since there was no impediment when Henry the Third granted the site to my ancestor, Gilbert de la Poer, First Baron Exham, in 1261.

Of my family before this date there is no evil report, but something strange must have happened then. In one chronicle there is a reference to a de la Poer as "cursed of God" in 1307, whilst village legendry had nothing but evil and frantic fear to tell of the castle that went up on the foundations of the old temple and priory. The fireside tales were of the most grisly description, all the ghastlier because of their frightened reticence and cloudy evasiveness. They represented my ancestors as a race of hereditary daemons beside whom Gilles de Retz and the Marquis de Sade would seem the veriest tyros, and hinted whisperingly at their responsibility for the occasional disappearances of villagers through several generations.

The worst characters, apparently, were the barons and their direct heirs; at least, most was whispered about these. If of healthier inclinations, it was said, an heir would early and mysteriously die to make way for another more typical scion. There seemed to be an inner cult in the family, presided over by the head of the house, and sometimes closed except to a few members. Temperament rather than ancestry was evidently the basis of this cult, for it was entered by several who married into the family. Lady Margaret Trevor from Cornwall, wife of Godfrey, the second son of the fifth baron, became a favourite bane of children all over the countryside, and the daemon heroine of a particularly horrible old ballad not yet extinct near the Welsh border. Preserved in balladry, too, though not illustrating the same point, is the hideous tale of Lady Mary de la Poer, who shortly after her marriage to the Earl of Shrewsfield was

103

killed by him and his mother, both of the slayers being absolved and blessed by the priest to whom they confessed what they dared not repeat to the world.

These myths and ballads, typical as they were of crude superstition, repelled me greatly. Their persistence, and their application to so long a line of my ancestors, were especially annoying; whilst the imputations of monstrous habits proved unpleasantly reminiscent of the one known scandal of my immediate forebears – the case of my cousin, young Randolph Delapore of Carfax, who went among the negroes and became a voodoo priest after he returned from the Mexican War.

I was much less disturbed by the vaguer tales of wails and howlings in the barren, windswept valley beneath the limestone cliff; of the graveyard stenches after the spring rains; of the floundering, squealing white thing on which Sir John Clave's horse had trod one night in a lonely field; and of the servant who had gone mad at what he saw in the priory in the full light of day. These things were hackneyed spectral lore, and I was at that time a pronounced sceptic. The accounts of vanished peasants were less to be dismissed, though not especially significant in view of mediaeval custom. Prying curiosity meant death, and more than one severed head had been publicly shown on the bastions – now effaced – around Exham Priory.

A few of the tales were exceedingly picturesque, and made me wish I had learnt more of the comparative mythology in my youth. There was, for instance, the belief that a legion of bat-winged devils kept witches' sabbath each night at the priory – a legion whose sustenance might explain the disproportionate abundance of coarse vegetables harvested in the vast gardens. And, most vivid of all, there was the dramatic epic of the rats – the scampering army of obscene vermin which had burst forth from the castle three months after the tragedy that doomed it to desertion – the lean, filthy, ravenous army which had swept all before it and devoured fowl, cats, dogs, hogs, sheep, and even two hapless human beings before its fury was spent. Around that unforgettable rodent army a whole separate cycle of myths revolves, for it scattered among the village homes and brought curses and horrors in its train.

Such was the lore that assailed me as I pushed to completion, with an elderly obstinacy, the work of restoring my ancestral home. It must not be imagined for a moment that these tales formed my principal psychological environment. On the other hand, I was constantly praised and encouraged by Capt. Norrys and the antiquarians who surrounded and aided me. When the task was done, over two years after its commencement, I viewed the great rooms, wainscoted walls, vaulted ceilings, mullioned windows, and broad staircases with a pride which fully compensated for the prodigious expense of the restoration.

Every attribute of the Middle Ages was cunningly reproduced and the new parts blended perfectly with the original walls and foundations. The seat of my fathers was complete, and I looked forward to redeeming at last the local fame of the line which ended in me. I could reside here permanently, and prove that a de la Poer (for I had adopted again the original spelling of the name) need not be a fiend. My comfort was perhaps augmented by the fact that, although Exham Priory was mediaevally fitted, its interior was in truth wholly new and free from old vermin and old ghosts alike.

As I have said, I moved in on 16 July 1923. My household consisted of seven servants and nine cats, of which latter species I am particularly fond. My eldest cat, "Nigger-Man", was seven years old and had come with me from my home in Bolton, Massachusetts; the others I had accumulated whilst living with Capt. Norrys' family during the restoration of the priory.

For five days our routine proceeded with the utmost placidity, my time being spent mostly in the codification of old family data. I had now obtained some very circumstantial accounts of the final tragedy and flight of Walter de la Poer, which I conceived to be the probable contents of the hereditary paper lost in the fire at Carfax. It appeared that my ancestor was accused with much reason of having killed all the other members of his household, except four servant confederates, in their sleep, about two weeks after a shocking discovery which changed his whole demeanour, but which, except by implication, he disclosed to no-one save perhaps the servants who assisted him and afterwards fled beyond reach.

This deliberate slaughter, which included a father, three brothers, and two sisters, was largely condoned by the villagers, and so slackly treated by the law that its perpetrator escaped honoured, unharmed, and undisguised to Virginia; the general whispered sentiment being that he had purged the land of an immemorial curse. What discovery had prompted an act so terrible, I could scarcely even conjecture. Walter de la Poer must have known for years the sinister tales about his family, so that this material could have given him no fresh impulse. Had he, then, witnessed some appalling ancient rite, or stumbled upon some frightful and revealing symbol in the priory or its vicinity? He was reputed to have been a shy, gentle youth in England. In Virginia he seemed not so much hard or bitter as harassed and apprehensive. He was spoken of in the diary of another gentleman adventurer, Francis Harley of Bellview, as a man of unexampled justice, honour, and delicacy.

On 22 July occurred the first incident which, though lightly dismissed at the time, takes on a preternatural significance in relation to later events. It was so simple as to be almost negligible, and could not possibly have been noticed under the circumstances; for it must be recalled that since I was in a building practically fresh and new except for the walls, and surrounded by a well-balanced staff of servitors, apprehension would have been absurd despite the locality.

What I afterward remembered is merely this – that my old black cat, whose moods I know so well, was undoubtedly alert and anxious to an extent wholly out of keeping with his natural character. He roved from room to room, restless and disturbed, and sniffed constantly about the walls which formed part of the Gothic structure. I realize how trite this sounds – like the inevitable dog in the ghost story, which always growls before his master sees the sheeted figure – yet I cannot consistently suppress it.

The following day a servant complained of restlessness among all the cats in the house. He came to me in my study, a lofty west room on the second storey, with groined arches, black oak panelling, and a triple Gothic window overlooking the limestone cliff and desolate valley; and even as he spoke I saw the jetty form of Nigger-Man creeping along the west wall and scratching at the new panels which overlaid the ancient stone.

I told the man that there must be some singular odour or emanation from the old stonework, imperceptible to human senses, but affecting the delicate organs of cats even through the new woodwork. This I truly believed, and when the fellow suggested the presence of mice or rats, I mentioned that there had been no rats there for three hundred years, and that even the field mice of the surrounding country could hardly be found in these high walls, where they had never been known to stray. That afternoon I called on Capt. Norrys, and he assured me that it would be quite incredible for field mice to infest the priory in such a sudden and unprecedented fashion.

That night, dispensing as usual with a valet, I retired in the west tower chamber which I had chosen as my own, reached from the study by a stone staircase and short gallery – the former partly ancient, the latter entirely restored. This room was circular, very high, and without wains-coting, being hung with arras which I had myself chosen in London.

Seeing that Nigger-Man was with me, I shut the heavy Gothic door and retired by the light of the electric bulbs which so cleverly counterfeited candles, finally switching off the light and sinking on the carved and canopied four-poster, with the venerable cat in his accustomed place across my feet. I did not draw the curtains, but gazed out at the narrow window which I faced. There was a suspicion of aurora in the sky, and the delicate traceries of the window were pleasantly silhouetted.

At some time I must have fallen quietly asleep, for I recall a distinct sense of leaving strange dreams, when the cat started violently from his placid position. I saw him in the faint auroral glow, head strained forward, forefeet on my ankles, and hind feet stretched behind. He was looking intensely at a point on the wall somewhat west of the window, a point which to my eye had nothing to mark it, but towards which all my attention was now directed.

And as I watched, I knew that Nigger-Man was not vainly excited. Whether the arras actually moved I cannot say. I think it did, very slightly. But what I can swear to is that behind it I heard a low, distinct scurrying of rats or mice. In a moment the cat had jumped bodily on the screening tapestry, bringing the affected section to the floor with his weight, and exposing a damp, ancient wall of stone; patched here and there by the restorers, and devoid of any trace of rodent prowlers.

Nigger-Man raced up and down the floor by this part of the wall, clawing the fallen arras and seemingly trying at times to insert a paw between the wall and the oaken floor. He found nothing, and after a time returned wearily to his place across my feet. I had not moved, but I did not sleep again that night.

In the morning I questioned all the servants, and found that none of them had noticed anything unusual, save that the cook remembered the actions of a cat which had rested on her windowsill. This cat had howled at some unknown hour of the night, awaking the cook in time for her to see him dart purposefully out of the open door down the stairs. I drowsed away the noontime, and in the afternoon called again on Capt. Norrys, who became exceedingly interested in what I told him. The odd incidents – so slight yet so curious – appealed to his sense of the picturesque and elicited from him a number of reminiscences of local ghostly lore. We were genuinely perplexed at the presence of rats, and Norrys lent me some traps and Paris green, which I had the servants place in strategic localities when I returned.

I retired early, being very sleepy, but was harassed by dreams of the most horrible sort. I seemed to be looking down from an immense height upon a twilit grotto, knee-deep with filth, where a white-bearded daemon swineherd drove about with his staff a flock of fungous, flabby beasts whose appearance filled me with unutterable loathing. Then, as the swine-herd paused and nodded over his task, a mighty swarm of rats rained down on the stinking abyss and fell to devouring beasts and man alike.

From this terrific vision I was abruptly awakened by the motions of Nigger-Man, who had been sleeping as usual across my feet. This time I did not have to question the source of his snarls and hisses, and of the fear which made him sink his claws into my ankle, unconscious of their effect; for on every side of the chamber the walls were alive with nauseous sound – the verminous slithering of ravenous, gigantic rats. There was now no aurora to show the state of the arras – the fallen section of which had been replaced – but I was not too frightened to switch on the light.

As the bulbs leapt into radiance I saw a hideous shaking all over the tapestry, causing the somewhat peculiar designs to execute a singular dance of death. This motion disappeared almost at once, and the sound with it. Springing out of bed, I poked at the arras with the long handle of a warming-pan that rested near, and lifted one section to see what lay beneath. There was nothing but the patched stone wall, and even the cat had lost his tense realization of abnormal presences. When I examined the circular trap that had been placed in the room, I found all of the openings sprung, though no trace remained of what had been caught and had escaped.

Further sleep was out of the question, so lighting a candle, I opened the door and went out in the gallery towards the stairs to my study, Nigger-Man following at my heels. Before we had reached the stone steps, however, the cat darted ahead of me and vanished down the ancient flight. As I descended the stairs myself, I became suddenly aware of sounds in the great room below; sounds of a nature which could not be mistaken.

The oak-panelled walls were alive with rats, scampering and milling whilst Nigger-Man was racing about with the fury of a baffled hunter. Reaching the bottom, I switched on the light, which did not this time cause the noise to subside. The rats continued their riot, stampeding with such force and distinctness that I could finally assign to their motions a definite direction. These creatures, in numbers apparently inexhaustible, were engaged in one stupendous migration from inconceivable heights to some depth conceivably or inconceivably below.

I now heard steps in the corridor, and in another moment two servants pushed open the massive door. They were searching the house for some unknown source of disturbance which had thrown all the cats into a snarling panic and caused them to plunge precipitately down several flights of stairs and squat, yowling, before the closed door to the sub-cellar. I asked them if they had heard the rats, but they replied in the negative. And when I turned to call their attention to the sounds in the panels, I realized that the noise had ceased.

With the two men, I went down to the door of the sub-cellar, but found the cats already dispersed. Later I resolved to explore the crypt below, but for the present I merely made a round of the traps. All were sprung, yet all were tenantless. Satisfying myself that no-one had heard the rats save the felines and me, I sat in my study till morning, thinking profoundly and recalling every scrap of legend I had unearthed concerning the building I inhabited. I slept some in the forenoon, leaning back in the one comfortable library chair which my mediaeval plan of furnishing could not banish. Later I telephoned to Capt. Norrys, who came over and helped me explore the sub-cellar.

Absolutely nothing untoward was found, although we could not repress a thrill at the knowledge that this vault was built by Roman hands. Every low arch and massive pillar was Roman – not the debased Romanesque of the bungling Saxons, but the severe and harmonious classicism of the age of the Caesars; indeed, the walls abounded with inscriptions familiar to the antiquarians who had repeatedly explored the place – things like "P. GETAE. PROP... TEMP... DONA..." and "L. PRAEC... VS... PONTIFI... ATYS..."

The reference to Atys made me shiver, for I had read Catullus and knew something of the hideous rites of the Eastern god, whose worship was so mixed with that of Cybele. Norrys and I, by the light of lanterns, tried to interpret the odd and nearly effaced designs on certain irregularly rectangular blocks of stone generally held to be altars, but could make nothing of them. We remembered that one pattern, a sort of rayed sun, was held by students to imply a non-Roman origin suggesting that these altars had merely been adopted by the Roman priests from some older and perhaps aboriginal temple on the same site. On one of these blocks were some brown stains which made me wonder. The largest, in the centre of the room, had certain features on the upper surface which indicated its connection with fire – probably burnt offerings.

Such were the sights in that crypt before whose door the cats howled, and where Norrys and I now determined to pass the night. Couches were brought down by the servants, who were told not to mind any nocturnal actions of the cats, and Nigger-Man was admitted as much for help as for companionship. We decided to keep the great oak door – a modern replica with slits for ventilation – tightly closed; and, with this attended to, we retired with lanterns still burning to await whatever might occur.

The vault was very deep in the foundations of the priory, and undoubtedly far down on the face of the beetling limestone cliff overlooking the waste valley. That it had been the goal of the scuffling and unexplainable rats I could not doubt, though why, I could not tell. As we lay there expectantly, I found my vigil occasionally mixed with half-formed dreams from which the uneasy motions of the cat across my feet would rouse me.

These dreams were not wholesome, but horribly like the one I had had the night before. I saw again the twilit grotto, and the swineherd with his unmentionable fungous beasts wallowing in filth, and as I looked at these things they seemed nearer and more distinct – so distinct that I could almost observe their features. Then I did observe the flabby features of one of them – and awakened with such a scream that Nigger-Man started up, whilst Capt. Norrys, who had not slept, laughed considerably. Norrys might have laughed more – or perhaps less – had he known what it was that made me scream. But I did not remember myself till later. Ultimate horror often paralyses memory in a merciful way.

Norrys waked me when the phenomena began. Out of the same frightful dream I was called by his gentle shaking and his urging to listen to the cats. Indeed, there was much to listen to, for beyond the closed door at the head of the stone steps was a veritable nightmare of feline yelling and clawing, whilst Nigger-Man, unmindful of his kindred outside, was running excitedly round the bare stone walls, in which I heard the same babel of scurrying rats that had troubled me the night before.

An acute terror now rose within me, for here were anomalies which nothing normal could well explain. These rats, if not the creatures of a madness which I shared with the cats alone, must be burrowing and sliding in Roman walls I had thought to be solid limestone blocks... unless perhaps the action of water through more than seventeen centuries had eaten winding tunnels which rodent bodies had worn clear and ample... But even so, the spectral horror was no less; for if these were living vermin why did not Norrys hear their disgusting commotion? Why did he urge me to watch Nigger-Man and listen to the cats outside, and why did he guess wildly and vaguely at what could have aroused them?

By this time I had managed to tell him, as rationally as I could, what I thought I was hearing, my ears gave me the last fading impression of scurrying; which had retreated *still downward*, far underneath this deepest of sub-cellars till it seemed as if the whole cliff below were riddled with questing rats. Norrys was not as sceptical as I had anticipated, but instead seemed profoundly moved. He motioned to me to notice that the cats at the door had ceased their clamour, as if giving up the rats for lost; whilst Nigger-Man had a burst of renewed restlessness, and was clawing frantically around the bottom of the large stone altar in the centre of the room, which was nearer Norrys' couch than mine.

My fear of the unknown was at this point very great. Something astounding had occurred, and I saw that Capt. Norrys, a younger, stouter, and presumably more naturally materialistic man, was affected fully as much as myself – perhaps because of his lifelong and intimate familiarity with local legend. We could for the moment do nothing but watch the old black cat as he pawed with decreasing fervour at the base of the altar, occasionally looking up and mewing to me in that persuasive manner which he used when he wished me to perform some favour for him.

Norrys now took a lantern close to the altar and examined the place where Nigger-Man was pawing; silently kneeling and scraping away the lichens of the centuries which joined the massive pre-Roman block to the tessellated floor. He did not find anything, and was about to abandon his efforts when I noticed a trivial circumstance which made me shudder, even though it implied nothing more than I had already imagined.

I told him of it, and we both looked at its almost imperceptible manifestation with the fixedness of fascinated discovery and acknowledgment. It was only this – that the flame of the lantern set down near the altar was slightly but certainly flickering from a draught of air which it had not before received, and which came indubitably from the crevice between floor and altar where Norrys was scraping away the lichens.

We spent the rest of the night in the brilliantly-lighted study, nervously discussing what we should do next. The discovery that some vault deeper than the deepest known masonry of the Romans underlay this accursed pile, some vault unsuspected by the curious antiquarians of three centuries, would have been sufficient to excite us without any background of the sinister. As it was, the fascination became two-fold; and we paused in doubt whether to abandon our search and quit the priory forever in superstitious caution, or to gratify our sense of adventure and brave whatever horrors might await us in the unknown depths.

By morning we had compromised, and decided to go to London to gather a group of archaeologists and scientific men fit to cope with the mystery. It should be mentioned that before leaving the sub-cellar we had vainly tried to move the central altar which we now recognized as the gate to a new pit of nameless fear. What secret would open the gate, wiser men than we would have to find.

During many days in London Capt. Norrys and I presented our facts, conjectures, and legendary anecdotes to five eminent authorities, all men who could be trusted to respect any family disclosures which future explorations might develop. We found most of them little disposed to scoff but, instead, intensely interested and sincerely sympathetic. It is hardly necessary to name them all, but I may say that they included Sir William Brinton, whose excavations in the Troad excited most of the world in their day. As we all took the train for Anchester I felt myself poised on the brink of frightful revelations, a sensation symbolized by the air of mourning among the many Americans at the unexpected death of the President on the other side of the world.

On the evening of 7 August we reached Exham Priory, where the servants assured me that nothing unusual had occurred. The cats, even old Nigger-Man, had been perfectly placid; and not a trap in the house had been sprung. We were to begin exploring on the following day, awaiting which I assigned well-appointed rooms to all my guests.

I myself retired in my own tower chamber, with Nigger-Man across my feet. Sleep came quickly, but hideous dreams assailed me. There was a vision of a Roman feast like that of Trimalchio, with a horror in a covered platter. Then came that damnable, recurrent thing about the swineherd and his filthy drove in the twilit grotto. Yet when I awoke it was full daylight, with normal sounds in the house below. The rats, living or spectral, had not troubled me; and Nigger-Man was still quietly asleep. On going down, I found that the same tranquillity had prevailed elsewhere; a condition which one of the assembled servants – a fellow named Thornton, devoted to the psychic – rather absurdly laid to the fact that I had now been shown the thing which certain forces had wished to show me.

All was now ready, and at 11 A.M. our entire group of seven men, bearing powerful electric searchlights and implements of excavation, went down to the sub-cellar and bolted the door behind us. Nigger-Man was with us, for the investigators found no occasion to despise his excitability, and were indeed anxious that he be present in case of obscure rodent manifestations. We noted the Roman inscriptions and unknown altar designs only briefly, for three of the savants had already seen them, and all knew their characteristics. Prime attention was paid to the momentous central altar, and within an hour Sir William Brinton had caused it to tilt backward, balanced by some unknown species of counterweight.

There now lay revealed such a horror as would have overwhelmed us had we not been prepared. Through a nearly square opening in the tiled floor, sprawling on a flight of stone steps so prodigiously worn that it was little more than an inclined plane at the centre, was a ghastly array of human or semi-human bones. Those which retained their collocation as skeletons showed attitudes of panic fear, and over all were the marks of rodent gnawing. The skulls denoted nothing short of utter idiocy, cretinism, or primitive semi-apedom.

Above the hellishly littered steps arched a descending passage seemingly chiselled from the solid rock, and conducting a current of air. This current was not a sudden and noxious rush as from a closed vault, but a cool breeze with something of freshness in it. We did not pause long, but shiveringly began to clear a passage down the steps. It was then that Sir William, examining the hewn walls, made the odd observation that the passage, according to the direction of the strokes, must have been chiselled *from beneath*.

I must be very deliberate now, and choose my words. After ploughing down a few steps amidst the gnawed bones we saw that there was light ahead; not any mystic phosphorescence, but a filtered daylight which could not come except from un-known fissures in the cliff that over-looked the waste valley. That such fissures had escaped notice from outside was hardly remarkable, for not only is the valley wholly uninhabited, but the cliff is so high and beetling that only an aeronaut could study its face in detail. A few steps more, and our breaths were literally snatched from us by what we saw; so literally that Thornton, the psychic investigator, actually fainted in the arms of the dazed man who stood behind him. Norrys, his plump face utterly white and flabby, simply cried out inarticulately; whilst I think that what I did was to gasp or hiss, and cover my eyes.

The man behind me – the only one of the party older than I – croaked the hackneyed "My God!" in the most cracked voice I ever heard. Of seven cultivated men, only Sir William Brinton retained his composure, a thing the more to his credit because he led the party and must have seen the sight first.

It was a twilit grotto of enormous height, stretching away farther than any eye could see; a subterraneous world of limitless mystery and horrible suggestion. There were buildings and other archi-tectural remains – in one terrified glance I saw a weird pattern of tumuli, a savage circle of monoliths, a low-domed Roman ruin, a sprawling Saxon pile, and an early English edifice of wood – but all these were dwarfed by the ghoulish spectacle presented by the general surface of the ground. For yards about the steps extended an insane tangle of human bones, or bones at least as human as those on the steps. Like a foamy sea they stretched, some fallen apart, but others wholly or partly articulated as skeletons; these latter invariably in postures of daemoniac frenzy, either fighting off some menace or clutching other forms with cannibal intent.

When Dr Trask, the anthropologist, stopped to classify the skulls, he found a degraded mixture which utterly baffled him. They were mostly lower than the Piltdown man in the scale of evolution, but in every case definitely human. Many were of higher grade, and a very few were the skulls of supremely and sensitively developed types. All the bones were gnawed, mostly by rats, but somewhat by others of the half-human drove. Mixed with them were many tiny bones of rats – fallen members of the lethal army which closed the ancient epic.

I wonder that any man among us lived and kept his sanity through that hideous day of discovery. Not Hoffman nor Huysmans could conceive a scene more wildly incredible, more frenetically repellent, or more Gothically grotesque than the twilit grotto through which we seven staggered; each stumbling on revelation after revelation, and trying to keep for the nonce from thinking of the events which must have taken place there three hundred, or a thousand, or two thousand or ten thousand years ago. It was the antechamber of hell, and poor Thornton fainted again when Trask told him that some of the skeleton things must have descended as quadrupeds through the last twenty or more generations.

Horror piled on horror as we began to interpret the architectural remains. The quadruped things – with their occasional recruits from the biped class – had been kept in stone pens, out of which they must have broken in their last delirium of hunger or rat-fear. There had been great herds of them, evidently fattened on the coarse vegetables whose remains could be found as a sort of poisonous ensilage at the bottom of the huge stone bins older than Rome. I knew now why my ancestors had had such excessive gardens – would to heaven I could forget! The purpose of the herds I did not have to ask.

Sir William, standing with his searchlight in the Roman ruin, translated aloud the most shocking ritual I have ever known; and told of the diet of the antediluvian cult which the priests of Cybele found and mingled with their own. Norrys, used as he was to the trenches, could not walk straight when he came out of the English building. It was a butcher shop and kitchen – he had expected that – but it was too much to see familiar English implements in such a place, and to read familiar English graffiti there, some as recent as 1610. I could not go in that building – that building whose daemon activities were stopped only by the dagger of my ancestor Walter de la Poer.

What I did venture to enter was the low Saxon building whose oaken door had fallen, and there I found a terrible row of ten stone cells with rusty bars. Three had tenants, all skeletons of high grade, and on the bony forefinger of one I found a seal ring with my own coat-of-arms. Sir William found a vault with far older cells below the Roman chapel, but these cells were empty. Below them was a low crypt with cases of formally arranged bones, some of them bearing terrible parallel inscriptions carved in Latin, Greek, and the tongue of Phrygia.

Meanwhile, Dr Trask had opened one of the prehistoric tumuli, and brought to light skulls which were slightly more human than a gorilla's, and which bore indescribably ideographic carvings. Through all this horror my cat stalked unperturbed. Once I saw him monstrously perched atop a mountain of bones, and wondered at the secrets that might lie behind his yellow eyes.

Having grasped to some slight degree the frightful revelations of this twilit area – an area so hideously foreshadowed by my recurrent dream – we turned to that apparently boundless depth of midnight cavern where no ray of light from the cliff could penetrate. We shall never know what sightless Stygian worlds yawn beyond the little distance we went, for it was decided that such secrets are not good for mankind. But there was plenty to engross us close at hand, for we had not gone far before the searchlights showed that accursed infinity of pits in which the rats had feasted, and whose sudden lack of replenishment had driven the ravenous rodent army first to turn on the living herds of starving things, and then to burst forth from the priory in that historic orgy of devastation which the peasants will never forget.

God! those carrion black pits of sawed, picked bones and opened skulls! Those nightmare chasms choked with the pithecanthropoid, Celtic, Roman, and English bones of countless unhallowed centuries! Some of them were full, and none can say how deep they had once been. Others were still bottomless to our searchlights, and peopled by unnamable fancies. What, I thought, of the hapless rats that stumbled into such traps amidst the blackness of their quests in this grisly Tartarus?

Once my foot slipped near a horribly yawning brink, and I had a moment of ecstatic fear. I must have been musing a long time, for I could not see any of the party but plump Capt. Norrys. Then there came a sound from that inky, boundless, farther distance that I thought I knew; and I saw my old black cat dart past me like a winged Egyptian god, straight into the illimitable gulf of the unknown. But I was not far behind, for there was no doubt after another second. It was the eldritch scurrying of those fiend-born rats, always questing for new horrors, and determined to lead me on even unto those grinning caverns of earth's centre where Nyarlathotep, the mad faceless god, howls blindly in the darkness to the piping of two amorphous idiot flute-players.

My searchlight expired, but still I ran. I heard voices, and yowls, and echoes, but above all there gently rose that impious, insidious scurrying; gently rising, rising, as a stiff bloated corpse gently rises above an oily river that flows under the endless onyx bridges to a black, putrid sea.

Something bumped into me – some-thing soft and plump. It must have been the rats; the viscous, gelatinous, ravenous army that feast on the dead and the living... Why shouldn't rats eat a de la Poer as a de la Poer eats forbidden things?... The war ate my boy, damn them all... and the Yanks ate Carfax with flames and burnt Grandsire Delapore and the secret... No, no, I tell you, I am not that daemon swineherd in the twilit grotto! It was *not* Edward Norrys' fat face on that flabby fungous thing! Who says I am a de la Poer? He lived, but my boy died!... Shall a Norrys hold the land of a de la Poer?... It's voodoo, I tell you... that spotted snake... Curse you, Thornton, I'll teach you to faint at what my family do!... 'Sblood, thou stinkard, I'll learn ye how to gust... wolde ye swynke me thilke wys?... *Magna Mater! Magna Mater!... Atys... Dia ad aghaidh's ad aodaun... agus bas dunach ort! Dhonas 's dholas ort, agus leat-sa!... Ungl... unl... rrlh... chchch...*

This is what they say I said when they found me in the blackness after three hours; found me crouching in the blackness over the plump, half-eaten body of Capt. Norrys, with my own cat leaping and tearing at my throat. Now they have blown up Exham Priory, taken my Nigger-Man away from me, and shut me into this barred room at Hanwell with fearful whispers about my heredity and experience. Thornton is in the next room, but they prevent me from talking to him. They are trying, too, to suppress most of the facts concerning the priory. When I speak of poor Norrys they accuse me of this hideous thing, but they must know that I did not do it. They must know it was the rats; the slithering scurrying rats whose scampering will never let me sleep; the daemon rats that race behind the padding in this room and beckon me down to greater horrors than I have ever known; the rats they can never hear; the rats, the rats in the walls.

THE LOVED DEAD

(with C. M. Eddy)

It's midnight. Before dawn they will find me and take me to a black cell where I shall languish interminably, while insatiable desires gnaw at my vitals and wither up my heart, till at last I become one with the dead that I love.

My seat is the fetid hollow of an aged grave; my desk is the back of a fallen tombstone worn smooth by devastating centuries; my only light is that of the stars and a thin-edged moon, yet I can see as clearly as though it were mid-day. Around me on every side, sepulchral sentinels guarding unkempt graves, the tilting, decrepit headstones lie half-hidden in masses of nauseous, rotting vegetation. Above the rest, silhouetted against the living sky, an august monument lifts its austere, tapering spire like the spectral chieftain of a Lemurian horde. The air is heavy with the noxious odours of fungi and the scent of damp, mouldy earth, but to me it is the aroma of Elysium. It is still – terrifyingly still – with a silence whose very profundity bespeaks the solemn and the hideous. Could I choose my habitation it would be in the heart of some such city of putrefying flesh and crumbling bones; for their nearness sends ecstatic thrills through my soul, causing the stagnant blood to race through my veins and my torpid heart to pound with delirious joy – for the presence of death is life to me!

My early childhood was one long, prosaic and monotonous apathy. Strictly ascetic, wan, pallid, undersized and subject to protracted spells of morbid moroseness, I was ostracized by the healthy, normal youngsters of my own age. They dubbed me a spoil-sport, an "old woman", because I had no interest in the rough, childish games they played, or any stamina to participate in them had I so desired.

Like all rural villages, Fenham had its quota of poison-tongued gossips. Their prying imaginations hailed my lethargic temperament as some abhorrent ab-normality; they compared me with my parents and shook their heads in ominous doubt at the vast difference. Some of the more superstitious openly pronounced me a changeling while others who knew something of my ancestry called attention to the vague mysterious rumours concerning a great-grand-uncle who had been burned at the stake as a necromancer.

117

Had I lived in some larger town, with greater opportunities for congenial companionship, perhaps I could have overcome this early tendency to be a recluse. As I reached my teens I grew even more sullen, morbid, and apathetic. My life lacked motivation. I seemed in the grip of something that dulled my senses, stunted my development, retarded my activities, and left me unaccountably dissatisfied.

I was sixteen when I attended my first funeral. A funeral in Fenham was a pre-eminent social event, for our town was noted for the longevity of its inhabitants. When, moreover, the funeral was that of such a well-known character as my grand-father, it was safe to assume that the townspeople would turn out *en masse* to pay homage to his memory. Yet I did not view the approaching ceremony with even latent interest. Anything that tended to lift me out of my habitual inertia held for me only the promise of physical and mental disquietude. In deference to my parents' importunings, mainly to give myself relief from their caustic condemnations of what they chose to call my unfilial attitude, I agreed to accompany them.

There was nothing out of the ordinary about my grandfather's funeral unless it was the voluminous array of floral tributes; but this, remember, was my first initiation to the solemn rites of such an occasion. Something about the darkened room, the oblong coffin with its sombre drapings, the banked masses of fragrant blooms, the dolorous manifestations of the assembled villagers, stirred me from my normal listlessness and arrested my attention. Roused from my momentary reverie by a nudge from my mother's sharp elbow, I followed her across the room to where the body of my grandparent lay.

For the first time I was face to face with Death. I looked down upon the calm placid face lined with its multitudinous wrinkles, and saw nothing to cause so much of sorrow. Instead, it seemed to me that my grandfather was immeasurably content, blandly satisfied. I felt swayed by some strange discordant sense of elation. So slowly, so stealthily had it crept over me, that I could scarcely define its coming. As I mentally review that portentous hour it seems that it must have originated with my first glimpse of that funeral scene, silently strengthening its grip with subtle insidiousness. A baleful malignant influence that seemed to emanate from the corpse itself held me with magnetic fascination. My whole being seemed charged with some ecstatic electrifying force, and I felt my form straighten without conscious volition. My eyes were trying to burn beneath the closed lids of the dead man's and read some secret message they concealed. My heart gave a sudden leap of unholy glee, and pounded against my ribs with demoniacal force as if to free itself from the confining walls of my frail frame. Wild, wanton, soul-satisfying sensuality engulfed me. Once more the vigorous prod of a maternal elbow jarred me into activity. I had made my way to the sable-shrouded coffin with leaden tread; I walked away with new-found animation.

I accompanied the cortege to the cemetery, my whole physical being permeated with this mystic enlivening influence. It was as if I had quaffed deep draughts of some exotic elixir – some abominable concoction brewed from blasphemous formulae in the archives of Belial.

The townsfolk were so intent upon the ceremony that the radical change in my demeanour passed unnoticed by all save my father and my mother, but in the fortnight that followed, the village busybodies found fresh material for their vitriolic tongues in my altered bearing. At the end of the fortnight, however, the potency of the stimulus began to lose its effectiveness. Another day or two and I had completely reverted to my old-time languor, though not to the complete and engulfing insipidity of the past. Before, there had been an utter lack of desire to emerge from the enervation; now vague and indefinable unrest disturbed me. Outwardly I had become myself again, and the scandal-mongers turned to some more engrossing subject. Had they even so much as dreamed the true cause of my exhilaration they would have shunned me as if I were a filthy, leprous thing. Had I visioned the execrable power behind my brief period of elation I would have locked myself forever from the rest of the world and spent my remaining years in penitent solitude.

Tragedy often runs in trilogies, hence despite the proverbial longevity of our townspeople, the next five years brought the death of both my parents. My mother went first, in an accident of the most unexpected nature; and so genuine was my grief that I was honestly surprised to find its poignancy mocked and contradicted by that almost forgotten feeling of supreme and diabolical ecstasy. Once more my heart leaped wildly within me, once more it pounded at trip-hammer speed and sent the hot blood coursing through my veins with meteoric fever. I shook from my shoulders the harassing cloak of stagnation only to replace it with the infinitely more horrible burden of loathsome, unhallowed desire. I haunted the deathchamber where the body of my mother lay, my soul athirst for the devilish nectar that seemed to saturate the air of the darkened room. Every breath strengthened me, lifted me to towering heights of seraphic satisfaction. I knew, now, that it was but a sort of drugged delirium which must soon pass and leave me correspondingly weakened by its malign power, yet I could no more control my longing than I could untwist the Gordian knots in the already tangled skein of my destiny.

I knew, too, that through some strange satanic curse my life depended upon the dead for its motive force; that there was a singularity in my makeup which responded only to the awesome presence of some lifeless clod. A few days later, frantic for the bestial intoxicant on which the fullness of my existence depended, I interviewed Fenham's sole undertaker and talked him into taking me on as a sort of apprentice.

The shock of my mother's demise had visibly affected my father. I think that if I had broached the idea of such *outré* employment at any other time he would have been emphatic in his refusal. As it was he nodded acquiescence after a moment's sober thought. How little did I dream that he would be the object of my first practical lesson!

He, too, died suddenly; developing some hitherto unsuspected heart affliction. My octogenarian employer tried his best to dissuade me from the unthinkable task of embalming his body, nor did he detect the rapturous glint in my eyes as I finally won him over to my damnable point of view. I cannot hope to express the reprehensible, the unutterable thoughts that swept in tumultous waves of passion through my racing heart as I laboured over the lifeless clay. Unsurpassed love was the keynote of these concepts, a love greater – far greater – than any I had ever borne him while he was alive.

My father was not a rich man, but he had possessed enough of worldly goods to make him comfortably independent. As his sole heir I found myself in rather a paradoxical position. My early youth had totally failed to fit me for contact with the modern world, yet the primitive life of Fenham with its attendant isolation defeated my sole motive in arranging my indenture.

After settling the estate it proved an easy matter to secure my release and I headed for Bayboro, a city some fifty miles away. Here my year of apprenticeship stood me in good stead. I had no trouble in establishing a favourable connection that maintained the largest funeral parlours in the city. I even prevailed upon them to let me sleep upon the premises – for already the proximity of the dead was becoming an obsession.

I applied myself to my task with unwonted zeal. No case was too gruesome for my impious sensibilities, and I soon became master at my chosen vocation. Every fresh corpse brought into the establishment meant a fulfilled promise of ungodly gladness, of irreverent grati-fication; a return of that rapturous tumult of the arteries which transformed my grisly task into one of beloved devotion – yet every carnal satiation exacted its toll. I came to dread the days that brought no dead for me to gloat over, and prayed to all the obscene gods of the nethermost abysses to bring swift, sure death upon the residents of the city.

Then came the nights when a skulking figure stole surreptitiously through the shadowy areas of the suburbs; pitchdark nights when the midnight moon was obscured by heavy lowering clouds. It was a furtive figure that blended with the trees and cast fugitive glances over its shoulder; a figure bent on some malignant mission. After one of those prowlings the morning papers would scream to their sensation-mad clientele the details of some nightmare crime; column on column of lurid gloating over abominable atrocities; paragraph on paragraph of impossible solutions and extravagant, conflicting suspicions. Through it all I felt a supreme sense of security, for who would for a moment suspect an employee in an undertaking establishment, where Death was supposedly an everyday affair, of seeking surcease from unnameable urgings in the cold-blooded slaughter of his fellow-beings? I planned each crime with maniacal cunning, varying the manner of my murders so that no-one would even dream that all were the work of one blood-stained pair of hands. The aftermath of each nocturnal venture was an ecstatic hour of pleasure, pernicious and unalloyed; a pleasure always heightened by the chance that its delicious source might be later be assigned to my gloating administrations in the course of my regular occupation. Sometimes that double and ultimate pleasure did occur – O rare and delicious memory!

During long nights when I clung to the shelter of my sanctuary, I was prompted by the mausoleum silence to devise new and unspeakable ways of lavishing my affections upon the dead that I loved – the dead that gave me life!

One morning Mr Gresham came much earlier than usual – came to find me stretched out upon a cold slab deep in ghoulish slumber, my arms wrapped about the stark, stiff, naked body of a fetid corpse! He roused me from my salacious dreams, his eyes filled with mingled detestation and pity. Gently but firmly he told me that I needed a long rest from the repellent tasks my vocation required, that my impressionable youth was too deeply affected by the dismal atmosphere of my environment. How little did he know of the demoniacal desires that spurred me on in my disgusting infirmities! I was wise enough to see that argument would only strengthen his belief in my potential madness – it was far better to leave than to invite discovery of the motive underlying my action.

After this I dared not stay long in one place for fear some overt act would bare my secret from city to city, town to town. I worked in morgues, around cemeteries, once in a crematory – anywhere that afforded me an opportunity to be near the dead that I so craved.

Then came the World War. I was one of the first to go across, one of the last to return. Four years of blood-red charnel Hell... sickening slime of rain and rotten trenches... deafening bursting of hysterical shells... monotonous droning of sardonic bullets... smoking frenzies of Phlegethon's fountains... stifling fumes of murderous gases... grotesque remnants of smashed and shredded bodies... four years of trans-cendent satisfaction.

In every wanderer there is a latent urge to return to the scenes of his childhood. A few months later found me making my way through the familiar byways of Fenham. Vacant dilapidated farm houses lined the adjacent roadsides, while the years had brought equal retro-gression to the town itself. A mere handful of the houses were occupied, but among those was the one I had once called home. The tangled, weed-choked driveway, the broken window-panes, the uncared-for acres that stretched behind, all bore mute confirmation of the tales that guarded inquiries had elicited – that it now sheltered a dissolute drunkard who eked out a meagre existence from the chores his few neighbours gave him out of sympathy for the mistreated wife and undernourished child who shared his lot. All in all, the glamour surrounding my youthful environment was entirely dispelled; so, prompted by some errant foolhardy thought, I next turned my step toward Bayboro.

Here, too, the years had brought changes, but in reverse order. The small city I remembered had almost doubled in size despite its wartime depopulation. Instinctively I sought my former place of employment, finding it still there but with an unfamiliar name and "successor to" above the door, for the influenza epidemic had claimed Mr Gresham, while the boys were overseas. Some fateful mood impelled me to ask for work. I referred to my tutelage under Mr. Gresham with some trepidation, but my fears were groundless – my late employer had carried the secret of my unethical conduct with him to the grave. An opportune vacancy ensured my immediate re-installation.

Then came vagrant haunting memories of scarlet nights of impious pilgrimages, and an uncontrollable desire to renew those illicit joys. I cast caution to the winds and launched upon another series of damnable debaucheries. Once more the yellow sheets found welcome material in the devilish details of my crimes, comparing them to the red weeks of horror that had appalled the city years before. Once more the police sent out their dragnet and drew into its enmeshing folds – nothing!

My thirst for the noxious nectar of the dead grew to a consuming fire, and I began to shorten the periods between my odious exploits. I realized that I was treading on dangerous ground, but demoniac desire gripped me in its torturing tentacles and urged me on.

All this time my mind was becoming more and more benumbed to any influence except the satiation of my insane longings. Little details vitally important to one bent on such escapades escaped me. Somehow, somewhere, I left a vague trace, an elusive clue, behind – not enough to warrant my arrest, but sufficient to turn the tide of suspicion in my direction. I sensed this espionage, yet was helpless to stem the surging demand for more dead to quicken my enervated soul.

Then came the night when the shrill whistle of the police roused me from my fiendish gloating over the body of my latest victim, a gory razor still clutched tightly in my hand. With one dexterous motion I closed the blade and thrust it into the pocket of the coat I wore. Nightsticks beat a lusty tattoo upon the door. I crashed the window with a chair, thanking Fate I had chosen one of the cheaper tenement districts for my locale. I dropped into a dingy alley as blue-coated forms burst through the shattered door. Over shaky fences, through filthy back yards, past squalid ramshackle houses, down dimly-lighted narrow streets I fled. I thought at once of the wooded marshes that lay beyond the city and stretched for half a hundred miles till they touched the outskirts of Fenham. If I could reach this goal I would be temporarily safe. Before dawn I was plunging headlong through the foreboding wasteland, stumbling over the rotting roots of half-dead trees whose naked branches stretched out like grotesque arms striving to encumber me with mocking embraces.

The imps of the nefarious gods to whom I offered my idolatrous prayers must have guided my footsteps through that menacing morass. A week later – wan, bedraggled, and emaciated – I lurked in the woods a mile from Fenham. So far I had eluded my pursuers, yet I dared not show myself, for I knew that the alarm must have been sent broadcast. I vaguely hoped I had thrown them off the trail. After that first frenetic night I had heard no sound of alien voices, no crashing of heavy bodies through the underbrush. Perhaps they had concluded that my body lay hidden in some stagnant pool or had vanished forever in the tenacious quagmire.

Hunger gnawed at my vitals with poignant pangs, thirst left my throat parched and dry. Yet far worse was the unbearable hunger of my starving soul for the stimulus I found only in the nearness of the dead. My nostrils quivered in sweet recollection. No longer could I delude myself with the thought that this desire was a mere whim of the heated imagination. I knew now that it was an integral part of life itself; that without it I should burn out like an empty lamp. I summoned all my remaining energy to fit me for the task of satisfying my accursed appetite. Despite the peril attending my move I set out to reconnoitre, skirting the sheltering shadows like an obscene wraith. Once more I felt that strange sensation of being led by some unseen satellite of Satan. Yet even my sin-steeped soul revolted for a moment when I found myself before my native abode, the scene of my youthful hermitage.

Then these disquieting memories faded. In their place came overwhelming lustful desire. Behind the rotting walls of this old house lay my prey. A moment later I had raised one of the shattered windows and climbed over the sill. I listened for a moment, every sense alert, every muscle tensed for action. The silence reassured me. With cat-like tread I stole through the familiar rooms until stertorous snores indicated the place where I was to find surcease from my sufferings. I allowed myself a sigh of anticipated ecstasy as I pushed open the door of the bedchamber. Panther-like I made my way to the supine form stretched out in a drunken stupor. The wife and child – where were they? – well, they could wait.

Hours later I was again the fugitive, but a new-found stolen strength was mine. Three silent forms slept to wake no more. It was not until the garish light of day penetrated my hiding-place that I visualized the certain consequences of my rashly purchased belief. By this time the bodies must have been discovered. Even the most obtuse of the rural police must surely link the tragedy with my flight from the nearby city. Besides, for the first time I had been careless enough to leave some tangible proof of my identity – my finger-prints on the throats of the newly dead. All day I shivered in nervous apprehension. The mere crackling of a dry twig beneath my feet conjured mental images that appalled me. That night, under cover of the protecting darkness, I skirted Fenham and made for the woods that lay beyond. Before dawn came the first definite hint of renewed pursuit – the distant baying of hounds.

Through the long night I pressed on, but by morning I could feel my artificial strength ebbing. Noon brought once more the insistent call of the contaminating curse, and I knew that I must fall by the way unless I could once more experience that exotic intoxication that came only with the proximity of the loved dead. I had travelled in a wide semicircle. If I pushed steadily ahead, midnight would bring me to the cemetery where I had laid my parents years before. My only hope, I felt certain, lay in reaching this goal before I was overtaken. With silent prayer to the devils that dominated my destiny I turned leaden feet in the direction of my last stronghold.

God! Can it be that a scant twelve hours have passed since I started for my ghostly sanctuary? I have lived an eternity in each leaden hour. But I have reached a rich reward. The noxious odours of this neglected spot are frankincense to my suffering soul!

The first streaks of dawn are greying the horizon. They are coming! My sharp ears catch the far-off howling of the dogs! It is but a matter of minutes before they find me and shut me away forever from the rest of the world, to spend my days in ravaging yearnings till at last I join the dead I love!

They shall not take me! A way of escape is open! A coward's choice, perhaps, but better – far better – than endless months of nameless misery. I will leave this record behind me that some soul may perhaps understand why I make this choice.

The razor! It has nestled forgotten in my pocket since my flight from Bayboro. Its blood-stained blade gleams oddly in the waning light of the thin-edged moon. One slashing stroke across my left wrist and deliverance is assured...

Warm, fresh blood spatters grotesque patterns on dingy, decrepit slabs... phantasmal hordes swarm over the rotting graves... spectral fingers beckon me... ethereal fragments of unwritten melodies rise in celestial crescendo... distant stars dance drunkenly in demonic accom-paniment... a thousand tiny hammers beat hideous dissonances on anvils inside my chaotic brain... grey ghosts of slaughtered spirits parade in mocking silence before me... scorched tongues of invisible flame sear the brand of Hell upon my sickened soul... I can... write... no... more...

THE SHUNNED HOUSE

I

From even the greatest of horrors irony is seldom absent. Sometimes it enters directly into the composition of the events, while sometimes it relates only to their fortuitous position among persons and places. The latter sort is splendidly exemplified by a case in the ancient city of Providence, where in the late forties Edgar Allan Poe used to sojourn often during his unsuccessful wooing of the gifted poetess, Mrs. Whitman. Poe generally stopped at the Mansion House in Benefit Street — the renamed Golden Ball Inn whose roof has sheltered Washington, Jefferson, and Lafayette — and his favourite walk led northward along the same street to Mrs. Whitman's home and the neighbouring hillside churchyard of St. John's, whose hidden expanse of eighteenth-century gravestones had for him a peculiar fascination.

Now the irony is this. In this walk, so many times repeated, the world's greatest master of the terrible and the bizarre was obliged to pass a particular house on the eastern side of the street; a dingy, antiquated structure perched on the abruptly rising side-hill, with a great unkempt yard dating from a time when the region was partly open country. It does not appear that he ever wrote or spoke of it, nor is there any evidence that he even noticed it. And yet that house, to the two persons in possession of certain information, equals or outranks in horror the wildest phantasy of the genius who so often passed it unknowingly, and stands starkly leering as a symbol of all that is unutterably hideous.

The house was — and for that matter still is — of a kind to attract the attention of the curious. Originally a farm or semi-farm building, it followed the average New England colonial lines of the middle eighteenth century — the prosperous peaked-roof sort, with two stories and dormerless attic, and with the Georgian doorway and interior panelling dictated by the progress of taste at that time. It faced south, with one gable end buried to the lower windows in the eastward rising hill, and the other exposed to the foundations toward the street. Its construction, over a century and a half ago, had followed the grading and straightening of the road in that especial vicinity; for Benefit Street — at first called Back Street — was laid out as a lane winding amongst the graveyards of the first settlers, and straightened only when the removal of the bodies to the North Burial Ground made it decently possible to cut through the old family plots.

At the start, the western wall had lain some twenty feet up a precipitous lawn from the roadway; but a widening of the street at about the time of the Revolution sheared off most of the intervening space, exposing the foundations so that a brick basement wall had to be made, giving the deep cellar a street frontage with door and two windows above ground, close to the new line of public travel. When the sidewalk was laid out a century ago the last of the intervening space was removed; and Poe in his walks must have seen only a sheer ascent of dull grey brick flush with the sidewalk and surmounted at a height of ten feet by the antique shingled bulk of the house proper.

The farm-like grounds extended back very deeply up the hill, almost to Wheaton Street. The space south of the house, abutting on Benefit Street, was of course greatly above the existing sidewalk level, forming a terrace bounded by a high bank wall of damp, mossy stone pierced by a steep flight of narrow steps which led inward between canyon-like surfaces to the upper region of mangy lawn, rheumy brick walls, and neglected gardens whose dismantled cement urns, rusted kettles fallen from tripods of knotty sticks, and similar paraphernalia set off the weather-beaten front door with its broken fanlight, rotting Ionic pilasters, and wormy triangular pediment.

What I heard in my youth about the shunned house was merely that people died there in alarmingly great numbers. That, I was told, was why the original owners had moved out some twenty years after building the place. It was plainly unhealthy, perhaps because of the dampness and fungous growth in the cellar, the general sickish smell, the draughts of the hallways, or the quality of the well and pump water. These things were bad enough, and these were all that gained belief among the persons whom I knew. Only the notebooks of my antiquarian uncle, Dr. Elihu Whipple, revealed to me at length the darker, vaguer surmises which formed an undercurrent of folklore among old-time servants and humble folk; surmises which never travelled far, and which were largely forgotten when Providence grew to be a metropolis with a shifting modern population.

The general fact is, that the house was never regarded by the solid part of the community as in any real sense "haunted". There were no widespread tales of rattling chains, cold currents of air, extinguished lights, or faces at the window. Extremists sometimes said the house was "unlucky", but that is as far as even they went. What was really beyond dispute is that a frightful proportion of persons died there; or more accurately, had died there, since after some peculiar happenings over sixty years ago the building had become deserted through the sheer impossibility of renting it. These persons were not all cut off suddenly by any one cause; rather did it seem that their vitality was insidiously sapped, so that each one died the sooner from whatever tendency to weakness he may have naturally had. And those who did not die displayed in varying degree a type of anaemia or consumption, and sometimes a decline of the mental faculties, which spoke ill for the salubriousness of the building. Neighbouring houses, it must be added, seemed entirely free from the noxious quality.

This much I knew before my insistent questioning led my uncle to shew me the notes which finally embarked us both on our hideous investigation. In my childhood the shunned house was vacant, with barren, gnarled, and terrible old trees, long, queerly pale grass, and nightmarishly misshapen weeds in the high terraced yard where birds never lingered. We boys used to overrun the place, and I can still recall my youthful terror not only at the morbid strangeness of this sinister vegetation, but at the eldritch atmosphere and odour of the dilapidated house, whose unlocked front door was often entered in quest of shudders. The small-paned windows were largely broken, and a nameless air of desolation hung round the precarious panelling, shaky interior shutters, peeling wall-paper, falling plaster, rickety staircases, and such fragments of battered furniture as still remained. The dust and cobwebs added their touch of the fearful; and brave indeed was the boy who would voluntarily ascend the ladder to the attic, a vast raftered length lighted only by small blinking windows in the gable ends, and filled with a massed wreckage of chests, chairs, and spinning-wheels which infinite years of deposit had shrouded and festooned into monstrous and hellish shapes.

But after all, the attic was not the most terrible part of the house. It was the dank, humid cellar which somehow exerted the strongest repulsion on us, even though it was wholly above ground on the street side, with only a thin door and window-pierced brick wall to separate it from the busy sidewalk. We scarcely knew whether to haunt it in spectral fascination, or to shun it for the sake of our souls and our sanity. For one thing, the bad odour of the house was strongest there; and for another thing, we did not like the white fungous growths which occasionally sprang up in rainy summer weather from the hard earth floor. Those fungi, grotesquely like the vegetation in the yard outside, were truly horrible in their outlines; detestable parodies of toadstools and Indian pipes, whose like we had never seen in any other situation. They rotted quickly, and at one stage became slightly phosphorescent; so that nocturnal passers-by sometimes spoke of witch-fires glowing behind the broken panes of the foetor-spreading windows.

We never – even in our wildest Hallowe'en moods – visited this cellar by night, but in some of our daytime visits could detect the phosphorescence, especially when the day was dark and wet. There was also a subtler thing we often thought we detected – a very strange thing which was, however, merely suggestive at most. I refer to a sort of cloudy whitish pattern on the dirt floor – a vague, shifting deposit of mould or nitre which we sometimes thought we could trace amidst the sparse fungous growths near the huge fireplace of the basement kitchen. Once in a while it struck us that this patch bore an uncanny resemblance to a doubled-up human figure, though generally no such kinship existed, and often there was no whitish deposit whatever. On a certain rainy afternoon when this illusion seemed phenomenally strong, and when, in addition, I had fancied I glimpsed a kind of thin, yellowish, shimmering exhalation rising from the nitrous pattern toward the yawning fireplace, I spoke to my uncle about the matter. He smiled at this odd conceit, but it seemed that his smile was tinged with reminiscence. Later I heard that a similar notion entered into some of the wild ancient tales of the common folk – a notion likewise alluding to ghoulish, wolfish shapes taken by smoke from the great chimney, and queer contours assumed by certain of the sinuous tree-roots that thrust their way into the cellar through the loose foundation-stones.

II

Not till my adult years did my uncle set before me the notes and data which he had collected concerning the shunned house. Dr. Whipple was a sane, conservative physician of the old school, and for all his interest in the place was not eager to encourage young thoughts toward the abnormal. His own view, postulating simply a building and location of markedly unsanitary qualities, had nothing to do with abnormality; but he realised that the very picturesqueness which aroused his own interest would in a boy's fanciful mind take on all manner of gruesome imaginative associations.

The doctor was a bachelor; a white-haired, clean-shaven, old-fashioned gentleman, and a local historian of note, who had often broken a lance with such controversial guardians of tradition as Sidney S. Rider and Thomas W.

Bicknell. He lived with one manservant in a Georgian homestead with knocker and iron-railed steps, balanced eerily on a steep ascent of North Court Street beside the ancient brick court and colony house where his grandfather – a cousin of that celebrated privateersman, Capt. Whipple, who burnt His Majesty's armed schooner *Gaspee* in 1772 – had voted in the legislature on May 4, 1776, for the independence of the Rhode Island Colony. Around him in the damp, low-ceiled library with the musty white panelling, heavy carved overmantel, and small-paned, vine-shaded windows, were the relics and records of his ancient family, among which were many dubious allusions to the shunned house in Benefit Street. That pest spot lies not far distant – for Benefit runs ledgewise just above the court-house along the precipitous hill up which the first settlement climbed.

When, in the end, my insistent pestering and maturing years evoked from my uncle the hoarded lore I sought, there lay before me a strange enough chronicle. Long-winded, statistical, and drearily genealogical as some of the matter was, there ran through it a continuous thread of brooding, tenacious horror and preternatural malevolence which impressed me even more than it had impressed the good doctor. Separate events fitted together uncannily, and seemingly irrelevant details held mines of hideous possibilities. A new and burning curiosity grew in me, compared to which my boyish curiosity was feeble and inchoate. The first revelation led to an exhaustive research, and finally to that shuddering quest which proved so disastrous to myself and mine. For at last my uncle insisted on joining the search I had commenced, and after a certain night in that house he did not come away with me. I am lonely without that gentle soul whose long years were filled only with honour, virtue, good taste, benevolence, and learning. I have reared a marble urn to his memory in St. John's churchyard – the place that Poe loved – the hidden grove of giant willows on the hill, where tombs and headstones huddle quietly between the hoary bulk of the church and the houses and bank walls of Benefit Street.

The history of the house, opening amidst a maze of dates, revealed no trace of the sinister either about its construction or about the prosperous and honourable family who built it. Yet from the first a taint of calamity, soon increased to boding significance, was apparent. My uncle's carefully compiled record began with the building of the structure in 1763, and followed the theme with an unusual amount of detail. The shunned house, it seems, was first inhabited by William Harris and his wife Rhoby Dexter, with their children, Elkanah, born in 1755, Abigail, born in 1757, William, Jr., born in 1759, and

Ruth, born in 1761. Harris was a substantial merchant and seaman in the West India trade, connected with the firm of Obadiah Brown and his nephews. After Brown's death in 1761, the new firm of Nicholas Brown & Co. made him master of the brig *Prudence*, Providence-built, of 120 tons, thus enabling him to erect the new homestead he had desired ever since his marriage.

The site he had chosen – a recently straightened part of the new and fashionable Back Street, which ran along the side of the hill above crowded Cheapside – was all that could be wished, and the building did justice to the location. It was the best that moderate means could afford, and Harris hastened to move in before the birth of a fifth child which the family expected. That child, a boy, came in December; but was still-born. Nor was any child to be born alive in that house for a century and a half.

The next April sickness occurred among the children, and Abigail and Ruth died before the month was over. Dr. Job Ives diagnosed the trouble as some infantile fever, though others declared it was more of a mere wasting-away or decline. It seemed, in any event, to be contagious; for Hannah Bowen, one of the two servants, died of it in the following June. Eli Liddeason, the other servant, constantly complained of weakness; and would have returned to his father's farm in Rehoboth but for a sudden attachment for Mehitabel Pierce, who was hired to succeed Hannah. He died the next year – a sad year indeed, since it marked the death of William Harris himself, enfeebled as he was by the climate of Martinique, where his occupation had kept him for considerable periods during the preceding decade.

The widowed Rhoby Harris never recovered from the shock of her husband's death, and the passing of her first-born Elkanah two years later was the final blow to her reason. In 1768 she fell victim to a mild form of insanity, and was thereafter confined to the upper part of the house; her elder maiden sister, Mercy Dexter, having moved in to take charge of the family. Mercy was a plain, raw-boned woman of great strength; but her health visibly declined from the time of her advent. She was greatly devoted to her unfortunate sister, and had an especial affection for her only surviving nephew William, who from a sturdy infant had become a sickly, spindling lad. In this year the servant Mehitabel died, and the other servant, Preserved Smith, left without coherent explanation – or at least, with only some wild tales and a complaint that he disliked the smell of the place. For a time Mercy could secure no more help, since the seven deaths and case of madness, all occurring within five years' space, had begun to set in motion the body of fireside rumour which later became so bizarre. Ultimately, however, she obtained new servants from out of town; Ann White, a morose woman from that part of North Kingstown now set off as the township of Exeter, and a capable Boston man named Zenas Low.

It was Ann White who first gave definite shape to the sinister idle talk. Mercy should have known better than to hire anyone from the Nooseneck Hill country, for that remote bit of backwoods was then, as now, a seat of the most uncomfortable superstitions. As lately as 1892 an Exeter community exhumed a dead body and ceremoniously burnt its heart in order to prevent certain alleged visitations injurious to the public health and peace, and one may imagine the point of view of the same section in 1768. Ann's tongue was perniciously active, and within a few months Mercy discharged her, filling her place with a faithful and amiable Amazon from Newport, Maria Robbins.

Meanwhile poor Rhoby Harris, in her madness, gave voice to dreams and imaginings of the most hideous sort. At times her screams became insupportable, and for long periods she would utter shrieking horrors which necessitated her son's temporary residence with his cousin, Peleg Harris, in Presbyterian-Lane near the new college building. The boy would seem to improve after these visits, and had Mercy been as wise as she was well-meaning, she would have let him live permanently with Peleg. Just what Mrs. Harris cried out in her fits of violence, tradition hesitates to say; or rather, presents such extravagant accounts that they nullify themselves through sheer absurdity. Certainly it sounds absurd to hear that a woman educated only in the rudiments of French often shouted for hours in a coarse and idiomatic form of that language, or that the same person, alone and guarded, complained wildly of a staring thing which bit and chewed at her. In 1772 the servant Zenas died, and when Mrs. Harris heard of it she laughed with a shocking delight utterly foreign to her. The next year she herself died, and was laid to rest in the North Burial Ground beside her husband.

Upon the outbreak of trouble with Great Britain in 1775, William Harris, despite his scant sixteen years and feeble constitution, managed to enlist in the Army of Observation under General Greene; and from that time on enjoyed a steady rise in health and prestige. In 1780, as a Captain in Rhode Island forces in New Jersey under Colonel Angell, he met and married Phebe Hetfield of Elizabethtown, whom he brought to Providence upon his honourable discharge in the following year.

The young soldier's return was not a thing of unmitigated happiness. The house, it is true, was still in good condition; and the street had been widened and changed in name from Back Street to Benefit Street. But Mercy Dexter's once robust frame had undergone a sad and curious decay, so that she was now a stooped and pathetic figure with hollow voice and disconcerting pallor – qualities shared to a singular degree by the one remaining servant Maria. In the autumn of 1782 Phebe Harris gave birth to a still-born daughter, and on the fifteenth of the next May Mercy Dexter took leave of a useful, austere, and virtuous life.

William Harris, at last thoroughly convinced of the radically unhealthful nature of his abode, now took steps toward quitting it and closing it forever. Securing temporary quarters for himself and his wife at the newly opened Golden Ball Inn, he arranged for the building of a new and finer house in Westminster Street, in the growing part of the town across the Great Bridge. There, in 1785, his son Dutee was born; and there the family dwelt till the encroachments of commerce drove them back across the river and over the hill to Angell Street, in the newer East Side residence district, where the late Archer Harris built his sumptuous but hideous French-roofed mansion in 1876. William and Phebe both succumbed to the yellow fever epidemic of 1797, but Dutee was brought up by his cousin Rathbone Harris, Peleg's son.

Rathbone was a practical man, and rented the Benefit Street house despite William's wish to keep it vacant. He considered it an obligation to his ward to make the most of all the boy's property, nor did he concern himself with the deaths and illnesses which caused so many changes of tenants, or the steadily growing aversion with which the house was generally regarded. It is likely that he felt only vexation when, in 1804, the town council ordered him to fumigate the place with sulphur, tar, and gum camphor on account of the much-discussed deaths of four persons, presumably caused by the then diminishing fever epidemic. They said the place had a febrile smell.

Dutee himself thought little of the house, for he grew up to be a privateersman, and served with distinction on the *Vigilant* under Capt. Cahoone in the War of 1812. He returned unharmed, married in 1814, and became a father on that memorable night of September 23, 1815, when a great gale drove the waters of the bay over half the town, and floated a tall sloop well up Westminster Street so that its masts almost tapped the Harris windows in symbolic affirmation that the new boy, Welcome, was a seaman's son.

Welcome did not survive his father, but lived to perish gloriously at Fredericksburg in 1862. Neither he nor his son Archer knew of the shunned house as other than a nuisance almost impossible to rent – perhaps on account of the mustiness and sickly odour of unkempt old age. Indeed, it never was rented after a series of deaths culminating in 1861, which the excitement of the war tended to throw into obscurity. Carrington Harris, last of the male line, knew it only as a deserted and somewhat picturesque centre of legend until I told him my experience. He had meant to tear it down and build an apartment house on the site, but after my account decided to let it stand, install plumbing, and rent it. Nor has he yet had any difficulty in obtaining tenants. The horror has gone.

III

It may well be imagined how powerfully I was affected by the annals of the Harrises. In this continuous record there seemed to me to brood a persistent evil beyond anything in Nature as I had known it; an evil clearly connected with the house and not with the family. This impression was confirmed by my uncle's less systematic array of miscellaneous data – legends transcribed from servant gossip, cuttings from the papers, copies of death-certificates by fellow-physicians, and the like. All of this material I cannot hope to give, for my uncle was a tireless antiquarian and very deeply interested in the shunned house; but I may refer to several dominant points which earn notice by their recurrence through many reports from diverse sources. For example, the servant gossip was practically unanimous in attributing to the fungous and malodorous *cellar* of the house a vast supremacy in evil influence. There had been servants – Ann White especially – who would not use the cellar kitchen, and at least three well-defined legends bore upon the queer quasi-human or diabolic outlines assumed by tree-roots and patches of mould in that region. These latter narratives interested me profoundly, on account of what I had seen in my boyhood, but I felt that most of the significance had in each case been largely obscured by additions from the common stock of local ghost lore.

Ann White, with her Exeter superstition, had promulgated the most extravagant and at the same time most consistent tale; alleging that there must lie buried beneath the house one of those vampires – the dead who retain their bodily form and live on the blood or breath of the living – whose hideous legions send their preying shapes or spirits abroad by night. To destroy a vampire one must, the grandmothers say, exhume it and burn its heart, or at least drive a stake through that organ; and Ann's dogged insistence on a search under the cellar had been prominent in bringing about her discharge.

Her tales, however, commanded a wide audience, and were the more readily accepted because the house indeed stood on land once used for burial purposes. To me their interest depended less on this circumstance than on the peculiarly appropriate way in which they dovetailed with certain other things – the complaint of the departing servant Preserved Smith, who had preceded Ann and never heard of her, that something "sucked his breath" at night; the death-certificates of fever victims of 1804, issued by Dr. Chad Hopkins, and shewing the four deceased persons all unaccountably lacking in blood; and the obscure passages of poor Rhoby Harris's ravings, where she complained of the sharp teeth of a glassy-eyed, half-visible presence.

Free from unwarranted superstition though I am, these things produced in me an odd sensation, which was intensified by a pair of widely separated newspaper cuttings relating to deaths in the shunned house – one from the *Providence Gazette and Country-Journal* of April 12, 1815, and the other from the *Daily Transcript and Chronicle* of October 27, 1845 – each of which detailed an appallingly grisly circumstance whose duplication was remarkable. It seems that in both instances the dying person, in 1815 a gentle old lady named Stafford and in 1845 a school-teacher of middle age named Eleazar Durfee, became transfigured in a horrible way; glaring glassily and attempting to bite the throat of the attending physician. Even more puzzling, though, was the final case which put an end to the renting of the house – a series of anaemia deaths preceded by progressive madnesses wherein the patient would craftily attempt the lives of his relatives by incisions in the neck or wrist.

This was in 1860 and 1861, when my uncle had just begun his medical practice; and before leaving for the front he heard much of it from his elder professional colleagues. The really inexplicable thing was the way in which the victims – ignorant people, for the ill-smelling and widely shunned house could now be rented to no others – would babble maledictions in French, a language they could not possibly have studied to any extent. It made one think of poor Rhoby Harris nearly a century before, and so moved my uncle that he commenced collecting historical data on the house after listening, some time subsequent to his return from the war, to the first-hand account of Drs. Chase and Whitmarsh. Indeed, I could see that my uncle had thought deeply on the subject, and that he was glad of my own interest – an open-minded and sympathetic interest which enabled him to discuss with me matters at which others would merely have laughed. His fancy had not gone so far as mine, but he felt that the place was rare in its imaginative potentialities, and worthy of note as an inspiration in the field of the grotesque and macabre.

For my part, I was disposed to take the whole subject with profound seriousness, and began at once not only to review the evidence, but to accumulate as much more as I could. I talked with the elderly Archer Harris, then owner of the house, many times before his death in 1916; and obtained from him and his still surviving maiden sister Alice an authentic corroboration of all the family data my uncle had collected. When, however, I asked them what connexion with France or its language the house could have, they confessed themselves as frankly baffled and ignorant as I. Archer knew nothing, and all that Miss Harris could say was that an old allusion her grandfather, Dutee Harris, had heard of might have shed a little light. The old seaman, who had survived his son Welcome's death in battle by two years, had not himself known the legend; but recalled that his earliest nurse, the ancient Maria Robbins, seemed darkly aware of something that might have lent a weird significance to the French ravings of Rhoby Harris, which she had so often heard during the last days of that hapless woman. Maria had been at the shunned house from 1769 till the removal of the family in 1783, and had seen Mercy Dexter die. Once she hinted to the child Dutee of a somewhat peculiar circumstance in Mercy's last moments, but he had soon forgotten all about it save that it was something peculiar. The granddaughter, moreover, recalled even this much with difficulty. She and her brother were not so much interested in the house as was Archer's son Carrington, the present owner, with whom I talked after my experience.

Having exhausted the Harris family of all the information it could furnish, I turned my attention to early town records and deeds with a zeal more penetrating than that which my uncle had occasionally shewn in the same work. What I wished was a comprehensive history of the site from its very settlement in 1636 – or even before, if any Narragansett Indian legend could be unearthed to supply the data. I found, at the start, that the land had been part of the long strip of home lot granted originally to John Throckmorton; one of many similar strips beginning at the Town Street beside the river and extending up over the hill to a line roughly corresponding with the modern Hope Street. The Throckmorton lot had later, of course, been much subdivided; and I became very assiduous in tracing that section through which Back or Benefit Street was later run. It had, a rumour indeed said, been the Throckmorton graveyard; but as I examined the records more carefully, I found that the graves had all been transferred at an early date to the North Burial Ground on the Pawtucket West Road.

Then suddenly I came – by a rare piece of chance, since it was not in the main body of records and might easily have been missed – upon something which aroused my keenest eagerness, fitting in as it did with several of the queerest phases of the affair. It was the record of a lease, in 1697, of a small tract of ground to an Etienne Roulet and wife. At last the French element had appeared – that, and another deeper element of horror which the name conjured up from the darkest recesses of my weird and heterogeneous reading – and I feverishly studied the platting of the locality as it had been before the cutting through and partial straightening of Back Street between 1747 and 1758. I found what I had half expected, that where the shunned house now stood the Roulets had laid out their graveyard behind a one-story and attic cottage, and that no record of any transfer of graves existed. The document, indeed, ended in much confusion; and I was forced to ransack both the Rhode Island Historical Society and Shepley Library before I could find a local door which the name Etienne Roulet would unlock. In the end I did find something; something of such vague but monstrous import that I set about at once to examine the cellar of the shunned house itself with a new and excited minuteness.

The Roulets, it seemed, had come in 1696 from East Greenwich, down the west shore of Narragansett Bay. They were Huguenots from Caude, and had encountered much opposition before the Providence selectmen allowed them to settle in the town. Unpopularity had dogged them in East Greenwich, whither they had come in 1686, after the revocation of the Edict of Nantes, and rumour said that the cause of dislike extended beyond mere racial and national prejudice, or the land disputes which involved other French settlers with the English in rivalries which not even Governor Andros could quell. But their ardent Protestantism – too ardent, some whispered – and their evident distress when virtually driven from the village down the bay, had moved the sympathy of the town fathers. Here the strangers had been granted a haven; and the swarthy Etienne Roulet, less apt at agriculture than at reading queer books and drawing queer diagrams, was given a clerical post in the warehouse at Pardon Tillinghast's wharf, far south in Town Street. There had, however, been a riot of some sort later on – perhaps forty years later, after old Roulet's death – and no one seemed to hear of the family after that.

For a century and more, it appeared, the Roulets had been well remembered and frequently discussed as vivid incidents in the quiet life of a New England seaport. Etienne's son Paul, a surly fellow whose erratic conduct had probably provoked the riot which wiped out the family, was particularly a source of speculation; and though Providence never shared the witchcraft panics of her Puritan neighbours, it was freely intimated by old wives that his prayers were neither uttered at the proper time nor directed toward the proper object. All this had undoubtedly formed the basis of the legend known by old Maria Robbins. What relation it had to the French ravings of Rhoby Harris and other inhabitants of the shunned house, imagination or future discovery alone could determine. I wondered how many of those who had known the legends realised that additional link with the terrible which my wide reading had given me; that ominous item in the annals of morbid horror which tells of the creature Jacques Roulet, of Caude, who in 1598 was condemned to death as a daemoniac but afterward saved from the stake by the Paris parliament and shut in a madhouse. He had been found covered with blood and shreds of flesh in a wood, shortly after the killing and rending of a boy by a pair of wolves. One wolf was seen to lope away unhurt. Surely a pretty hearthside tale, with a queer significance as to name and place; but I decided that the Providence gossips could not have generally known of it. Had they known, the coincidence of names would have brought some drastic and frightened action – indeed, might not its limited whispering have precipitated the final riot which erased the Roulets from the town?

I now visited the accursed place with increased frequency; studying the unwholesome vegetation of the garden, examining all the walls of the building, and poring over every inch of the earthen cellar floor. Finally, with Carrington Harris's permission, I fitted a key to the disused door opening from the cellar directly upon Benefit Street, preferring to have a more immediate access to the outside world than the dark stairs, ground floor hall, and front door could give. There, where morbidity lurked most thickly, I searched and poked during long afternoons when the sunlight filtered in through the cobwebbed above-ground windows, and a sense of security glowed from the unlocked door which placed me only a few feet from the placid sidewalk outside. Nothing new rewarded my efforts – only the same depressing mustiness and faint suggestions of noxious odours and nitrous outlines on the floor – and I fancy that many pedestrians must have watched me curiously through the broken panes.

At length, upon a suggestion of my uncle's, I decided to try the spot nocturnally; and one stormy midnight ran the beams of an electric torch over the mouldy floor with its uncanny shapes and distorted, half-phosphorescent fungi. The place had dispirited me curiously that evening, and I was almost prepared when I saw – or thought I saw – amidst the whitish deposits a particularly sharp definition of the "huddled form" I had suspected from boyhood. Its clearness was astonishing and unprecedented – and as I watched I seemed to see again the thin, yellowish, shimmering exhalation which had startled me on that rainy afternoon so many years before.

Above the anthropomorphic patch of mould by the fireplace it rose; a subtle, sickish, almost luminous vapour which as it hung trembling in the dampness seemed to develop vague and shocking suggestions of form, gradually trailing off into nebulous decay and passing up into the blackness of the great chimney with a foetor in its wake. It was truly horrible, and the more so to me because of what I knew of the spot. Refusing to flee, I watched it fade – and as I watched I felt that it was in turn watching me greedily with eyes more imaginable than visible. When I told my uncle about it he was greatly aroused; and after a tense hour of reflection, arrived at a definite and drastic decision. Weighing in his mind the importance of the matter, and the significance of our relation to it, he insisted that we both test – and if possible destroy – the horror of the house by a joint night or nights of aggressive vigil in that musty and fungus-cursed cellar.

IV

On Wednesday, June 25, 1919, after a proper notification of Carrington Harris which did not include surmises as to what we expected to find, my uncle and I conveyed to the shunned house two camp chairs and a folding camp cot, together with some scientific mechanism of greater weight and intricacy. These we placed in the cellar during the day, screening the windows with paper and planning to return in the evening for our first vigil. We had locked the door from the cellar to the ground floor; and having a key to the outside cellar door, we were prepared to leave our expensive and delicate apparatus – which we had obtained secretly and at great cost – as many days as our vigils might need to be protracted. It was our design to sit up together till very late, and then watch singly till dawn in two-hour stretches, myself first and then my companion; the inactive member resting on the cot.

The natural leadership with which my uncle procured the instruments from the laboratories of Brown University and the Cranston Street Armoury, and instinctively assumed direction of our venture, was a marvellous commentary on the potential vitality and resilience of a man of eighty-one. Elihu

Whipple had lived according to the hygienic laws he had preached as a physician, and but for what happened later would be here in full vigour today. Only two persons suspect what did happen – Carrington Harris and myself. I had to tell Harris because he owned the house and deserved to know what had gone out of it. Then too, we had spoken to him in advance of our quest; and I felt after my uncle's going that he would understand and assist me in some vitally necessary public explanations. He turned very pale, but agreed to help me, and decided that it would now be safe to rent the house.

To declare that we were not nervous on that rainy night of watching would be an exaggeration both gross and ridiculous. We were not, as I have said, in any sense childishly superstitious, but scientific study and reflection had taught us that the known universe of three dimensions embraces the merest fraction of the whole cosmos of substance and energy. In this case an overwhelming preponderance of evidence from numerous authentic sources pointed to the tenacious existence of certain forces of great power and, so far as the human point of view is concerned, exceptional malignancy. To say that we actually believed in vampires or werewolves would be a carelessly inclusive statement. Rather must it be said that we were not prepared to deny the possibility of certain unfamiliar and unclassified modifications of vital force and attenuated matter; existing very infrequently in three-dimensional space because of its more intimate connexion with other spatial units, yet close enough to the boundary of our own to furnish us occasional manifestations which we, for lack of a proper vantage-point, may never hope to understand.

In short, it seemed to my uncle and me that an incontrovertible array of facts pointed to some lingering influence in the shunned house; traceable to one or another of the ill-favoured French settlers of two centuries before, and still operative through rare and unknown laws of atomic and electronic motion. That the family of Roulet had possessed an abnormal affinity for outer circles of entity – dark spheres which for normal folk hold only repulsion and terror – their recorded history seemed to prove. Had not, then, the riots of those bygone seventeen-thirties set moving certain kinetic patterns in the morbid brain of one or more of them – notably the sinister Paul Roulet – which obscurely survived the bodies murdered and buried by the mob, and continued to function in some multiple-dimensioned space along the original lines of force determined by a frantic hatred of the encroaching community?

Such a thing was surely not a physical or biochemical impossibility in the light of a newer science which includes the theories of relativity and intra-atomic action. One might easily imagine an alien nucleus of substance or energy, formless or otherwise, kept alive by imperceptible or immaterial subtractions from the life-force or bodily tissues and fluids of other and more palpably living things into which it penetrates and with whose fabric it sometimes completely merges itself. It might be actively hostile, or it might be dictated merely by blind motives of self-preservation. In any case such a monster must of necessity be in our scheme of things an anomaly and an intruder, whose extirpation forms a primary duty with every man not an enemy to the world's life, health, and sanity.

What baffled us was our utter ignorance of the aspect in which we might encounter the thing. No sane person had even seen it, and few had ever felt it definitely. It might be pure energy – a form ethereal and outside the realm of substance – or it might be partly material; some unknown and equivocal mass of plasticity, capable of changing at will to nebulous approximations of the solid, liquid, gaseous, or tenuously unparticled states. The anthropomorphic patch of mould on the floor, the form of the yellowish vapour, and the curvature of the tree-roots in some of the old tales, all argued at least a remote and reminiscent connexion with the human shape; but how representative or permanent that similarity might be, none could say with any kind of certainty.

We had devised two weapons to fight it; a large and specially fitted Crookes tube operated by powerful storage batteries and provided with peculiar screens and reflectors, in case it proved intangible and opposable only by vigorously destructive ether radiations, and a pair of military flame-throwers of the sort used in the world-war, in case it proved partly material and susceptible of mechanical destruction – for like the superstitious Exeter rustics, we were prepared to burn the thing's heart out if heart existed to burn. All this aggressive mechanism we set in the cellar in positions carefully arranged with reference to the cot and chairs, and to the spot before the fireplace where the mould had taken strange shapes. That suggestive patch, by the way, was only faintly visible when we placed our furniture and instruments, and when we returned that evening for the actual vigil. For a moment I half doubted that I had ever seen it in the more definitely limned form – but then I thought of the legends.

Our cellar vigil began at 10 p.m., daylight saving time, and as it continued we found no promise of pertinent developments. A weak, filtered glow from the rain-harassed street-lamps outside, and a feeble phosphorescence from the detestable fungi within, shewed the dripping stone of the walls, from which all traces of whitewash had vanished; the dank, foetid, and mildew-tainted hard earth floor with its obscene fungi; the rotting remains of what had been stools, chairs, and tables, and other more shapeless furniture; the heavy planks and massive beams of the ground floor overhead; the decrepit plank door leading to bins and chambers beneath other parts of the house; the crumbling stone staircase with ruined wooden hand-rail; and the crude and cavernous fireplace of blackened brick where rusted iron fragments revealed the past presence of hooks, andirons, spit, crane, and a door to the Dutch oven – these things, and our austere cot and camp chairs, and the heavy and intricate destructive machinery we had brought.

We had, as in my own former explorations, left the door to the street unlocked; so that a direct and practical path of escape might lie open in case of manifestations beyond our power to deal with. It was our idea that our continued nocturnal presence would call forth whatever malign entity lurked there; and that being prepared, we could dispose of the thing with one or the other of our provided means as soon as we had recognised and observed it sufficiently. How long it might require to evoke and extinguish the thing, we had no notion. It occurred to us, too, that our venture was far from safe; for in what strength the thing might appear no one could tell. But we deemed the game worth the hazard, and embarked on it alone and unhesitatingly; conscious that the seeking of outside aid would only expose us to ridicule and perhaps defeat our entire purpose. Such was our frame of mind as we talked – far into the night, till my uncle's growing drowsiness made me remind him to lie down for his two-hour sleep.

Something like fear chilled me as I sat there in the small hours alone – I say alone, for one who sits by a sleeper is indeed alone; perhaps more alone than he can realise. My uncle breathed heavily, his deep inhalations and exhalations accompanied by the rain outside, and punctuated by another nerve-racking sound of distant dripping water within – for the house was repulsively damp even in dry weather, and in this storm positively swamp-like. I studied the loose, antique masonry of the walls in the fungus-light and the feeble rays which stole in from the street through the screened windows; and once, when the noisome atmosphere of the place seemed about to sicken me, I opened the door and looked up and down the street, feasting my eyes on familiar sights and my nostrils on the wholesome air. Still nothing occurred to reward my watching; and I yawned repeatedly, fatigue getting the better of apprehension.

Then the stirring of my uncle in his sleep attracted my notice. He had turned restlessly on the cot several times during the latter half of the first hour, but now he was breathing with unusual irregularity, occasionally heaving a sigh which held more than a few of the qualities of a choking moan. I turned my electric flashlight on him and found his face averted, so rising and crossing to the other side of the cot, I again flashed the light to see if he seemed in any pain. What I saw unnerved me most surprisingly, considering its relative triviality. It must have been merely the association of any odd circumstance with the sinister nature of our location and mission, for surely the circumstance was not in itself frightful or unnatural. It was merely that my uncle's facial expression, disturbed no doubt by the strange dreams which our situation prompted, betrayed considerable agitation, and seemed not at all characteristic of him. His habitual expression was one of kindly and well-bred calm, whereas now a variety of emotions seemed struggling within him. I think, on the whole, that it was this variety which chiefly disturbed me. My uncle, as he gasped and tossed in increasing perturbation and with eyes that had now started open, seemed not one but many men, and suggested a curious quality of alienage from himself.

All at once he commenced to mutter, and I did not like the look of his mouth and teeth as he spoke. The words were at first indistinguishable, and then – with a tremendous start – I recognised something about them which filled me with icy fear till I recalled the breadth of my uncle's education and the interminable translations he had made from anthropological and antiquarian articles in the *Revue des Deux Mondes*. For the venerable Elihu Whipple was muttering in *French*, and the few phrases I could distinguish seemed connected with the darkest myths he had ever adapted from the famous Paris magazine.

Suddenly a perspiration broke out on the sleeper's forehead, and he leaped abruptly up, half awake. The jumble of French changed to a cry in English, and the hoarse voice shouted excitedly, "My breath, my breath!" Then the awakening became complete, and with a subsidence of facial expression to the normal state my uncle seized my hand and began to relate a dream whose nucleus of significance I could only surmise with a kind of awe.

He had, he said, floated off from a very ordinary series of dream-pictures into a scene whose strangeness was related to nothing he had ever read. It was of this world, and yet not of it – a shadowy geometrical confusion in which could be seen elements of familiar things in most unfamiliar and perturbing combinations. There was a suggestion of queerly disordered pictures superimposed one upon another; an arrangement in which the essentials of time as well as of space seemed dissolved and mixed in the most illogical fashion. In this kaleidoscopic vortex of phantasmal images were occasional snapshots, if one might use the term, of singular clearness but unaccountable heterogeneity.

Once my uncle thought he lay in a carelessly dug open pit, with a crowd of angry faces framed by straggling locks and three-cornered hats frowning down on him. Again he seemed to be in the interior of a house – an old house, apparently – but the details and inhabitants were constantly changing, and he could never be certain of the faces or the furniture, or even of the room itself, since doors and windows seemed in just as great a state of flux as the more presumably mobile objects. It was queer – damnably queer – and my uncle spoke almost sheepishly, as if half expecting not to be believed, when he declared that of the strange faces many had unmistakably borne the features of the Harris family. And all the while there was a personal sensation of choking, as if some pervasive presence had spread itself through his body and sought to possess itself of his vital processes. I shuddered at the thought of those vital processes, worn as they were by eighty-one years of continuous functioning, in conflict with unknown forces of which the youngest and strongest system might well be afraid; but in another moment reflected that dreams are only dreams, and that these uncomfortable visions could be, at most, no more than my uncle's reaction to the investigations and expectations which had lately filled our minds to the exclusion of all else.

Conversation, also, soon tended to dispel my sense of strangeness; and in time I yielded to my yawns and took my turn at slumber. My uncle seemed now very wakeful, and welcomed his period of watching even though the nightmare had aroused him far ahead of his allotted two hours. Sleep seized me quickly, and I was at once haunted with dreams of the most disturbing kind. I felt, in my visions, a cosmic and abysmal loneness; with hostility surging from all sides upon some prison where I lay confined. I seemed bound and gagged, and taunted by the echoing yells of distant multitudes who thirsted for my blood. My uncle's face came to me with less pleasant associations than in waking hours, and I recall many futile struggles and attempts to scream. It was not a pleasant sleep, and for a second I was not sorry for the echoing shriek which clove through the barriers of dream and flung me to a sharp and startled awakeness in which every actual object before my eyes stood out with more than natural clearness and reality.

V

I had been lying with my face away from my uncle's chair, so that in this sudden flash of awakening I saw only the door to the street, the more northerly window, and the wall and floor and ceiling toward the north of the room, all photographed with morbid vividness on my brain in a light brighter than the glow of the fungi or the rays from the street outside. It was not a strong or even a fairly strong light; certainly not nearly strong enough to read an average book by. But it cast a shadow of myself and the cot on the floor, and had a yellowish, penetrating force that hinted at things more potent than luminosity. This I perceived with unhealthy sharpness despite the fact that two of my other senses were violently assailed. For on my ears rang the reverberations of that shocking scream, while my nostrils revolted at the stench which filled the place. My mind, as alert as my senses, recognised the gravely unusual; and almost automatically I leaped up and turned about to grasp the destructive instruments which we had left trained on the mouldy spot before the fireplace. As I turned, I dreaded what I was to see; for the scream had been in my uncle's voice, and I knew not against what menace I should have to defend him and myself.

Yet after all, the sight was worse than I had dreaded. There are horrors beyond horrors, and this was one of those nuclei of all dreamable hideousness which the cosmos saves to blast an accursed and unhappy few. Out of the fungus-ridden earth steamed up a vaporous corpse-light, yellow and diseased, which bubbled and lapped to a gigantic height in vague outlines half-human and half-monstrous, through which I could see the chimney and fireplace beyond. It was all eyes – wolfish and mocking – and the rugose insect-like head dissolved at the top to a thin stream of mist which curled putridly about and finally vanished up the chimney. I say that I saw this thing, but it is only in conscious retrospection that I ever definitely traced its damnable approach to form. At the time it was to me only a seething, dimly phosphorescent cloud of fungous loathsomeness, enveloping and dissolving to an abhorrent plasticity the one object to which all my attention was focussed. That object was my uncle – the venerable Elihu Whipple – who with blackening and decaying features leered and gibbered at me, and reached out dripping claws to rend me in the fury which this horror had brought.

It was a sense of routine which kept me from going mad. I had drilled myself in preparation for the crucial moment, and blind training saved me. Recognising the bubbling evil as no substance reachable by matter or material chemistry, and therefore ignoring the flame-thrower which loomed on my left, I threw on the current of the Crookes tube apparatus, and focussed toward that scene of immortal blasphemousness the strongest ether radiations which man's art can arouse from the spaces and fluids of Nature. There was a bluish haze and a frenzied sputtering, and the yellowish phosphorescence grew dimmer to my eyes. But I saw the dimness was only that of contrast, and that the waves from the machine had no effect whatever.

Then, in the midst of that daemoniac spectacle, I saw a fresh horror which brought cries to my lips and sent me fumbling and staggering toward that unlocked door to the quiet street, careless of what abnormal terrors I loosed upon the world, or what thoughts or judgments of men I brought down upon my head. In that dim blend of blue and yellow the form of my uncle had commenced a nauseous liquefaction whose essence eludes all description, and in which there played across his vanishing face such changes of identity as only madness can conceive. He was at once a devil and a multitude, a charnel-house and a pageant. Lit by the mixed and uncertain beams, that gelatinous face assumed a dozen – a score – a hundred – aspects; grinning, as it sank to the ground on a body that melted like tallow, in the caricatured likeness of legions strange and yet not strange.

I saw the features of the Harris line, masculine and feminine, adult and infantile, and other features old and young, coarse and refined, familiar and unfamiliar. For a second there flashed a degraded counterfeit of a miniature of poor mad Rhoby Harris that I had seen in the School of Design Museum, and another time I thought I caught the raw-boned image of Mercy Dexter as I recalled her from a painting in Carrington Harris's house. It was frightful beyond conception; toward the last, when a curious blend of servant and baby visages flickered close to the fungous floor where a pool of greenish grease was spreading, it seemed as though the shifting features fought against themselves, and strove to form contours like those of my uncle's kindly face. I like to think that he existed at that moment, and that he tried to bid me farewell. It seems to me I hiccoughed a farewell from my own parched throat as I lurched out into the street; a thin stream of grease following me through the door to the rain-drenched sidewalk.

The rest is shadowy and monstrous. There was no one in the soaking street, and in all the world there was no one I dared tell. I walked aimlessly south past College Hill and the Athenaeum, down Hopkins Street, and over the bridge to the business section where tall buildings seemed to guard me as modern material things guard the world from ancient and unwholesome wonder. Then grey dawn unfolded wetly from the east, silhouetting the archaic hill and its venerable steeples, and beckoning me to the place where my terrible work was still unfinished. And in the end I went, wet, hatless, and dazed in the morning light, and entered that awful door in Benefit Street which I had left ajar, and which still swung cryptically in full sight of the early householders to whom I dared not speak.

The grease was gone, for the mouldy floor was porous. And in front of the fireplace was no vestige of the giant doubled-up form in nitre. I looked at the cot, the chairs, the instruments, my neglected hat, and the yellowed straw hat of my uncle. Dazedness was uppermost, and I could scarcely recall what was dream and what was reality. Then thought trickled back, and I knew that I had witnessed things more horrible than I had dreamed. Sitting down, I tried to conjecture as nearly as sanity would let me just what had happened, and how I might end the horror, if indeed it had been real. Matter it seemed not to be, nor ether, nor anything else conceivable by mortal mind. What, then, but some exotic *emanation*; some vampirish vapour such as Exeter rustics tell of as lurking over certain churchyards? This I felt was the clue, and again I looked at the floor before the fireplace where the mould and nitre had taken strange forms. In ten minutes my mind was made up, and taking my hat I set out for home, where I bathed, ate, and gave by telephone an order for a pickaxe, a spade, a military gas-mask, and six carboys of sulphuric acid, all to be delivered the next morning at the cellar door of the shunned house in Benefit Street. After that I tried to sleep; and failing, passed the hours in reading and in the composition of inane verses to counteract my mood.

At 11 a.m. the next day I commenced digging. It was sunny weather, and I was glad of that. I was still alone, for as much as I feared the unknown horror I sought, there was more fear in the thought of telling anybody. Later I told Harris only through sheer necessity, and because he had heard odd tales from old people which disposed him ever so little toward belief. As I turned up the stinking black earth in front of the fireplace, my spade causing a viscous yellow ichor to ooze from the white fungi which it severed, I trembled at the dubious thoughts of what I might uncover. Some secrets of inner earth are not good for mankind, and this seemed to me one of them.

My hand shook perceptibly, but still I delved; after a while standing in the large hole I had made. With the deepening of the hole, which was about six feet square, the evil smell increased; and I lost all doubt of my imminent contact with the hellish thing whose emanations had cursed the house for over a century and a half. I wondered what it would look like – what its form and substance would be, and how big it might have waxed through long ages of life-sucking. At length I climbed out of the hole and dispersed the heaped-up dirt, then arranging the great carboys of acid around and near two sides, so that when necessary I might empty them all down the aperture in quick succession. After that I dumped earth only along the other two sides; working more slowly and donning my gas-mask as the smell grew. I was nearly unnerved at my proximity to a nameless thing at the bottom of a pit.

Suddenly my spade struck something softer than earth. I shuddered, and made a motion as if to climb out of the hole, which was now as deep as my neck. Then courage returned, and I scraped away more dirt in the light of the electric torch I had provided. The surface I uncovered was fishy and glassy – a kind of semi-putrid congealed jelly with suggestions of translucency. I scraped further, and saw that it had form. There was a rift where a part of the substance was folded over. The exposed area was huge and roughly cylindrical; like a mammoth soft blue-white stovepipe doubled in two, its largest part some two feet in diameter. Still more I scraped, and then abruptly I leaped out of the hole and away from the filthy thing; frantically unstopping and tilting the heavy carboys, and precipitating their corrosive contents one after another down that charnel gulf and upon the unthinkable abnormality whose titan elbow I had seen.

The blinding maelstrom of greenish-yellow vapour which surged tempestuously up from that hole as the floods of acid descended, will never leave my memory. All along the hill people tell of the yellow day, when virulent and horrible fumes arose from the factory waste dumped in the Providence River, but I know how mistaken they are as to the source. They tell, too, of the hideous roar which at the same time came from some disordered water-pipe or gas main underground – but again I could correct them if I dared. It was unspeakably shocking, and I do not see how I lived through it. I did faint after emptying the fourth carboy, which I had to handle after the fumes had begun to penetrate my mask; but when I recovered I saw that the hole was emitting no fresh vapours.

The two remaining carboys I emptied down without particular result, and after a time I felt it safe to shovel the earth back into the pit. It was twilight before I was done, but fear had gone out of the place. The dampness was less foetid, and all the strange fungi had withered to a kind of harmless greyish powder which blew ash-like along the floor. One of earth's nethermost terrors had perished forever; and if there be a hell, it had received at last the daemon soul of an unhallowed thing. And as I patted down the last spadeful of mould, I shed the first of the many tears with which I have paid unaffected tribute to my beloved uncle's memory.

The next spring no more pale grass and strange weeds came up in the shunned house's terraced garden, and shortly afterward Carrington Harris rented the place. It is still spectral, but its strangeness fascinates me, and I shall find mixed with my relief a queer regret when it is torn down to make way for a tawdry shop or vulgar apartment building. The barren old trees in the yard have begun to bear small, sweet apples, and last year the birds nested in their gnarled boughs.

THE HORROR AT RED HOOK

There are sacraments of evil as well as of good about us, and we live and move to my belief in an unknown world, a place where there are caves and shadows and dwellers in twilight. It is possible that man may sometimes return on the track of evolution, and it is my belief that an awful lore is not yet dead.

— Arthur Machen

I

Not many weeks ago, on a street corner in the village of Pascoag, Rhode Island, a tall, heavily built, and wholesome-looking pedestrian furnished much speculation by a singular lapse of behaviour. He had, it appears, been descending the hill by the road from Chepachet; and encountering the compact section, had turned to his left into the main thoroughfare where several modest business blocks convey a touch of the urban. At this point, without visible provocation, he committed his astonishing lapse; staring queerly for a second at the tallest of the buildings before him, and then, with a series of terrified, hysterical shrieks, breaking into a frantic run which ended in a stumble and fall at the next crossing. Picked up and dusted off by ready hands, he was found to be conscious, organically unhurt, and evidently cured of his sudden nervous attack. He muttered some shamefaced explanations involving a strain he had undergone, and with downcast glance turned back up the Chepachet road, trudging out of sight without once looking behind him. It was a strange incident to befall so large, robust, normal-featured, and capable-looking a man, and the strangeness was not lessened by the remarks of a bystander who had recognised him as the boarder of a well-known dairyman on the outskirts of Chepachet.

He was, it developed, a New York police detective named Thomas F. Malone, now on a long leave of absence under medical treatment after some disproportionately arduous work on a gruesome local case which accident had made dramatic. There had been a collapse of several old brick buildings during a raid in which he had shared, and something about the wholesale loss of life, both of prisoners and of his companions, had peculiarly appalled him. As a result, he had acquired an acute and anomalous horror of any buildings even

150

remotely suggesting the ones which had fallen in, so that in the end mental specialists forbade him the sight of such things for an indefinite period. A police surgeon with relatives in Chepachet had put forward that quaint hamlet of wooden colonial houses as an ideal spot for the psychological convalescence; and thither the sufferer had gone, promising never to venture among the brick-lined streets of larger villages till duly advised by the Woonsocket specialist with whom he was put in touch. This walk to Pascoag for magazines had been a mistake, and the patient had paid in fright, bruises, and humiliation for his disobedience.

So much the gossips of Chepachet and Pascoag knew; and so much, also, the most learned specialists believed. But Malone had at first told the specialists much more, ceasing only when he saw that utter incredulity was his portion. Thereafter he held his peace, protesting not at all when it was generally agreed that the collapse of certain squalid brick houses in the Red Hook section of Brooklyn, and the consequent death of many brave officers, had unseated his nervous equilibrium. He had worked too hard, all said, in trying to clean up those nests of disorder and violence; certain features were shocking enough, in all conscience, and the unexpected tragedy was the last straw. This was a simple explanation which everyone could understand, and because Malone was not a simple person he perceived that he had better let it suffice. To hint to unimaginative people of a horror beyond all human conception – a horror of houses and blocks and cities leprous and cancerous with evil dragged from elder worlds – would be merely to invite a padded cell instead of a restful rustication, and Malone was a man of sense despite his mysticism. He had the Celt's far vision of weird and hidden things, but the logician's quick eye for the outwardly unconvincing; an amalgam which had led him far afield in the forty-two years of his life, and set him in strange places for a Dublin University man born in a Georgian villa near Phoenix Park.

And now, as he reviewed the things he had seen and felt and apprehended, Malone was content to keep unshared the secret of what could reduce a dauntless fighter to a quivering neurotic; what could make old brick slums and seas of dark, subtle faces a thing of nightmare and eldritch portent. It would not be the first time his sensations had been forced to bide uninterpreted – for was not his very act of plunging into the polyglot abyss of New York's underworld a freak beyond sensible explanation? What could he tell the prosaic of the antique witcheries and grotesque marvels discernible to sensitive eyes amidst the poison cauldron where all the varied dregs of unwholesome ages mix their venom and perpetuate their obscene terrors? He had seen the hellish green flame of secret wonder in this blatant, evasive welter of outward greed and inward blasphemy, and had smiled gently when all the New Yorkers he knew scoffed at his experiment in police work. They had been very witty and cynical, deriding his fantastic pursuit of unknowable mysteries and assuring him that in these days New York held nothing but cheapness and vulgarity. One of them had wagered him a heavy sum that he could not – despite many poignant things to his credit in the *Dublin Review* – even write a truly interesting story of New York low life; and now, looking back, he perceived that cosmic irony had justified the prophet's words while secretly confuting their flippant meaning. The horror, as glimpsed at last, could not make a story – for like the book cited by Poe's German authority, *es lasst sich nicht lesen* – "it does not permit itself to be read."

II

To Malone the sense of latent mystery in existence was always present. In youth he had felt the hidden beauty and ecstasy of things, and had been a poet; but poverty and sorrow and exile had turned his gaze in darker directions, and he had thrilled at the imputations of evil in the world around. Daily life had for him come to be a phantasmagoria of macabre shadow-studies; now glittering and leering with concealed rottenness as in Beardsley's best manner, now hinting terrors behind the commonest shapes and objects as in the subtler and less obvious work of Gustave Doré. He would often regard it as merciful that most persons of high intelligence jeer at the inmost mysteries; for, he argued, if superior minds were ever placed in fullest contact with the secrets preserved by ancient and lowly cults, the resultant abnormalities would soon not only wreck the world, but threaten the very integrity of the universe. All this reflection was no doubt morbid, but keen logic and a deep sense of humour ably offset it. Malone was satisfied to let his notions remain as half-spied and forbidden visions to be lightly played with; and hysteria came only when duty flung him into a hell of revelation too sudden and insidious to escape.

He had for some time been detailed to the Butler Street station in Brooklyn when the Red Hook matter came to his notice. Red Hook is a maze of hybrid squalor near the ancient waterfront opposite Governor's Island, with dirty highways climbing the hill from the wharves to that higher ground where the decayed lengths of Clinton and Court Streets lead off toward the Borough Hall. Its houses are mostly of brick, dating from the first quarter to the middle of the nineteenth century, and some of the obscurer alleys and byways have that alluring antique flavour which conventional reading leads us to call "Dickensian". The population is a hopeless tangle and enigma; Syrian, Spanish, Italian, and negro elements impinging upon one another, and fragments of Scandinavian and American belts lying not far distant. It is a babel of sound and filth, and sends out strange cries to answer the lapping of oily waves at its grimy piers and the monstrous organ litanies of the harbour whistles. Here long ago a brighter picture dwelt, with clear-eyed mariners on the lower streets and homes of taste and substance where the larger houses line the hill. One can trace the relics of this former happiness in the trim shapes of the buildings, the occasional graceful churches, and the evidences of original art and background in bits of detail here and there – a worn flight of steps, a battered doorway, a wormy pair of decorative columns or pilasters, or a fragment of once green space with bent and rusted iron railing. The houses are generally in solid blocks, and now and then a many-windowed cupola arises to tell of days when the households of captains and ship-owners watched the sea.

From this tangle of material and spiritual putrescence the blasphemies of a hundred dialects assail the sky. Hordes of prowlers reel shouting and singing along the lanes and thoroughfares, occasional furtive hands suddenly extinguish lights and pull down curtains, and swarthy, sin-pitted faces disappear from windows when visitors pick their way through. Policemen despair of order or reform, and seek rather to erect barriers protecting the outside world from the contagion. The clang of the patrol is answered by a kind of spectral silence, and such prisoners as are taken are never communicative. Visible offences are as varied as the local dialects, and run the gamut from the smuggling of rum and prohibited aliens through diverse stages of lawlessness and obscure vice to murder and mutilation in their most abhorrent guises. That these visible affairs are not more frequent is not to the neighbour-hood's credit, unless the power of concealment be an art demanding credit. More people enter Red Hook than leave it – or at least, than leave it by the landward side – and those who are not loquacious are the likeliest to leave.

Malone found in this state of things a faint stench of secrets more terrible than any of the sins denounced by citizens and bemoaned by priests and philanthropists. He was conscious, as one who united imagination with scientific knowledge, that modern people under lawless conditions tend uncannily to repeat the darkest instinctive patterns of primitive half-ape savagery in their daily life and ritual observances; and he had often viewed with an anthropologist's shudder the chanting, cursing processions of blear-eyed and pockmarked young men which wound their way along in the dark small hours of morning. One saw groups of these youths incessantly; sometimes in leering vigils on street corners, sometimes in doorways playing eerily on cheap instruments of music, sometimes in stupefied dozes or indecent dialogues around cafeteria tables near Borough Hall, and sometimes in whispering converse around dingy taxicabs drawn up at the high stoops of crumbling and closely shuttered old houses. They chilled and fascinated him more than he dared confess to his associates on the force, for he seemed to see in them some monstrous thread of secret continuity; some fiendish, cryptical, and ancient pattern utterly beyond and below the sordid mass of facts and habits and haunts listed with such conscientious technical care by the police. They must be, he felt inwardly, the heirs of some shocking and primordial tradition; the sharers of debased and broken scraps from cults and ceremonies older than mankind. Their coherence and definiteness suggested it, and it shewed in the singular suspicion of order which lurked beneath their squalid disorder. He had not read in vain such treatises as Miss Murray's *Witch-Cult In Western Europe*, and knew that up to recent years there had certainly survived among peasants and furtive folk a frightful and clandestine system of assemblies and orgies descended from dark religions antedating the Aryan world, and appearing in popular legends as Black Masses and Witches' Sabbaths. That these hellish vestiges of old Turanian-Asiatic magic and fertility-cults were even now wholly dead he could not for a moment suppose, and he frequently wondered how much older and how much blacker than the very worst of the muttered tales some of them might really be.

III

It was the case of Robert Suydam which took Malone to the heart of things in Red Hook. Suydam was a lettered recluse of ancient Dutch family, possessed originally of barely independent means, and inhabiting the spacious but ill-preserved mansion which his grandfather had built in Flatbush when that village was little more than a pleasant group of colonial cottages surrounding the steepled and ivy-clad Reformed Church with its iron-railed yard of Netherlandish gravestones. In his lonely house, set back from Martense Street amidst a yard of venerable trees, Suydam had read and brooded for some six decades except for a period a generation before, when he had sailed for the old world and remained there out of sight for eight years. He could afford no servants, and would admit but few visitors to his absolute solitude; eschewing close friendships and receiving his rare acquaintances in one of the three ground-floor rooms which he kept in order – a vast, high-ceiled library whose walls were solidly packed with tattered books of ponderous, archaic, and vaguely repellent aspect. The growth of the town and its final absorption in the Brooklyn district had meant nothing to Suydam, and he had come to mean less and less to the town. Elderly people still pointed him out on the streets, but to most of the recent population he was merely a queer, corpulent old fellow whose unkempt white hair, stubbly beard, shiny black clothes, and gold-headed cane earned him an amused glance and nothing more. Malone did not know him by sight till duty called him to the case, but had heard of him indirectly as a really profound authority on mediaeval superstition, and had once idly meant to look up an out-of-print pamphlet of his on the Kabbalah and the Faustus legend, which a friend had quoted from memory.

Suydam became a "case" when his distant and only relatives sought court pronouncements on his sanity. Their action seemed sudden to the outside world, but was really undertaken only after prolonged observation and sorrowful debate. It was based on certain odd changes in his speech and habits; wild references to impending wonders, and unaccountable hauntings of disreputable Brooklyn neighbourhoods. He had been growing shabbier and shabbier with the years, and now prowled about like a veritable mendicant; seen occasionally by humiliated friends in subway stations, or loitering on the benches around Borough Hall in conversation with groups of swarthy, evil-looking strangers. When he spoke it was to babble of unlimited powers almost within his grasp, and to repeat with knowing leers such mystical words or names as "Sephiroth", "Ashmodal", and "Samaël". The court action revealed that he was using up his income and wasting his principal in the purchase of curious tomes imported from London and Paris, and in the maintenance of a squalid basement flat in the Red Hook district where he spent nearly every night, receiving odd delegations of mixed rowdies and foreigners, and apparently conducting some kind of ceremonial service behind the green blinds of secretive windows. Detectives assigned to follow him reported strange cries and chants and prancing of feet filtering out from these nocturnal rites, and shuddered at their peculiar ecstasy and abandon despite the commonness of weird orgies in that sodden section. When, however, the matter came to a hearing, Suydam managed to preserve his liberty. Before the judge his manner grew urbane and reasonable, and he freely admitted the queerness of demeanour and extravagant cast of language into which he had fallen through excessive devotion to study and research. He was, he said, engaged in the investigation of certain details of European tradition which required the closest contact with foreign groups and their songs and folk dances. The notion that any low secret society was preying upon him, as hinted by his relatives, was obviously absurd; and shewed how sadly limited was their under-standing of him and his work. Triumphing with his calm explanations, he was suffered to depart unhindered; and the paid detectives of the Suydams, Cor- lears, and Van Brunts were withdrawn in resigned disgust.

It was here that an alliance of Federal inspectors and police, Malone with them, entered the case. The law had watched the Suydam action with interest, and had in many instances been called upon to aid the private detectives. In this work it developed that Suydam's new associates were among the blackest and most vicious criminals of Red Hook's devious lanes, and that at least a third of them were known and repeated offenders in the matter of thievery, disorder, and the importation of illegal immigrants. Indeed, it would not have been too much to say that the old scholar's particular circle coincided almost perfectly with the worst of the organised cliques which smuggled ashore certain nameless and unclassified Asian dregs wisely turned back by Ellis Island. In the teeming rookeries of Parker Place – since renamed – where Suydam had his basement flat, there had grown up a very unusual colony of unclassified slant- eyed folk who used the Arabic alphabet but were eloquently repudiated by the great mass of Syrians in and around Atlantic Avenue. They could all have been deported for lack of credentials, but legalism is slow-moving, and one does not disturb Red Hook unless publicity forces one to.

These creatures attended a tumbledown stone church, used on Wednesdays as a dance-hall, which reared its Gothic buttresses near the vilest part of the waterfront. It was nominally Catholic; but priests throughout Brooklyn denied the place all standing and authenticity, and policemen agreed with them when they listened to the noises it emitted at night. Malone used to fancy he heard terrible cracked bass notes from a hidden organ far underground when the church stood empty and unlighted, whilst all observers dreaded the shrieking and drumming which accom-panied the visible services. Suydam, when questioned, said he thought the ritual was some remnant of Nestorian Christianity tinctured with the Shamanism of Tibet. Most of the people, he conjectured, were of Mongol stock, originating somewhere in or near Kurdistan and Malone could not help recalling that Kurdistan is the land of the Yezidis, last survivors of the Persian devil-worshippers. However this may have been, the stir of the Suydam investigation made it certain that these unauthorised new-comers were flooding Red Hook in increasing numbers; entering through some marine conspiracy unreached by revenue officers and harbour police, overrunning Parker Place and rapidly spreading up the hill, and welcomed with curious fraternalism by the other assorted denizens of the region. Their squat figures and characteristic squinting physiognomies, grotesquely combined with flashy American clothing, appeared more and more numerously among the loafers and nomad gangsters of the Borough Hall section; till at length it was deemed necessary to compute their numbers, ascertain their sources and occupations, and find if possible a way to round them up and deliver them to the proper immigration authorities. To this task Malone was assigned by agreement of Federal and city forces, and as he commenced his canvass of Red Hook he felt poised upon the brink of nameless terrors, with the shabby, unkempt figure of Robert Suydam as arch-fiend and adversary.

IV

Police methods are varied and ingenious. Malone, through unostentatious rambles, carefully casual conversations, well-timed offers of hip-pocket liquor, and judicious dialogues with frightened prisoners, learned many isolated facts about the movement whose aspect had become so menacing. The newcomers were indeed Kurds, but of a dialect obscure and puzzling to exact philology. Such of them as worked lived mostly as dock-hands and unlicenced pedlars, though frequently serving in Greek restaurants and tending corner news stands. Most of them, however, had no visible means of support; and were obviously connected with underworld pursuits, of which smuggling and "bootlegging" were the least indescribable. They had come in steamships, apparently tramp freighters, and had been unloaded by stealth on moonless nights in rowboats which stole under a certain wharf and followed a hidden canal to a secret subterranean pool beneath a house. This wharf, canal, and house Malone could not locate, for the memories of his informants were exceedingly confused, while their speech was to a great extent beyond even the ablest interpreters; nor could he gain any real data on the reasons for their systematic importation. They were reticent about the exact spot from which they had come, and were never sufficiently off guard to reveal the agencies which had sought them out and directed their course.

Indeed, they developed something like acute fright when asked the reasons for their presence. Gangsters of other breeds were equally taciturn, and the most that could be gathered was that some god or great priest-hood had promised them unheard-of powers and supernatural glories and rulerships in a strange land.

The attendance of both newcomers and old gangsters at Suydam's closely guarded nocturnal meetings was very regular, and the police soon learned that the erstwhile recluse had leased additional flats to accommodate such guests as knew his password; at last occupying three entire houses and permanently harbouring many of his queer companions. He spent but little time now at his Flatbush home, apparently going and coming only to obtain and return books; and his face and manner had attained an appalling pitch of wildness. Malone twice interviewed him, but was each time brusquely repulsed. He knew nothing, he said, of any mysterious plots or movements; and had no idea how the Kurds could have entered or what they wanted. His business was to study undisturbed the folklore of all the immigrants of the district; a business with which policemen had no legitimate concern. Malone mentioned his admiration for Suydam's old brochure on the Kabbalah and other myths, but the old man's softening was only momentary. He sensed an intrusion, and rebuffed his visitor in no uncertain way; till Malone withdrew disgusted, and turned to other channels of information.

What Malone would have unearthed could he have worked continuously on the case, we shall never know. As it was, a stupid conflict between city and Federal authority suspended the investigations for several months, during which the detective was busy with other assignments. But at no time did he lose interest, or fail to stand amazed at what began to happen to Robert Suydam. just at the time when a wave of kidnappings and disappearances spread its excitement over New York, the unkempt scholar embarked upon a metamorphosis as startling as it was absurd. One day he was seen near Borough Hall with clean-shaved face, well-trimmed hair, and tastefully immaculate attire, and on every day thereafter some obscure improvement was noticed in him. He maintained his new fastidiousness without interruption, added to it an unwonted sparkle of eye and crispness of speech, and began little by little to shed the corpulence which had so long deformed him. Now frequently taken for less than his age, he acquired an elasticity of step and buoyancy of demeanour to match the new tradition, and shewed a curious darkening of the hair which somehow did not suggest dye. As the months passed, he commenced to dress less and less conservatively, and finally astonished his new friends by renovating and redecorating his Flatbush mansion, which he threw open in a series of receptions, summoning all the acquaintances he could remember, and extending a special welcome to the fully forgiven relatives who had so lately sought his restraint. Some attended through curiosity, others through duty; but all were suddenly charmed by the dawning grace and urbanity of the former hermit. He had, he asserted, accomplished most of his allotted work; and having just inherited some property from a half-forgotten European friend, was about to spend his remaining years in a brighter second youth which ease, care, and diet had made possible to him. Less and less was he seen at Red Hook, and more and more did he move in the society to which he was born. Policemen noted a tendency of the gangsters to congregate at the old stone church and dance-hall instead of at the basement flat in Parker Place, though the latter and its recent annexes still overflowed with noxious life.

Then two incidents occurred – wide enough apart, but both of intense interest in the case as Malone envisaged it. One was a quiet announcement in the *Eagle* of Robert Suydam's engagement to Miss Cornelia Gerritsen of Bayside, a young woman of excellent position, and distantly related to the elderly bridegroom-elect; whilst the other was a raid on the dance-hall church by city police, after a report that the face of a kidnapped child had been seen for a second at one of the basement windows. Malone had participated in this raid, and studied the place with much care when inside. Nothing was found – in fact, the building was entirely deserted when visited – but the sensitive Celt was vaguely disturbed by many things about the interior. There were crudely painted panels he did not like – panels which depicted sacred faces with peculiarly worldly and sardonic expressions, and which occasionally took liberties that even a layman's sense of decorum could scarcely countenance. Then, too, he did not relish the Greek inscription on the wall above the pulpit; an ancient incantation which he had once stumbled upon in Dublin college days, and which read, literally translated,

"O friend and companion of night, thou who rejoicest in the baying of dogs and spilt blood, who wanderest in the midst of shades among the tombs, who longest for blood and bringest terror to mortals, Gorgo, Mormo, thousand-faced moon, look favourably on our sacrifices!"

When he read this he shuddered, and thought vaguely of the cracked bass organ notes he fancied he had heard beneath the church on certain nights. He shuddered again at the rust around the rim of a metal basin which stood on the altar, and paused nervously when his nostrils seemed to detect a curious and ghastly stench from somewhere in the neighbourhood. That organ memory haunted him, and he explored the basement with particular assiduity before he left. The place was very hateful to him; yet after all, were the blasphemous panels and inscriptions more than mere crudities perpetrated by the ignorant?

By the time of Suydam's wedding the kidnapping epidemic had become a popular newspaper scandal. Most of the victims were young children of the lowest classes, but the increasing number of disappearances had worked up a sentiment of the strongest fury. Journals clamoured for action from the police, and once more the Butler Street station sent its men over Red Hook for clues, discoveries, and criminals. Malone was glad to be on the trail again, and took pride in a raid on one of Suydam's Parker Place houses. There, indeed, no stolen child was found, despite the tales of screams and the red sash picked up in the areaway; but the paintings and rough inscriptions on the peeling walls of most of the rooms, and the primitive chemical laboratory in the attic, all helped to convince the detective that he was on the track of something tremendous. The paintings were appalling – hideous monsters of every shape and size, and parodies on human outlines which cannot be described. The writing was in red, and varied from Arabic to Greek, Roman, and Hebrew letters. Malone could not read much of it, but what he did decipher was portentous and cabbalistic enough. One frequently repeated motto was in a sort of Hebraised Hellenistic Greek, and suggested the most terrible daemon-evocations of the Alexandrian decadence:

HEL • HELOYM • SOTHER • EMMANVEL • SABAOTH • AGLA
TETRAGRAMMATON • AGYROS • OTHEOS • ISCHYROS
ATHANATOS • IEHOVA • VA • ADONAI • SADAY
HOMOVSION • MESSIAS • ESCHEREHEYE

Circles and pentagrams loomed on every hand, and told indubitably of the strange beliefs and aspirations of those who dwelt so squalidly here. In the cellar, however, the strangest thing was found – a pile of genuine gold ingots covered carelessly with a piece of burlap, and bearing upon their shining surfaces the same weird hieroglyphics which also adorned the walls. During the raid the police encountered only a passive resistance from the squinting Orientals that swarmed from every door. Finding nothing relevant, they had to leave all as it

160

was; but the precinct captain wrote Suydam a note advising him to look closely to the character of his tenants and protégés in view of the growing public clamour.

V

Then came the June wedding and the great sensation. Flatbush was gay for the hour about high noon, and pennanted motors thronged the streets near the old Dutch church where an awning stretched from door to highway. No local event ever surpassed the Suydam-Gerritsen nuptials in tone and scale, and the party which escorted bride and groom to the Cunard Pier was, if not exactly the smartest, at least a solid page from the Social Register. At five o'clock adieux were waved, and the ponderous liner edged away from the long pier, slowly turned its nose seaward, discarded its tug, and headed for the widening water spaces that led to old world wonders. By night the outer harbour was cleared, and late passengers watched the stars twinkling above an unpolluted ocean.

Whether the tramp steamer or the scream was first to gain attention, no-one can say. Probably they were simultaneous, but it is of no use to calculate. The scream came from the Suydam stateroom, and the sailor who broke down the door could perhaps have told frightful things if he had not forthwith gone completely mad – as it is, he shrieked more loudly than the first victims, and thereafter ran simpering about the vessel till caught and put in irons. The ship's doctor who entered the stateroom and turned on the lights a moment later did not go mad, but told nobody what he saw till afterward, when he corresponded with Malone in Chepachet. It was murder – strangulation – but one need not say that the clawmark on Mrs. Suydam's throat could not have come from her hus - band's or any other human hand, or that upon the white wall there flickered for an instant in hateful red a legend which, later copied from memory, seems to have been nothing less than the fearsome Chaldee letters of the word "LILITH". One need not mention these things because they vanished so quickly – as for Suydam, one could at least bar others from the room until one knew what to think oneself. The doctor has distinctly assured Malone that he did not see *IT*. The open porthole, just before he turned on the lights, was clouded for a second with a certain phosphorescence, and for a moment there seemed to echo in the night outside the suggestion of a faint and hellish tittering; but no real outline met the eye. As proof, the doctor points to his continued sanity.

Then the tramp steamer claimed all attention. A boat put off, and a horde of swart, insolent ruffians in officers' dress swarmed aboard the temporarily halted Cunarder. They wanted Suydam or his body – they had known of his trip, and for certain reasons were sure he would die. The captain's deck was almost a pan-demonium; for at the instant, between the doctor's report from the stateroom and the demands of the men from the tramp, not even the wisest and gravest seaman could think what to do. Suddenly the leader of the visiting mariners, an Arab with a hatefully negroid mouth, pulled forth a dirty, crumpled paper and handed it to the captain. It was signed by Robert Suydam, and bore the following odd message:

"In case of sudden or unexplained accident or death on my part, please deliver me or my body unquestioningly into the hands of the bearer and his associates. Everything, for me, and perhaps for you, depends on absolute compliance. Explanations can come later – do not fail me now.
   – ROBERT SUYDAM."

Captain and doctor looked at each other, and the latter whispered something to the former. Finally they nodded rather helplessly and led the way to the Suydam stateroom. The doctor directed the captain's glance away as he unlocked the door and admitted the strange seamen, nor did he breathe easily till they filed out with their burden after an unaccountably long period of preparation. It was wrapped in bedding from the berths, and the doctor was glad that the outlines were not very revealing. Somehow the men got the thing over the side and away to their tramp steamer without uncovering it. The Cunarder started again, and the doctor and a ship's undertaker sought out the Suydam stateroom to perform what last services they could. Once more the physician was forced to reticence and even to mendacity, for a hellish thing had happened. When the undertaker asked him why he had drained off all of Mrs. Suydam's blood, he neglected to affirm that he had not done so; nor did he point to the vacant bottle-spaces on the rack, or to the odour in the sink which shewed the hasty disposition of the bottles' original contents. The pockets of those men – if men they were – had bulged damnably when they left the ship. Two hours later, and the world knew by radio all that it ought to know of the horrible affair.

VI

That same June evening, without having heard a word from the sea, Malone was desperately busy among the alleys of Red Hook. A sudden stir seemed to permeate the place, and as if apprised by "grapevine telegraph" of something singular, the denizens clustered expectantly around the dance-hall church and the houses in Parker Place. Three children had just disappeared – blue-eyed Norwegians from the streets toward Gowanus – and there were rumours of a mob forming among the sturdy Vikings of that section. Malone had for weeks been urging his colleagues to attempt a general clean-up; and at last, moved by conditions more obvious to their common sense than the conjectures of a Dublin dreamer, they had agreed upon a final stroke. The unrest and menace of this evening had been the deciding factor, and just about midnight a raiding party recruited from three stations descended upon Parker Place and its environs. Doors were battered in, stragglers arrested, and candlelighted rooms forced to disgorge unbelievable throngs of mixed foreigners in figured robes, mitres, and other inexplicable devices. Much was lost in the melée, for objects were thrown hastily down unexpected shafts, and betraying odours deadened by the sudden kindling of pungent incense. But spattered blood was everywhere, and Malone shuddered whenever he saw a brazier or altar from which the smoke was still rising.

He wanted to be in several places at once, and decided on Suydam's basement flat only after a messenger had reported the complete emptiness of the dilapidated dance-hall church. The flat, he thought, must hold some clue to a cult of which the occult scholar had so obviously become the centre and leader; and it was with real expectancy that he ransacked the musty rooms, noted their vaguely charnel odour, and examined the curious books, instruments, gold ingots, and glass-stoppered bottles scattered carelessly here and there. Once a lean, black-and-white cat edged between his feet and tripped him, overturning at the same time a beaker half full of a red liquid. The shock was severe, and to this day Malone is not certain of what he saw; but in dreams he still pictures that cat as it scuttled away with certain monstrous alterations and peculiarities. Then came the locked cellar door, and the search for something to break it down. A heavy stool stood near, and its tough seat was more than enough for the antique panels. A crack formed and enlarged, and the whole door gave way – but from the *other* side; whence poured a howling tumult of ice-cold wind with all the stenches of the bottomless pit, and whence reached a sucking force not of earth or heaven, which, coiling sentiently about the paralysed detective, dragged him through the aperture and down unmeasured spaces filled with whispers and wails, and gusts of mocking laughter.

Of course it was a dream. All the specialists have told him so, and he has nothing to prove the contrary. Indeed, he would rather have it thus; for then the sight of old brick slums and dark foreign faces would not eat so deeply into his soul. But at the time it was all horribly real, and nothing can ever efface the memory of those nighted crypts, those titan arcades, and those half-formed shapes of hell that strode gigantically in silence holding half-eaten things whose still surviving portions screamed for mercy or laughed with madness. Odours of incense and corruption joined in sickening concert, and the black air was alive with the cloudy, semi-visible bulk of shapeless elemental things with eyes. Somewhere dark sticky water was lapping at onyx piers, and once the shivery tinkle of raucous little bells pealed out to greet the insane titter of a naked phosphorescent thing which swam into sight, scrambled ashore, and climbed up to squat leeringly on a carved golden pedestal in the background.

Avenues of limitless night seemed to radiate in every direction, till one might fancy that here lay the root of a contagion destined to sicken and swallow cities, and engulf nations in the foetor of hybrid pestilence. Here cosmic sin had entered, and festered by unhallowed rites had commenced the grinning march of death that was to rot us all to fungous abnormalities too hideous for the grave's holding. Satan here held his Babylonish court, and in the blood of stainless childhood the leprous limbs of phos-phorescent Lilith were laved. Incubi and succubae howled praise to Hecate, and headless moon-calves bleated to the Magna Mater. Goats leaped to the sound of thin accursed flutes, and aegipans chased endlessly after misshapen fauns over rocks twisted like swollen toads. Moloch and Astaroth were not absent; for in this quintessence of all damnation the bounds of consciousness were let down, and man's fancy lay open to vistas of every realm of horror and every forbidden dimension that evil had power to mould. The world and Nature were helpless against such assaults from unsealed wells of night, nor could any sign or prayer check the Walpurgis-riot of horror which had come when a sage with the hateful key had stumbled on a horde with the locked and brimming coffer of transmitted daemon-lore.

Suddenly a ray of physical light shot through these phantasms, and Malone heard the sound of oars amidst the blasphemies of things that should be dead. A boat with a lantern in its prow darted into sight, made fast to an iron ring in the slimy stone pier, and vomited forth several dark men bearing a long burden swathed in bedding. They took it to the naked phosphorescent thing on the carved golden pedestal, and the thing tittered and pawed at the bedding. Then they unswathed it, and propped upright before the pedestal the gangrenous corpse of a corpulent old man with stubbly beard and unkempt white hair. The phosphorescent thing tittered again, and the men produced bottles from their pockets and anointed its feet with red, whilst they afterward gave the bottles to the thing to drink from.

All at once, from an arcaded avenue leading endlessly away, there came the daemoniac rattle and wheeze of a blasphemous organ, choking and rumbling out the mockeries of hell in a cracked, sardonic bass. In an instant every moving entity was electrified; and forming at once into a ceremonial procession, the nightmare horde slithered away in quest of the sound – goat, satyr, and aegipan, incubus, succuba, and lemur, twisted toad and shapeless elemental, dog-faced howler and silent strutter in darkness – all led by the abominable naked phosphorescent thing that had squatted on the carved golden throne, and that now strode insolently bearing in its arms the glassy-eyed corpse of the corpulent old man. The strange dark men danced in the rear, and the whole column skipped and leaped with Dionysiac fury. Malone staggered after them a few steps, delirious and hazy, and doubtful of his place in this or in any world. Then he turned, faltered, and sank down on the cold damp stone, gasping and shivering as the daemon organ croaked on, and the howling and drumming and tinkling of the mad procession grew fainter and fainter.

Vaguely he was conscious of chanted horrors and shocking croakings afar off. Now and then a wall or whine of ceremonial devotion would float to him through the black arcade, whilst eventually there rose the dreadful Greek incantation whose text he had read above the pulpit of that dance-hall church.

"O friend and companion of night, thou who rejoicest in the baying of dogs *[here a hideous howl burst forth]* and spilt blood *[here nameless sounds vied with morbid shriekings]*, who wanderest in the midst of shades among the tombs *[here a whistling sigh occurred]*, who longest for blood and bringest terror to mortals *[short, sharp cries from myriad throats]*, Gorgo *[repeated with ecstasy]*, thousand-faced moon *[sighs and flute notes]*, look favourably on our sacrifices!"

As the chant closed, a general shout went up, and hissing sounds nearly drowned the croaking of the cracked bass organ. Then a gasp as from many throats, and a babe] of barked and bleated words: "Lilith, Great Lilith, behold the Bride-groom!" More cries, a clamour of rioting, and the sharp, clicking footfalls of a running figure. The footfalls approached, and Malone raised himself to his elbow to look.

The luminosity of the crypt, lately diminished, had now slightly increased; and in that devil-light there appeared the fleeing form of that which should not flee or feel or breathe – the glassy-eyed, gangrenous corpse of the corpulent old man, now needing no support, but animated by some infernal sorcery of the rite just closed. After it raced the naked, tittering, phosphorescent thing that belonged on the carven pedestal, and still farther behind panted the dark men, and all the dread crew of sentient loath-somenesses. The corpse was gaining on its pursuers, and seemed bent on a definite object, straining with every rotting muscle toward the carved golden pedestal, whose necromantic importance was evidently so great. Another moment and it had reached its goal, whilst the trailing throng laboured on with more frantic speed. But they were too late, for in one final spurt of strength which ripped tendon from tendon and sent its noisome bulk floundering to the floor in a state of jellyish dissolution, the staring corpse which had been Robert Suydam achieved its object and its triumph. The push had been tremendous, but the force had held out; and as the pusher collapsed to a muddy blotch of corruption the pedestal he had pushed tottered, tipped, and finally careened from its onyx base into the thick waters below, sending up a parting gleam of carven gold as it sank heavily to undreamable gulfs of lower Tartarus. In that instant, too, the whole scene of horror faded to nothingness before Malone's eyes; and he fainted amidst a thunderous crash which seemed to blot out all the evil universe.

VII

Malone's dream, experienced in full before he knew of Suydam's death and transfer at sea, was curiously supplemented by some odd realities of the case; though that is no reason why anyone should believe it. The three old houses in Parker Place, doubtless long rotten with decay in its most insidious form, collapsed without visible cause while half the raiders and most of the prisoners were inside; and of both the greater number were instantly killed. Only in the basements and cellars was there much saving of life, and Malone was lucky to have been deep below the house of Robert Suydam. For he really was there, as no-one is disposed to deny. They found him unconscious by the edge of a night-black pool, with a grotesquely horrible jumble of decay and bone, identifiable through dental work as the body of Suydam, a few feet away. The case was plain, for it was hither that the smugglers' underground canal led; and the men who took Suydam from the ship had brought him home. They themselves were never found, or at least never identified; and the ship's doctor is not yet satisfied with the simple certitudes of the police.

Suydam was evidently a leader in extensive man-smuggling operations, for the canal to his house was but one of several subterranean channels and tunnels in the neighbourhood. There was a tunnel from this house to a crypt beneath the dance-hall church; a crypt accessible from the church only through a narrow secret passage in the north wall, and in whose chambers some singular and terrible things were discovered. The croaking organ was there, as well as a vast arched chapel with wooden benches and a strangely figured altar. The walls were lined with small cells, in seventeen of which – hideous to relate – solitary prisoners in a state of complete idiocy were found chained, including four mothers with infants of disturbingly strange appearance. These infants died soon after exposure to the light; a circumstance which the doctors thought rather merciful. Nobody but Malone, among those who inspected them, remembered the sombre question of old Delrio: *"An sint unquam daemones incubi et succubae, et an ex tali congressu proles nasci queat?"*

Before the canals were filled up they were thoroughly dredged, and yielded forth a sensational array of sawed and split bones of all sizes. The kidnapping epidemic, very clearly, had been traced home; though only two of the surviving prisoners' could by any legal thread be connected with it. These men are now in prison, since they failed of conviction as accessories in the actual murders. The carved golden pedestal or throne so often mentioned by Malone as of primary occult importance was never brought to light, though at one place under the Suydam house the canal was observed to sink into a well too deep for dredging. It was choked up at the mouth and cemented over when the cellars of the new houses were made, but Malone often speculates on what lies beneath. The police, satisfied that they had shattered a dangerous gang of maniacs and man-smugglers, turned over to the Federal authorities the unconvicted Kurds, who before their deportation were conclusively found to belong to the Yezidi clan of devil-worshippers. The tramp ship and its crew remain an elusive mystery, though cynical detectives are once more ready to combat its smuggling and rum-running ventures. Malone thinks these detectives shew a sadly limited perspective in their lack of wonder at the myriad unexplainable details, and the suggestive obscurity of the whole case; though he is just as critical of the newspapers, which saw only a morbid sensation and gloated over a minor sadist cult which they might have proclaimed a horror from the universe's very heart. But he is content to rest silent in Chepachet, calming his nervous system and praying that time may gradually transfer his terrible experience from the realm of present reality to that of picturesque and semi-mythical remoteness.

Robert Suydam sleeps beside his bride in Greenwood Cemetery. No funeral was held over the strangely released bones, and relatives are grateful for the swift oblivion which overtook the case as a whole. The scholar's connection with the Red Hook horrors, indeed, was never emblazoned by legal proof; since his death forestalled the inquiry he would otherwise have faced. His own end is not much mentioned, and the Suydams hope that posterity may recall him only as a gentle recluse who dabbled in harmless magic and folklore.

As for Red Hook – it is always the same. Suydam came and went; a terror gathered and faded; but the evil spirit of darkness and squalor broods on amongst the mongrels in the old brick houses, and prowling bands still parade on unknown errands past windows where lights and twisted faces unaccountably appear and disappear. Age-old horror is a hydra with a thousand heads, and the cults of darkness are rooted in blasphemies deeper than the well of Democritus. The soul of the beast is omnipresent and triumphant, and Red Hook's legions of blear-eyed, pockmarked youths still chant and curse and howl as they file from abyss to abyss, none knows whence or whither, pushed on by blind laws of biology which they may never understand. As of old, more people enter Red Hook than leave it on the landward side, and there are already rumours of new canals running underground to certain centres of traffic in liquor and less mentionable things.

The dance-hall church is now mostly a dance-hall, and queer faces have appeared at night at the windows. Lately a policeman expressed the belief that the filled-up crypt has been dug out again, and for no simply explainable purpose. Who are we to combat poisons older than history and mankind? Apes danced in Asia to those horrors, and the cancer lurks secure and spreading where furtiveness hides in rows of decaying brick.

Malone does not shudder without cause – for only the other day an officer overheard a swarthy squinting hag teaching a small child some whispered patois in the shadow of an areaway. He listened, and thought it very strange when he heard her repeat over and over again,

"O friend and companion of night, thou who rejoicest in the baying of dogs and spilt blood, who wanderest in the midst of shades among the tombs, who longest for blood and bringest terror to mortals, Gorgo, Mormo, thousand-faced moon, look favourably on our sacrifices!"

IN THE VAULT

(Dedicated to C. W. Smith, from whose suggestion the central situation is taken)

There is nothing more absurd, as I view it, than that conventional association of the homely and the wholesome which seems to pervade the psychology of the multitude. Mention a bucolic Yankee setting, a bungling and thick-fibred village undertaker, and a careless mishap in a tomb, and no average reader can be brought to expect more than a hearty albeit grotesque phase of comedy. God knows, though, that the prosy tale which George Birch's death permits me to tell has in it aspects beside which some of our darkest tragedies are light.

Birch acquired a limitation and changed his business in 1881, yet never discussed the case when he could avoid it. Neither did his old physician Dr. Davis, who died years ago. It was generally stated that the affliction and shock were results of an unlucky slip whereby Birch had locked himself for nine hours in the receiving tomb of Peck Valley Cemetery, escaping only by crude and disastrous mechanical means; but while this much was undoubtedly true, there were other and blacker things which the man used to whisper to me in his drunken delirium toward the last. He confided in me because I was his doctor, and because he probably felt the need of confiding in someone else after Davis died. He was a bachelor, wholly without relatives.

Birch, before 1881, had been the village undertaker of Peck Valley; and was a very calloused and primitive specimen even as such specimens go. The practices I heard attributed to him would be unbelievable today, at least in a city; and even Peck Valley would have shuddered a bit had it known the easy ethics of its mortuary artist in such debatable matters as the ownership of costly "laying-out" apparel invisible beneath the casket's lid, and the degree of dignity to be maintained in posing and adapting the unseen members of lifeless tenants to containers not always calculated with sublimest accuracy. Most distinctly Birch was lax, insensitive, and professionally undesirable; yet I still think he was not an evil man. He was merely crass of fibre and function – thoughtless, careless, and liquorish, as his easily avoidable accident proves, and without that modicum of imagination which holds the average citizen within certain limits fixed by taste.

Just where to begin Birch's story I can hardly decide, since I am no

169

practiced teller of tales. I suppose one should start in the cold December of 1880, when the ground froze and the cemetery delvers found they could dig no more graves till spring. Fortunately the village was small and the death rate low, so that it was possible to give all of Birch's inanimate charges a temporary haven in the single antiquated receiving tomb. The undertaker grew doubly lethargic in the bitter weather, and seemed to outdo even himself in carelessness. Never did he knock together flimsier and ungainlier caskets, or disregard more flagrantly the needs of the rusty lock on the tomb door which he slammed open and shut with such nonchalant abandon.

At last the spring thaw came, and graves were laboriously prepared for the nine silent harvests of the grim reaper which waited in the tomb. Birch, though dreading the bother of removal and interment, began his task of transference one disagreeable April morning, but ceased before noon because of a heavy rain that seemed to irritate his horse, after having laid but one mortal tenement to its permanent rest. That was Darius Peck, the nonagenarian, whose grave was not far from the tomb. Birch decided that he would begin the next day with little old Matthew Fenner, whose grave was also near by; but actually postponed the matter for three days, not getting to work till Good Friday, the 15th. Being without superstition, he did not heed the day at all; though ever afterward he refused to do anything of importance on that fateful sixth day of the week. Certainly, the events of that evening greatly changed George Birch.

On the afternoon of Friday, April 15th, then, Birch set out for the tomb with horse and wagon to transfer the body of Matthew Fenner. That he was not perfectly sober, he subsequently admitted; though he had not then taken to the wholesale drinking by which he later tried to forget certain things. He was just dizzy and careless enough to annoy his sensitive horse, which as he drew it viciously up at the tomb neighed and pawed and tossed its head, much as on that former occasion when the rain had vexed it. The day was clear, but a high wind had sprung up; and Birch was glad to get to shelter as he unlocked the iron door and entered the side-hill vault. Another might not have relished the damp, odorous chamber with the eight carelessly placed coffins; but Birch in those days was insensitive, and was concerned only in getting the right coffin for the right grave. He had not forgotten the criticism aroused when Hannah Bixby's relatives, wishing to transport her body to the cemetery in the city whither they had moved, found the casket of Judge Capwell beneath her headstone.

The light was dim, but Birch's sight was good, and he did not get Asaph Sawyer's coffin by mistake, although it was very similar. He had, indeed, made

170

that coffin for Matthew Fenner; but had cast it aside at last as too awkward and flimsy, in a fit of curious sentimentality aroused by recalling how kindly and generous the little old man had been to him during his bankruptcy five years before. He gave old Matt the very best his skill could produce, but was thrifty enough to save the rejected specimen, and to use it when Asaph Sawyer died of a malignant fever. Sawyer was not a lovable man, and many stories were told of his almost inhuman vindictiveness and tenacious memory for wrongs real or fancied. To him Birch had felt no compunction in assigning the carelessly made coffin which he now pushed out of the way in his quest for the Fenner casket.

It was just as he had recognised old Matt's coffin that the door slammed to in the wind, leaving him in a dusk even deeper than before. The narrow transom admitted only the feeblest of rays, and the overhead ventilation funnel virtually none at all; so that he was reduced to a profane fumbling as he made his halting way among the long boxes toward the latch. In this funereal twilight he rattled the rusty handles, pushed at the iron panels, and wondered why the massive portal had grown so suddenly recalcitrant. In this twilight, too, he began to realise the truth and to shout loudly as if his horse outside could do more than neigh an unsympathetic reply. For the long-neglected latch was obviously broken, leaving the careless undertaker trapped in the vault, a victim of his own oversight.

The thing must have happened at about three-thirty in the afternoon. Birch, being by temperament phlegmatic and practical, did not shout long; but proceeded to grope about for some tools which he recalled seeing in a corner of the tomb. It is doubtful whether he was touched at all by the horror and exquisite weirdness of his position, but the bald fact of imprisonment so far from the daily paths of men was enough to exasperate him thoroughly. His day's work was sadly interrupted, and unless chance presently brought some rambler hither, he might have to remain all night or longer. The pile of tools soon reached, and a hammer and chisel selected, Birch returned over the coffins to the door. The air had begun to be exceedingly unwholesome; but to this detail he paid no attention as he toiled, half by feeling, at the heavy and corroded metal of the latch. He would have given much for a lantern or bit of candle; but lacking these, bungled semi-sightlessly as best he might.

When he perceived that the latch was hopelessly unyielding, at least to such meagre tools and under such tenebrous conditions as these, Birch glanced about for other possible points of escape. The vault had been dug from a hillside, so that the narrow ventilation funnel in the top ran through several feet of earth, making this direction utterly useless to consider. Over the door, however, the high, slit-like transom in the brick facade gave promise of possible enlargement to a diligent worker; hence upon this his eyes long rested as he racked his brains for means to reach it. There was nothing like a ladder in the tomb, and the coffin niches on the sides and rear – which Birch seldom took the trouble to use – afforded no ascent to the space above the door. Only the coffins themselves remained as potential stepping-stones, and as he considered these he speculated on the best mode of arranging them. Three coffin-heights, he reckoned, would permit him to reach the transom; but he could do better with four. The boxes were fairly even, and could be piled up like blocks; so he began to compute how he might most stably use the eight to rear a scalable platform four deep. As he planned, he could not but wish that the units of his contemplated staircase had been more securely made. Whether he had imagination enough to wish they were empty, is strongly to be doubted.

Finally he decided to lay a base of three parallel with the wall, to place upon this two layers of two each, and upon these a single box to serve as the platform. This arrangement could be ascended with a minimum of awkwardness, and would furnish the desired height. Better still, though, he would utilise only two boxes of the base to support the superstructure, leaving one free to be piled on top in case the actual feat of escape required an even greater altitude. And so the prisoner toiled in the twilight, heaving the unresponsive remnants of mortality with little ceremony as his miniature Tower of Babel rose course by course. Several of the coffins began to split under the stress of handling, and he planned to save the stoutly built casket of little Matthew Fenner for the top, in order that his feet might have as certain a surface as possible. In the semi-gloom he trusted mostly to touch to select the right one, and indeed came upon it almost by accident, since it tumbled into his hands as if through some odd volition after he had unwittingly placed it beside another on the third layer.

The tower at length finished, and his aching arms rested by a pause during which he sat on the bottom step of his grim device, Birch cautiously ascended with his tools and stood abreast of the narrow transom. The borders of the space were entirely of brick, and there seemed little doubt but that he could shortly chisel away enough to allow his body to pass. As his hammer blows began to fall, the horse outside whinnied in a tone which may have been encouraging and may have been mocking. In either case it would have been appropriate; for the unexpected tenacity of the easy-looking brickwork was surely a sardonic commentary on the vanity of mortal hopes, and the source of a task whose performance deserved every possible stimulus.

Dusk fell and found Birch still toiling. He worked largely by feeling now, since newly gathered clouds hid the moon; and though progress was still slow, he felt heartened at the extent of his encroachments on the top and bottom of the aperture. He could, he was sure, get out by midnight – though it is characteristic of him that this thought was untinged with eerie implications. Undisturbed by oppressive reflections on the time, the place, and the company beneath his feet, he philosophically chipped away the stony brickwork; cursing when a fragment hit him in the face, and laughing when one struck the increasingly excited horse that pawed near the cypress tree. In time the hole grew so large that he ventured to try his body in it now and then, shifting about so that the coffins beneath him rocked and creaked. He would not, he found, have to pile another on his platform to make the proper height; for the hole was on exactly the right level to use as soon as its size might permit.

It must have been midnight at least when Birch decided he could get through the transom. Tired and perspiring despite many rests, he descended to the floor and sat a while on the bottom box to gather strength for the final wriggle and leap to the ground outside. The hungry horse was neighing repeatedly and almost uncannily, and he vaguely wished it would stop. He was curiously unelated over his impending escape, and almost dreaded the exertion, for his form had the indolent stoutness of early middle age. As he remounted the splitting coffins he felt his weight very poignantly; especially when, upon reaching the topmost one, he heard that aggravated crackle which bespeaks the wholesale rending of wood. He had, it seems, planned in vain when choosing the stoutest coffin for the platform; for no sooner was his full bulk again upon it than the rotting lid gave way, jouncing him two feet down on a surface which even he did not care to imagine. Maddened by the sound, or by the stench which billowed forth even to the open air, the waiting horse gave a scream that was too frantic for a neigh, and plunged madly off through the night, the wagon rattling crazily behind it.

Birch, in his ghastly situation, was now too low for an easy scramble out of the enlarged transom; but gathered his energies for a determined try. Clutching the edges of the aperture, he sought to pull himself up, when he noticed a queer retardation in the form of an apparent drag on both his ankles. In another moment he knew fear for the first time that night; for struggle as he would, he could not shake clear of the unknown grasp which held his feet in relentless captivity. Horrible pains, as of savage wounds, shot through his calves;

and in his mind was a vortex of fright mixed with an unquenchable materialism that suggested splinters, loose nails, or some other attribute of a breaking wooden box. Perhaps he screamed. At any rate he kicked and squirmed frantically and automatically whilst his consciousness was almost eclipsed in a half-swoon.

Instinct guided him in his wriggle through the transom, and in the crawl which followed his jarring thud on the damp ground. He could not walk, it appeared, and the emerging moon must have witnessed a horrible sight as he dragged his bleeding ankles toward the cemetery lodge; his fingers clawing the black mould in brainless haste, and his body responding with that maddening slowness from which one suffers when chased by the phantoms of nightmare. There was evidently, however, no pursuer; for he was alone and alive when Armington, the lodge-keeper, answered his feeble clawing at the door.

Armington helped Birch to the outside of a spare bed and sent his little son Edwin for Dr. Davis. The afflicted man was fully conscious, but would say nothing of any consequence; merely muttering such things as "oh, my ankles!", "let go!", or "shut in the tomb". Then the doctor came with his medicine-case and asked crisp questions, and removed the patient's outer clothing, shoes, and socks. The wounds – for both ankles were frightfully lacerated about the Achilles' tendons – seemed to puzzle the old physician greatly, and finally almost to frighten him. His questioning grew more than medically tense, and his hands shook as he dressed the mangled members; binding them as if he wished to get the wounds out of sight as quickly as possible.

For an impersonal doctor, Davis' ominous and awestruck cross-examination became very strange indeed as he sought to drain from the weakened undertaker every least detail of his horrible experience. He was oddly anxious to know if Birch were sure – absolutely sure – of the identity of that top coffin of the pile; how he had chosen it, how he had been certain of it as the Fenner coffin in the dusk, and how he had distinguished it from the inferior duplicate coffin of vicious Asaph Sawyer. Would the firm Fenner casket have caved in so readily? Davis, an old-time village practitioner, had of course seen both at the respective funerals, as indeed he had attended both Fenner and Sawyer in their last illnesses. He had even wondered, at Sawyer's funeral, how the vindictive farmer had managed to lie straight in a box so closely akin to that of the diminutive Fenner.

After a full two hours Dr. Davis left, urging Birch to insist at all times that his wounds were caused entirely by loose nails and splintering wood. What else, he added, could ever in any case be proved or believed? But it would be well to say as little as could be said, and to let no other doctor treat the wounds. Birch heeded this advice all the rest of his life till he told me his story; and when I saw the scars – ancient and whitened as they then were – I agreed that he was wise in so doing. He always remained lame, for the great tendons had been severed; but I think the greatest lameness was in his soul. His thinking processes, once so phlegmatic and logical, had become ineffaceably scarred; and it was pitiful to note his response to certain chance allusions such as "Friday", "tomb", "coffin", and words of less obvious concatenation. His frightened horse had gone home, but his frightened wits never quite did that. He changed his business, but something always preyed upon him. It may have been just fear, and it may have been fear mixed with a queer belated sort of remorse for bygone crudities. His drinking, of course, only aggravated what it was meant to alleviate.

When Dr. Davis left Birch that night he had taken a lantern and gone to the old receiving tomb. The moon was shining on the scattered brick fragments and marred facade, and the latch of the great door yielded readily to a touch from the outside. Steeled by old ordeals in dissecting rooms, the doctor entered and looked about, stifling the nausea of mind and body that everything in sight and smell induced. He cried aloud once, and a little later gave a gasp that was more terrible than a cry. Then he fled back to the lodge and broke all the rules of his calling by rousing and shaking his patient, and hurling at him a succession of shuddering whispers that seared into the bewildered ears like the hissing of vitriol.

"It was Asaph's coffin, Birch, just as I thought! I knew his teeth, with the front ones missing on the upper jaw – never, for God's sake, shew those wounds! The body was pretty badly gone, but if ever I saw vindictiveness on any face – or former face. . . . You know what a fiend he was for revenge – how he ruined old Raymond thirty years after their boundary suit, and how he stepped on the puppy that snapped at him a year ago last August. . . . He was the devil incarnate, Birch, and I believe his eye-for-an-eye fury could beat old Father Death himself. God, what a rage! I'd hate to have it aimed at me!

"Why did you do it, Birch? He was a scoundrel, and I don't blame you for giving him a cast-aside coffin, but you always did go too damned far! Well enough to skimp on the thing some way, but you knew what a little man old Fenner was.

"I'll never get the picture out of my head as long as I live. You kicked hard, for Asaph's coffin was on the floor. His head was broken in, and everything was tumbled about. I've seen sights before, but there was one thing too much here. An eye for an eye! Great heavens, Birch, but you got what you deserved.

The skull turned my stomach, but the other was worse – *those ankles cut neatly off to fit Matt Fenner's cast-aside coffin!*"

PICKMAN'S MODEL

You needn't think I'm crazy, Eliot – plenty of others have queerer prejudices than this. Why don't you laugh at Oliver's grand-father, who won't ride in a motor? If I don't like that damned subway, it's my own business; and we got here more quickly anyhow in the taxi. We'd have had to walk up the hill from Park Street if we'd taken the car.

I know I'm more nervous than I was when you saw me last year, but you don't need to hold a clinic over it. There's plenty of reason, God knows, and I fancy I'm lucky to be sane at all. Why the third degree? You didn't use to be so inquisitive.

Well, if you must hear it, I don't know why you shouldn't. Maybe you ought to, anyhow, for you kept writing me like a grieved parent when you heard I'd begun to cut the Art Club and keep away from Pickman. Now that he's disappeared I go round to the club once in a while, but my nerves aren't what they were.

No, I don't know what's become of Pickman, and I don't like to guess. You might have surmised I had some inside information when I dropped him – and that's why I don't want to think where he's gone. Let the police find what they can – it won't be much, judging from the fact that they don't know yet of the old North End place he hired under the name of Peters. I'm not sure that I could find it again myself – not that I'd ever try, even in broad daylight! Yes, I do know, or am afraid I know, why he maintained it. I'm coming to that. And I think you'll understand before I'm through why I don't tell the police. They would ask me to guide them, but I couldn't go back there even if I knew the way. There was something there – and now I can't use the subway or (and you may as well have your laugh at this, too) go down into cellars any more.

I should think you'd have known I didn't drop Pickman for the same silly reasons that fussy old women like Dr Reid or Joe Minot or Rosworth did. Morbid art doesn't shock me, and when a man has the genius Pickman had I feel it an honour to know him, no matter what direction his work takes. Boston never had a greater painter than Richard Upton Pickman. I said it at first and I say it still, and I never swerved an inch, either, when he showed that "Ghoul Feeding". That, you remember, was when Minot cut him.

You know, it takes profound art and profound insight into Nature to turn out stuff like Pickman's. Any magazine-cover hack can splash paint around wildly and call it a nightmare or a Witches' Sabbath or a portrait of the devil, but only a great painter can make such a thing really scare or ring true. That's because only a real artist knows the actual anatomy of the terrible or the physiology of fear – the exact sort of lines and proportions that connect up with latent instincts or hereditary memories of fright, and the proper colour contrasts and lighting effects to stir the dormant sense of strangeness. I don't have to tell you why a Fuseli really brings a shiver while a cheap ghost-story frontis-piece merely makes us laugh. There's something those fellows catch – beyond life – that they're able to make us catch for a second. Doré had it. Sime has it. Angarola of Chicago has it. And Pickman had it as no man ever had it before or – I hope to Heaven – ever will again.

Don't ask me what it is they see. You know, in ordinary art, there's all the difference in the world between the vital, breathing things drawn from Nature or models and the artificial truck that commercial small fry reel off in a bare studio by rule. Well, I should say that the really weird artist has a kind of vision which makes models, or summons up what amounts to actual scenes from the spectral world he lives in. Anyhow, he manages to turn out results that differ from the pretender's mince-pie dreams in just about the same way that the life painter's results differ from the concoctions of a correspondence-school cartoonist. If I had ever seen what Pickman saw – but no! Here, let's have a drink before we get any deeper. Gad, I wouldn't be alive if I'd ever seen what that man – if he was a man – saw!

You recall that Pickman's *forte* was faces. I don't believe anybody since Goya could put so much of sheer hell into a set of features or a twist of expression. And before Goya you have to go back to the mediaeval chaps who did the gargoyles and chimaeras on Notre Dame and Mont Saint-Michel. They believed all sorts of things – and maybe they saw all sorts of things, too, for the Middle Ages had some curious phases. I remember your asking Pickman yourself once, the year before you went away, wherever in thunder he got such ideas and visions. Wasn't that a nasty laugh he gave you? It was partly because of that laugh that Reid dropped him. Reid, you know, had just taken up comparative pathology, and was full of pompous "inside stuff" about the biological or evolutionary significance of this or that mental or physical symptom. He said Pickman repelled him more and more every day, and almost frightened him towards the last – that the fellow's features and expression were slowly developing in a way he didn't like; in a way that wasn't human. He had a lot of talk about diet, and said Pickman must be abnormal and eccentric to the last degree. I suppose you told Reid, if you and he had any correspondence over it, that he'd let Pickman's paintings get on his nerves or harrow up his imagination. I know I told him that myself – *then*.

But keep in mind that I didn't drop Pickman for anything like this. On the contrary, my admiration for him kept growing; for that "Ghoul Feeding" was a tremendous achievement. As you know, the club wouldn't exhibit it, and the Museum of Fine Arts wouldn't accept it as a gift; and I can add that nobody would buy it, so Pickman had it right in his house till he went. Now his father has it in Salem – you know Pickman comes of old Salem stock, and had a witch ancestor hanged in 1692.

I got into the habit of calling on Pickman quite often, especially after I began making notes for a monograph on weird art. Probably it was his work which put the idea into my head, and anyhow, I found him a mine of data and suggestions when I came to develop it. He showed me all the paintings and drawings he had about; including some pen-and-ink sketches that would, I verily believe, have got him kicked out of the club if many of the members had seen them. Before long I was pretty nearly a devotee, and would listen for hours like a schoolboy to art theories and philosophic speculations wild enough to qualify him for the Danvers asylum. My hero-worship, coupled with the fact that people generally were commencing to have less and less to do with him, made him get very confidential with me; and one evening he hinted that if I were fairly close-mouthed and none too squeamish, he might show me something rather unusual – something a bit stronger than anything he had in the house.

"You know," he said, "there are things that won't do for Newbury Street – things that are out of place here, and that can't be conceived here, anyhow. It's my business to catch the overtones of the soul, and you won't find those in a parvenu set of artificial streets on made land. Back Bay isn't Boston – it isn't anything yet, because it's had no time to pick up memories and attract local spirits. If there are any ghosts here, they're the tame ghosts of a salt marsh and a shallow cove; and I want human ghosts – the ghosts of beings highly organized enough to have looked on hell and know the meaning of what they saw.

"The place for an artist to live is the North End. If any aesthete were sincere, he'd put up with the slums for the sake of the massed traditions. God, man! Don't you realize that places like that weren't merely made, but actually grew? Generation after generation lived and felt and died there, and in days when people weren't afraid to live and feel and die. Don't you know there was a mill on Copp's Hill in 1632, and that half the present streets were laid out by 1650? I can show you houses that have stood two centuries and a half and more; houses that have witnessed what would make a modern house crumble into powder. What do moderns know of life and the forces behind it? You call the Salem witchcraft a delusion, but I'll wager my four-times-great-grandmother could have told you things. They hanged her on Gallows Hill, with Cotton Mather looking sanctimoniously on. Mather, damn him, was afraid somebody might succeed in kicking free of this accursed cage of monotony – I wish someone had laid a spell on him or sucked his blood in the night!

"I can show you a house he lived in, and I can show you another one he was afraid to enter in spite of all his fine bold talk. He knew things he didn't dare put into that stupid *Magnalia* or that puerile *Wonders Of The Invisible World*. Look here, do you know the whole North End once had a set of tunnels that kept certain people in touch with each other's houses, and the burying ground, and the sea? Let them prosecute and persecute above ground – things went on every day that they couldn't reach, and voices laughed at night that they couldn't place!

"Why, man, out of ten surviving houses built before 1700 and not moved since I'll wager that in eight I can show you something queer in the cellar. There's hardly a month that you don't read of workmen finding bricked-up arches and wells leading nowhere in this or that old place as it comes down – you could see one near Henchman Street from the elevated last year. There were witches and what their spells summoned; pirates and what they brought in from the sea; smugglers; privateers – and I tell you, people knew how to live, and how to enlarge the bounds of life, in the old time! This wasn't the only world a bold and wise man could know – faugh! And to think of today in contrast, with such pale-pink brains that even a club of supposed artists gets shudders and convulsions if a picture goes beyond the feelings of a Beacon Street tea-table!

"The only saving grace of the present is that it's too damned stupid to question the past very closely. What do maps and records and guidebooks really tell of the North End? Bah! At a guess I'll guarantee to lead you to thirty or forty alleys and networks of alleys north of Prince Street that aren't suspected by ten living beings outside of the foreigners that swarm them. And what do those Dagoes know of their meaning? No, Thurber, these ancient places are dreaming gorgeously and overflowing with wonder and terror and escapes from the commonplace, and yet there's not a living soul to understand or profit by them.

Or rather, there's only one living soul – for I haven't been digging around in the past for nothing!

"See here, you're interested in this sort of thing. What if I told you that I've got another studio up there, where I can catch the night-spirit of antique horror and paint things that I couldn't even think of in Newbury Street? Naturally I don't tell those cursed old maids at the club – with Reid, damn him, whispering even as it is that I'm a sort of monster bound down the toboggan of reverse evolution. Yes, Thurber, I decided long ago that one must paint terror as well as beauty from life, so I did some exploring in places where I had reason to know terror lives.

"I've got a place that I don't believe three living Nordic men besides myself have ever seen. It isn't so very far from the elevated as distance goes, but it's centuries away as the soul goes. I took it because of the queer old brick well in the cellar – one of the sort I told you about. The shack's almost tumbling down so that nobody else would live there, and I'd hate to tell you how little I pay for it. The windows are boarded up, but I like that all the better, since I don't want daylight for what I do. I paint in the cellar, where the inspiration is thickest, but I've other rooms furnished on the ground floor. A Sicilian owns it, and I've hired it under the name of Peters.

"Now if you're game, I'll take you there tonight. I think you'd enjoy the pictures, for, as I said, I've let myself go a bit there. It's no vast tour – I sometimes do it on foot, for I don't want to attract attention with a taxi in such a place. We can take the shuttle at the South Station for Battery Street, and after that the walk isn't much."

Well, Eliot, there wasn't much for me to do after that harangue but to keep myself from running instead of walking for the first vacant cab we could sight. We changed to the elevated at the South Station, and at about twelve o'clock had climbed down the steps at Battery Street and struck along the old waterfront past Constitution Wharf. I didn't keep track of the cross streets, and can't tell you which it was we turned up, but I know it wasn't Greenough Lane.

When we did turn, it was to climb through the deserted length of the oldest and dirtiest alley I ever saw in my life, with crumbling-looking gables, broken small-paned windows, and archaic chimneys that stood out half-disintegrated against the moonlit sky. I don't believe there were three houses in sight that hadn't been standing in Cotton Mather's time – certainly I glimpsed at least two with an overhang, and once I thought I saw a peaked roof-line of the almost forgotten pre-gambrel type, though antiquarians tell us there are none left in Boston.

From that alley, which had a dim light, we turned to the left into an equally silent and still narrower alley with no light at all: and in a minute made what I think was an obtuse-angled bend towards the right in the dark. Not long after this Pickman produced a flashlight and revealed an antediluvian ten-panelled door that looked damnably worm-eaten. Unlocking it, he ushered me into a barren hallway with what was once splendid dark-oak panelling – simple, of course, but thrillingly suggestive of the times of Andros and Phipps, and the Witchcraft. Then he took me through a door on the left, lighted an oil lamp, and told me to make myself at home.

Now, Eliot, I'm what the man in the street would call fairly "hard-boiled", but I'll confess that what I saw on the walls of that room gave me a bad turn. They were his pictures, you know – the ones he couldn't paint or even show in Newbury Street – and he was right when he said he had "let himself go." Here – have another drink – I need one anyhow!

There's no use in my trying to tell you what they were like, because the awful, the blasphemous horror, and the unbelievable loathsomeness and moral foetor came from simple touches quite beyond the power of words to classify. There was none of the exotic technique you see in Sidney Sime, none of the trans-Saturnian landscapes and lunar fungi that Clark Ashton Smith uses to freeze the blood. The backgrounds were mostly old churchyards, deep woods, cliffs by the sea, brick tunnels, ancient panelled rooms, or simple vaults of masonry. Copp's Hill Burying Ground, which could not be many blocks away from this very house, was a favourite scene. The madness and monstrosity lay in the figures in the foreground – for Pickman's morbid art was pre-eminently one of daemoniac por-traiture. These figures were seldom completely human, but often approached humanity in varying degree. Most of the bodies, while roughly bipedal, had a forward slumping, and a vaguely canine cast. The texture of the majority was a kind of unpleasant rubberiness. Ugh! I can see them now! Their occupations – well, don't ask me to be too precise. They were usually feeding – I won't say on what. They were sometimes shown in groups in cemeteries or underground passages, and often appeared to be in battle over their prey – or rather, their treasure-trove. And what damnable expressiveness Pickman some-times gave the sightless faces of this charnel booty! Occasionally the things were shown leaping through open windows at night, or squatting on the chests of sleepers, worrying at their throats. One canvas showed a ring of them baying about a hanged witch on Gallows Hill, whose dead face held a close kinship to

182

theirs.

But don't get the idea that it was all this hideous business of theme and setting which struck me faint. I'm not a three-year-old kid, and I'd seen much like this before. It was the faces, Eliot, those accursed faces, that leered and slavered out of the canvas with the very breath of life! By God, man, I verily believe they were alive! That nauseous wizard had waked the fires of hell in pigment, and his brush had been a nightmare-spawning wand. Give me that decanter, Eliot!

There was one thing called "The Lesson" – Heaven pity me, that I ever saw it! Listen – can you fancy a squatting circle of nameless doglike things in a churchyard teaching a small child how to feed like themselves? The price of a changeling, I suppose – you know the old myth about how the weird people leave their spawn in cradles in exchange for the human babes they steal. Pickman was showing what happens to those stolen babes – how they grow up – and then I began to see a hideous relationship in the faces of the human and nonhuman figures. He was, in all his gradations of morbidity between the frankly non-human and the degradedly human, establishing a sardonic linkage and evolution. The dog-things were developed from mortals!

And no sooner had I wondered what he made of their own young as left with mankind in the form of changelings, than my eye caught a picture embodying that very thought. It was that of an ancient Puritan interior – a heavily beamed room with lattice windows, a settle, and clumsy seventeenth-century furniture, with the family sitting about while the father read from the Scriptures. Every face but one showed nobility and reverence, but that one reflected the mockery of the pit. It was that of a young man in years, and no doubt belonged to a supposed son of that pious father, but in essence it was the kin of unclean things. It was their changeling – and in a spirit of supreme irony Pickman had given the features a very perceptible resemblance to his own.

By this time Pickman had lighted a lamp in an adjoining room and was politely holding open the door for me; asking me if I would care to see his "modern studies." I hadn't been able to give him much of my opinions – I was too speechless with fright and loathing – but I think he fully understood and felt highly complimented. And now I want to assure you again, Eliot, that I'm no mollycoddle to scream at anything which shows a bit of departure from the usual. I'm middle-aged and decently sophisticated, and I guess you saw enough of me in France to know I'm not easily knocked out. Remember, too, that I'd just about recovered my wind and gotten used to those frightful pictures which turned colonial New England into a kind of annexe of hell. Well, in spite of all this, that next room forced a real scream out of me, and I had to clutch at the doorway to keep from keeling over. The other chamber had shown a pack of ghouls and witches over-running the world of our forefathers, but this one brought the horror right into our own daily life!

Gad, how that man could paint! There was a study called "Subway Accident", in which a flock of the vile things were clambering up from some unknown cata-comb through a crack in the floor of the Boylston Street subway and attacking a crowd of people on the platform. Another showed a dance on Copp's Hill among the tombs with the background of today. Then there were any number of cellar views, with monsters creeping in through holes and rifts in the masonry and grinning as they squatted behind barrels or furnaces and waited for their first victim to descend the stairs. One disgusting canvas seemed to depict a vast cross-section of Beacon Hill, with ant-like armies of the mephitic monsters squeezing themselves through burrows that honeycombed the ground. Dances in the modern cemeteries were freely pictured, and another conception somehow shocked me more than all the rest – a scene in an unknown vault, where scores of the beasts crowded about one who held a well-known Boston guidebook and was evidently reading aloud. All were pointing to a certain passage, and every face seemed so distorted with epileptic and reverberant laughter that I almost thought I heard the fiendish echoes. The title of the picture was, "Holmes, Lowell and Longfellow Lie Buried in Mount Auburn."

As I gradually steadied myself and got readjusted to this second room of deviltry and morbidity, I began to analyse some of the points in my sickening loathing. In the first place, I said to myself, these things repelled because of the utter inhumanity and callous cruelty they showed in Pickman. The fellow must be a relentless enemy of all mankind to take such glee in the torture of brain and flesh and the degradation of the mortal tenement. In the second place, they terrified because of their very greatness. Their art was the art that convinced – when we saw the pictures we saw the daemons themselves and were afraid of them. And the queer part was, that Pickman got none of his power from the use of selectiveness or bizarrerie. Nothing was blurred, distorted, or conventionalized; outlines were sharp and lifelike, and the details were almost painfully defined. And the faces!

It was not any mere artist's interpretation that we saw; it was pandemonium itself, crystal clear in stark objectivity. That was it, by Heaven! The man was not a fantaisiste or romanticist at all – he did not even try to give us the churning, prismatic ephemera of dreams, but coldly and sardonically reflected some stable, mechanistic, and well-established horror-world which he saw fully, brilliantly, squarely, and unfalteringly. God knows what that world can have been, or where he ever glimpsed the blasphemous shapes that loped and trotted and crawled through it; but whatever the baffling source of his images, one thing was plain. Pickman was in every sense – in conception and in execution – a thorough, painstaking, and almost scientific *realist*.

My host was now leading the way down the cellar to his actual studio, and I braced myself for some hellish efforts among the unfinished canvases. As we reached the bottom of the damp stairs he turned his flashlight to a corner of the large open space at hand, revealing the circular brick curb of what was evidently a great well in the earthen floor. We walked nearer, and I saw that it must be five feet across, with walls a good foot thick and some six inches above the ground level – solid work of the seventeenth century, or I was much mistaken. That, Pickman said, was the kind of thing he had been talking about – an aperture of the network of tunnels that used to undermine the hill. I noticed idly that it did not seem to be bricked up, and that a heavy disc of wood formed the apparent cover. Thinking of the things this well must have been connected with if Pickman's wild hints had not been mere rhetoric, I shivered slightly; then turned to follow him up a step and through a narrow door into a room of fair size, provided with a wooden floor and furnished as a studio. An acetylene gas outfit gave the light necessary for work.

The unfinished pictures on easels or propped against the walls were as ghastly as the finished ones upstairs, and showed the painstaking methods of the artist. Scenes were blocked out with extreme care, and pencilled guide lines told of the minute exactitude which Pickman used in getting the right perspective and proportions. The man was great – I say it even now, knowing as much as I do. A large camera on a table excited my notice, and Pickman told me that he used it in taking scenes for backgrounds, so that he might paint them from photographs in the studio instead of carting his outfit around the town for this or that view. He thought a photograph quite as good as an actual scene or model for sustained work, and declared he employed them regularly.

There was something very disturbing about the nauseous sketches and half-finished monstrosities that leered round from every side of the room, and when Pickman suddenly unveiled a huge canvas on the side away from the light I could not for my life keep back a loud scream – the second I had emitted that night. It echoed and echoed through the dim vaultings of that ancient and nitrous cellar, and I had to choke back a flood of reaction that threatened to burst out as hysterical laughter. Merciful Creator! Eliot, but I don't know how much was real and how much was feverish fancy. It doesn't seem to me that earth can hold a dream like that!

It was a colossal and nameless blasphemy with glaring red eyes, and it held in bony claws a thing that had been a man, gnawing at the head as a child nibbles at a stick of candy. Its position was a kind of crouch, and as one looked one felt that at any moment it might drop its present prey and seek a juicier morsel. But damn it all, it wasn't even the fiendish subject that made it such an immortal fountain-head of all panic – not that, nor the dog face with its pointed ears, bloodshot eyes, flat nose, and drooling lips. It wasn't the scaly claws nor the mould-caked body nor the half-hooved feet – none of these, though any one of them might well have driven an excitable man to madness.

It was the technique, Eliot – the cursed, the impious, the unnatural technique! As I am a living being, I never elsewhere saw the actual breath of life so fused into a canvas. The monster was there – it glared and gnawed and gnawed and glared – and I knew that only a suspension of Nature's laws could ever let a man paint a thing like that without a model – without some glimpse of the nether world which no mortal unsold to the Fiend has ever had.

Pinned with a thumb-tack to a vacant part of the canvas was a piece of paper now badly curled up – probably, I thought, a photograph from which Pickman meant to paint a background as hideous as the nightmare it was to enhance. I reached out to uncurl and look at it, when suddenly I saw Pickman start as if shot. He had been listening with peculiar intensity ever since my shocked scream had waked un-accustomed echoes in the dark cellar, and now he seemed struck with a fright which, though not comparable to my own, had in it more of the physical than of the spiritual. He drew a revolver and motioned me to silence, then stepped out into the main cellar and closed the door behind him.

I think I was paralysed for an instant. Imitating Pickman's listening, I fancied I heard a faint scurrying sound somewhere, and a series of squeals or bleats in a direction I couldn't determine. I thought of huge rats and shuddered. Then there came a subdued sort of clatter which somehow set me all in gooseflesh – a furtive, groping kind of clatter, though I can't attempt to convey what I mean in words. It was like heavy wood falling on stone or brick – wood on brick – what did that make me think of?

It came again, and louder. There was a vibration as if the wood had fallen farther than it had fallen before. After that followed a sharp grating noise, a shouted gibberish from Pickman, and the deafening discharge of all six chambers of a revolver, fired spectacularly as a lion-tamer might fire in the air for effect. A muffled squeal or squawk, and a thud. Then more wood and brick grating, a pause, and the opening of the door – at which I'll confess I started violently. Pickman reappeared with his smoking weapon, cursing the bloated rats that infested the ancient well.

"The deuce knows what they eat, Thurber," he grinned, "for those archaic tunnels touched graveyard and witch-den and sea-coast. But whatever it is, they must have run short, for they were devilish anxious to get out. Your yelling stirred them up, I fancy. Better be cautious in these old places – our rodent friends are the one drawback, though I sometimes think they're a positive asset by way of atmosphere and colour."

Well, Eliot, that was the end of the night's adventure. Pickman had promised to show me the place, and Heaven knows he had done it. He led me out of that tangle of alleys in another direction, it seems, for when we sighted a lamp-post we were in a half-familiar street with monotonous rows of mingled tenement blocks and old houses. Charter Street, it turned out to be, but I was too flustered to notice just where we hit it. We were too late for the elevated, and walked back downtown through Hanover Street. I remember that walk. We switched from Tremont up Beacon, and Pickman left me at the corner of Joy, where I turned off. I never spoke to him again.

Why did I drop him? Don't be impatient. Wait till I ring for coffee. We've had enough of the other stuff, but I for one need something. No – it wasn't the paintings I saw in that place; though I'll swear they were enough to get him ostracized in nine-tenths of the homes and clubs of Boston, and I guess you won't wonder now why I have to steer clear of subways and cellars. It was – something I found in my coat the next morning. You know, the curled-up paper tacked to the frightful canvas in the cellar; the thing I thought was a photograph of some scene he meant to use as a background for that monster. That last scare had come while I was reaching to uncurl it, and it seems I had vacantly crumpled it into my pocket. But here's the coffee – take it black, Eliot, if you're wise.

Yes, that paper was the reason I dropped Pickman; Richard Upton Pickman, the greatest artist I have ever known – and the foulest being that ever leaped the bounds of life into the pits of myth and madness. Eliot – old Reid was right. He wasn't strictly human. Either he was born in strange shadow, or he'd found a way to unlock the forbidden gate. It's all the same now, for he's gone – back into the fabulous darkness he loved to haunt. Here, let's have the chandelier going.

Don't ask me to explain or even conjecture about what I burned. Don't ask me, either, what lay behind that mole-like scrambling Pickman was so keen to pass off as rats. There are secrets, you know, which might have come down from old Salem times, and Cotton Mather tells even stranger things. You know how damned lifelike Pickman's paintings were – how we all wondered where he got those faces.

Well – that paper wasn't a photograph of any background, after all. What it showed was simply the monstrous being he was painting on that awful canvas. It was the model he was using – and its background was merely the wall of the cellar studio in minute detail. But by God, Eliot, *it was a photograph from life*.

THE CALL OF CTHULHU

*Of such great powers or beings there may be conceivably a survival... a survival of a hugely
remote period when... consciousness was manifested perhaps, in shapes and forms long since
withdrawn before the tide of advancing humanity... forms of which poetry and legend alone have
caught a flying memory and called them gods, monsters, mythical beings of all sorts and kinds...*
                                                                – Algernon Blackwood

I : THE HORROR IN CLAY

The most merciful thing in the world, I think, is the inability of the human mind
to correlate all its contents. We live on a placid island of ignorance in the midst
of black seas of infinity, and it was not meant that we should voyage far.

The sciences, each straining in its own direction, have hitherto harmed
us little; but some day the piecing together of dissociated knowledge will open up
such terrifying vistas of reality, and of our frightful position therein, that we shall
either go mad from the revelation or flee from the deadly light into the peace and
safety of a new dark age.

Theosophists have guessed at the awesome grandeur of the cosmic
cycle wherein our world and human race form transient incidents. They have
hinted at strange survival in terms which would freeze the blood if not masked
by a bland optimism. But it is not from them that there came the single glimpse
of forbidden aeons which chills me when I think of it and maddens me when I
dream of it. That glimpse, like all dread glimpses of truth, flashed out from an
accidental piecing together of separated things – in this case an old newspaper
item and the notes of a dead professor. I hope that no-one else will accomplish
this piecing out; certainly, if I live, I shall never knowingly supply a link in so
hideous a chain. I think that the professor, too, intended to keep silent regarding
the part he knew, and that he would have destroyed his notes had not sudden
death seized him.

My knowledge of the thing began in the winter of 1926-7 with the
death of my great-uncle, George Gammell Angell, Professor Emeritus of Semitic
Languages in Brown University, Providence, Rhode Island. Professor Angell was
widely known as an authority on ancient inscriptions, and had frequently been

resorted to by the heads of prominent museums; so that his passing at the age of ninety-two may be recalled by many. Locally, interest was intensified by the obscurity of the cause of death. The professor had been stricken whilst returning from the Newport boat; falling suddenly, as witnesses said, after having been jostled by a nautical-looking negro who had come from one of the queer dark courts on the precipitous hillside which formed a short cut from the water-front to the deceased's home in Williams Street. Physicians were unable to find any visible disorder, but concluded after perplexed debate that some obscure lesion of the heart, induced by the brisk ascent of so steep a hill by so elderly a man, was responsible for the end. At the time I saw no reason to dissent from this dictum, but latterly I am inclined to wonder – and more than wonder.

As my great-uncle's heir and executor, for he died a childless widower, I was expected to go over his papers with some thoroughness; and for that purpose moved his entire set of files and boxes to my quarters in Boston. Much of the material which I correlated will be later published by the American Archaeological Society, but there was one box which I found exceedingly puzzling, and which I felt much averse from showing to other eyes. It had been locked, and I did not find the key till it occurred to me to examine the personal ring which the professor carried always in his pocket. Then, indeed, I succeeded in opening it, but when I did so seemed only to be confronted by a greater and more closely locked barrier. For what could be the meaning of the queer clay bas-relief and the disjointed jottings, ramblings and cuttings which I found? Had my uncle, in his latter years, become credulous of the most superficial impostures? I resolved to search out the eccentric sculptor responsible for this apparent disturbance of an old man's peace of mind.

The bas-relief was a rough rectangle less than an inch thick and about five by six inches in area; obviously of modern origin. Its designs, however, were far from modern in atmosphere and suggestion; for, although the vagaries of cubism and futurism are many and wild, they do not often reproduce that cryptic regularity which lurks in prehistoric writing. And writing of some kind the bulk of these designs seemed certainly to be; though my memory, despite much familiarity with the papers and collections of my uncle, failed in any way to identify this particular species, or even hint at its remotest affiliations.

Above these apparent hieroglyphics was a figure of evidently pictorial intent, though its impressionistic execution forbade a very clear idea of its nature. It seemed to be a sort of monster, or symbol representing a monster, of a form which only a diseased fancy could conceive. If I say that my somewhat extravagant imagination yielded simultaneous pictures of an octopus, a dragon, and a human caricature, I shall not be unfaithful to the spirit of the thing. A pulpy, tentacled head surmounted a grotesque and scaly body with rudimentary wings; but it was the *general outline* of the whole which made it most shockingly frightful. Behind the figure was a vague suggestion of a Cyclopean architectural background.

The writing accompanying this oddity was, aside from a stack of press cuttings, in Professor Angell's most recent hand; and made no pretension to literary style. What seemed to be the main document was headed "CTHULHU CULT" in characters painstakingly printed to avoid the erroneous reading of a word so unheard-of. This manuscript was divided into two sections, the first of which was headed "1925 – Dream and Dream Work of H. A. Wilcox, 7 Thomas St., Providence, R. I.", and the second "Narrative of Inspector John R. Legrasse, 121 Bienville St., New Orleans, La., at 1908 A. A. S. Mtg. – Notes on Same, & Prof. Webb's Acct." The other manuscript papers were all brief notes, some of them accounts of the queer dreams of different persons, some of them citations from theosophical books and magazines (notably W. Scott-Elliott's *Atlantis And The Lost Lemuria*), and the rest comments on long-surviving secret societies and hidden cults, with references to passages in such mythological and anthropological source-books as Frazer's *Golden Bough* and Miss Murray's *Witch-Cult In Western Europe*. The cuttings largely alluded to *outré* mental illness and outbreaks of group folly or mania in the spring of 1925.

The first half of the principal manuscript told a very peculiar tale. It appears that on 1 March 1925, a thin, dark young man of neurotic and excited aspect had called upon Professor Angell bearing the singular clay bas-relief, which was then exceedingly damp and fresh. His card bore the name of Henry Anthony Wilcox, and my uncle had recognized him as the youngest son of an excellent family slightly known to him, who had latterly been studying sculpture at the Rhode Island School of Design and living alone at the Fleur-de-Lys Building near that institution. Wilcox was a precocious youth of known genius but great eccentricity, and had from childhood excited attention through the strange stories and odd dreams he was in the habit of relating. He called himself "psychically hypersensitive", but the staid folk of the ancient commercial city dismissed him as merely "queer". Never mingling much with his kind, he had dropped gradually from social visibility, and was now known only to a small group of aesthetes from other towns. Even the Providence Art Club, anxious to preserve its conservatism, had found him quite hopeless.

On the occasion of the visit, ran the professor's manuscript, the sculptor abruptly asked for the benefit of his host's archaeological knowledge in identifying the hieroglyphics on the bas-relief. He spoke in a dreamy, stilted manner which suggested pose and alienated sympathy; and my uncle showed some sharpness in replying, for the conspicuous freshness of the tablet implied kinship with anything but archaeology. Young Wilcox's rejoinder, which impressed my uncle enough to make him recall and record it verbatim, was of a fantastically poetic cast which must have typified his whole conversation, and which I have since found highly characteristic of him. He said, "It is new, indeed, for I made it last night in a dream of strange cities; and dreams are older than brooding Tyre, or the contemplative Sphinx, or garden-girdled Babylon."

It was then that he began that rambling tale which suddenly played upon a sleeping memory and won the fevered interest of my uncle. There had been a slight earthquake tremor the night before, the most considerable felt in New England for some years; and Wilcox's imaginations had been keenly affected. Upon retiring, he had had an unprecedented dream of great Cyclopean cities of titan blocks and sky-flung monoliths, all dripping with green ooze and sinister with latent horror. Hieroglyphics had covered the walls and pillars, and from some undetermined point below had come a voice that was not a voice; a chaotic sensation which only fancy could transmute into sound, but which he attempted to render by the almost unpronounceable jumble of letters, *"Cthulhu fhtagn."*

This verbal jumble was the key to the recollection which excited and disturbed Professor Angell. He questioned the sculptor with scientific minuteness; and studied with almost frantic intensity the bas-relief on which the youth had found himself working, chilled and clad only in his night-clothes, when waking had stolen bewilderingly over him. My uncle blamed his old age, Wilcox afterward said, for his slowness in recognizing both hieroglyphics and pictorial design. Many of his questions seemed highly out of place to his visitor, especially those which tried to connect the latter with strange cults or societies; and Wilcox could not understand the repeated promises of silence which he was offered in exchange for an admission of membership in some widespread mystical or paganly religious body. When Professor Angell became convinced that the sculptor was indeed ignorant of any cult or system of cryptic lore, he besieged his visitor with demands for future reports of dreams. This bore regular fruit, for after the first interview the manuscript records daily calls of the young man, during which he related startling fragments of nocturnal imagery whose burden was always some terrible Cyclopean vista of dark and dripping stone, with a subterrene voice or intelligence shouting monotonously in enigmatical sense-impacts uninscribable save as gibberish. The two sounds most frequently repeated are those rendered by the letters *"Cthulhu"* and *"R'lyeh"*.

On 23 March, the manuscript continued, Wilcox failed to appear; and inquiries at his quarters revealed that he had been stricken with an obscure sort of fever and taken to the home of his family in Waterman Street. He had cried out in the night, arousing several other artists in the building, and had manifested since then only alternations of unconsciousness and delirium. My uncle at once telephoned the family, and from that time forward kept close watch of the case; calling often at the Thayer Street office of Dr Tobey, whom he learned to be in charge. The youth's febrile mind, apparently, was dwelling on strange things; and the doctor shuddered now and then as he spoke of them. They included not only a repetition of what he had formerly dreamed, but touched wildly on a gigantic thing "miles high" which walked or lumbered about. He at no time fully described this object but occasional frantic words, as repeated by Dr Tobey, convinced the professor that it must be identical with the nameless monstrosity he had sought to depict in his dream-sculpture. Reference to this object, the doctor added, was invariably a prelude to the young man's subsidence into lethargy. His temperature, oddly enough, was not greatly above normal; but the whole condition was otherwise such as to suggest true fever rather than mental disorder.

On 2 April at about 3 P.M. every trace of Wilcox's malady suddenly ceased. He sat upright in bed, astonished to find himself at home and completely ignorant of what had happened in dream or reality since the night of 22 March. Pronounced well by his physician, he returned to his quarters in three days; but to Professor Angell he was of no further assistance. All traces of strange dreaming had vanished with his recovery, and my uncle kept no record of his night-thoughts after a week of pointless and irrelevant accounts of thoroughly usual visions.

Here the first part of the manuscript ended, but references to certain of the scattered notes gave me much material for thought – so much, in fact, that only the ingrained scepticism then forming my philosophy can account for my continued distrust of the artist. The notes in question were those descriptive of the dreams of various persons covering the same period as that in which young Wilcox had had his strange visitations. My uncle, it seems, had quickly instituted a prodigiously far-flung body of inquiries amongst nearly all the friends whom he could question without impertinence, asking for nightly reports of their dreams, and the dates of any notable visions for some time past. The reception of his request seems to have been varied; but he must, at the very least, have received more responses than any ordinary man could have handled without a secretary. This original correspondence was not preserved, but his notes formed a thorough and really significant digest. Average people in society and business — New England's traditional "salt of the earth" — gave an almost completely negative result, though scattered cases of uneasy but formless nocturnal impressions appear here and there, always between 23 March and 2 April — the period of young Wilcox's delirium. Scientific men were little more affected, though four cases of vague description suggest fugitive glimpses of strange landscapes, and in one case there is mentioned a dread of something abnormal.

It was from the artists and poets that the pertinent answers came, and I know that panic would have broken loose had they been able to compare notes. As it was, lacking their original letters, I half suspected the compiler of having asked leading questions, or of having edited the correspondence in corroboration of what he had latently resolved to see. That is why I continued to feel that Wilcox, somehow cognizant of the old data which my uncle had possessed, had been imposing on the veteran scientist. These responses from aesthetes told a disturbing tale. From 28 February to 2 April a large proportion of them had dreamed very bizarre things, the intensity of the dreams being immeasurably the stronger during the period of the sculptor's delirium. Over a fourth of those who reported anything, reported scenes and half-sounds not unlike those which Wilcox had described; and some of the dreamers confessed acute fear of the gigantic nameless thing visible towards the last. One case, which the note describes with emphasis, was very sad. The subject, a widely known architect with leanings towards theosophy and occultism, went violently insane on the date of young Wilcox's seizure, and expired several months later after incessant screamings to be saved from some escaped denizen of hell. Had my uncle referred to these cases by name instead of merely by number, I should have attempted some corroboration and personal investigation; but as it was, I succeeded in tracing down only a few. All of these, however, bore out the notes in full. I have often wondered if all the objects of the professor's questioning felt as puzzled as did this fraction. It is well that no explanation shall ever reach them.

The press cuttings, as I have intimated, touched on cases of panic, mania, and eccentricity during the given period. Professor Angell must have employed a cutting bureau, for the number of extracts was tremendous, and the sources scattered throughout the globe. Here was a nocturnal suicide in London, where a lone sleeper had leaped from a window after a shocking cry. Here likewise a rambling letter to the editor of a paper in South America, where a fanatic deduces a dire future from visions he has seen. A dispatch from California describes a theosophist colony as donning white robes *en masse* for some "glorious fulfilment" which never arrives, whilst items from India speak guardedly of serious native unrest towards the end of March. Voodoo orgies multiply in Haiti, and African outposts report ominous mutterings. American officers in the Philippines find certain tribes bothersome about this time, and New York policemen are mobbed by hysterical Levantines on the night of 22-23 March. The west of Ireland, too, is full of wild rumour and legendry, and a fantastic painter named Ardois-Boonot hangs a blasphemous *Dream Landscape* in the Paris spring salon of 1926. And so numerous are the recorded troubles in insane asylums that only a miracle can have stopped the medical fraternity from noting strange parallelisms and drawing mystified conclusions. A weird bunch of cuttings, all told; and I can at this date scarcely envisage the callous rationalism with which I set them aside. But I was then convinced that young Wilcox had known of the older matters mentioned by the professor.

II : THE TALE OF INSPECTOR LEGRASSE

The old matters which had made the sculptor's dream and bas-relief so significant to my uncle formed the subject of the second half of his long manuscript. Once before, it appears, Professor Angell had seen the hellish outlines of the nameless monstrosity, puzzled over the unknown hieroglyphics, and heard the ominous syllables which can be rendered only as *"Cthulhu"*; and all this in so stirring and horrible a connection that it is small wonder he pursued young Wilcox with queries and demands for data.

This earlier experience had come in 1908, seventeen years before, when the American Archaeological Society held its annual meeting in St Louis. Professor Angell, as befitted one of his authority and attainments, had had a prominent part in all the deliberations, and was one of the first to be approached by the several outsiders who took advantage of the convocation to offer questions for correct answering and problems for expert solution.

The chief of these outsiders, and in a short time the focus of interest for the entire meeting, was a commonplace-looking middle-aged man who had travelled all the way from New Orleans for certain special information unobtainable from any local source. His name was John Raymond Legrasse, and he was by profession an inspector of police. With him he bore the subject of his visit, a grotesque, repulsive, and apparently very ancient stone statuette whose origin he was at a loss to determine.

It must not be fancied that Inspector Legrasse had the least interest in archaeology. On the contrary, his wish for enlightenment was prompted by purely professional considerations. The statuette, idol, fetish, or whatever it was, had been captured some months before in the wooden swamps south of New Orleans during a raid on a supposed voodoo meeting; and so singular and hideous were the rites connected with it, that the police could not but realize that they had stumbled on a dark cult totally unknown to them, and infinitely more diabolic than even the blackest of the African voodoo circles. Of its origin, apart from the erratic and unbelievable tales extorted from the captured members, absolutely nothing was to be discovered; hence the anxiety of the police for any antiquarian lore which might help them to place the frightful symbol, and through it track down the cult to its fountain-head.

Inspector Legrasse was scarcely prepared for the sensation which his offering created. One sight of the thing had been enough to throw the assembled men of science into a state of tense excitement, and they lost no time in crowding around him to gaze at the diminutive figure whose utter strangeness and air of genuinely abysmal antiquity hinted so potently at unopened and archaic vistas. No recognized school of sculpture had animated this terrible object, yet centuries and even thousands of years seemed recorded in its dim and greenish surface of unplaceable stone.

The figure, which was finally passed slowly from man to man for close and careful study, was between seven and eight inches in height, and of exquisitely artistic workmanship. It represented a monster of vaguely anthropoid outline, but with an octopus-like head whose face was a mass of feelers, a scaly, rubbery-looking body, prodigious claws on hind and fore feet, and long, narrow wings behind. This thing, which seemed instinct with a fearsome and unnatural malignancy, was of a somewhat bloated corpulence, and squatted evilly on a rectangular block or pedestal covered with undecipherable characters. The tips of the wings touched the back edge of the block, the seat occupied the centre, whilst the long, curved claws of the doubled-up, crouching hind legs gripped the front edge and extended a quarter of the way down towards the bottom of the pedestal. The cephalopod head was bent forward, so that the ends of the facial feelers brushed the backs of huge fore-paws which clasped the croucher's elevated knees. The aspect of the whole was abnormally lifelike, and the more subtly fearful because its source was so totally unknown. Its vast, awesome, and incalculable age was unmistakable; yet not one link did it show with any known type of art belonging to civilization's youth – or indeed to any other time.

Totally separate and apart, its very material was a mystery; for the soapy, greenish-black stone with its golden or iridescent flecks and striations resembled nothing familiar to geology or mineralogy. The characters along the base were equally baffling; and no member present, despite a representation of half the world's expert learning in this field, could form the least notion of even their remotest linguistic kinship. They, like the subject and material, belonged to something horribly remote and distinct from mankind as we know it; something frightfully suggestive of old and unhallowed cycles of life in which our world and our conceptions have no part.

And yet, as the members severally shook their heads and confessed defeat at the inspector's problem, there was one man in that gathering who suspected a touch of bizarre familiarity in the monstrous shape and writing, and who presently told with some diffidence of the odd trifle he knew. This person was the late William Channing Webb, professor of anthropology in Princeton University, and an explorer of no slight note.

Professor Webb had been engaged, forty-eight years before, in a tour of Greenland and Iceland in search of some Runic inscriptions which he failed to unearth; and whilst high up on the West Greenland coast had encountered a singular tribe or cult of degenerate Eskimos whose religion, a curious form of devil-worship, chilled him with its deliberate bloodthirstiness and repulsiveness. It was a faith of which other Eskimos knew little, and which they mentioned only with shudders, saying that it had come down from horribly ancient aeons before ever the world was made. Besides nameless rites and human sacrifices there were certain queer hereditary rituals addressed to a supreme elder devil or *tornasuk*; and of this Professor Webb had taken a careful phonetic copy from an aged *angekok* or wizard-priest, expressing the sounds in Roman letters as best he knew how. But just now of prime significance was the fetish which this cult had cherished, and around which they danced when the aurora leaped high over the ice cliffs. It was, the professor stated, a very crude bas-relief of stone, comprising a hideous picture and some cryptic writing. And as far as he could tell, it was a rough parallel in all essential features of the bestial thing now lying before the meeting.

These data, received with suspense and astonishment by the assembled members, proved doubly exciting to Inspector Legrasse; and he began at once to ply his informant with questions. Having noted and copied an oral ritual among the swamp cult-worshippers his men had arrested, he besought the professor to remember as best he might the syllables taken down amongst the diabolist Eskimos. There then followed an exhaustive comparison of details, and a moment of really awed silence when both detective and scientist agreed on the virtual identity of the phrase common to two hellish rituals so many worlds of distance apart. What, in substance, both the Eskimo wizards and the Louisiana swamp-priests had chanted to their kindred idols was something very like this – the word-divisions being guessed at from traditional breaks in the phrase as chanted aloud:

"Ph'nglui mglw'nafh Cthulhu R'lyeh wgah'nagl fhtagn."

Legrasse had one point in advance of Professor Webb, for several among his mongrel prisoners had repeated to him what older celebrants had told them the words meant. This text, as given, ran something like this:

"In his house at R'lyeh dead Cthulhu waits dreaming."

And now, in response to a general urgent demand, Inspector Legrasse related as fully as possible his experience with the swamp worshippers; telling a story to which I could see my uncle attached profound significance. It savoured of the wildest dreams of myth-maker and theosophist, and disclosed an astonishing degree of cosmic imagination among such half-castes and pariahs as might be least expected to possess it.

On 1 November 1907, there had come to New Orleans police a frantic summons from the swamp and lagoon country to the south. The squatters there, mostly primitive but good-natured descendants of Lafitte's men, were in the grip of stark terror from an unknown thing which had stolen upon them in the night. It was voodoo, apparently, but voodoo of a more terrible sort than they had ever known; and some of their women and children had dis-appeared since the malevolent tom-tom had begun its incessant beating far within the black haunted woods where no dweller ventured. There were insane shouts and harrowing screams, soul-chilling chants and dancing devil-flames; and, the frightened messenger added, the people could stand it no more.

So a body of twenty police, filling two carriages and an automobile, had set out in the late afternoon with the shivering squatter as a guide. At the end of the passable road they alighted, and for miles splashed on in silence through the terrible cypress woods where day never came. Ugly roots and malignant hanging nooses of Spanish moss beset them, and now and then a pile of dank stones or fragments of a rotting wall intensified by its hint of morbid habitation a depression which every malformed tree and every fungous islet combined to create. At length the squatter settlement, a miserable huddle of huts, hove in sight; and hysterical dwellers ran out to cluster around the group of bobbing lanterns. The muffled beat of tom-toms was now faintly audible far, far ahead; and a curdling shriek came at infrequent intervals when the wind shifted. A reddish glare, too, seemed to filter through the pale undergrowth beyond endless avenues of forest night. Reluctant even to be left alone again, each one of the cowed squatters refused point-blank to advance another inch towards the scene of unholy worship, so Inspector Legrasse and his nineteen colleagues plunged on unguided into black arcades of horror that none of them had ever trod before.

The region now entered by the police was one of traditionally evil repute, substantially unknown and untraversed by white men. There were legends of a hidden lake unglimpsed by mortal sight, in which dwelt a huge, formless white polypus thing with luminous eyes; and squatters whispered that bat-winged devils flew up out of caverns in inner earth to worship it at midnight. They said it had been there before D'Iberville, before La Salle, before the Indians, and before even the wholesome beasts and birds of the woods. It was nightmare itself, and to see it was to die. But it made men dream, and so they knew enough to keep away. The present voodoo orgy was, indeed, on the merest fringe of this abhorred area, but that location was bad enough; hence perhaps the very place of the worship had terrified the squatters more than the shocking sounds and incidents.

Only poetry or madness could do justice to the noises heard by Legrasse's men as they ploughed on through the black morass towards the red glare and the muffled tom-toms. There are vocal qualities peculiar to men, and vocal qualities peculiar to beasts; and it is terrible to hear the one when the source should yield the other. Animal fury and orgiastic licence here whipped themselves to demoniac heights by howls and squawking ecstasies that tore and reverberated through those nighted woods like pestilential tempests from the gulfs of hell. Now and then the less organized ululations would cease, and from what seemed a well-drilled chorus of hoarse voices would rise in singsong chant that hideous phrase or ritual:

"Ph'nglui mglw'nafh Cthulhu R'lyeh wgah'nagl fhtagn."

Then the men, having reached a spot where the trees were thinner, came suddenly in sight of the spectacle itself. Four of them reeled, one fainted, and two were shaken into a frantic cry which the mad cacophony of the orgy fortunately deadened. Legrasse dashed swamp water on the face of the fainting man, and all stood trembling and nearly hypnotized with horror.

In a natural glade of the swamp stood a grassy island of perhaps an acre's extent, clear of trees and tolerably dry. On this now leaped and twisted a more in-describable horde of human abnormality than any but a Sime or an Angarola could paint. Void of clothing, this hybrid spawn were braying, bellowing and writhing about a monstrous ring-shaped bonfire; in the centre of which, revealed by occasional rifts in the curtain of flame, stood a great granite monolith some eight feet in height; on top of which, incongruous in its diminutiveness, rested the noxious carven statuette. From a wide circle of ten scaffolds set up at regular intervals with the flame-girt monolith as a centre hung, head downward, the oddly marred bodies of the helpless squatters who had dis-appeared. It was inside this circle that the ring of worshippers jumped and roared, the general direction of the mass motion being from left to right in endless bacchanale between the ring of bodies and the ring of fire.

It may have been only imagination and it may have been only echoes which induced one of the men, an excitable Spaniard, to fancy he heard antiphonal responses to the ritual from some far and unillumined spot deeper within the wood of ancient legendry and horror. This man, Joseph D. Galvez, I later met and questioned; and he proved distractingly imaginative. He indeed went so far as to hint of the faint beating of great wings, and of a glimpse of shining eyes and moun-tainous white bulk beyond the remotest trees – but I suppose he had been hearing too much native superstition.

Actually, the horrified pause of the men was of comparatively brief duration. Duty came first; and although there must have been nearly a hundred mongrel celebrants in the throng, the police relied on their firearms and plunged deter-minedly into the nauseous rout. For five minutes the resultant din and chaos were beyond description. Wild blows were struck, shots were fired, and escapes were made; but in the end Legrasse was able to count some forty-seven sullen prisoners, whom he forced to dress in haste and fall into line between two rows of policemen. Five of the worshippers lay dead, and two severely wounded ones were carried away on improvised stretchers by their fellow-prisoners. The image on the monolith, of course, was carefully removed and carried back by Legrasse.

Examined at headquarters after a trip of intense strain and weariness, the prisoners all proved to be men of a very low, mixed-blooded, and mentally aberrant type. Most were seamen, and a sprinkling of negroes and mulattos, largely West Indians or Brava Portuguese from the Cape Verde Islands, gave a colouring of voodooism to the heterogeneous cult. But before many questions were asked, it became manifest that something far deeper and older than negro fetishism was involved. Degraded and ignorant as they were, the creatures held with surprising consistency to the central idea of their loathsome faith.

They worshipped, so they said, the Great Old Ones who lived ages before there were any men, and who came to the young world out of the sky. These Old Ones were gone now, inside the earth and under the sea; but their dead bodies had told their secrets in dreams to the first man, who formed a cult which had never died. This was that cult, and the prisoners said it had always existed and always would exist, hidden in distant wastes and dark places all over the world until the time when the great priest Cthulhu, from his dark house in the mighty city of R'lyeh under the waters, should rise and bring the earth again beneath his sway. Some day he would call, when the stars were ready, and the secret cult would always be waiting to liberate him.

Meanwhile no more must be told. There was a secret which even torture could not extract. Mankind was not absolutely alone among the conscious things of earth, for shapes came out of the dark to visit the faithful few. But these were not the Great Old Ones. No man had ever seen the Old Ones. The carven idol was great Cthulhu, but none might say whether or not the others were precisely like him. No-one could read the old writing now, but things were told by word of mouth. The chanted ritual was not the secret − that was never spoken aloud, only whispered. The chant meant only this:

"In his house at R'lyeh dead Cthulhu waits dreaming."

Only two of the prisoners were found sane enough to be hanged, and the rest were committed to various institutions. All denied a part in the ritual murders, and averred that the killing had been done by Black-winged Ones which had come to them from their immemorial meeting-place in the haunted wood. But of those mysterious allies no coherent account could ever be gained. What the police did extract came mainly from an immensely aged mestizo named Castro, who claimed to have sailed to strange ports and talked with undying leaders of the cult in the mountains of China.

Old Castro remembered bits of hideous legend that paled the speculations of theosophists and made man and the world seem recent and transient indeed. There had been aeons when other Things ruled on the earth, and They had had great cities. Remains of Them, he said the deathless Chinamen had told him, were still to be found as Cyclopean stones on islands in the Pacific. They all died vast epochs of time before man came, but there were arts which could revive Them when the stars had come round again to the right positions in the cycle of eternity. They had, indeed, come themselves from the stars, and brought Their images with Them.

These Great Old Ones, Castro continued, were not composed altogether of flesh and blood. They had shape – for did not this star-fashioned image prove it? – but that shape was not made of matter. When the stars were right, They could plunge from world to world through the sky; but when the stars were wrong, They could not live. But although They no longer lived, They would never really die. They all lay in stone houses in Their great city of R'lyeh, preserved by the spells of mighty Cthulhu for a glorious resurrection when the stars and the earth might once more be ready for Them. But at that time some force from outside must serve to liberate Their bodies. The spells that preserved Them intact likewise prevented Them from making an initial move, and They could only lie awake in the dark and think whilst uncounted millions of years rolled by. They knew all that was occurring in the universe, for Their mode of speech was transmitted thought. Even now They talked in Their tombs. When, after infinities of chaos, the first men came, the Great Old Ones spoke to the sensitive among them by moulding their dreams; for only thus could Their language reach the fleshy minds of mammals.

Then, whispered Castro, those first men formed the cult around small idols which the Great Ones showed them; idols brought in dim eras from dark stars. That cult would never die till the stars came right again, and the secret priests would take great Cthulhu from His tomb to revive His subjects and resume His rule of earth. The time would be easy to know, for then mankind would have become as the Great Old Ones; free and wild and beyond good and evil, with laws and morals thrown aside and all men shouting and killing and revelling in joy. Then the liberated Old Ones would teach them new ways to shout and kill and revel and enjoy themselves, and all the earth would flame with a holocaust of ecstasy and freedom. Meanwhile the cult, by appropriate rites, must keep alive the memory of those ancient ways and shadow forth the prophecy of their return.

In the elder time chosen men had talked with the entombed Old Ones in dreams, but then something had happened. The great stone city R'lyeh, with its monoliths and sepulchres, had sunk beneath the waves; and the deep waters, full of the one primal mystery through which not even thought can pass, had cut off the spectral intercourse. But memory never died, and high priests said that the city would rise again when the stars were right. Then came out of the earth the black spirits of earth, mouldy and shadowy, and full of dim rumours picked up in caverns beneath forgotten sea-bottoms. But of them old Castro dared not speak much. He cut himself off hurriedly, and no amount of persuasion or subtlety could elicit more in this direction. The size of the Old Ones, too, he curiously declined to mention. Of the cult, he said that he thought the centre lay amid the pathless deserts of Arabia, where Irem, the City of Pillars, dreams hidden and untouched. It was not allied to the European witch-cult, and was virtually unknown beyond its members. No book had ever really hinted of it, though the deathless Chinamen said that there were double meanings in the *Necronomicon* of the mad Arab Abdul Alhazred which the initiated might read as they chose, especially the much-discussed couplet:

That is not dead which can eternal lie,
And with strange aeons even death may die.

Legrasse, deeply impressed and not a little bewildered, had inquired in vain concerning the historic affiliations of the cult. Castro, apparently, had told the truth when he said that it was wholly secret. The authorities at Tulane University could shed no light upon either cult or image, and now the detective had come to the highest authorities in the country and met with no more than the Greenland tale of Professor Webb.

The feverish interest aroused at the meeting by Legrasse's tale, corroborated as it was by the statuette, is echoed in the subsequent correspondence of those who attended; although scant mention occurs in the formal publication of the society. Caution is the first care of those accustomed to face occasional charlatanry and imposture. Legrasse for some time lent the image to Professor Webb, but at the latter's death it was returned to him and remains in his possession, where I viewed it not long ago. It is truly a terrible thing, and unmistakably akin to the dream-sculpture of young Wilcox.

That my uncle was excited by the tale of the sculptor I did not wonder, for what thoughts must arise upon hearing, after a knowledge of what Legrasse had learned of the cult, of a sensitive young man, who had dreamed not only the figure and exact hieroglyphics of the swamp-found image and the Greenland devil tablet, but had come in his dreams upon at least three of the precise words of the formula uttered alike by Eskimo diabolists and mongrel Louisianans? Professor Angell's instant start on an investigation of the utmost thoroughness was eminently natural; though privately I suspected young Wilcox of having heard of the cult in some indirect way, and of having invented a series of dreams to heighten and continue the mystery at my uncle's expense. The dream-narratives and cuttings collected by the professor were, of course, strong corroboration; but the rationalism of my mind and the extravagance of the whole subject led me to adopt what I thought the most sensible conclusions. So, after thoroughly studying the manuscript again and correlating the theosophical and anthropological notes with the cult narrative of Legrasse, I made a trip to Providence to see the sculptor and give him the rebuke I thought proper for so boldly imposing upon a learned and aged man.

Wilcox still lived alone in the Fleur-de-Lys Building in Thomas Street, a hideous Victorian imitation of seventeenth-century Breton architecture which flaunts its stuccoed front amidst the lovely Colonial houses on the ancient hill, and under the very shadow of the finest Georgian steeple in America. I found him at work in his rooms, and at once conceded from the specimens scattered about that his genius is indeed profound and authentic. He will, I believe, be heard from some time as one of the great decadents; for he has crystallized in clay and will one day mirror in marble those nightmares and fantasies which Arthur Machen evokes in prose, and Clark Ashton Smith makes visible in verse and in painting.

Dark, frail, and somewhat unkempt in aspect, he turned languidly at my knock and asked me my business without rising. When I told him who I was, he displayed some interest; for my uncle had excited his curiosity in probing his strange dreams, yet had never explained the reason for the study. I did not enlarge his knowledge in this regard, but sought with some subtlety to draw him out.

In a short time I became convinced of his absolute sincerity for he spoke of the dreams in a manner none could mistake. They and their subconscious residuum had influenced his art profoundly, and he showed me a morbid statue whose contours almost made me shake with the potency of its black suggestion. He could not recall having seen the original of this thing except in his own dream bas-relief, but the outlines had formed themselves insensibly under his hands. It was, no doubt, the giant shape he had raved of in delirium. That he really knew nothing of the hidden cult, save from hat my uncle's relentless catechism had let fall, he soon made clear; and again I strove to think of some way in which he could possibly have received the weird impressions.

He talked of his dreams in a strangely poetic fashion; making me see with terrible vividness the damp Cyclopean city of slimy green stone – whose geometry, he oddly said, was all wrong – and hear with frightened expectancy the ceaseless, half-mental calling from underground:

"Cthulhu fhtagn, Cthulhu fhtagn."

These words had formed part of that dread ritual which told of dead Cthulhu's dream-vigil in his stone vault at R'lyeh, and I felt deeply moved despite my rational beliefs. Wilcox, I was sure, had heard of the cult in some casual way, and had soon forgotten it amidst the mass of his equally weird reading and imagining. Later, by virtue of its sheer impressiveness, it had found subconscious expression in dreams, in the bas-relief, and in the terrible statue I now beheld; so that his imposture upon my uncle had been a very innocent one. The youth was of a type, at once slightly affected and slightly ill-mannered, which I could never like; but I was willing enough now to admit both his genius and his honesty. I took leave of him amicably, and wished him all the success his talent promised.

The matter of the cult still remained to fascinate me, and at times I had visions of personal fame from researches into its origin and connections. I visited New Orleans, talked with Legrasse and others of that old-time raiding-party, saw the frightful image, and even questioned such of the mongrel prisoners as still survived. Old Castro, unfortunately, had been dead for some years. What I now heard so graphically at first hand, though it was really no more than a detailed confirmation of what my uncle had written, excited me afresh; for I felt sure that I was on the track of a very real, very secret, and very ancient religion whose discovery would make me an anthropologist of note. My attitude was still one of absolute materialism as I wish it still were, and I discounted with a most inexplicable perversity the coincidence of the dream notes and odd cuttings collected by Professor Angell.

One thing which I began to suspect, and which I now fear I know, is that my uncle's death was far from natural. He fell on a narrow hill street leading up from an ancient waterfront swarming with foreign mongrels, after a careless push from a negro sailor. I did not forget the mixed blood and marine pursuits of the cult-members in Louisiana, and would not be surprised to learn of secret methods and poison needles as ruthless and as anciently known as the cryptic rites and beliefs. Legrasse and his men, it is true, have been let alone; but in Norway a certain seaman who saw things is dead. Might not the deeper inquiries of my uncle after encountering the sculptor's data have come to sinister ears? I think Professor Angell died because he knew too much, or because he was likely to learn too much. Whether I shall go as he did remains to be seen, for I have learned much now.

III : THE MADNESS FROM THE SEA

If heaven ever wishes to grant me a boon, it will be a total effacing of the results of a mere chance which fixed my eye on a certain stray piece of shelf-paper. It was nothing on which I would naturally have stumbled in the course of my daily round, for it was an old number of an Australian journal, *Sydney Bulletin* for 18 April 1925. It had escaped even the cutting bureau which had at the time of its issuance been avidly collecting material for my uncle's research.

I had largely given over my inquiries into what Professor Angell called the "Cthulhu Cult", and was visiting a learned friend of Paterson, New Jersey; the curator of a local museum and a mineralogist of note. Examining one day the reserve specimens roughly set on the storage shelves in a rear room of the museum, my eye was caught by an odd picture in one of the old papers spread beneath the stones. It was the *Sydney Bulletin* I have mentioned, for my friend has wide affiliations in all conceivable foreign parts; and the picture was a half-tone cut of a hideous stone image almost identical with that which Legrasse had found in the swamp.

Eagerly clearing the sheet of its precious contents, I scanned the item in detail, and was disappointed to find it of only moderate length. What it suggested, however, was of portentous significance to my flagging quest; and I carefully tore it out for immediate action. It read as follows:

MYSTERY DERELICT FOUND AT SEA

Vigilant Arrives with Helpless Armed New Zealand Yacht in Tow. One Survivor and Dead Man Found Aboard. Tale of Desperate Battle and Deaths at Sea. Rescued Seaman Refuses Particulars of Strange Experience. Odd Idol Found in His Possession. Inquiry to Follow.

The Morrison Co's freighter *Vigilant*, bound from Valparaiso, arrived this morning at its wharf in Darling Harbour having in tow the battled and disabled but heavily armed steam yacht *Alert* of Dunedin, NZ, which was sighted 12 April in S. Latitude 340° 21', W. Longitude 152° 17', with one living and one dead man aboard.

The *Vigilant* left Valparaiso 25 March, and on 2 April was driven considerably south of her course by exceptionally heavy storms and monster waves. On 12 April the derelict was sighted; and though apparently deserted, was found upon boarding to contain one survivor in a half-delirious condition and one man who had evidently been dead for more than a week.

The living man was clutching a horrible stone idol of unknown origin, about a foot in height, regarding whose nature authorities at Sydney University, the Royal Society, and the Museum in College Street all profess complete bafflement, and which the survivor says he found in the cabin of the yacht, in a small carved shrine of common pattern.

This man, after recovering his senses, told an exceedingly strange story of piracy and slaughter. He is Gustaf Johansen, a Norwegian of some intelligence, and had been second mate of the two-masted schooner *Emma* of Auckland, which sailed for Callao 20 February, with a complement of eleven men.

The *Emma*, he says, was delayed and thrown widely south of her course by the great storm of 1 March, and on 22 March, in S. Latitude 490° 51', W. Longitude 128° 34', encountered the *Alert*, manned by a queer and evil-looking crew of Kanakas and half-castes. Being ordered peremptorily to turn back, Capt. Collins refused; whereupon the strange crew began to fire savagely and without warning upon the schooner with a peculiarly heavy battery of brass cannon forming part of the yacht's equipment.

The *Emma*'s men showed fight, says the survivor, and though the schooner began to sink from shots beneath the waterline they managed to heave alongside their enemy and board her, grappling with the savage crew on the yacht's deck, and being forced to kill them all, the number being slightly superior, because of their particularly abhorrent and desperate though rather clumsy mode of fighting.

Three of *Emma*'s men, including Capt. Collins and First Mate Green, were killed; and the remaining eight under Second Mate Johansen proceeded to navigate the captured yacht, going ahead in their original direction to see if any reason for their ordering back had existed.

The next day, it appears, they raised and landed on a small island, although none is known to exist in that part of the ocean; and six of the men somehow died ashore, though Johansen is queerly reticent about this part of his story and speaks only of their falling into a rock chasm.

Later, it seems, he and one companion boarded the yacht and tried to manage her, but were beaten about by the storm of 2 April.

From that time till his rescue on the 12th, the man remembers little, and he does not even recall when William Briden, his companion, died. Briden's death reveals no apparent cause, and was probably due to excitement or exposure.

Cable advices from Dunedin report that the *Alert* was well known there as an island trader, and bore an evil reputation along the waterfront. It was owned by a curious group of half-castes whose frequent meetings and night trips to the woods attracted no little curiosity; and it had set sail in great haste just after the storm and earth tremors of 1 March.

Our Auckland correspondent gives the *Emma* and her crew an excellent reputation, and Johansen is described as a sober and worthy man.

The admiralty will institute an inquiry on the whole matter, beginning tomorrow, at which every effort will be made to induce Johansen to speak more freely than he has done hitherto.

This was all, together with the picture of the hellish image; but what a train of ideas it started in my mind! Here were new treasuries of data on the Cthulhu Cult, and evidence that it had strange interests at sea as well as on land. What motive prompted the hybrid crew to order back the *Emma* as they sailed about with their hideous idol? What was the unknown island on which six of the *Emma*'s crew had died, and about which the mate Johansen was so secretive? What had the vice-admiralty's investigation brought out, and what was known of the noxious cult in Dunedin? And most marvellous of all, what deep and more than natural linkage of dates was this which gave a malign and now undeniable significance to the various turns of events so carefully noted by my uncle?

1 March – our 28 February according to the International Date Line – the earthquake and storm had come. From Dunedin the *Alert* and her noisome crew had darted eagerly forth as if imperiously summoned, and on the other side of the earth poets and artists had begun to dream of a strange, dank Cyclopean city whilst a young sculptor had moulded in his sleep the form of the dreaded Cthulhu. 23 March the crew of the *Emma* landed on an unknown island and left six men dead; and on that date the dreams of sensitive men assumed a heightened vividness and darkened with dread of a giant monster's malign pursuit, whilst an architect had gone mad and a sculptor had lapsed suddenly into delirium! And what of this storm of 2 April – the date on which all dreams of the dank city ceased, and Wilcox emerged unharmed from the bondage of strange fever? What of all this – and of those hints of old Castro about the sunken, star-born Old Ones and their coming reign; their faithful cult *and their mastery of dreams?* Was I tottering on the brink of cosmic horrors beyond man's power to bear? If so, they must be horrors of the mind alone, for in some way the second of April had put a stop to whatever monstrous menace had begun its seige of mankind's soul.

That evening, after a day of hurried cabling and arranging, I bade my host adieu and took a train for San Francisco. In less than a month I was in Dunedin: where, however, I found that little was known of the strange cult-members who had lingered in the old sea taverns. Waterfront scum was far too common for special mention; though there was vague talk about one inland trip these mongrels had made, during which faint drumming and red flame were noted on the distant hills.

In Auckland I learned that Johansen had returned *with yellow hair turned white* after a perfunctory and inconclusive questioning at Sydney, and had thereafter sold his cottage in West Street and sailed with his wife to his old home in Oslo. Of his stirring experience he would tell his friends no more than he had told the admiralty officials, and all they could do was to give me his Oslo address.

After that I went to Sydney and talked profitlessly with seamen and members of the vice-admiralty court. I saw the *Alert*, now sold and in commercial use, in Circular Quay at Sydney Cove, but gained nothing from its noncommittal bulk. The crouching image with its cuttlefish head, dragon body, scaly wings, and hiero-glyphed pedestal, was preserved in the Museum at Hyde Park; and I studied it long and well, finding it a thing of balefully exquisite workmanship, and with the same utter mystery, terrible antiquity, and unearthly strangeness of material which I had noted in Legrasse's smaller specimen. Geologists, the curator told me, had found it a monstrous puzzle; for they vowed that the world held no rock like it. Then I thought with a shudder of what old Castro had told Legrasse about the primal Great Ones: "They had come from the stars, and had brought Their images with Them."

Shaken with such a mental revolution as I had never before known, I now resolved to visit Mate Johansen in Oslo. Sailing for London, I re-embarked at once for the Norwegian capital; and one autumn day landed at the trim wharves in the shadow of the Egeberg.

Johansen's address, I discovered, lay in the Old Town of King Harold Haardrada, which kept alive the name of Oslo during all the centuries that the greater city masqueraded as "Christiania." I made the brief trip by taxicab, and knocked with palpitant heart at the door of a neat and ancient building with plastered front. A sad-faced woman in black answered my summons, and I was stung with disappointment when she told me in halting English that Gustaf Johansen was no more.

He had not long survived his return, said his wife, for the doings at sea in 1925 had broken him. He had told her no more than he had told the public, but had left a long manuscript – of "technical matters" as he said – written in English, evidently in order to safeguard her from the peril of casual perusal. During a walk through a narrow lane near the Gothenburg dock, a bundle of papers falling from an attic window had knocked him down. Two Lascar sailors at once helped him to his feet, but before the ambulance could reach him he was dead. Physicians found no adequate cause for the end, and laid it to heart trouble and a weakened constitution.

I now felt gnawing at my vitals that dark terror which will never leave me till I, too, am at rest; "accidentally" or otherwise. Persuading the widow that my connection with her husband's "technical matters" was sufficient to entitle me to his manuscript, I bore the document away and began to read it on the London boat.

It was a simple, rambling thing – a naïve sailor's effort at a postfacto diary – and strove to recall day by day that last awful voyage. I cannot attempt to transcribe it verbatim in all its cloudiness and redundance, but I will tell its gist enough to show why the sound of the water against the vessel's sides became so unendurable to me that I stopped my ears with cotton.

Johansen, thank God, did not know quite all, even though he saw the city and the Thing, but I shall never sleep calmly again when I think of the horrors that lurk ceaselessly behind life in time and in space, and of those unhallowed blasphemies from elder stars which dream beneath the sea, known and favoured by a nightmare cult ready and eager to loose them on the world whenever another earthquake shall heave their monstrous stone city again to the sun and air.

Johansen's voyage had begun just as he told it to the vice-admiralty. The *Emma*, in ballast, had cleared Auckland on 20 February, and had felt the full force of that earthquake-born tempest which must have heaved up from the sea-bottom the horrors that filled men's dreams. Once more under control, the ship was making good progress when held up by the *Alert* on 22 March, and I could feel the mate's regret as he wrote of her bombardment and sinking. Of the swarthy cult-fiends on the *Alert* he speaks with significant horror. There was some peculiarly abominable quality about them which made their destruction seem almost a duty, and Johansen shows ingenuous wonder at the charge of ruthlessness brought against his party during the proceedings of the court of inquiry. Then, driven ahead by curiosity in their captured yacht under Johansen's command, the men sight a great stone pillar sticking out of the sea, and in S. Latitude 47° 9', W. Longitude 126° 43', come upon a coastline of mingled mud, ooze, and weedy Cyclopean masonry which can be nothing less than the tangible substance of earth's supreme terror – the nightmare corpse-city of R'lyeh, that was built in measureless aeons behind history by the vast, loathsome shapes that seeped down from the dark stars. There lay great Cthulhu and his hordes, hidden in green slimy vaults and sending out at last, after cycles incalculable, the thoughts that spread fear to the dreams of the sensitive and called imperiously to the faithful to come on a pilgrimage of liberation and restoration. All this Johansen did not suspect, but God knows he soon saw enough!

I suppose that only a single mountain-top, the hideous monolith-crowned citadel whereon great Cthulhu was buried, actually emerged from the waters. When I think of the *extent* of all that may be brooding down there I almost wish to kill myself forthwith. Johansen and his men were awed by the cosmic majesty of this dripping Babylon of elder daemons, and must have guessed without guidance that it was nothing of this or any sane planet. Awe at the unbelievable size of the greenish stone blocks, at the dizzying height of the great carven monolith, and at the stupefying identity of the colossal statues and bas-reliefs with the queer image found in the shrine on the *Alert*, is poignantly visible in every line of the mate's frightened description.

Without knowing what futurism is like, Johansen achieved something very close to it when he spoke of the city; for instead of describing any definite structure or building, he dwells only on the broad impressions of vast angles and stone surfaces – surfaces too great to belong to anything right or proper for this earth, and impious with horrible images and hieroglyphs. I mention his talk about *angles* because it suggests something Wilcox had told me of his awful dreams. He had said that the *geometry* of the dream-place he saw was abnormal, non-Euclidean, and loath-somely redolent of spheres and dimensions apart from ours. Now an unlettered seaman felt the same thing whilst gazing at the terrible reality.

Johansen and his men landed at a sloping mud-bank on this monstrous acropolis, and clambered slipperily up over titan oozy blocks which could have been no mortal staircase. The very sun of heaven seemed distorted when viewed through the polarizing miasma welling out from this sea-soaked perversion, and twisted menace and suspense lurked leeringly in those crazily elusive angles of carven rock where a second glance showed concavity after the first showed convexity.

Something very like fright had come over all the explorers before anything more definite than rock and ooze and weed was seen. Each would have fled had he not feared the scorn of the others, and it was only half-heartedly that they searched – vainly, as it proved – for some portable souvenir to bear away.

It was Rodriguez the Portuguese who climbed up the foot of the monolith and shouted of what he had found. The rest followed him, and looked curiously at the immense carved door with the now familiar squid-dragon bas-relief. It was, Johansen said, like a great barn-door; and they all felt that it was a door because of the ornate lintel, threshold, and jambs around it, though they could not decide whether it lay flat like a trap-door or slantwise like an outside cellar-door. As Wilcox would have said, the geometry of the place was all wrong. One could not be sure that the sea and the ground were horizontal, hence the relative position of everything else seemed fantasmally variable.

Briden pushed at the stone in several places without result. Then Donovan felt over it delicately around the edge, pressing each point separately as he went. He climbed interminably along the grotesque stone moulding – that is, one would call it climbing if the thing was not after all horizontal – and the men wondered how any door in the universe could be so vast. Then, very softly and slowly, the acre-great panel began to give inward at the top; and they saw that it was balanced.

212

Donovan slid or somehow propelled himself down or along the jamb and rejoined his fellows, and everyone watched the queer recession of the monstrously carven portal. In this fantasy of prismatic distortion it moved anomalously in a diagonal way, so that all the rules of matter and perspective seemed upset.

The aperture was black with a darkness almost material. That tenebrous-ness was indeed a *positive quality*; for it obscured such parts of the inner walls as ought to have been revealed, and actually burst forth like smoke from its aeon-long imprisonment, visibly darkening the sun as it slunk away into the shrunken and gibbous sky on flapping membranous wings. The odour arising from the newly opened depths was intolerable, and at length the quick-eared Hawkins thought he heard a nasty, slopping sound down there. Everyone listened, and everyone was listening still when It lumbered slobberingly into sight and gropingly squeezed Its gelatinous green immensity through the black doorway into the tainted outside air of that poison city of madness.

Poor Johansen's handwriting almost gave out when he wrote of this. Of the six men who never reached the ship, he thinks two perished of pure fright in that accursed instant. The Thing cannot be described – there is no language for such abysms of shrieking and immemorial lunacy, such eldritch contradictions of all matter, force, and cosmic order. A mountain walked or stumbled. God! What wonder that across the earth a great architect went mad, and poor Wilcox raved with fever in that telepathic instant? The Thing of the idols, the green, sticky spawn of the stars, had awaked to claim his own. The stars were right again, and what an age-old cult had failed to do by designs, a band of innocent sailors had done by accident. After vigintillions of years great Cthulhu was loose again, and ravening for delight.

Three men were swept up by the flabby claws before anybody turned. God rest them, if there be any rest in the universe. They were Donovan, Guerrera and Angstrom. Parker slipped as the other three were plunging frenziedly over endless vistas of green-crusted rock to the boat, and Johansen swears he was swallowed up by an angle of masonry which shouldn't have been there; an angle which was acute, but behaved as if it were obtuse. So only Briden and Johansen reached the boat, and pulled desperately for the *Alert* as the mountainous monstrosity flopped down the slimy stones and hesitated, floundering at the edge of the water.

Steam had not been suffered to go down entirely, despite the departure of all hands for the shore; and it was the work of only a few moments of feverish rushing up and down between wheels and engines to get the *Alert* under way. Slowly, amidst the distorted horrors of the indescribable scene, she began to churn the lethal waters; whilst on the masonry of that charnel shore that was not of earth the titan Thing from the stars slavered and gibbered like Polypheme cursing the fleeing ship of Odysseus. Then, bolder than the storied Cyclops, great Cthulhu slid greasily into the water and began to pursue with vast wave-raising strokes of cosmic potency. Briden looked back and went mad, laughing at intervals till death found him one night in the cabin whilst Johansen was wandering deliriously.

But Johansen had not given out yet. Knowing that the Thing could surely overtake the *Alert* until steam was fully up, he resolved on a desperate chance; and, setting the engine for full speed, ran lightning-like on deck and reversed the wheel. There was a mighty eddying and foaming in the noisome brine, and as the steam mounted higher and higher the brave Norwegian drove his vessel head on against the pursuing jelly which rose above the unclean froth like the stern of a demon galleon. The awful squid-head with writhing feelers came nearly up to the bowsprit of the sturdy yacht, but Johansen drove on relentlessly.

There was a bursting as of an exploding bladder, a slushy nastiness as of a cloven sunfish, a stench as of a thousand opened graves, and a sound that the chronicler would not put on paper. For an instant the ship was befouled by an acrid and blinding green cloud, and then there was only a venomous seething astern; where – God in heaven! – the scattered plasticity of that nameless sky-spawn was nebulously recombining in its hateful original form, whilst its distance widened every second as the *Alert* gained impetus from its mounting steam.

That was all. After that Johansen only brooded over the idol in the cabin and attended to a few matters of food for himself and the laughing maniac by his side. He did not try to navigate after the first bold flight; for the reaction had taken something out of his soul. Then came the storm of 2 April, and a gathering of the clouds about his consciousness. There is a sense of spectral whirling through liquid gulfs of infinity, of dizzying rides through reeling universes on a comet's tail, and of hysterical plunges from the pit to the moon and from the moon back again to the pit, all livened by a cachinnating chorus of the distorted, hilarious elder gods and the green, bat-winged mocking imps of Tartarus.

Out of that dream came rescue – the *Vigilant*, the vice-admiralty court, the streets of Dunedin, and the long voyage back home to the old house by the Egeberg. He could not tell – they would think him mad. He would write of what he knew before death came, but his wife must not guess. Death would be a boon if only it could blot out the memories.

That was the document I read, and now I have placed it in the tin box beside the bas-relief and the papers of Professor Angell. With it shall go this record of mine – this test of my own sanity, wherein is pieced together that which I hope may never be pieced together again. I have looked upon all that the universe has to hold of horror, and even the skies of spring and the flowers of summer must ever afterward be poison to me. But I do not think my life will be long. As my uncle went, as poor Johansen went, so shall I go. I know too much, and the cult still lives.

Cthulhu still lives, too, I suppose, again in that chasm of stone which has shielded him since the sun was young. His accursed city is sunken once more, for the *Vigilant* sailed over the spot after the April storm; but his ministers on earth still bellow and prance and play around idol-capped monoliths in lonely places. He must have been trapped by the sinking whilst within his black abyss, or else the world would by now be screaming with fright and frenzy. Who knows the end? What has risen may sink, and what has sunk may rise. Loathsomeness waits and dreams in the deep, and decay spreads over the tottering cities of men. A time will come – but I must not and cannot think! Let me pray that, if I do not survive this manuscript, my executors may put caution before audacity and see that it meets no other eye.

THE COLOUR OUT OF SPACE

West of Arkham the hills rise wild, and there are valleys with deep woods that no axe has ever cut. There are dark narrow glens where the trees slope fantastically, and where thin brooklets trickle without ever having caught the glint of sunlight. On the gentler slopes there are farms, ancient and rocky, with squat, moss-coated cottages brooding eternally over old New England secrets in the lee of great ledges; but these are all vacant now; the wide chimneys crumbling and the shingled sides bulging perilously beneath low gambrel roofs.

The old folk have gone away, and foreigners do not like to live there. French-Canadians have tried it, Italians have tried it, and the Poles have come and departed. It is not because of anything that can be seen or heard or handled, but because of something that is imagined. The place is not good for imagination, and does not bring restful dreams at night. It must be this which keeps the foreigners away, for old Ammi Pierce has never told them of anything he recalls from the strange days. Ammi, whose head has been a little queer for years, is the only one who still remains, or who ever talks of the strange days; and he dares to do this because his house is so near the open fields and the travelled roads around Arkham.

There was once a road over the hills and through the valleys, that ran straight where the blasted heath is now; but people ceased to use it and a new road was laid curving far toward the south. Traces of the old one can still be found amidst the weeds of a returning wilderness, and some of them will doubtless linger even when half the hollows are flooded for the new reservoir. Then the dark woods will be cut down and the blasted heath will slumber far below blue waters whose surface will mirror the sky and ripple in the sun. And the secrets of the strange days will be one with the deep's secrets; one with the hidden lore of old ocean, and all the mystery of primal earth.

When I went into the hills and vales to survey for the new reservoir they told me the place was evil. They told me this in Arkham, and because that is a very old town full of witch legends I thought the evil must be something which grandams had whispered to children through centuries. The name "blasted heath" seemed to me very odd and theatrical, and I wondered how it had come into the folklore of a Puritan people. Then I saw that dark westward tangle of glens and slopes for myself, and ceased to wonder at anything beside its own elder mystery. It was morning when I saw it, but shadow lurked always there. The trees grew too thickly, and their trunks were too big for any healthy New England wood. There was too much silence in the dim alleys between them, and the floor was too soft with the dank moss and mattings of infinite years of decay.

In the open spaces, mostly along the line of the old road, there were little hillside farms; sometimes with all the buildings standing, sometimes with only one or two, and sometimes with only a lone chimney or fast-filling cellar. Weeds and briers reigned, and furtive wild things rustled in the undergrowth. Upon every-thing was a haze of restlessness and oppression; a touch of the unreal and the grotesque, as if some vital element of perspective or chiaroscuro were awry. I did not wonder that the foreigners would not stay, for this was no region to sleep in. It was too much like a landscape of Salvator Rosa; too much like some forbidden wood-cut in a tale of terror.

But even all this was not so bad as the blasted heath. I knew it the moment I came upon it at the bottom of a spacious valley; for no other name could fit such a thing, or any other thing fit such a name. It was as if the poet had coined the phrase from having seen this one particular region. It must, I thought as I viewed it, be the outcome of a fire; but why had nothing new ever grown over those five acres of grey desolation that sprawled open to the sky like a great spot eaten by acid in the woods and fields? It lay largely to the north of the ancient road line, but encroached a little on the other side. I felt an odd reluctance about approaching, and did so at last only because my business took me through and past it. There was no vegetation of any kind on that broad expanse, but only a fine grey dust or ash which no wind seemed ever to blow about. The trees near it were sickly and stunted, and many dead trunks stood or lay rotting at the rim. As I walked hurriedly by I saw the tumbled bricks and stones of an old chimney and cellar on my right, and the yawning black maw of an abandoned well whose stagnant vapours played strange tricks with the hues of the sunlight. Even the long, dark woodland climb beyond seemed welcome in contrast, and I marvelled no more at the frightened whispers of Arkham people. There had been no house or ruin near; even in the old days the place must have been lonely and remote. And at twilight, dreading to repass that ominous spot, I walked circuitously back to the town by the curving road on the south. I vaguely wished some clouds would gather, for an odd timidity about the deep skyey voids above had crept into my soul.

In the evening I asked old people in Arkham about the blasted heath, and what was meant by that phrase "strange days" which so many evasively muttered. I could not, however, get any good answers, except that all the mystery was much more recent than I had dreamed. It was not a matter of old legendry at all, but something within the lifetime of those who spoke. It had happened in the 'eighties, and a family had disappeared or was killed. Speakers would not be exact; and because they all told me to pay no attention to old Ammi Pierce's crazy tales, I sought him out the next morning, having heard that he lived alone in the ancient tottering cottage where the trees first begin to get very thick. It was a fearsomely ancient place, and had begun to exude the faint miasmal odour which clings about houses that have stood too long. Only with persistent knocking could I rouse the aged man, and when he shuffled timidly to the door I could tell he was not glad to see me. He was not so feeble as I had expected; but his eyes drooped in a curious way, and his unkempt clothing and white beard made him seem very worn and dismal.

Not knowing just how he could best be launched on his tales, I feigned a matter of business; told him of my surveying, and asked vague questions about the district. He was far brighter and more educated than I had been led to think, and before I knew it had grasped quite as much of the subject as any man I had talked with in Arkham. He was not like other rustics I had known in the sections where reservoirs were to be. From him there were no protests at the miles of old wood and farmland to be blotted out, though perhaps there would have been had not his home lain outside the bounds of the future lake. Relief was all that he showed; relief at the doom of the dark ancient valleys through which he had roamed all his life. They were better under water now – better under water since the strange days. And with this opening his husky voice sank low, while his body leaned forward and his right forefinger began to point shakily and impressively.

It was then that I heard the story, and as the rambling voice scraped and whispered on I shivered again and again despite the summer day. Often I had to recall the speaker from ramblings, piece out scientific points which he knew only by a fading parrot memory of professors' talk, or bridge over gaps where his sense of logic and continuity broke down. When he was done I did not wonder that his mind had snapped a trifle, or that the folk of Arkham would not speak much of the blasted heath. I hurried back before sunset to my hotel, unwilling to have the stars come out above me in the open; and the next day returned to Boston to give up my position. I could not go into that dim chaos of old forest and slope again, or face another time that grey blasted heath where the black well yawned deep beside the tumbled bricks and stones. The reservoir will soon be built now, and all those elder secrets will be safe forever under watery fathoms. But even then I do not believe I would like to visit that country by night – at least not when the sinister stars are out; and nothing could bribe me to drink the new city water of Arkham.

It all began, old Ammi said, with the meteorite. Before that time there had been no wild legends at all since the witch trials, and even then these western woods were not feared half so much as the small island in the Miskatonic where the devil held court beside a curious stone altar older than the Indians. These were not haunted woods, and their fantastic dusk was never terrible till the strange days. Then there had come that white noontide cloud, that string of explosions in the air, and that pillar of smoke from the valley far in the wood. And by night all Arkham had heard of the great rock that fell out of the sky and bedded itself in the ground beside the well at the Nahum Gardner place. That was the house which had stood where the blasted heath was to come – the trim white Nahum Gardner house amidst its fertile gardens and orchards.

Nahum had come to town to tell people about the stone, and dropped in at Ammi Pierce's on the way. Ammi was forty then, and all the queer things were fixed very strongly in his mind. He and his wife had gone with the three professors from Miskatonic University who hastened out the next morning to see the weird visitor from unknown stellar space, and had wondered why Nahum had called it so large the day before. It had shrunk, Nahum said, as he pointed out the big brownish mound above the ripped earth and charred grass near the archaic well-sweep in his front yard; but the wise men answered that stones do not shrink. Its heat lingered persistently, and Nahum declared it had glowed faintly in the night. The professors tried it with a geologist's hammer and found it was oddly soft. It was, in truth, so soft as to be almost plastic; and they gouged rather than chipped a specimen to take back to the college for testing. They took it in an old pail borrowed from Nahum's kitchen, for even the small piece refused to grow cool. On the trip back they stopped at Ammi's to rest, and seemed thoughtful when Mrs Pierce remarked that the fragment was growing smaller and burning the bottom of the pail. Truly, it was not large, but perhaps they had taken less than they thought.

The day after that – all this was in June of '82 – the professors had trooped out again in a great excitement. As they passed Ammi's they told him what queer things the specimen had done, and how it had faded wholly away when they put it in a glass beaker. The beaker had gone, too, and the wise men talked of the strange stone's affinity for silicon. It had acted quite unbelievably in that well-ordered laboratory; doing nothing at all and showing no occluded gases when heated on charcoal, being wholly negative in the borax bead, and soon proving itself absolutely non-volatile at any producible temperature, including that of the oxy-hydrogen blowpipe. On an anvil it appeared highly malleable, and in the dark its luminosity was very marked. Stubbornly refusing to grow cool, it soon had the college in a state of real excitement; and when upon heating before the spectroscope it displayed shining bands unlike any known colours of the normal spectrum there was much breathless talk of new elements, bizarre optical properties, and other things which puzzled men of science are wont to say when faced by the unknown.

Hot as it was, they tested it in a crucible with all the proper reagents. Water did nothing. Hydrochloric acid was the same. Nitric acid and even aqua regia merely hissed and spattered against its torrid invulnerability. Ammi had difficulty in recalling all these things, but recognized some solvents as I mentioned them in the usual order of use. There were ammonia and caustic soda, alcohol and ether, nauseous carbon disulphide and a dozen others; but although the weight grew steadily less as time passed, and the fragment seemed to be slightly cooling, there was no change in the solvents to show that they had attacked the substance at all. It was a metal, though, beyond a doubt. It was magnetic, for one thing; and after its immersion in the acid solvents there seemed to be faint traces of the Widmänstätten figures found on meteoric iron. When the cooling had grown very considerable, the testing was carried on in glass; and it was in a glass beaker that they left all the chips made of the original fragment during the work. The next morning both chips and beaker were gone without trace, and only a charred spot marked the place on the wooden shelf where they had been.

All this the professors told Ammi as they paused at his door, and once more he went with them to see the stony messenger from the stars, though this time his wife did not accompany him. It had now most certainly shrunk, and even the sober professors could not doubt the truth of what they saw. All around the dwindling brown lump near the well was a vacant space, except where the earth had caved in; and whereas it had been a good seven feet across the day before, it was now scarcely five. It was still hot, and the sages studied its surface curiously as they detached another and larger piece with hammer and chisel. They gouged deeply this time, and as they pried away the smaller mass they saw that the core of the thing was not quite homogeneous.

They had uncovered what seemed to be the side of a large coloured globule embedded in the substance. The colour, which resembled some of the bands in the meteor's strange spectrum, was almost impossible to describe; and it was only by analogy that they called it colour at all. Its texture was glossy, and upon tapping it appeared to promise both brittleness and hollowness. One of the professors gave it a smart blow with a hammer, and it burst with a nervous little pop. Nothing was emitted, and all trace of the thing vanished with the puncturing. It left behind a hollow spherical space about three inches across, and all thought it probable that others would be discovered as the enclosing substance wasted away.

Conjecture was vain; so after a futile attempt to find additional globules by drilling, the seekers left again with their new specimen – which proved, however, as baffling in the laboratory as its predecessor. Aside from being almost plastic, having heat, magnetism, and slight luminosity, cooling slightly in powerful acids, possessing an unknown spectrum, wasting away in air, and attacking silicon compounds with mutual destruction as a result, it presented no identifying features whatsoever; and at the end of the tests the college scientists were forced to own that they could not place it. It was nothing of this earth, but a piece of the great outside; and as such dowered with outside properties and obedient to outside laws.

That night there was a thunderstorm, and when the professors went out to Nahum's the next day they met with a bitter disappointment. The stone, magnetic as it had been, must have had some peculiar electrical property; for it had "drawn the lightning", as Nahum said, with a singular persistence. Six times within an hour the farmer saw the lightning strike the furrow in the front yard, and when the storm was over nothing remained but a ragged pit by the ancient well-sweep, half-choked with a caved-in earth. Digging had borne no fruit, and the scientists verified the fact of the utter vanishment. The failure was total; so that nothing was left to do but go back to the laboratory and test again the disappearing fragment left carefully cased in lead. That fragment lasted a week, at the end of which nothing of value had been learned of it. When it had gone, no residue was left behind, and in time the professors felt scarcely sure they had indeed seen with waking eyes that cryptic vestige of the fathomless gulfs outside; that lone, weird message from other universes and other realms of matter, force, and entity.

As was natural, the Arkham papers made much of the incident with its collegiate sponsoring, and sent reporters to talk with Nahum Gardner and his family. At least one Boston daily also sent a scribe, and Nahum quickly became a kind of local celebrity. He was a lean, genial person of about fifty, living with his wife and three sons on the pleasant farmstead in the valley. He and Ammi exchanged visits frequently, as did their wives; and Ammi had nothing but praise for him after all these years. He seemed slightly proud of the notice his place had attracted, and talked often of the meteorite in the succeeding weeks. That July and August were hot; and Nahum worked hard at his haying in the ten-acre pasture across Chapman's Brook; his rattling wain wearing deep ruts in the shadowy lanes between. The labour tired him more than it had in other years, and he felt that age was beginning to tell on him.

Then fell the time of fruit and harvest. The pears and apples slowly ripened, and Nahum vowed that his orchards were prospering as never before. The fruit was growing to phenomenal size and unwonted gloss, and in such abundance that extra barrels were ordered to handle the future crop. But with the ripening came sore disappointment, for of all that gorgeous array of specious lusciousness not one single jot was fit to eat. Into the fine flavour of the pears and apples had crept a stealthy bitterness and sickishness, so that even the smallest bites induced a lasting disgust. It was the same with the melons and tomatoes, and Nahum sadly saw that his entire crop was lost. Quick to connect events, he declared that the meteorite had poisoned the soil, and thanked Heaven that most of the other crops were in the upland lot along the road.

Winter came early, and was very cold. Ammi saw Nahum less often than usual, and observed that he had begun to look worried. The rest of his family too, seemed to have grown taciturn; and were far from steady in their church-going or their attendance at the various social events of the countryside. For this reserve or melancholy no cause could be found, though all the household confessed now and then to poorer health and a feeling of vague disquiet. Nahum himself gave the most definite statement of anyone when he said he was disturbed about certain footprints in the snow. They were the usual winter prints of red squirrels, white rabbits, and foxes, but the brooding farmer professed to see something not quite right about their nature and arrangement. He was never specific, but appeared to think that they were not as characteristic of the anatomy and habits of squirrels and rabbits and foxes as they ought to be. Ammi listened without interest to this talk until one night when he drove past Nahum's house in his sleigh on the way back from Clark's Corners. There had been a moon, and a rabbit had run across the road, and the leaps of that rabbit were longer than either Ammi or his horse liked. The latter, indeed, had almost run away when brought up by a firm rein. Thereafter Ammi gave Nahum's tales more respect, and wondered why the Gardner dogs seemed so cowed and quivering every morning. They had, it developed, nearly lost the spirit to bark.

In February the McGregor boys from Meadow Hill were out shooting wood-chucks, and not far from the Gardner place bagged a very peculiar specimen. The proportions of its body seemed slightly altered in a queer way impossible to describe, while its face had taken on an expression which no-one ever saw in a woodchuck before. The boys were genuinely frightened, and threw the thing away at once, so that only their grotesque tales of it ever reached the people of the countryside. But the shying of horses near Nahum's house had now become an acknowledged thing, and all the basis for a cycle of whispered legend was fast taking form.

People vowed that the snow melted faster around Nahum's than it did anywhere else, and early in March there was an awed discussion in Potter's general store at Clark's Corners. Stephen Rice had driven past Gardner's in the morning, and had noticed the skunk-cabbages coming up through the mud by the woods across the road. Never were things of such size seen before, and they held strange colours that could not be put into any words. Their shapes were monstrous, and the horse had snorted at an odour which struck Stephen as wholly unprecedented. That afternoon several persons drove past to see the abnormal growth, and all agreed that plants of that kind ought never to sprout in a healthy world. The bad fruit of the fall before was freely mentioned, and it went from mouth to mouth that there was poison in Nahum's ground. Of course it was the meteorite; and remembering how strange the men from the college had found that stone to be, several farmers spoke about the matter to them.

One day they paid Nahum a visit; but having no love of wild tales and folklore were very conservative in what they inferred. The plants were certainly odd, but all skunk-cabbages are more or less odd in shape and hue. Perhaps some mineral element from the stone had entered the soil, but it would soon be washed away. And as for the footprints and frightened horses – of course this was mere country talk which such a phenomenon as the aerolite would be certain to start. There was really nothing for serious men to do in cases of wild gossip, for superstitious rustics will say and believe anything. And so all through the strange days the professors stayed away in contempt. Only one of them, when given two phials of dust for analysis in a police job over a year and a half later, recalled that the queer colour of that skunk-cabbage had been very like one of the anomalous bands of light shown by the meteor fragment in the college spectroscope, and like the brittle globule found imbedded in the stone from the abyss. The samples in this analysis case gave the same odd bands at first, though later they lost the property.

The trees budded prematurely around Nahum's, and at night they swayed ominously in the wind. Nahum's second son Thaddeus, a lad of fifteen, swore that they swayed also when there was no wind; but even the gossips would not credit this. Certainly, however, restlessness was in the air. The entire Gardner family developed the habit of stealthy listening, though not for any sound which they could consciously name. The listening was, indeed, rather a product of moments when consciousness seemed half to slip away. Unfortunately such moments increased week by week, till it became common speech that "something was wrong with all Nahum's folks". When the early saxifrage came out it had another strange colour; not quite that of the skunk-cabbage, but plainly related and equally unknown to anyone who saw it. Nahum took some blossoms to Arkham and showed them to the editor of the *Gazette*, but that dignitary did no more than write a humorous article about them, in which the dark fears of rustics were held up to polite ridicule. It was a mistake of Nahum's to tell a stolid city man about the way the great, overgrown mourning-cloak butterflies behaved in connection with these saxifrages.

April brought a kind of madness to the country folk, and began that disuse of the road past Nahum's which led to its ultimate abandonment. It was the vegetation. All the orchard trees blossomed forth in strange colours, and through the stony soil of the yard and adjacent pasturage there sprang up a bizarre growth which only a botanist could connect with the proper flora of the region. No sane wholesome colours were anywhere to be seen except in the green grass and leafage; but everywhere were those hectic and prismatic variants of some diseased, underlying primary tone without a place among the known tints of earth. The "Dutchman's breeches" became a thing of sinister menace, and the bloodroots grew insolent in their chromatic perversion. Ammi and the Gardners thought that most of the colours had a sort of haunting familiarity, and decided that they reminded one of the brittle globule in the meteor. Nahum ploughed and sowed the ten-acre pasture and the upland lot, but did nothing with the land around the house. He knew it would be of no use, and hoped that the summer's strange growths would draw all the poison from the soil. He was prepared for almost anything now, and had grown used to the sense of something near him waiting to be heard. The shunning of his house by neighbours told on him, of course; but it told on his wife more. The boys were better off, being at school each day; but they could not help being frightened by the gossip.

Thaddeus, an especially sensitive youth, suffered the most.

In May the insects came, and Nahum's place became a nightmare of buzzing and crawling. Most of the creatures seemed not quite usual in their aspects and motions, and their nocturnal habits contradicted all former experience. The Gardners took to watching at night – watching in all directions at random for something – they could not tell what. It was then that they all owned that Thaddeus had been right about the trees. Mrs Gardner was the next to see it from the window as she watched the swollen boughs of a maple against a moonlit sky. The boughs surely moved, and there was no wind. It must be the sap. Strangeness had come into everything growing now. Yet it was none of Nahum's family at all who made the next discovery. Familiarity had dulled them, and what they could not see was glimpsed by a timid windmill salesman from Bolton who drove by one night in ignorance of the country legends. What he told in Arkham was given a short paragraph in the *Gazette*; and it was there that all the farmers, Nahum included, saw it first. The night had been dark and the buggy-lamps faint, but around a farm in the valley which everyone knew from the account must be Nahum's, the darkness had been less thick. A dim though distinct luminosity seemed to inhere in all the vegetation, grass, leaves, and blossoms alike, while at one moment a detached piece of the phosphorescence appeared to stir furtively in the yard near the barn.

The grass had so far seemed untouched, and the cows were freely pastured in the lot near the house, but towards the end of May the milk began to be bad. Then Nahum had the cows driven to the uplands, after which this trouble ceased. Not long after this the change in grass and leaves became apparent to the eye. All the verdure was going grey, and was developing a highly singular quality of brittleness. Ammi was now the only person who ever visited the place, and his visits were becoming fewer and fewer. When school closed the Gardners were virtually cut off from the world, and sometimes let Ammi do their errands in town. They were failing curiously both physically and mentally, and no-one was surprised when the news of Mrs Gardner's madness stole around.

It happened in June, about the anniversary of the meteor's fall, and the poor woman screamed about things in the air which she could not describe. In her raving there was not a single specific noun, but only verbs and pronouns. Things moved and changed and fluttered, and ears tingled to impulses which were not wholly sounds. Something was taken away – she was being drained of something – some-thing was fastening itself on her that ought not to be – someone must make it keep off – nothing was ever still in the night – the walls and windows shifted. Nahum did not send her to the county asylum, but let her wander about the house as long as she was harmless to herself and others. Even when her expression changed he did nothing. But when the boys grew afraid of her, and Thaddeus nearly fainted at the way she made faces at him, he decided to keep her locked in the attic. By July she had ceased to speak and crawled on all fours, and before that month was over Nahum got the mad notion that she was slightly luminous in the dark, as he now clearly saw was the case with the nearby vegetation.

It was a little before this that the horses had stampeded. Something had aroused them in the night, and their neighing and kicking in their stalls had been terrible. There seemed virtually nothing to do to calm them, and when Nahum opened the stable door they all bolted out like frightened woodland deer. It took a week to track all four, and when found they were seen to be quite useless and unmanageable. Something had snapped in their brains, and each one had to be shot for its own good. Nahum borrowed a horse from Ammi for his haying, but found it would not approach the barn. It shied, balked, and whinnied, and in the end he could do nothing but drive it into the yard while the men used their own strength to get the heavy wagon near enough the hayloft for convenient pitching. And all the while the vegetation was turning grey and brittle. Even the flowers whose hues had been so strange were greying now, and the fruit was coming out grey and dwarfed and tasteless. The asters and goldenrod bloomed grey and distorted, and the roses and zinnias and hollyhocks in the front yard were such blasphemous-looking things that Nahum's oldest boy Zenas cut them down. The strangely puffed insects died about that time, even the bees that had left their hives and taken to the woods.

By September all the vegetation was fast crumbling to a greyish powder, and Nahum feared that the trees would die before the poison was out of the soil. His wife now had spells of terrific screaming, and he and the boys were in a constant state of nervous tension. They shunned people now, and when school opened the boys did not go. But it was Ammi, on one of his rare visits, who first realized that the well water was no longer good. It had an evil taste that was not exactly foetid nor exactly salty, and Ammi advised his friend to dig another well on higher ground to use till the soil was good again. Nahum, however, ignored the warning, for he had by that time become calloused to strange and unpleasant things. He and the boys continued to use the tainted supply, drinking it as listlessly and mechanically as they ate their meagre and ill-cooked meals and did their thankless and monotonous chores through the aimless days. There was something of stolid resignation about them all, as if they walked half in another world between lines of nameless guards to a certain and familiar doom.

Thaddeus went mad in September after a visit to the well. He had gone with a pail and had come back empty-handed, shrieking and waving his arms, and sometimes lapsing into an inane titter or a whisper about "the moving colours down there." Two in one family was pretty bad, but Nahum was very brave about it. He let the boy run about for a week until he began stumbling and hurting himself, and then he shut him in an attic room across the hall from his mother's. The way they screamed at each other from behind their locked doors was very terrible, especially to little Merwin, who fancied they talked in some terrible language that was not of earth. Merwin was getting frightfully imaginative, and his restlessness was worse after the shutting away of the brother who had been his greatest playmate.

Almost at the same time the mortality among the livestock commenced. Poultry turned greyish and died very quickly, their meat being found dry and noisome upon cutting. Hogs grew inordinately fat, then suddenly began to undergo loathsome changes which no-one could explain. Their meat was of course useless, and Nahum was at his wits' end. No rural veterinary would approach his place, and the city veterinary from Arkham was openly baffled. The swine began growing grey and brittle and falling to pieces before they died, and their eyes and muzzles developed singular alterations. It was very inexplicable, for they had never been fed from the tainted vegetation. Then some-thing struck the cows. Certain areas or sometimes the whole body would be uncannily shrivelled or compressed, and atrocious collapses or disintegrations were common. In the last stages – and death was always the result – there would be a greying and turning brittle like that which beset the hogs. There could be no question of poison, for all the cases occurred in a locked and undisturbed barn. No bites of prowling things could have brought the virus, for what live beast of earth can pass through solid obstacles? It must be only natural disease – yet what disease could wreak such results was beyond any mind's guessing. When the harvest came there was not an animal surviving on the place, for the stock and poultry were dead and the dogs had run away. These dogs, three in number, had all vanished one night and were never heard of again. The five cats had left some time before, but their going was scarcely noticed since there now seemed to be no mice, and only Mrs Gardner had made pets of the graceful felines.

On the nineteenth of October Nahum staggered into Ammi's house with hideous news. The death had come to poor Thaddeus in his attic room, and it had come in a way which could not be told. Nahum had dug a grave in the railed family plot behind the farm, and had put therein what he found. There could have been nothing from outside, for the small barred window and locked door were intact; but it was much as it had been in the barn. Ammi and his wife consoled the stricken man as best as they could, but shuddered as they did so. Stark terror seemed to cling round the Gardners and all they touched, and the very presence of one in the house was a breath from regions unnamed and unnameable. Ammi accom-panied Nahum home with the greatest reluctance, and did what he might to calm the hysterical sobbing of little Merwin. Zenas needed no calming. He had come of late to do nothing but stare into space and obey what his father told him; and Ammi thought that his fate was very merciful. Now and then Merwin's screams were answered faintly from the attic, and in response to an inquiring look Nahum said that his wife was getting very feeble. When night approached, Ammi managed to get away; for not even friendship could make him stay in that spot when the faint glow of the vegetation began and the trees may or may not have swayed without wind. It was really lucky for Ammi that he was not more imaginative. Even as things were, his mind was bent ever so slightly; but had he been able to connect and reflect upon all the portents around him he must inevitably have turned a total maniac. In the twilight he hastened home, the screams of the mad woman and the nervous child ringing horribly in his ears.

Three days later Nahum burst into Ammi's kitchen in the early morning, and in the absence of his host stammered out a desperate tale once more, while Mrs Pierce listened in a clutching fright. It was little Merwin this time. He was gone. He had gone out late at night with a lantern and pail for water, and had never come back. He'd been going to pieces for days, and hardly knew what he was about. Screamed at everything. There had been a frantic shriek from the yard then, but before the father could get to the door the boy was gone. There was no glow from the lantern he had taken, and of the child himself no trace. At the time Nahum thought the lantern and pail were gone too; but when dawn came, and the man had plodded back from his all-night search of the woods and fields, he had found some very curious things near the well. There was a crushed and apparently somewhat melted mass of iron which had certainly been the lantern; while a bent handle and twisted iron hoops beside it, both half-fused, seemed to hint at the remnants of the pail. That was all. Nahum was past imagining, Mrs Pierce was blank, and Ammi, when he had reached home and heard the tale, could give no guess. Merwin was gone, and there would be no use in telling the people around, who shunned all Gardners now. No use, either, in telling the city people at Arkham who laughed at everything. Thad was gone, and now Merwin was gone. Something was creeping and creeping and waiting to be seen and heard. Nahum would go soon, and he wanted Ammi to look after his wife and Zenas if they survived him. It must all be a judgment of some sort; though he could not fancy what for, since he had always walked uprightly in the Lord's ways so far as he knew.

For over two weeks Ammi saw nothing of Nahum; and then, worried about what might have happened, he overcame his fears and paid the Gardner place a visit. There was no smoke from the great chimney, and for a moment the visitor was apprehensive of the worst. The aspect of the whole farm was shocking – greyish withered grass and leaves on the ground, vines falling in brittle wreckage from archaic walls and gables, and great bare trees clawing up at the grey November sky with a studied malevolence which Ammi could not but feel had come from some subtle change in the tilt of the branches. But Nahum was alive, after all. He was weak, and lying on a couch in the low-ceilinged kitchen, but perfectly conscious and able to give simple orders to Zenas. The room was deadly cold; and as Ammi visibly shivered, the host shouted huskily to Zenas for more wood. Wood, indeed, was sorely needed; since the cavernous fireplace was unlit and empty, with a cloud of soot blowing about in the chill wind that came down the chimney. Presently Nahum asked him if the extra wood had made him any more comfort-able, and then Ammi saw what had happened. The stoutest cord had broken at last, and the hapless farmer's mind was proof against more sorrow.

Questioning tactfully, Ammi could get no clear data at all about the missing Zenas. "In the well – he lives in the well" was all that the clouded father would say. Then there flashed across the visitor's mind a sudden thought of the mad wife, and he changed his line of inquiry. "Nabby? Why, here she is!" was the surprised response of poor Nahum, and Ammi soon saw that he must search for himself. Leaving the harmless babbler on the couch, he took the keys from their nail beside the door and climbed the creaking stairs to the attic. It was very close and noisome up there, and no sound could be heard from any direction. Of the four doors in sight only one was locked, and on this he tried various keys of the ring he had taken. The third key proved the right one, and after some fumbling Ammi threw open the low white door.

It was quite dark inside, for the window was small and half-obscured by the crude wooden bars; and Ammi could see nothing at all on the wide-planked floor. The stench was beyond enduring, and before proceeding further he had to retreat to another room and return with his lungs filled with breathable air. When he did enter he saw something dark in the corner, and upon seeing it more clearly he screamed outright. While he screamed he thought a momentary cloud eclipsed the window, and a second later he felt himself brushed as if by some hateful current of vapour. Strange colours danced before his eyes; and had not a present horror numbed him he would have thought of the globule in the meteor that the geologist's hammer had shattered, and of the morbid vegetation that had sprouted in the spring. As it was he thought only of the blasphemous monstrosity which confronted him, and which all too clearly had shared the nameless fate of young Thaddeus and the livestock. But the terrible thing about the horror was that it very slowly and perceptibly moved as it continued to crumble.

Ammi would give me no added particulars of this scene, but the shape in the corner does not reappear in his tale as a moving object. There are things which cannot be mentioned, and what is done in common humanity is sometimes cruelly judged by the law. I gathered that no moving thing was left in that attic room, and that to leave anything capable of motion there would have been a deed so monstrous as to damn any accountable being to eternal torment. Anyone but a stolid farmer would have fainted or gone mad, but Ammi walked conscious through that low doorway and locked the accursed secret behind him. There would be Nahum to deal with now; he must be fed and tended, and removed to some place where he could be cared for.

Commencing his descent of the dark stairs, Ammi heard a thud below him. He even thought a scream had been suddenly choked off, and recalled nervously the clammy vapour which had brushed by him in that frightful room above. What presence had his cry and entry started up? Halted by some vague fear, he heard still further sounds below. Indubitably there was a sort of heavy dragging, and a most detestably sticky noise as of some fiendish and unclean species of suction. With an associative sense goaded to feverish heights, he thought unaccountably of what he had seen upstairs. Good God! What eldritch dream-world was this into which he had blundered? He dared move neither backward nor forward, but stood there trembling at the black curve of the boxed-in staircase. Every trifle of the scene burned itself into his brain. The sounds, the sense of dread expectancy, the darkness, the steepness of the narrow steps – and merciful Heaven! – the faint but unmistakable luminosity of all the woodwork in sight; steps, sides, exposed laths, and beams alike.

Then there burst forth a frantic whinny from Ammi's horse outside, followed at once by a clatter which told of a frenzied runaway. In another moment horse and buggy had gone beyond earshot, leaving the frightened man on the dark stairs to guess what had sent them. But that was not all. There had been another sound out there. A sort of liquid splash – water – it must have been the well. He had left Hero untied near it, and a buggy-wheel must have brushed the coping and knocked in a stone. And still the pale phosphorescence glowed in that detestably ancient wood-work. God! how old the house was! Most of it built before 1670, and the gambrel roof no later than 1730.

A feeble scratching on the floor downstairs now sounded distinctly, and Ammi's grip tightened on a heavy stick he had picked up in the attic for some purpose. Slowly nerving himself, he finished his descent and walked boldly toward the kitchen. But he did not complete the walk, because what he sought was no longer there. It had come to meet him, and it was still alive after a fashion. Whether it had crawled or whether it had been dragged by any external forces, Ammi could not say; but the death had been at it. Everything had happened in the last half-hour, but collapse, greying, and disintegration were already far advanced. There was a horrible brittleness, and dry fragments were scaling off. Ammi could not touch it, but looked horrifiedly into the distorted parody that had been a face. "What was it, Nahum – what was it?" he whispered, and the cleft, bulging lips were just able to crackle out a final answer.

"Nothin'... nothin'... the colour... it burns... cold an' wet, but it burns... it lived in the well... I seen it... a kind of smoke... jest like the flowers last spring... the well shone at night... Thad an' Merwin an' Zenas... everything alive... suckin' the life out of everything... in that stone... it must a' come in that stone... pizened the whole place... dun't know what it wants... that round thing them men from the college dug outen the stone... they smashed it... it was that same colour... jest the same, like the flowers an' plants... must a' ben more of 'em... seeds... seeds... they growed... I seen it the fust time this week... must a' got strong on Zenas... he was a big boy, full o' life... it beats down your mind an' then gets ye... burns ye up... in the well water... you was right about that... evil water... Zenas never come back from the well... can't git away... draws ye... ye know summ'at's comin' but tain't no use... I seen it time an' agin senct Zenas was took... whar's Nabby, Ammi?... my head's no good... dun't know how long since I fed her... it'll git her ef we ain't keerful... jest a colour... her face is gittin' to hev that colour sometimes towards night... an' it burns an sucks... it come from some place whar things ain't as they is here... one o' them professors said so... he was right... look out, Ammi,

231

it'll do suthin' more... sucks the life out..."

But that was all. That which spoke could speak no more because it had completely caved in. Ammi laid a red checked tablecloth over what was left and reeled out the back door into the fields. He climbed the slope to the ten-acre pasture and stumbled home by the north road and the woods. He could not pass that well from which his horses had run away. He had looked at it through the window, and had seen that no stone was missing from the rim. Then the lurching buggy had not dislodged anything after all – the splash had been something else – something which went into the well after it had done with poor Nahum...

When Ammi reached his house the horses and buggy had arrived before him and thrown his wife into fits of anxiety. Reassuring her without explanations, he set out at once for Arkham and notified the authorities that the Gardner family was no more. He indulged in no details, but merely told of the deaths of Nahum and Nabby, that of Thaddeus being already known, and mentioned that the cause seemed to be the same strange ailment which had killed the live-stock. He also stated that Merwin and Zenas had dis-appeared. There was considerable questioning at the police station, and in the end Ammi was compelled to take three officers to the Gardner farm, together with the coroner, the medical examiner, and the veterinary who had treated the diseased animals. He went much against his will, for the afternoon was advancing and he feared the fall of night over that accursed place, but it was some comfort to have so many people with him.

The six men drove out in a democrat-wagon, following Ammi's buggy, and arrived at the pest-ridden farmhouse about four o'clock. Used as the officers were to gruesome experiences, not one remained unmoved at what was found in the attic and under the red checked tablecloth on the floor below. The whole aspect of the farm with its grey desolation was terrible enough, but those two crumbling objects were beyond all bounds. No-one could look long at them, and even the medical examiner admitted that there was very little to examine. Specimens could be analysed, of course, so he busied himself in obtaining them – and here it develops that a very puzzling aftermath occurred at the college laboratory where the two phials of dust were finally taken. Under the spectroscope both samples gave off an unknown spectrum, in which many of the baffling bands were precisely like those which the strange meteor had yielded in the previous year. The property of emitting this spectrum vanished in a month, the dust thereafter consisting mainly of alkaline phosphates and carbonates.

Ammi would not have told the men about the well if he had thought they meant to do anything then and there. It was getting toward sunset, and he was anxious to be away. But he could not help glancing nervously at the stony kerb by the great sweep, and when a detective questioned him he admitted that Nahum had feared something down there – so much so that he had never even thought of searching it for Merwin or Zenas. After that nothing would do but that they empty and explore the well immediately, so Ammi had to wait trembling while pail after pail of rank water was hauled up and splashed on the soaking ground outside. The men sniffed in disgust at the fluid, and toward the last held their noses against the foetor they were uncovering. It was not so long a job as they had feared it would be, since the water was phenomenally low. There is no need to speak too exactly of what they found. Merwin and Zenas were both there, in part, though the vestiges were mainly skeletal. There were also a small deer and a large dog in about the same state, and a number of bones of small animals. The ooze and slime at the bottom seemed inexplicably porous and bubbling, and a man who descended on hand-holds with a long pole found that he could sink the wooden shaft to any depth in the mud of the floor without meeting any solid obstruction.

Twilight had now fallen, and lanterns were brought from the house. Then, when it was seen that nothing further could be gained from the well, everyone went indoors and conferred in the ancient sitting-room while the intermittent light of a spectral half-moon played wanly on the grey desolation outside. The men were frankly nonplussed by the entire case, and could find no convincing common element to link the strange vegetable conditions, the unknown disease of live-stock and humans, and the unaccountable deaths of Merwin and Zenas in the tainted well. They had heard the common country talk, it is true; but could not believe that anything contrary to natural law had occurred. No doubt the meteor had poisoned the soil, but the illness of persons and animals who had eaten nothing grown in that soil was another matter. Was it the well water? Very possibly. It might be a good idea to analyse it. But what peculiar madness could have made both boys jump into the well? Their deeds were so similar – and the fragments showed that they had both suffered from the grey brittle death. Why was everything so grey and brittle?

It was the coroner, seated near a window overlooking the yard, who first noticed the glow about the well. Night had fully set in, and all the abhorrent grounds seemed faintly luminous with more than the fitful moonbeams; but this new glow was something definite and distinct, and appeared to shoot up from the black pit like a softened ray from a searchlight, giving dull reflections in the little ground pools where the water had been emptied. It had a very queer colour, and as all the men clustered round the window Ammi gave a violent start. For this strange beam of ghastly miasma was to him of no unfamiliar hue. He had seen that colour before, and feared to think what it might mean. He had seen it in the nasty brittle globule in that aerolite two summers ago, had seen it in the crazy vegetation of the springtime, and had thought he had seen it for an instant that very morning against the small barred window of that terrible attic room where nameless things had happened. It had flashed there a second, and a clammy and hateful current of vapour had brushed past him – and then poor Nahum had been taken by something of that colour. He had said so at the last – said it was like the globule and the plants. After that had come the runaway in the yard and the splash in the well – and now that well was belching forth to the night a pale insidious beam of the same demoniac tint.

It does credit to the alertness of Ammi's mind that he puzzled even at that tense moment over a point which was essentially scientific. He could not but wonder at his gleaning of the same impression from a vapour glimpsed in the daytime, against a window opening on the morning sky, and from a nocturnal exhalation seen as a phosphorescent mist against the black and blasted landscape. It wasn't right – it was against Nature – and he thought of those terrible last words of his stricken friend, "It come from some place whar things ain't as they is here... one o' them professors said so..."

All three horses outside, tied to a pair of shrivelled saplings by the road, were now neighing and pawing frantically. The wagon driver started for the door to do something, but Ammi laid a shaky hand on his shoulder. "Duon't go out thar," he whispered. "They's more to this nor what we know. Nahum said somethin' lived in the well that sucks your life out. He said it must be some'at growed from a round ball like one we all seen in the meteor stone that fell a year ago June. Sucks an' burns, he said, an' is jest a cloud of colour like that light out thar now, that ye can hardly see an' can't tell what it is. Nahum thought it feeds on everything livin' an' gits stronger all the time. He said he seen it this last week. It must be somethin' from away off in the sky like the men from the college last year says the meteor stone was. The way it's made an' the way it works ain't like no way o' God's world. It's summ'at from beyond."

So the men paused indecisively as the light from the well grew stronger and the hitched horses pawed and whinnied in increasing frenzy. It was truly an awful moment; with terror in that ancient and accursed house itself, four monstrous sets of fragments – two from the house and two from the well – in the woodshed behind, and that shaft of unknown and unholy iridescence from the slimy depths in front. Ammi had restrained the driver on impulse, forgetting how uninjured he himself was after the clammy brushing of that coloured vapour in the attic room, but perhaps it is just as well that he acted as he did. No-one will ever know what was abroad that night; and though the blasphemy from beyond had not so far hurt any human of unweakened mind, there is no telling what it might not have done at that last moment, with its seemingly increased strength and the special signs of purpose it was soon to display beneath the half-clouded moonlit sky.

All at once one of the detectives at the window gave a short, sharp gasp. The others looked at him, and then quickly followed his own gaze upward to the point at which its idle straying had suddenly arrested. There was no need for words. What had been disputed in country gossip was disputable no longer, and it is because of the thing which every man of that party agreed in whispering later on, that the strange days are never talked about in Arkham. It is necessary to premise that there was no wind at that hour of the evening. One did arise not long afterward, but there was absolutely none then. Even the dry tips of the lingering hedge-mustard, grey and blighted, and the fringe on the roof of the standing democrat-wagon were unstirred. And yet amid that tense, godless calm the high bare boughs of all the trees in the yard were moving. They were twitching morbidly and spasmodically, clawing in convulsive and epileptic madness at the moonlit clouds; scratching impotently in the noxious air as if jerked by some allied and bodiless line of linkage with subterrene writhing and struggling below the black roots.

Not a man breathed for several seconds. Then a cloud of darker depth passed over the moon, and the silhouette of clutching branches faded out momentarily. At this there was a general cry; muffled with awe, but husky and almost identical from every throat. For the terror had not faded with the silhouette, and in a fearsome instant of deeper darkness the watchers saw wriggling at that tree-top height a thousand tiny points of faint and unhallowed radiance, tipping each bough like the fire of St Elmo or the flames that come down on the apostles' heads at Pentecost. It was a monstrous constellation of unnatural light, like a glutted swarm of corpse-fed fireflies dancing hellish sarabands over an accursed marsh; and its colour was that same nameless intrusion which Ammi had come to recognize and dread. All the while the shaft of phosphorescence from the well was getting brighter and brighter, bringing, to the minds of the huddled men, a sense of doom and abnormality. It was no longer *shining* out; it was *pouring* out; and as the shapeless stream of unplaceable colour left the well it seemed to flow directly into the sky.

The veterinary shivered, and walked to the front door to drop the heavy extra bar across it. Ammi shook no less, and had to tug and point for lack of controllable voice when he wished to draw notice to the growing luminosity of the trees. The neighing and stamping of the horses had become utterly frightful, but not a soul of that group in the old house would have ventured forth for any earthly reward. With the moments the shining of the trees increased, while their restless branches seemed to strain more and more toward verticality. The wood of the well-sweep was shining now, and presently a police-man dumbly pointed to some wooden sheds and bee-hives near the stone wall on the west. They were commencing to shine, too, though the tethered vehicles of the visitors seemed so far unaffected. Then there was a wild commotion and clopping in the road, and as Ammi quenched the lamp for better seeing they realized that the span of frantic greys had broken their sapling and run off with the democrat-wagon.

The shock served to loosen several tongues, and embarrassed whispers were exchanged. "It spreads on everything organic that's been around here," muttered the medical examiner. No-one replied, but the man who had been in the well gave a hint that his long pole must have stirred up something intangible. "It was awful," he added. "There was no bottom at all, just ooze and bubbles and the feeling of something lurking under there." Ammi's horse still pawed and screamed deafeningly in the road outside, and nearly drowned its owner's faint quaver as he mumbled his formless reflections. "It come from that stone – it growed down thar – it got everything livin' – it fed itself on 'em, mind and body – Thad an' Merwin, Zenas an' Nabby – Nahum was the last – they all drunk the water – it got strong on 'em – it come from beyond, what things ain't like they be here – now it's goin' home—"

At this point, as the column of unknown colour flared suddenly stronger and stronger and began to weave itself into fantastic suggestions of shape which each spectator later described differently, there came from poor tethered Hero such a sound as no man before or since ever heard from a horse. Every person in that low-pitched sitting room stopped his ears, and Ammi turned away from the window in horror and nausea. Words could not convey it – when Ammi looked again the hapless beast lay huddled inert on the moonlit round between the splintered shafts of the buggy. That was the last of Hero till they buried him the next day. But the present was no time to mourn, for almost at this instant a detective silently called attention to something terrible in the very

236

room with them. In the absence of the lamplight it was clear that a faint phosphorescence had begun to pervade the entire apartment. It glowed on the broad-planked floor and the fragment of rag carpet, and shimmered over the sashes of the small-paned windows. It ran up and down the exposed corner-posts, coruscated about the shelf and mantel, and infected the very doors and furniture. Each minute saw it strengthen, and at last it was very plain that healthy living things must leave that house.

Ammi showed them the back door and the path up through the fields to the ten-acre pasture. They walked and stumbled as in a dream, and did not dare look back till they were far away on the high ground. They were glad of the path, for they could not have gone the front way, by that well. It was bad enough passing the glowing barn and sheds, and those shining orchard trees with their gnarled, fiendish contours; but thank Heaven the branches did their worst twisting high up. The moon went under some very black clouds as they crossed the rustic bridge over Chapman's Brook, and it was blind groping from there to the open meadows.

When they looked back toward the valley and the distant Gardner place at the bottom they saw a fearsome sight. All the farm was shining with the hideous unknown blend of colour: trees, buildings, and even such grass and herbage as had not been wholly changed to lethal grey brittleness. The boughs were all straining skyward, tipped with tongues of foul flame, and lambent tricklings of the same monstrous fire were creeping about the ridgepoles of the house, barn and sheds. It was a scene from a vision of Fuseli, and over all the rest reigned that riot of luminous amorphousness, that alien and undimensioned rainbow of cryptic poison from the well – seething, feeling, lapping, reaching, scintillating, straining, and malignly bubbling in its cosmic and unrecognizable chromaticism.

Then without warning the hideous thing shot vertically up toward the sky like a rocket or meteor, leaving behind no trail and disappearing through a round and curiously regular hole in the clouds before any man could gasp or cry out. No watcher can ever forget that sight, and Ammi stared blankly at the stars of Cygnus, Deneb twinkling above the others, where the unknown colour had melted into the Milky Way. But his gaze was the next moment called swiftly to earth by the crackling in the valley. It was just that. Only a wooden ripping and crackling, and not an explosion, as so many others of the party vowed. Yet the outcome was the same, for in one feverish kaleidoscopic instant there burst up from that doomed and accursed farm a gleaming eruptive cataclysm of unnatural sparks and substance; blurring the glance of the few who saw it, and sending forth to the zenith a bombarding cloudburst of such coloured and fantastic fragments as our universe must needs disown. Through quickly re-closing vapours they followed the great morbidity that had vanished, and in another second they had vanished too. Behind and below was only a darkness to which the men dared not return, and all about was a mounting wind which seemed to sweep down in black, frore gusts from interstellar space. It shrieked and howled, and lashed the fields and distorted woods in a mad cosmic frenzy, till soon the trembling party realized it would be no use waiting for the moon to show what was left down there at Nahum's.

Too awed even to hint theories, the seven shaking men trudged back toward Arkham by the north road. Ammi was worse than his fellows, and begged them to see him inside his own kitchen, instead of keeping straight on to town. He did not wish to cross the blighted wind-whipped woods alone to his home on the main road. For he had had an added shock that the others were spared, and was crushed forever with a brooding fear he dared not even mention for many years to come. As the rest of the watchers on that tempestuous hill had stolidly set their faces toward the road, Ammi had looked back in an instant at the shadowed valley of desolation so lately sheltering his ill-starred friend. And from that stricken, faraway spot he had seen something feebly rise only to sink down again upon the place from which the great shapeless horror had shot into the sky. It was just a colour – but not any colour of our earth or heavens. And because Ammi recognized that colour, and knew that this last faint remnant must still lurk down there in the well, he has never been quite right since.

Ammi could never go near the place again. It is forty-four years now since the horror happened, but he has never been there, and will be glad when the new reservoir blots it out. I shall be glad, too, for I do not like the way the sunlight changed colour around the mouth of that abandoned well I passed. I hope the water will always be very deep – but even so, I shall never drink it. I do not think I shall visit the Arkham country hereafter. Three of the men who had been with Ammi returned the next morning to see the ruins by daylight, but there were not any real ruins. Only the bricks of the chimney, the stones of the cellar, some mineral and metallic litter here and there, and the rim of that nefandous well. Save for Ammi's dead horse, which they towed away and buried, and the buggy which they shortly returned to him, everything that had ever been living had gone. Five eldritch acres of dusty grey desert remained, nor has anything ever grown there since. To this day it sprawls open to the sky like a great spot eaten by acid in the woods and fields, and the few who have ever dared glimpse it in spite of the rural tales have named it "the blasted heath".

The rural tales are queer. They might be even queerer if city men and college chemists could be interested enough to analyse the water from that disused well, or the grey dust that no wind seems to disperse. Botanists, too, ought to study the stunted flora on the borders of that spot, for they might shed light on the country notion that the blight is spreading – little by little, perhaps an inch a year. People say the colour of the neighbouring herbage is not quite right in the spring, and that wild things leave queer prints in the light winter snow. Snow never seems quite so heavy on the blasted heath as it is elsewhere. Horses – the few that are left in this motor age – grow skittish in the silent valley; and the hunters cannot depend on their dogs too near the splotch of greyish dust. They say the mental influences are very bad, too; numbers went queer in the years after Nahum's taking, and always they lacked the power to get away. Then the stronger-minded folk all left the region, and only the foreigners tried to live in the crumbling old homesteads. They could not stay, though; and one sometimes wonders what insight beyond ours their wild, weird stories of whispered magic have given them. Their dreams at night, they protest, are very horrible in that grotesque country; and surely the very look of the dark realm is enough to stir a morbid fancy. No traveller has ever escaped a sense of strangeness in those deep ravines, and artists shiver as they paint thick woods whose mystery is as much of the spirit as of the eye. I myself am curious about the sensation I derived from my one lone walk before Ammi told me his tale. When twilight came I had vaguely wished some clouds would gather, for an odd timidity about the deep skyey voids above had crept into my soul.

Do not ask me for my opinion. I do not know – that is all. There was no-one but Ammi to question; for Arkham people will not talk about the strange days, and all three professors who saw the aerolite and its coloured globule are dead. There were other globules – depend upon that. One must have fed itself and escaped, and probably there was another which was too late. No doubt it is still down the well – I know there was something wrong with the sunlight I saw above the miasmal brink. The rustics say the blight creeps an inch a year, so perhaps there is a kind of growth or nourishment even now. But whatever daemon hatching is there, it must be tethered to something or else it would quickly spread. Is it fastened to the roots of those trees that claw the air? One of the current Arkham tales is about fat oaks that shine and move as they ought not to do at night.

What it is, only God knows. In terms of matter I suppose the things Ammi described would be called a gas, but this gas obeyed the laws that are not of our cosmos. This was no fruit of such worlds and suns as shine on the telescopes and photographic plates of our observatories. This was no breath from the skies whose motions and dimensions our astronomers measure or deem too vast to measure. It was just a colour out of space – a frightful messenger from unformed realms of infinity beyond all Nature as we know it; from realms whose mere existence stuns the brain and numbs us with the black extra-cosmic gulfs it throws open before our frenzied eyes.

I doubt very much if Ammi consciously lied to me, and I do not think his tale was all a freak of madness as the townsfolk had forewarned. Something terrible came to the hills and valleys on that meteor, and something terrible – though I know not in what proportion – still remains. I shall be glad to see the water come. Meanwhile I hope nothing will happen to Ammi. He saw so much of the thing – and its influence was so insidious. Why has he never been able to move away? How clearly he recalled those dying words of Nahum's – "can't git away – draws ye – ye know summ'at's comin' but t'ain't no use–". Ammi is such a good old man – when the reservoir gang gets to work I must write the chief engineer to keep a sharp watch on him. I would hate to think of him as the grey, twisted, brittle monstrosity which persists more and more in troubling my sleep.